**Hermit or not, I'd heard whis**

I'd been living with a woman I considered fay for years. I'd seen a lot of unexplainable happenings with my own two eyes. Mary May wasn't only an eccentric old woman. She could predict the rain in the turn of a leaf. She could time the birth of a baby—goat or human—almost to the second. She could take the fire out of a burn and a wart from the skin with a pass of one gnarled hand. What did I have to fear from "witches"? There were darker things. Still, the old house creaked around me as the night wind picked up and whistled over the vine-covered shingles. Boards settled in the rafters and on the turret stairs. Not footsteps. Only age and the change in temperature as evening deepened and cool mountain air permeated cracks and crevices of the old house. I shivered, although the rock walls around me had stood for a hundred years or more.

*Here be witches and wayward girls grown into lonely women spooked by the wind.*

# Praise for
## *Wildwood Whispers*

"A feast for the senses. *Wildwood Whispers* is everything I love in a book, and I fell under its spell. Willa Reece has written a magical, romantic tale about our essential connections to nature and to each other." —Sarah Addison Allen, *New York Times* bestselling author

"Willa Reece has perfectly infused magic, suspense, and a love of nature deep into the pages of this novel. Ultimately filled with hope, love, and the power of growth and resilience, *Wildwood Whispers* is a thought-provoking, memorable debut."
—Heather Webber, *USA Today* bestselling
author of *Midnight at the Blackbird Café*

"Dark, tender, and thought-provoking, *Wildwood Whispers* is a beautifully woven tale of fantasy, feminism, and mystery set in rural Appalachia." —Constance Sayers, author of *A Witch in Time*

"A lovely tale of sisterly love, the power of inheritance, and the many magics of the natural world. Readers will love Reece's wonderful wisewomen and cheer for the abandoned baby who grows up to find her true home. A deeply satisfying read!"
—Louisa Morgan, author of *The Age of Witches*

"The Appalachian Mountains are alive with magic in this folksy, feminist contemporary fantasy.... Mel's story is full of human compassion and animal wisdom that will charm readers. This works both as a contemporary fairy tale and a slow-burning romance—and fans of both genres will appreciate this walk through the wild woods."
—*Publishers Weekly*

"A wonderful, heartfelt novel full of intuitive nature-based magic, wisewomen, and found family."

—Luanne G. Smith, author of *The Vine Witch*

"Willa Reece's *Wildwood Whispers* will cast a spell on its readers. Rich with imagination and rooting itself in the tendrils of rural Appalachia, the story will pull you in and never let go. A glorious read."

—Lydia Kang, author of *Opium and Absinthe*

"A beautifully written debut spun from love, suspense, and a deep connection with nature that simply entrances. *Wildwood Whispers* is an unforgettable tale."

—Tish Thawer, author of *The Witches of BlackBrook*

"Reece's poignant writing style truly captured the vivid *s* of small-town Appalachia. Readers craving a witchy story full of found family, lush nature, and small-town secrets will find it utterly enchanting."        —Hester Fox, author of *The Witch of Willow Hall*

"A sweet tale of self-discovery, but it's also a story of the way women and marginalized communities have always been underestimated by those with power."        —*Culturess*

# Wildwood Magic

**By Willa Reece**

*Wildwood Whispers*
*Wildwood Magic*

# WildWood Magic

## WILLA REECE

REDHOOK

Cover design by Lisa Marie Pompilio
Cover illustration by Mike Heath | Magnus Creative
Cover copyright © 2023 by Hachette Book Group, Inc.
Author photograph by Norris Hancock

Redhook Books/Orbit
Hachette Book Group
1290 Avenue of the Americas
New York, NY 10104
hachettebookgroup.com

First Edition: July 2023

Redhook is an imprint of Orbit, a division of Hachette Book Group.
The Redhook name and logo are trademarks of Hachette Book Group, Inc.

The publisher is not responsible for websites (or their content) that are not owned by the publisher.

The Hachette Speakers Bureau provides a wide range of authors for speaking events. To find out more, go to hachettespeakersbureau.com or email HachetteSpeakers@hbgusa.com.

Redhook books may be purchased in bulk for business, educational, or promotional use. For information, please contact your local bookseller or the Hachette Book Group Special Markets Department at special.markets@hbgusa.com.

Library of Congress Cataloging-in-Publication Data
Names: Reece, Willa, author.
Title: Wildwood magic / Willa Reece.
Description: First edition. | New York, NY : Redhook, [2023]
Identifiers: LCCN 2022045283 | ISBN 9780316591812 (trade paperback) |
    ISBN 9780316591799 (ebook)
Classification: LCC PS3608.A69775 W54 2023 | DDC 813/.6—dc23
LC record available at https://lccn.loc.gov/2022045283

ISBNs: 9780316591812 (trade paperback), 9780316591799 (ebook)

Printed in the United States of America

LSC-C

Printing 1, 2023

*For Granny*

# Prologue

*Rachel*
*Morgan's Gap, Virginia, 1959*

*A breeze showed me the way.*

I slipped from the hot, frenzied crowd in the revival tent, going under and out a loose flap in the heavy canvas like a much younger child. The wind rustled the musty fabric, even though I hadn't felt it on my own flushed skin. Sister Fay and the other matrons' attention was focused on the cheap portable podium at the front of the crowd. They were all red too—from the closeness and the summer heat and the fervor of the other revival attendees.

And Brother Tate.

As the preacher yelled about the fire that would consume nonbelievers, I was suddenly sure that the hellfire he wanted them to fear was actually here, already inside them, burning all the people around me from the inside out.

I'd seen this fire before in Sister Fay's eyes whenever I "strayed from the path." As far as I could tell—and I'd had all of my thirteen years to figure it out—you strayed when you asked questions or when you were too slow, too quick, too anything but obedient with your eyes cast down and your shoulders bowed to take up less space.

*Invisible.*

It had gotten harder and harder to hide in plain sight as my body resisted my attempts to stay small. I could—most of the time—control my voice and my eyes, but I couldn't help what was becoming a lean, gawky figure with hands, feet and shoulders too big to be unnoticed.

And breasts.

Soft fullness that only stood out more because the rest of me was so bony.

Growing.

The white patent-leather Mary Janes Sister Fay had forced onto my feet that morning pinched my toes and made me walk in tiny mincing steps both unnatural and highly ineffective for getting very far very fast. Since Sister Fay was always telling me to slow down, it would have been pointless and probably painful to complain. Much more painful than pinched toes or the blisters I would surely have come morning.

Morning was my goal.

Tonight, when I'd followed the crowd into the tent to find creaky folding chairs for all the smaller children in the back, I'd felt exposed when Brother Tate had singled me out. He'd commented on what a good girl I was to help the sisters shepherd the little ones into place. But I hadn't felt good. The praise had made the hair rise up on the back of my neck and the palms of my hands go wet in a scared, cold sweat that wouldn't wipe away on my skirts no matter how hard I tried.

No wonder the sudden fluttering movement of loose canvas caught my attention. *Here*, it seemed to say. *Look. Here. A way out.* I dropped down to my knees and left the pounding fist of the preacher and the brimstone he shouted about behind. I didn't even dust off the faded cotton of my Sunday dress when I got back to my feet on the other side.

I just started walking.

Away from the repurposed circus tent. Away from the strange fire in people's eyes.

There was nowhere for me to go. I'd been left at the girls' home as a baby with no hint of my heritage save for the "mark of her mother's sins" on my left shoulder. Sister Fay often used a green birch on the pale strawberry birthmark as if to flay it away. But the pink patch of skin was always there when the switch marks healed.

Since I had no *where* to go, I aimed for a *when*. Morning. With my toes pinched and no flashlight, it was a mountainous goal for a girl who couldn't even manage to be seen and not heard, but the sunrise called to me from somewhere down the long stretch of country road that disappeared out of sight on the horizon. It seemed right to take one step after another away from the tent and in the opposite direction of the Home for Wayward Girls.

I wasn't running away. All I'd ever known was the home and the Sect women who ran it. The sisters who fed, clothed and never once spared us the rod were harsh but familiar. It was the growing that frightened me, and the Sect men who noticed it.

Around the cleared fairgrounds, where the circus tent squatted with no calliope music or balloons or fried funnel cakes, was a wilderness of trees. That's where the breeze came from, fresh and oh-so-appealing on my face and arms. There wouldn't be any monkeys there or brightly colored tropical birds, but I liked it anyway, so different and peaceful compared to the city and the circus tent.

But it was also dark and shadowy, a jungle waiting for me to explore.

Like something out of the books I had to sneak around to read.

So I would walk until morning, and no matter what happened after that, every step I took on my own surrounded by the whispering woods was a step no one could ever take away. Not Brother Tate nor all his followers put together.

The Mary Janes were in my hand by the time I began to see the tops of smaller trees against a lightening sky. Hours before, when the cars from the revival had begun to drive past me in a steady stream of headlights, I dodged onto a side road and continued to walk. Eventually I decided to take the shoes off to relieve my toes and ease the busted blisters on my heels. I didn't throw the shoes into the shadows where the forest began and the dirt track stopped. Even then, with the tent behind me and all those steps between me and the sisters, I shuddered at the punishment I would surely face if they found me without the shoes.

They weren't mine. They were used for a time and then passed on to the next girl and the next. I gripped them tightly in my fist and walked on, taking more steps against the even tighter hopelessness of those never-ending "next girls" who would also own nothing. Not the clothes on their backs nor the skin beneath them either. Not even the thoughts in their heads were supposed to be theirs.

Mine always were, though. Deep down. Where no one could see. I had thoughts that were all my own. I thought about pearls and presidents, about *Betty and Veronica*. I thought about miniskirts and marches. About forbidden newspapers and Nancy Drew. All bits and pieces of news, books, comics and magazines I'd managed to sneak beneath the sisters' watchful eyes.

When a pink glow softened the sky and revealed the hush of dawn mist around me, morning became too obvious to ignore. A terrible weight settled heavy on my shoulders as the gently warming dew on ground and grass began to rise. I was exhausted. Tired from my long, lonely journey through the night, but also tired from other things.

The switch.

My unstoppable growth.

Brother Tate's bloodshot eyes.

My feet slowed to a standstill. The dirt road continued around the next curve, but down below the worn track, the forest opened up into an orchard. In the soft, rosy light, the branches were bowed, heavy with the growth of thousands of pale green globes—apples, standing out lighter and brighter than the leaves around them.

My stomach clenched and growled. I clutched it with my free hand and limped off the road toward the trees. There was no hellfire here. No need for invisibility. There was only the cool moisture rising up from the ground through the trees, kissing my cheeks and the ripening apples.

It was a simple, hushed welcome I hadn't felt in the tent or in all the years prior. I was close kin to the birds beginning to wake and the insects scrambling up, up, up stalks and trunks to warm their wings and antennae in the sun.

I walked through the meandering rows, around and around, as if drawn forward by a tugged string that was anchored deep in my chest. The cold moisture on the ground soothed and numbed my feet. The wet grass was a sweet relief. As was the cover soon provided by the larger, older trees in the middle of the orchard. From sapling to sprawling grandfather I walked until I came to a small rise in what must have been the dead center of the former field.

Maybe the center of the whole wilderness on top of Sugarloaf Mountain.

There the largest apple tree of all grew in an impressive display of gnarled limbs stretching up toward the sky from a trunk that made me think of the elephants I'd seen in a picture book once, left near a garbage pail on the street because of its torn pages. Trash to someone else, but a treasure to me. In spite of its size and the rough, wrinkled bark that proclaimed its great age, the tree on the rise was loaded with more apples than all the trees around it.

The tug on the string in my chest eased.

Once I reached the shelter of its canopy, I stopped and looked up, my attention called to thousands of shadowy crevices and hollows, a leafy universe of fairy nooks and butterfly bowers. I wanted to leap for the lowest branch and pull myself up into the fruit-heavy tree.

My stomach gurgled again, tempted by the abundance within reach.

*Thou shalt not steal.*

There were some things the matrons got wrong. I was sure of it. But my inner voice said that not stealing was one of the few they got right. So instead of grabbing a green apple and sinking my teeth into its tart goodness, I dropped to the ground at the base of the tree. Hot tears mixed with the cool dew on my cheeks as I gave in to sleep.

The young girl slept while the world around her woke up.

A flock of barn swallows darted from their colony under the metal eaves of an all-but-deserted shed to swoop acrobatically over a nearby meadow. Bees that had waited for the rising sun to dry the dew and the misty air hummed about their summer business, finding wildflowers on the ground now that the apple blossoms were gone. Far in the distance, a rooster crowed and a cow lowed for the maid who would milk it, then open the gate so it could roam the pasture until evening.

*Thud.* An apple fell.

*Thud. Thud.*

Then another and another.

The last rolled across the grass to stop against the sleeping girl's hip. A passerby might have looked up into the old tree to see if a squirrel had dislodged the fruit, for it was far too soon for so many unripened apples to fall.

But no one passed and the girl slept on, sheltered by the First Tree, the greatest tree, on the rise.

*Siobhán*
*Northern Ireland, 1879*

*Siobhán Wright sewed the precious apple seeds into the lining of her petticoat. She placed the blind-hem stitches snugly together—whip, whip, whip—with light thread that disappeared against the coarsely woven linen. The same way her mother had shown her to secretly stash the coins and Grandmother's hammered copper ring, which her grandfather had worked into the shape of a tree with twining, twisting roots that mirrored its branches. No one paid any mind to a girl's patched undergarments.*

*Even when they were doing their best to get into them.*

*She had never met her grandparents. The Great Hunger had taken both of them in Black '47 before she was born. Gone too soon. So many had died younger than they should have during the hard times. Even a woodsman like her grandfather and a wisewoman like her grandmother hadn't been able to survive when the potatoes failed.*

*Permanently gnawing insides had driven many of their folk to set off in search of a better life in those days.*

*"You're young. Go. Survive," her mother had said when the famine came again.*

*Along with the seeds, coins and ring, Siobhán brought a small muslin bundle of dirt from her mother's herb garden, untainted and blessed. Her father had fashioned her a walnut chest. On it, he carved flocks of barn swallows. Fly…fly…fly away. First to Liverpool. She used the chest for the precious soil no one would want to steal and a few items of clothing. Some might have seen her inheritance as pitiful, but Siobhán knew better. Her family had given all they had left in the world for her journey to a new one.*

*She wouldn't let their sacrifice be in vain.*

Rachel
Morgan's Gap, 1959

The scent of baked apples teased me awake. Was that why I had dreamed about apple seeds? But it was the soft mattress ticking and the fresh downy pillow that caused me to sit up. My usual bed was a cot with only a thin rag mat to cover its springs. My only pillow was my own arms. To wake in an unfamiliar place made me instantly suspect that I was still wrapped in the dream that had seemed so real.

But it hadn't been a good dream, had it? My heart still thumped behind my ribs with the fear I'd felt alongside the girl from another time who'd sewn with the worn, calloused fingers of a much older person. She'd had a mother, but she'd been forced to leave her. I'd had a mother who had left me. Somehow the pain met and mixed and blended together.

I blinked. I rubbed sticky dried tears from the corners of my eyes. Dream world or not, I didn't want anyone to see that I'd cried. I noticed the shelves once my eyes cleared. The walls of the tiny bedroom were lined with horizontal boards, some bowed under the weight of the books, magazines and papers packed onto them.

Was I awake?

So often I had longed for more books in the barren places I knew, filled only with work and prayer.

"You need rest, but you need food more and I'm too old to carry you a tray. Come in the kitchen and eat."

I didn't startle when a woman spoke from the doorway. I had lots of practice hiding my natural reaction to things. But I didn't hesitate. The woman had already turned to walk away. I jumped up from the bed that wasn't a dream, noticing my sun-bleached homespun nightgown and the hewn log walls that showed around the edges of the shelves. I reached to run my fingers across the spines of the books. All real. There were wool stockings on my feet and a moist tingling around my toes and a slight numbness in my blistered heels. Someone had brought me in from the orchard. Someone had nursed me. The woman who led me into the kitchen couldn't have carried me. She was tiny and stooped, and when I got a better look at her face, I gasped because it was craggy and lined, as if she'd been baking pies for a thousand years.

None of the sisters at the Home for Wayward Girls were old. They were only worn. Faded around the edges like the tossed-aside newspapers they used to fill the cracks in the boards of the house in Richmond when the wind blew and there wasn't much coal.

I gaped at this ancient lady, forgetting my confusion, my hunger. The woman's long skirt was actually a pair of wide-legged trousers made of tartan wool in spite of the season. Her pants ended at her ankles, where dainty laced boots began. On top she wore a man's shirt with rolled sleeves where her arms poked out, freckled and sun browned. Her arms were corded like a man's, lean and tough, belying her age. Maybe she truly had carried me in from the orchard. But her wild mane of hair told the truth of her years. It was silver like moonlight all around her face and shoulders and down past her waist. Not braided or combed or twisted into shape or pinned or sprayed or tamed by curlers.

Her hair was free.

I quickly reached for my braids to find them as real and as painful at my temples as they'd ever been. The tight braids proved it. I was no longer dreaming.

The tempting scent of apple pie—cinnamon, brown sugar, baking crust and bubbling juice—distracted me from the mystery of how I came to wake in the house. My stomach had growled at dawn. Now it silently ached without the gumption to even gurgle, and my head felt light. Many times I'd been sent to bed without supper, but I'd never walked so long and so far on an empty stomach.

"Sit down before you fall down, girl," the old woman advised. She nodded her head curtly at a thick spindled chair, and I was glad it was already pulled out from the butcher-block table.

I sat with a plop that would have been punished back at the home.

But the woman only brought me a wedge of pie she must have cut to cool moments before. Buttery, flaky crust. Tender, spice-flecked chunks of apple only sweet enough to soften the bite of the tart fruit. The piece of pie was more than generous. A portion all of a quarter of the entire pastry.

I ate it all. Every bite. Every crumb. And then I stared forlornly at the thick juice left on the solid pottery plate. There wasn't a switch in sight, but I couldn't risk sopping up the juice with a finger. As if she sensed that I was still hungry, the old woman turned from the old ice box in the corner with a small pitcher of frothy milk and a muslin-wrapped hunk of cheese.

"This too. You need nourishment. More than I'll have time to give you. Can't be helped. We can only stir what we can," the old woman said.

I drank the mug of milk she poured me and ate the strong, cream-colored cheese. Both were rich and pungent. From a goat instead of a cow. Neither seemed to make it to my stomach. Like the pie, they soaked into my body on the way down. I felt better but not full, as if I was only getting started.

"Name's Mary. Remember it. Mary May. You'll need to know one day.

And don't forget the orchard called you. Ain't no child going to walk that far in the wee hours for nothing. Might seem it was for nothing, mind you. But don't give up. You've got a longer walk ahead. A long hard walk. And there's no shortcut. One foot in front of the other. That's all. She got here, didn't she? She knows how it's done!" The last was said to a goat that appeared at the screened door that opened out onto a stoop. It was a large billy with a gray beard down to its knobby knees, and it replied to Mary May as if participating in a conversation I could only half understand.

"I was walking away from the revival tent. Didn't have a place to be," I said.

The woman refilled my glass, and even though it was greedy I drank all of it down, only stopping between gulps to catch my breath.

"Away is a place, girl. The best place. And this particular mountain orchard is about as away as a body can get," Mary May said. "Roots twining down to the heart of the earth. Branches stretching up to the sky. Blossoms then fruits like they was plucked from the heavens."

I could feel the distance I'd traveled somewhere deeper than blistered skin. The air was different around me and the ground was sturdier beneath my feet. As if I'd been off balance before I got here. One step away from falling. But now, I was on solid footing. If this was away, I liked it.

"I've never seen so many apples in one place. You're going to have a good harvest," I said.

"So many apples right there for the picking, but you didn't, did you? Didn't take a one though you're a starving thing, gone all to growth, and nothing to fuel it by."

"It didn't seem right to take without asking. There was no one around."

"The trees will remember your courtesy. They always do," the old woman muttered. She nodded with every word she spoke as if she was carrying on a conversation with herself. "I reckon that was a little harder to resist," she continued. Her nod became specific, indicating something beside my plate, and I was startled by the tiny book I must have picked up from a shelf in the bedroom or hall as I passed. I was too used to grabbing reading materials wherever and whenever I could. The shelves hadn't stopped in the bedroom. The whole house was lined with them, and every one was full.

My cheeks heated. I picked up the book and held it out to Mary May. She didn't take it. Instead, she reached to push it back toward me.

"More than your belly is hungry. Any fool can see that. You keep it. Things that catch us like that are never happenstance. It's always best to listen when the world whispers. *When the wildwood whispers.* It's yours," Mary said. Her tone was scolding, but her eyes were bright. "It'll take more than goat's milk to fuel you for the journey ahead."

I looked down at the gift. It was no larger than the palm of my hand. The golden title glinted as I turned it to the light. *The Scarlet Letter* by Nathaniel Hawthorne.

Mary left the room while I read the first few pages. I hated to put it down when she came back with my petticoats in her hands.

"Aired these out on the line. Spot-cleaned your dress. No sense in catching trouble for moss stains," Mary said. She flipped the petticoats this way and that. "Senseless things. Hiding legs as if we don't all have them. We can make it useful with a few stitches, though, can't we?"

Mary sat at the table. I hadn't noticed the sewing basket she'd crooked over her arm under the petticoat. She placed it on the table in front of her and prepared a needle and white thread quickly with surprisingly nimble fingers. Then she folded the material of the petticoat until she'd fashioned a hidden sleeve on one side near the waist.

"Pockets are power. Up to you what you put in them, see? Only you decide. And no one needs to know," Mary said. She reached for the book and placed it in the pocket she'd made just big enough to hold it.

"And this too. A needle box. My mother made it a long time ago from a fallen branch of that apple tree you were sleeping under. There's several needles and some thread in there. For you."

She handed me the applewood needle box. It was a plain and smooth cylinder with no decoration except for the whorls of the aged wood. The bark had been removed and the wood polished by time and fingers. One side had been whittled down to fit into the other. I gently popped it open. The inside had been hollowed out to hold the needles. A small bit of red thread was wound around their silvery eyes.

There had been something in my dream about petticoats and hidden seeds. In all the time I'd been trying to read when the sisters forbade it, I hadn't thought of using the hated undergarments as a treasure trove.

I closed the needle box and slid it into the hidden pocket beside the book. Two gifts from a stranger who, although strange, seemed like someone I'd known for longer than a half an hour.

As Mary finished stitching, I carried the empty plate and glass to the sink. I tried not to stare, but the room was unusual beyond the quantity of books and papers stacked and piled on every surface. There were herbs bundled with twine and hung to dry in a sun-facing window—mint, dill and others I didn't recognize. Open shelves lined the tops of the walls, and from them green glass jars sparkled in the morning sunlight, their unlabeled contents made mysterious by the gleam. I thought I could see apple slices through a juicy haze and the thick, chunky texture of persimmon jam. From the exposed beams in the ceiling hung the dark flash of fire-scorched copper pots in various sizes and shapes from stewpot to footed cauldron. And, although there was a great old cast-iron stove, there was also a fireplace in the corner fitted up with a spit and other handles and holders the old woman must have used often, because they were worn smooth.

The stones of the hearth were blackened by soot all the way out to my toes. More blackened than years of an open flame would have accounted for. One corner stone had faint chiseled letters I could barely make out—"HONEYWICK"—and a date that was even more faded. In fact, it looked almost as if someone had scraped the date away so long ago that the scrapes themselves were half-hidden by soot.

"Honeywick," I deciphered out loud.

Mary *hmmm*ed behind me, but I couldn't tell if her noise was meant to be a yes or a no, or if it was merely a startled sound, as if my reading of the stone had disturbed her somehow. Whatever the case, I was discouraged from asking about the name or the mysterious date.

I turned politely away from the hearth toward an embroidery stand pushed to the side. It was also dark, as if many years of soot and smoke had colored the wood. And it was empty. Maybe that's why my fingers were immediately drawn to the carved edges of the hoop, or maybe it was a trick of the morning light that made the carefully crafted leaves seem to move.

There were apples among the leaves. Peeking out just as the green apples had peeked at me at dawn. One of the apples had been made to appear as if someone had taken a bite out of it. Love of the orchard shone through in every carefully placed etch of a long-ago blade.

Suddenly the hoop being empty made my chest tighten and my fingers twitch as if I'd touched a frayed cord with its innards showing. The phantom electricity startled me and I curled my hand against it, but I couldn't stay chastised for long.

There were many utensils hanging on hooks and nails around the fireplace, but one drew my attention more than the others. It wasn't my place to reach for the large wooden spoon and take it from the wall. I did it without thinking, driven by the need to look closer at the carving that wound around the handle.

It was a thin, graceful curve of a snake, a harmless one by the rounded shape of its head—garter or green. I was instantly charmed by the tilt of its eyes and the frozen flick of its tongue.

The carving of the serpent on the spoon hanging near the hoop was whimsical—a garden and a snake, but not a warning. A dare. The delicate snake was a rebel, not a devil. Me too, my heart whispered. Me too.

"Best put her back for now. There isn't time for all that. She's been hanging there for fifty years; another ten won't matter," Mary said.

I didn't want to hang the spoon back on the wall, but I did. I couldn't help it if my fingers traced the coils of the little snake or if I hesitated near the stand, afraid to touch it again, but longing to all the same. The strange tightness gripped my chest again. I rubbed my palm against the center of my ribs to try to loosen it, but it wouldn't ease.

Only the sound of a car's engine and tires on gravel finally made me turn toward the door. Mary sighed loudly, the billy goat cried out and ran away and a sheriff's deputy got out of a black-and-white painted Impala. The tightness was explained: The real world had come for me in this fairy-tale cottage I'd found. It had pulled into the front yard and even without flashing lights or sirens I was caught in its terrible clutches.

I'd tried to be careful, but someone must have seen me walking this way.

Mary May put her hands on her hips. She suddenly looked very small in comparison to the burly man whose knuckles made a terrible rat-a-tat-tat-tat on the frame of her screen door. He could see us in the kitchen. He frowned, as if runaway girl-children and wizened old women were nothing but trouble.

"You must be the girl who wandered off last night. They're breaking down the tent. Need to get you back to the folks you belong to," the deputy said. He pushed the door open and held it wide without coming inside or saying good morning to Mary May.

"Don't belong to nobody but herself," Mary May said, followed by a humph as if there was no use in arguing. "At least let the girl put her shoes on."

I was already buckling the Mary Janes, thankful for the treatment that made my heels numb so I could walk gingerly toward the man who still hadn't acknowledged the woman who scolded him.

"I got lost," I said, but he ignored that too. He put his hand on my back and pushed me toward the squad car so that I had to take several quick steps that made the blisters on my feet sting.

"Found, more like," Mary May said.

I looked over my shoulder and our eyes locked. She might be smaller than the deputy, and unable to keep him from taking me back to the Sect sisters, but the firm set to her jaw and the look on her face said that she wasn't as helpless as he and the world might think.

Her look gave me courage. My chest swelled against the tightness and I could suddenly breathe in a last gulp of baked-apple air.

"Hurry up. Get in." The deputy reached to push me forward again, but this time I was already moving and his fingers brushed harmlessly away. I opened the car door myself and climbed into the backseat.

My last view of Honeywick was through the back glass of the deputy's car. Like the hearth, the cottage was built entirely of blackened stone. But the cottage's rock walls were softened by an abundance of flowering vines that twined from foundation to roof and completely covered a small-towered turret on one side. Even all stained by soot or age or whatever had darkened its stones, the cottage, like the carved embroidery hoop and the snake spoon, looked like a fairy tale, one I was being taken away from too soon.

I turned around to face the road, but not before I had imagined myself turning down one corner of a storybook to mark the page.

# *One*

*Rachel*

*Richmond, Virginia, February 1965*

*M*y *secret was so* much a part of me it was hard to imagine, small and mysterious, and yet, as known as the beating of my heart. My very soul had split, and somewhere deep inside there was another, hidden away...for now.

And there was my problem. That tiny part of my soul was destined to become his...under his fist, under his heel, under his control.

The idea was a horror. I couldn't remember standing up from the doctor's desk. I couldn't remember the nurse's congratulations or taking my coat from the tree in the reception room. I must have buttoned the perfectly tailored herringbone tweed, automatically. I must have nodded and smiled. I had become so good at nodding and smiling.

Somehow, I maneuvered the sleek Oldsmobile station wagon home. Like the coat, the car had been his choice, one his followers would admire and envy. He chose everything for the same reason, including the new brick rancher in a neighborhood named after the church at its center.

His church. His home. His car. His wife.

He'd chosen me.

I'd been trying to come to grips with that realization for a long time.

Someone like Ezekiel wanted meek and mild. I'd been neat and clean and obedient by the time we'd met. What spirit I'd naturally had as a curious child had been bled out of me from the stripes the green birch switches made on my legs and back.

I parked the wagon in the carport, for once not noticing if the fenders were too close to the scrolling wrought iron supports. When my hands were no longer required for the steering wheel, they automatically went to my abdomen.

I needed whatever spirit I had left to rise.

He had wanted this more than the house or the car. More than my immaculate wardrobe. More than the church. And the church was his castle. The seat of his fiefdom. The baby was to be his heir, a prince to the kingdom he was building.

I hadn't known.

In the year since our marriage—straight from the girls' home to the good reverend's bed—I had learned a lot. Too much. And, in his eyes, never enough.

Now this. After months of trying.

His trying. My praying at first that it would happen quickly, then later, *please God*, never.

His first wife had died in a horrible boating accident, they said. Only the shell of a burnt-out motorboat and her remains had been recovered. He had survived, by the grace of God. I knew better. Had known for a while. Accidents happened a lot around my good reverend husband. Trips. Falls. Far too clumsy, silly girl. And always the knowledge that he was weighing your usefulness with a cold-blooded calculation that could easily be lost to rage in the blink of an eye.

His followers called it passion and they were drawn to it, but I'd often seen the flicker of fear in their eyes. Fear of his disapproval. Fear of failure. Fear of God. If they lived exactly as he told them to they would be spared the damnation we all deserve, he preached. They believed and drew others into their belief like a herd of nervous sheep. Here. Gather. Beneath his watchful eyes. Safety in numbers. It was a survival instinct a man like my husband naturally exploited, alternating easily between pulpit pounding and benevolent smiles.

A wolf in sheepdog's clothing.

I unlocked the side door and stepped into a kitchen so painstakingly kept (such pain!) the harvest gold appliances and orange Formica countertops were straight from a photograph and untouched by the meals prepared on them and with them. Cooking as a performance rather than for sustenance.

Now, a baby in my womb.

A child.

As innocent as I had been long ago and far away. The coat belonged on its designated hanger in the hall closet. I needed to exchange it for the cherry apron on its hook by the range.

I didn't.

It was Tuesday.

The meatloaf was already prepared in the refrigerator. Ready to go in the oven so it would be hot and fresh when he came through the door.

I knew the way he would want to be told. Perfect meal. Perfect silence. Speak when spoken to. He'd know I'd been to the doctor today. Every second of every day was directed by him. Master of all he surveyed. Like me, he'd come from less. Much less. But a humble servant of God could achieve great things. Terrible things. Things I wished to forget.

I'd asked the doctor to let me be the one to tell my husband. The doctor knew. He'd seen some of the bruises. I'd seen pity in his eyes and also resignation. Some husbands had tempers. Still, better to be respectably married. Small price to pay. I didn't know how long I stood indecisive, the hated coat shed into a pile on the immaculately hoovered floor. But I heard his car door slam. And knew without a doubt that I wouldn't tell him about the baby.

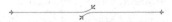

I hadn't kept the Oldsmobile on the road. Somewhere between the doctor's office and the carport I'd swung wide. I could vaguely recall the swerve, the correction. One tire had jolted in the rough grass beside the asphalt and a hubcap had been loosened. He always walked around the station wagon when I'd been out.

No meatloaf in the oven. Apron on its hook. My coat on the floor. By the time Reverend Gray found me at the end of the hall with one foot toward the front door and my hands on my stomach, he was already furious. To discipline he didn't have to be angry. He could easily point out my failings with carefully controlled slaps and pinches. Constant correction. But I'd learned long ago that the rage switch was always there waiting for me—or our future child—to flip.

I often wondered if it had been rage or calculation that had come for his first wife. She hadn't been able to conceive. He complained about it often. Her failure. And 1965 or not, divorce wasn't an option. Had he carefully planned the purchase of the motorboat? Had she known when he took her out on the maiden voyage with no life jacket? I could all too easily imagine him holding her under the water while she screamed, great bubbles filled with her last breaths breaking the roiling surface of the lake. The boat had run aground and burst into flames, they said. His first wife had burned with it. The reverend had walked away without a scratch. What a blessing.

I'd found all the old photographs of his first wife. I hadn't been consciously snooping. I couldn't help myself. Even his closet, filled with identical dark suits and striped ties, might have something to read on a rainy day when the chores were done and the rest of the day loomed ahead of me full of dread for when it was time for him to be home. Shoeboxes sometimes held newspaper clippings. But not this one. This one held pictures. And in every single one someone had burned out a woman's mouth. The blackened edges of burnt paper rimmed ashy holes. Like someone had kissed the woman with a cruel flame. Not someone. Him. He had done it, before or after. And then he had kept them all in a box like some kind of gruesome confession.

Or trophy.

*A long, unused fireplace match had been left in the box too.*

But worse than the match was the photograph of me from our wedding day. I hadn't posed. It was a candid snapshot. I'd never seen my own face look so tense, as if the muscles behind my lips, cheeks and eyes had cemented into an expression of dread. Even Mirror Me hid that fear, putting on a brave face. My photograph, smelling of sulfur and smoke, sat in the box with his dead wife's burnt-out lips and the unused match—waiting.

It had been dangerous to take the photograph, but I'd done it anyway. Since that first secret pocket Mary May had sewn for me, I'd always added hidden pockets to my petticoats and dresses. *Pockets are power*, she'd said. Only you decide what to put there. I'd placed the wedding day photograph in a succession of hidden pockets as a reminder of what I didn't want to be.

No power, hidden or otherwise, protected me from his fists when he got home that day. He sent me to clean myself up once he was finished. But only after I'd put the meatloaf in the oven and prepared him an iced tea. I'd done those things with blood dripping into my eye from a cut his wedding ring had caused on my brow.

Then I was sent to make myself presentable while he read the evening newspaper that was forbidden to me. The bathroom smelled cloyingly of the perfume he liked me to wear. The basket of first aid supplies were placed handily under the powder-blue sink.

As I washed up and masked the damage he'd done with cosmetics, I made a promise to the baby no more than a speck in my womb. My spirit had been tamped down, but not lost.

I vowed his match would never get the chance to turn my lips to ash.

*Away is a place.*

My hands wouldn't stop shaking. It was adrenaline, not fear. I held myself together against the rush in my blood and carefully tiptoed through deep shadows that still smelled faintly of meatloaf. The whole house was dark, but I couldn't risk turning on lights. One step after another, I avoided every single squeaky floorboard while Ezekiel snored.

I'd used the powder from too many of the pills I'd broken open and saved instead of taking them for my "nerves." After I'd cleaned up and reappeared to assure him I'd been properly chastised, I'd sprinkled the powder on top of his meatloaf. It had soaked into the tomato sauce and disappeared. I'd been sent to bed without supper. Ezekiel had gobbled up his portion.

Hitting me always increased his appetite.

The need for quiet didn't stop a soft nervous laugh from passing my swollen lip. I swallowed hard to tamp down any further sound out of fear of detection and also because my laugh had been eerie in the darkness, teetering on the edge of hysteria.

I couldn't waste time on a breakdown.

I had hidden one small overnight bag behind the vacuum in the hall closet. In it were some clothing, a few toiletries and my needle box. He regularly inspected for dust, but he never paid any attention to the tools for "women's work." Never once glanced in the broom closet. Or looked twice in my sewing basket. Never once worried about what I might be hiding in the bottles and jars in the kitchen. I hadn't learned the "lessons" he was always trying to teach me, but I had learned a few of my own.

I paused once I retrieved the bag and listened. For long seconds, there hadn't been a sound from upstairs. I strained my ears, not sure if I wanted to hear silence or his snoring resume. Finally, there was a snort and a sigh. Rustling movement as his body moved in his unnatural sleep. I wasn't a murderer. I should be glad.

But if I'm honest there was a disappointed twinge somewhere deep and dark inside of my heart.

I sat the bag down and donned my coat, taking the time to button it over my still flat abdomen.

"Here we go," I whispered. A flutter made me hesitate again, but the movement didn't repeat. Too soon. Only hunger. But I was still buoyed as if I had companionship in my mad endeavor.

I clutched keys in one hand and my bag in the other and rushed outside. Ezekiel wouldn't wake for hours. I'd waited for him to collapse into bed. I'd watched for midnight so the neighborhood would be asleep. Now, I hurried, puffs of white escaping my lips with every step.

I had to risk starting the station wagon.

Only one window down the street still emitted a faint glow. That was Mr. Farnham, who fell asleep in front of his new color television every night and slept by the light of the test pattern until *Captain Kangaroo* woke him in the morning. His wife always complained and I always tutted my understanding even though I couldn't imagine such a simple, ordinary marriage.

I fumbled for the right key after I'd quietly eased the door of the car shut. In my hurry, I'd accidentally closed the door on my coat, but I couldn't risk opening and closing it again. The rush of my blood in my ears urged me on. Hurry. Hurry. Hurry. With each beat of my heart. Away. Away. Away.

I forced my hand to steady and turned the ignition. The sudden roar of the engine made a gasp escape between teeth I hadn't known were gritted. There would be black marks on the cement of the driveway tomorrow morning because the tires skidded when I threw the car in reverse and hit the gas.

But only a slight squeal.

That was all.

This time I knew exactly where I was going. I'd planned and prepared for months. An old used Rambler was waiting for me by the river. I'd paid with precious cash I'd managed to save one dime and nickel at a time so Ezekiel wouldn't notice. A surprise for my husband, I'd said to the man who sold me the car. This time, I laughed out loud. Such a surprise.

I'd given the Rambler's owner an extra five dollars to park the car by the river and leave the key on the lip of the fender. Sure, lady. Lucky man to have such a pretty sweet wife. The powder from one more pill might have killed him. I clenched my hands on the steering wheel at the thought.

I wasn't a killer.

I carried new life inside of me. I didn't want my baby to have a murderer for a mother.

I tried not to drive the Oldsmobile too quickly through town. I was out in between *The Tonight Show* and the milk man. The city was all stillness while my heart raced and my blood rushed and my foot shook on the accelerator.

Every time I'd had errands over the past year I'd driven farther afield. Looking. Searching. Exploring the outskirts of the city. I'd finally found an accessible slope above the river with only a derelict factory in sight.

The perfect spot.

It had to be perfect.

There was a fresh pile of empty beer cans and the blackened remnants of a bonfire since I'd been here last. Thankfully, there was no one out in the cold tonight.

The station wagon was big, but the fishing hole beneath the bridge was bigger. Tonight, it was blacker than black, a deep dark place to pretend to drown. I sat for a while contemplating the nothingness. No lights. No other cars. No sound but the gurgle of current and the occasional hum of a big rig on the highway miles away.

I'd parked with the nose of the wagon tilted down the steep incline. I'd seen this in my mind a thousand times. But the pop of the emergency brake when I released it sounded louder than a gunshot and the door opened faster and heavier than I'd expected. I was holding on too tightly. Gravity and the door's weight pulled me out of the seat. The car was already picking up speed. I couldn't stay on my feet.

Worse than the fall was the sudden tug of my coat when I finally tried to let go.

It was still hung on the metal of the door. I scrabbled with legs and hands, tilting and twisting trying to break free. A screw. A latch. Something had me. I screamed. A thin cry of disbelief. Not like this. Not like this. The ground was hard and rough. Rocks and brambles tore at my face and clothes. I cried out again. There was no one to help me.

I had to help myself.

A flutter again, as if my baby was struggling too. Impossible to feel in the midst of being pulled to my death, but I felt it. I felt her. And then a sudden clear impulse to shed the hated coat that was dragging us both toward the river.

One button.

Two.

Three.

My legs found purchase in a tangled bush and the pull of the car worked in our favor. The coat was peeled from my straining body as several rattling jounces took the station wagon over the riverside cliff. The car hitting the water was a soft sound. Like a swallow. Like a gulp. My frantic breathing was louder. Hysterical hitches no pill could have calmed down.

I didn't care about my torn skin or clothes or about how black and blue wrestling with coat and car would make me tomorrow. At least there would be one. And another and another. Each one taking me and the baby further away from hell. As the river rushed into the windows I'd left cracked with a glorious sucking sound, I sat up shaking and reached for my stomach.

I prayed for another flutter. Just one. To the river. To the breeze. And for some reason I thought about apple trees from so long ago and far away. Please. Please. Please. I watched the station wagon disappear while I struggled to breathe. Finally, when the last of the roof vanished with a glug, there was a responding bubble from deep inside me.

"We're going away," I promised. But it took me several tries before I could stand. My ankle was sprained or worse. It hurt to draw breath so I suspected my ribs were also hurt, cracked from the violent tumble.

Wouldn't be the first time.

I limped up the hill toward the waiting Rambler, promising myself and my unborn daughter that it would be the last.

The heater in the Rambler was broken. By the time I found my destination my teeth were clicking together and my hands were numb on the steering wheel. I rolled down the window anyway. Just a crack. Just enough to allow a breeze that was bracingly familiar to caress my cold cheeks.

I didn't have a map and I didn't stop to buy one. I had to trust an old dusty memory of roads that existed only in my heart.

Up, up, up a mountain. Up out of the city and the lowlands into fresh-forested wilderness. The ribbon of road I followed, lit by headlights and starlight and a sliver of moon peeking now and then from skiffs of night clouds, became a hushed adventure populated only by a flash of fox, a startled and leaping buck, a rabbit that caused me to come to a sudden full stop with my foot hard on the brake, shaking at the close call, before it sprang away.

I hadn't climbed through a wardrobe, but I'd discovered a different world from the one I'd left down below.

Or rediscovered.

A weaving of skeletal trees lined the road, no matter how it twisted and turned, creating a sheltered pathway for my car and the creatures I encountered. More deer. I lost count. And a family of raccoons. The swoop of an owl silhouetted against the sky above a diorama of evergreen spikes.

*Hello*, I thought each time life presented itself. *Hello*. Tentative, but hopeful. Spurred onward and upward.

I wasn't surprised when I found the road that led to the orchard. I slowly drove down the rutted gravel, but I recalled it by once-upon-a-time footsteps, one after another.

Honeywick had always been with me. A secret I'd never shared with anyone else. There had never been anyone I could trust with that magical morning of pie and goat's milk. Of copper kettles and a whimsical wooden spoon. Of blackened stone and a vine-covered turret room.

And an empty embroidery hoop that had seemed to zap my fingers with a strange energy, which lingered years later whenever I took up needle and thread.

Never anyone else to share it with until now.

Windows glowed with welcoming light when I came around the final bend. The apple trees were dormant in the distance, sleeping through winter, but as I pulled up to the cottage, more covered in vines than I remembered, the front door opened and a familiar figure stood framed in the flicker of the hearth behind her.

There was only the slightest hint of dawn's pink on the horizon, but Mary May was up. I was tired, cold and bruised. I allowed myself to imagine she had been waiting for me, *for us* to arrive.

I parked and climbed from the car, stiff, but determined. There had been no flutter inside of me for hours now. Even though I had treated the journey like a story I shared out loud. Please be all right. Please. The journey from the chilled car to the open doorway was suddenly more daunting than all the miles I'd traveled to get to this point. Even than all the years.

"We're here," I said, to the baby, to Mary May, to the sleeping orchard and to myself. I stepped into the old woman's outstretched arms and she supported my weight with her wiry muscles and surprisingly strong, straight back. Her warmth and the scent of apples, cinnamon and savory browned butter enveloped me at the same time.

"And none too soon," she replied.

# Two

*Mary May*
*Morgan's Gap, May 1969*

*E ven in this hotter* than normal spring, when the wildwood was already rustling dryly in the hopes of a good long drink of rain, Mary May was cold. It was time. Well past time to go to ground like the ones before her had done when there was work left to do even though their years had run out.

But first an urgent task had come to her in the night, like the heavy atmosphere of a downpour the trees waited and waited for that just wouldn't start. Rachel was tossing and turning and muttering in her sleep when Mary made her way to the kitchen. "Hurry. Hurry. Hurry," the young woman told her pillows. Mary didn't go into her room to soothe her. No doubt Rachel felt the approaching storm as well. Not rain. There wouldn't be any rain on the mountain for a long while to come. Fear and fury sucked the life out of a body and the air. Mary could already feel what it would be like a few weeks from now when a miasma of distrust suffocated the town rising up from the people and places haunted by the past. Old prejudices against the different, against those touched by the fae, against *Other* no matter what that Other might be, lurked in the shadows of Morgan's Gap, waiting to be brought forward into the light.

Dreams were one way a wisewoman knew things.

There were no clouds. No ozone in the air. Only necessity so frightening it caused her usually steady hands to shake and the words on the recipe card she retrieved from the old tin box to blur.

The orchard nudged. The trees always knew. Maybe she was getting too old to listen, too far gone to understand. She'd known Rachel's baby was touched by the fae from the moment she'd cooed and blinked at the world when she was born rather than crying in protest at the sudden cold and bright light. Fairy shine some called it. Rachel had named her Pearl. Mary hadn't realized what unwanted attention the child might attract when she began to mature into her gifts.

Almost four already!

And Rachel wasn't equipped to help her daughter. Yet.

You couldn't hide a bright spark forever, and the child would be most vulnerable on the day of her birth, when the veil was thin and the fairy shine was on her.

Mary wrote the first three names, confidently pressing her pen to the faded card. Words had power. Names even more so. She wasn't as certain of the last name she committed to the card. She placed it on the very bottom at the edge where the worn paper had started to curl in on itself after so many years of use.

Maybe she shouldn't have included the last name at all. Fear caused even the wisest woman to teach skewed lessons. Yet, it wasn't her place to second-guess the intuition that nudged her pen across the page. She'd had more than enough years on this earth to know the energy between student and teacher flowed both ways. Knowledge. Ignorance. Fear. Courage. All of us a mixture of those things.

It had been years since she'd had anyone wiser to give instruction over her shoulder. This was her place. Her job. The tending. The harvesting. And providing a haven for the girl—now a woman full-grown—who needed a place to call home.

Mary May had welcomed Rachel back to the mountain. She'd helped her through the pregnancy. She'd even accepted the frightened insistence that the baby had to be given away.

*Her father was a murderer and there was always the chance that he might find me.*

Mary shivered, but this time it had nothing to do with being cold. The gathering storm wouldn't converge in one morning, but she had no time to pamper creaky joints and chilled bones. She must away. Her Billy, gone silent and still, told her. Her energy was fading, depleted as it had never been before. She'd lingered longer this time. Too long. For Rachel and the baby, now grown to precocious girl all eyes and curls like her mother. *Maybe she shouldn't be so quick to accuse others of teaching from a place of fear.*

There was so much for Rachel to learn. Mary had tried to give her time—to heal, to wake, to finally begin to live again, but the young woman had only drawn more deeply into herself.

Time had run out. For Mary May and for the girl the orchard had called. Silly of her to second-guess the wildwood's timing after all these years, of course. She would rest. Rachel would rise. It was only weakness to wonder and worry and doubt. She needed to trust in the trees as she had always done. Wildwood willing, she would sleep in its embrace and wake recharged. If not, she would find a deeper rest and only wake as leaf and limb and vine.

Thank the First Tree, there were others on the mountain. It would take more than one—no matter how extraordinary the one was—to help Morgan's Gap make it through the summer.

*Rachel*
*Morgan's Gap, May 1969*

Honeywick was never hushed.

Farm animals bleated, crowed and clucked. Mary May sang or clanged with a rhythmic rattle of pots and pans I'd grown so used to that her hustle was my meditation. That morning I'd washed my face, combed the chestnut curls that now grew long all the way to my waist and gotten dressed in my usual patched jumper before the silence penetrated my consciousness.

Complete. Silence.

Except for the sudden thudding of my heart in my ears.

My memory-fueled night had left me jumpy this morning. That was all. I scoffed at my pounding heart.

All was well and settled. Pearl was safe and I was...fine. I forced myself not to rush from the tiny bathroom addition to the centuries-old front room where the kitchen still welcomed infrequent visitors to the house, but my quickly donned canvas sneakers slapped on the uneven hall floor, staccato and strange all by themselves.

No songs. No fussing. No goat's greeting or cookery underway.

Mary's Market Day willow basket and her prized recipe box sat on the kitchen table. They brought me up short. I stood just inside the doorway from the hall trying to calm my breathing. Each breath in and out threatened to hitch in my throat, squeezed by (please God) unnecessary panic.

There must be a simple explanation.

But the blood rushing in my ears sounded like warning whispers.

It was unlike the elderly wisewoman to take the handwoven basket off its hook by the front door until it was time to fill it, and she always placed the painted metal recipe tin back on its shelf beside the chipped porcelain sugar bowl. So while the rooster crowed at the break of day, I forced myself forward to pick up one of the recipes Mary had left beside the open box.

The card was worn around the edges and smoothed by time and countless fingers. I scanned the neatly numbered steps to making apple cider, then placed the card back on the table. The other card, even more worn, was for making apple pie. There were fresh ink marks on the pie recipe in Mary May's wavering script—Mavis Hall, Truvy Rey and Jo Shively. Then, farther down, a hastily scrawled addition—Granny Ross. Why had Mary added the names to the recipe and why had she left the otherwise faded card on the table?

The house was still hushed. The market basket seemed expectant, waiting for its load of muslin-wrapped goat cheese rounds Mary traded for various and sundry necessities and treats as well as a precious few coins.

But Saturday was almost a week away.

The cookstove was cold and the kettle Mary used for tea every morning was still in the drainer beside the sink.

The small spiral staircase to Mary's bedroom was on the other side of the cottage at the end of a hall. I hesitated. I never intruded on her privacy. I'd never had any of my own before coming here, so it seemed a sacred thing, not to be disturbed. Still, this was practical. Checking on her well-being wouldn't be an intrusion, right? She was very old, after all. She might have fallen. She might be quietly sick in bed in need of nursing.

A circular room opened up at the top of the stairs, ringed by paned windows with glass so old it was wavy. They allowed only a hazy view of outside and the merest hint of rising sunbeams within. Dust motes floated on the light, drawing my eyes upward to the high rafted roof. Some of the honeysuckle vines from outside had found their way in to twine across the ceiling. There was no evidence of leaks, only a whimsy of living woven canopy instead of plaster.

Mary's bed sat empty, neatly made and spread with a colorful quilt. Her possessions lay in an ordinary tumble of everyday use.

One object caught my attention. In the middle of the table, as if it was a miniature barnyard, was a red clay statue of Billy, complete with his left crooked horn. With one hesitant finger, I touched the lifelike face. The room was eerily empty in spite of its clutter. Mary must be outside.

I skipped breakfast, washed and dressed quickly, so I could hurry to catch up with whatever task the elderly woman had gotten up to before sunrise. I tried to be a good assistant to my hostess, offering my younger back and hands in service to whatever she had going on each day.

But the real Billy wasn't in the doorway of the barn or anywhere else I would usually see him when Mary was tending to her daily business. The unlatched barn door creaked slightly on its hinges. The sound set my teeth on edge.

The long lone wooden match I'd dreamed about last night still haunted me. That was all.

The chickens were up with the rooster and hopefully poking through the gravel and dust. I shook off my unease and tossed them some cracked corn from the barrel. Their joy over breakfast came in the form of fluttering wings and scrambling for the best place to scratch among their brethren.

The familiar routine didn't make me relax because Mary was still nowhere to be seen.

Nanny goats stared out at me with big, unblinking eyes and bleated, puffs of dust around their feet punctuating their unease. It had been a dry winter and spring had arrived dry as well. The air was hot and heavy. The honeysuckle vine that nearly covered the blackened stone of Honeywick was wilting. The fragrance from the blossoms had gone faint on the breeze. Only a whiff of what it used to be.

"All right, ladies. What have you done with Billy?" I asked, only halfway joking.

I was used to following along with Mary's bustling routine. Suddenly, I was rudderless, drifting in the doldrums of a glassy sea. A familiar dread had risen up from my chest. I caught myself tense and bracing.

*For the next fist to fall.*

I didn't like my trepidation. Didn't like the familiarity of it after all this time. Not the dull thud of my heartbeat beneath a sharp ringing in my ears. Not the clammy sweat on my upper lip or the shaking in my fingers. Last night, I'd relived the night I'd left Richmond in my nightmares. It had brought the nightmare of my life with Ezekiel back to the forefront of my mind.

The sound of tires on gravel pulled my attention away from the nanny goats and my crippling physical reaction to Mary's disappearance. As if conjured by my thoughts, the tinker's truck pulled up the driveway.

His name was Michael Coombs. Most people called him Mack, but I thought of him as "the tinker" when I thought of him at all. *A broken man who repairs things.* Mary depended on him, as did many of the people around Morgan's Gap. His appearance was ordinary in an otherwise strange morning. And I liked ordinary above all else.

I moistened my lips, tasting an embarrassing amount of salt from where my nervous perspiration had dried in the sun. I rolled my shoulders. I put one foot in front of the other. I wasn't an abused child or a beaten wife. Not anymore.

"Mary called and asked me to come out and take a look at the cider press," the tinker said. His window was down, no doubt to catch as much as he could of the mountain breeze that would die before noon. I was startled, silent and motionless, by the need to make conversation on top of Mary's absence. I don't know why. He was all dungarees and tools as usual, as plain as could be. Except he wasn't plain, was he? In that moment, with his window down and his whole manner held still as if he was speaking to a deer that might startle away, I found myself staring at the shallow dimple in his chiseled chin, wondering if he had smiled, even once, since returning from Vietnam. "She said she was going away for a while," he continued.

"Away?" I echoed. I managed to close the lid of the chicken feed barrel. *Away is a place.* Why hadn't Mary told me she was leaving?

"She said you were going to make the cider this year. Asked me if I could help." He'd opened the door of his truck and stepped down without using the running board. He was a tall man and his polish-blackened boots squared off on the ground with the ease of practice. "Mary has early apples. Grow faster than most. Cider making is usually in late July. So at least that long."

He didn't act as if it was strange to remind me. I hadn't really been a part of any goings-on that involved anyone besides Mary May since I'd come here. I supposed everyone knew it. She was the one who managed the harvest, the cider making and especially the Market Days when Morgan's Gap was busy with locals bartering between each other for goods and services both simple and sublime. Mary's cider always fetched the best trades, but her goat cheese was also regularly in demand. "On account of the field apples," I'd heard her say. The goats loved the old bruised fruit she added to their feed and she swore it made their milk sweeter and the cheese she made from it richer and more filling. My part had always been hidden away, packing and unpacking her Market Day baskets.

I crammed my suddenly icy hands deep into the pockets of my coveralls. I liked pockets. I had ever since Mary had sewn me the first secret one. I kept my wedding day photograph buried deep in a pocket of an apron Mary had given me when I first came back to the orchard. Now the apron gift seemed portentous. It was one thing to help Mary with her tasks. It was another to take on her duties myself.

Two months alone. At least. There'd be no hiding away in that.

The very idea of facing a busy Morgan's Gap Market Day for the first time and alone made cold sweat break out on the back of my neck.

The tinker had continued on to the back of his truck where a cargo bed was lined by cedar rails much newer than the truck they framed. He'd come back from the war with a noticeable limp. "Such a shame," Mary said the townspeople whispered, as if bad luck might have followed the former quarterback home from the bloody jungles of Saigon. The injury still bothered him. I could tell. When he thought no one was looking, he would rub his upper thigh as if to ease the pain. He never caught my glances. We avoided eye contact altogether, like a shy dance, always looking away, away, away.

He lowered the tailgate with another practiced move, not even grunting, although the heavy rusted metal screeched in protest. Injured or not, he was a strong man, a working man. So unlike the Sect men I'd known who were all smooth hands and slicked back, plastic hair.

The truck bed was a jumble of tools and supplies, but he easily reached for an open toolbox with a slanted handle that must have weighed fifty pounds. He hoisted it out and turned back to face me, blowing a lock of dark brown hair back from where it had fallen in front of his eyes. Lots of returning soldiers let their hair grow long, I'd heard. The tinker certainly had. His head was thick with overgrown waves.

Our gazes bumped into each other, all clumsy and shocked. Distracted, I had stumbled in our dance. The one, two, three and one, two, three had skipped its measured beat and somehow I was at one when he was at three. And neither of us looked away. His eyes were blue. A dark, rich blue. Like the back of a barn swallow lit by the rising sun. But shadowed. Oh, God, so shadowed with shades of darkness I shouldn't be able to recognize, but I did. I'd seen shadows like those in my own eyes in the mirror.

I glanced away first.

"The cider press is in the barn," I stammered.

"All right. I'll get to work," the tinker said. He was always quiet, speaking sparingly with a deep, measured voice that flowed like liquid on the ears. If he'd seen anything unusual about my eyes, he hadn't let them shake him the way his had shaken me.

I don't know why I lingered near his truck when he walked away. I was drawn to the jumble that ended up being a fairly organized collection. There were neat coils of rope and boxes of bolts, nails and screws.

But it was the woodwork that caught my eye. The toys.

There were hand-carved trucks and cars. Limber Jack dolls fashioned out of walnut with their accompanying planks of wood that could be placed under a hip for the doll, suspended like a marionette in a child's hand, to tap dance upon. There was a hobby horse with a handsome carved head complete with a flowing mane and small wheels to hold the other end of its saddled stick. And there was a duck-and-ducklings pull toy painted yellow and attached to each other by string. There was also a bucket filled with smaller toys lashed to the side of the bed—simple wooden figures of people and animals, spiky jacks and hollowed-out whistles.

I hadn't expected to find colorful whimsy in the back of the tinker's truck. Or maybe something about the lettering on the side had clued me in that I might. A broken man who repaired things *and created happy new ones*. I was caught, fascinated by what this man's work said about him, even when he rarely said much at all. I found myself unable to put the duck and ducklings down after I'd picked them up for a closer look.

I turned from the truck, ducks held to my chest, and walked into the barn before I could change my mind.

# Three

*M*rs. Morgan lay not *in the manner of the deep but restless sleep laudanum gifted her, but sprawled, eyes half-open, mouth already stiffening in a rictus of despair.*

*The opiate liquid she regularly drank usually kept her nightmares at bay or at least made her forget them during the day. But now she looked as if her nightmares had materialized to drag her to hell.*

*Siobhán was struck still as a statue in the doorway of the steamship cabin she shared with her (former) mistress. Only her eyes moved, shifting her gaze back and forth between the new bottle she'd procured for Mrs. Morgan only yesterday—and the horror of its emptiness—and the corpse on the bed. It was many moments before she saw the spoon, usually used to carefully measure drafts, on the floor, longer still before the tangle of sheets wrapped around Mrs. Morgan's arms and the rent nightgown—once soft and luxurious, now torn to leave the vulnerable swell of one pale, cold breast bare.*

*Her feet propelled her back from the door, but not far. Only a few steps brought her body against the solid wall of Mr. Morgan.*

*A nightmare of her own.*

"Many barren women cannot live with the shame," Mr. Morgan said. His hands bit cruelly into Siobhán's upper arms, holding her, preventing her from escape. Useless to struggle. Better to pretend she believed what he said.

"Of course it was irresponsible of you to bring her more when I had expressly forbidden it. Did you also help her take it? Did you give her too much last night, Siobhán?" He spoke against her hair. The heat from his lips and tobacco-scented breath scalded her scalp.

It had been five years' work to obtain the position of lady's maid and companion to a wealthy coal baron's wife. She'd bided her time, always watching for an opportunity to fill a sudden, desperate need that would enable a clever woman to step in. The dream of traveling to America in first class rather than steerage had disintegrated once she'd met Penelope Morgan's husband.

"I should have known a delicate, highborn lady would be too weak to give me a son. I was too focused on her wealth and title. But I no longer need those things from a wife," Morgan continued.

Siobhán had seen him watching her from the start of the voyage. She'd adopted severity in her hair and she'd bound her chest. It had done her no good. He had overheard her mentioning her many brothers to Mrs. Morgan over tea. She'd seen the sharp speculation in his eyes.

"You will want for nothing," he said. His wife was still cooling on the bed several feet away. Mrs. Morgan had wanted kindness. A gentle hand. Love. "You will come with me to Virginia. You will not be named a murderess."

Siobhán was on a great ship in the middle of a churning sea. She closed her eyes and steadied her breathing. Her pulse slowed as she focused on the hidden seeds in her petticoat's hem. In the antechamber where she slept, the tiny wooden chest her father had carved waited under the cot with the blessed soil from her mother's herb garden. Holcomb Morgan was rich and powerful and perfectly capable of sending her to hang.

Virginia.

*For now, for the seeds and the soil and her family, she could only acquiesce.*

More often than not, since I'd sent Pearl away, I drank valerian tea before bed and rarely dreamed at all. She'd been so tiny and perfect, with one curled fist in her mouth and wrapped in a pale blue crocheted blanket Mary had started working on before I'd even arrived at her front door. I'd nursed her for several months until Mary said she was strong enough to be taken from my breast. But the memory of her—that cozy, powdery, yeasty scent unique to a baby's head, the exact yielding weight of her small body molding against mine, the grip of her small hand—stayed. And the memory of her would catch me unaware at times when I lifted a bag of flour or heard the bleating of the baby goats calling for their mothers.

Mary hadn't commented on my continued use of the tea. I'd diminished the tin on the counter several times. But that morning when I rose from my dreams where I'd been another woman from another time again, as desperate as I was, but twice as strong, I found the tin was missing from its place beside the stove.

There were still Morgans in this town, but our paths never crossed. My path rarely crossed with anyone if I could help it.

The absence of the tea felt like a message. Like the market basket and the cider card and the apple pie recipe placed where I would find them.

Laughter came to me on the breeze.

The day was sharp and cool and so bright I could easily wear a dimestore pair of white plastic sunglasses to hide my red-rimmed eyes. It wasn't Pearl's real birthday, but I always allowed myself to visit her on this day from afar, taking care not to be seen as I watched her celebrate.

Without me.

She was laughing and squealing with delight as only a lovingly indulged almost-four-year-old can, sunlight glinting off the gold-shot chestnut curls of her hair. I had cried that morning. Not something I normally did. But now, sheltered behind a copse of trees, my mouth curved into a smile.

Helen Newbill was a younger friend of Mary's. She was a midwife who'd never had any children of her own. Only she knew where Pearl had come from. And why her parentage needed to be hidden. She had picked the spring for Pearl's "birthday" and I liked her for it. New beginnings. Sunshine and balloons. Clowns and cupcakes.

In August I would quietly mark the exact moment of Pearl's birth, alone, the better to keep the precious secret of her to myself, but today she innocently enjoyed the celebration of her birth even if it wasn't held on the exact day she'd been born.

My arms still ached to hold her. There was a hollow in my chest where her love for me should be. But she was safe, deeply cared for and close enough for me to share her life in the only way possible—from a distance.

I was grateful for the clown-themed tablecloth and the bunch of balloons tied to one chair that bobbed merrily. Cheerful. Modern. Bringing me firmly back to the present. I was thrilled to see a handful of toddler friends come to celebrate with her and the pink frothy cupcakes her caretaker had made.

Helen and Pearl lived with a fat cat in a Queen Anne Victorian laced with gingerbread trim surrounded by a wrought-iron fence. It was a fairy-tale house complete with a flourishing kitchen garden that grew so abundantly it almost filled the entire backyard. Neighboring houses also had picturesque fences behind which children laughed and played within sight of a sleepy main street and no less than half a dozen steeples from around the town that peeked above rows of neatly planted maples and oaks.

I sang happy birthday under my breath. While we were singing, an old pickup truck pulled up to the curb. The tinker had finally arrived. His black truck had vintage-style lettering on the driver's-side door. The sign matched the rounded fenders and rust along the edges of the wheel wells.

I liked the curve and swirl of the letters that spelled out "Repairs," but that didn't explain why I had taken the risk. Mary's disappearance didn't explain it either. Being completely alone at Honeywick should have made me more cautious, not less so.

Pearl played with the duck tag-a-long for the rest of the party. The other children chased her around the yard about a million times. The tinker got a cupcake for his trouble and he chatted with the other adults while I watched from across the street.

I thought he spotted me once. His attention had focused on the park for several minutes too long. He hadn't given me away. He'd gone back to his lemonade, pausing only long enough to untangle the ducks half a dozen times before he took his leave. At the door of his truck he'd glanced toward the park again, but he didn't so much as nod in my direction.

When the last car had driven away and Pearl had gone inside, I finally rose from the bench to head home. Now I could celebrate that we'd made it through another year without detection.

My small blue Rambler wouldn't be familiar to anyone from my old life, but I hadn't driven to town. I always walked on the day of Pearl's party. It was best for me to slip in and out without notice. I'd headed out early to give myself plenty of time and I'd packed a flashlight in my purse for the long walk back.

I wasn't weak from hunger these days and my shoes fit fine.

If a feeling of being hunted sometimes woke me in the middle of the night, the memory of the sisters' burning eyes…and of my husband's fists…helped reassure me that I'd done better for my daughter than had ever been done for me.

I was well on my way at the outskirts of town when I heard the familiar rattle and rev of an engine pull up alongside me. I hadn't needed to turn on my flashlight, but I had. Its beam had given me the illusion of warmth and company as I left Pearl's laughter behind. I'd remembered more of a recent dream. *Siobhán*. It had replayed in my mind like a flickering memory of my own. Now I flicked off the light and turned to the tinker, who had his window rolled down.

"It'll be dark soon. Let me take you home," he said. He didn't ask if I was having car trouble or why I hadn't brought the Rambler to town. I'd been right. He'd seen me in the park. Between that and my purchase of the toy, he probably suspected why I might want to silently slip in and out of town.

Fear tightened my chest. I'd been so careful, for so long.

"I give people rides all the time. Practically a taxi service. Get in or I follow you all the way to the orchard. Mary wouldn't want you out here walking at night on your own."

The tightness in my chest eased slightly at his matter-of-fact tone. Mary trusted him, and it wasn't his fault I trusted no one. The quick ride he offered would be more discreet than a ten-mile hike, dark or not.

I walked around the front of the truck and used the running board to climb inside. Once I was settled he reached across me to help me pull the door shut. His nearness startled me into silent acceptance. The reach, the pull, the lean, our closeness, the whisper brush of our sleeves together were over in seconds. But my heart beat too fast, after. The cab was filled with the scent of sawdust—the sharp citrusy bite of cedar, the loamy richness of oak—and the vaguest hint of pipe tobacco.

"Thank you," I said, to break the spell cast by the scents and the silence following the slide of his sleeve against mine.

"No problem. Jack of all trades," he replied. "Or 'Mack' I should say."

I watched him from the corner of my eye as he gripped the knob to shift the truck into gear. He had rolled his window partially up while I'd walked around, but left it cracked for a breeze that made the pleasant scents in the cab swirl around my face.

The world had darkened enough that he needed to turn on the headlights. I held the switched-off flashlight tightly in my lap. The sheltered companionship of the truck's cab should have been comforting, but it wasn't. Pearl's greatest protection was my isolation. Besides, I didn't know how to sit companionably with a man.

I turned the radio on without asking permission. It was tuned to the only station we received in Morgan's Gap, so I only had to fiddle a little with the dial to get a clearer signal. Patsy Cline crooned in perfect accompaniment to the day I'd had. I turned her down so the lyrics weren't clear, only comforting noise to go along with the jangling, jostling rustle of the tinker's truck and its load.

From the rearview mirror, a wooden owl dangled. The awkward, jerky sway the truck's motion caused didn't do the majestic sweep of the owl's wingspan justice. I assumed the tinker had carved it midflight, every feather carefully rendered, quill by quill. I didn't mean to reach for it, but the move happened as if the owl was a magnet. I steadied it carefully with one finger and looked into its wide, staring eyes.

"I love him," I said. And it was true. Affection swelled in my heart for the carving that would have fit into the palm of my hand. So easy to love an inanimate object that posed no threat or possible loss.

"Everyone needs a mascot, I figure," the tinker replied.

He'd been a football star before he went to war. Even Mary May still talked about some of the feats he'd performed on the field, although I'd never known her to go to a game. Morgan's Gap's high school mascot was an eagle. Lots of people had brass eagles on their mailboxes and the courthouse flew the school banner complete with a garish cartoon bird under the United States flag. For some reason, I was suddenly, fiercely glad the tinker had picked this owl as his personal mascot. Things change. People change too. The man beside me wasn't a quarterback anymore. The graceful curves of the owl's wings and the big, watchful eyes on his face seemed more suited to a veteran with an artist's soul.

I lowered my hand to allow the owl to sway again.

"Mary goes wandering occasionally. She has for as long as I can remember," the tinker continued. Maybe he took my silence for sadness. And maybe he wasn't wrong. "Lots of old-timers on the mountain have what city folk would call peculiar ways. I find it best to leave them to it. Especially Miss Mary."

"She's very old. How could she get far without help?" I asked. In spite of the tinker's reassurance, I'd searched the whole farm several times for her and spent every moment expecting her footsteps on the stair. Mary hadn't wandered for as long as I'd known her, but Michael Coombs had known her much longer.

"I doubt she does much without help these days. But she has it. Everywhere she turns. You know that," he replied.

I did know. Mary kept to herself, but she had friends. Many as strange and fay as she was herself. Mack, the tinker.

Truvy Rey. Mavis Hall. Jo Shively. *And Granny Ross.*

Names left for me on a card like part of the recipe I should follow. I couldn't match the names to faces. I had only the vaguest idea of who the women were. I had become a hermit. For Pearl.

The thought left me with only the slightest pang that I might be hiding because it was easier to be alone.

The only illumination now was from the headlight beams in front of us and the faint glow from the radio. I didn't have to worry about the shadows in my eyes or his and I could freely trace his silhouette.

"I don't like pity," he suddenly said.

"Neither do I," I agreed.

I looked out the passenger window not realizing we'd come abreast of the field I usually made a point of avoiding. I had ghosts too. And this field was haunted by a giant circus tent with garish stripes of white and red.

Only this time the ghost solidified into something horribly real.

The red stripes had gone to faded pink.

The white had long turned to gray.

The stench of dry rotted canvas and sweat suddenly polluted the soft evening breeze. I coughed, gagging on what could only be an imagined smell. One that had lived a long time in a little girl's nightmares.

Headlights from dozens of vans circled like rounded wagons lit a frenzy of activity. Men in coveralls were hoisting ropes and welding hammers to anchor them to pikes on the ground.

"Stop," I said in a choked whisper.

Mack didn't ask why. He didn't hesitate. He responded to the urgency in my voice and pulled to the side of the road before we reached the field. I stretched to turn off the lights. We sat in silence while I tried to calm my panicked breathing. It wouldn't be the same tent. It wouldn't be the same people. Brother Tate had died years ago. A stroke had taken him in the middle of consummating his third marriage to a much younger woman. There were new matrons in charge at the girls' home. And yet, there were several dark sedans parked in the field.

Sect men always drove sedans the color of hearses. And just because their revivals hadn't traveled through Morgan's Gap in the last few years didn't mean we'd always be so lucky.

"Revival this weekend," Mack said. I had walked away from the Sect, but there was no "away" that was far enough to last. Hadn't I learned that lesson many years ago? I'd grown lax in my anonymity. I'd felt increasingly safer as Morgan's Gap had been skipped by the Sect's summer outreach year after year.

"Personally, I had my fill of fire and brimstone in the army. Kind of puts a man off those things," Mack said. The tent was all the way up now, an eyesore surrounded by ripped-up and smashed-down grass. The absence of other circus accouterments left it looking strange, a hulking thing repurposed for anything but levity and light.

"Or draws them to it," I said. "They gather in the lost ones. They fill the empty. I used to find anything I could to fill myself up—books, magazines, newspapers, music—to keep them out of my head."

"I'm going to drive on now, Rachel," Mack said. "I've seen the inside of Mary's house. Like a tattered and torn and well-loved library. You're full to bursting, I wager. Nothing to fear here."

I didn't protest. I had read every book Mary owned. Every magazine. And she'd brought me more. From the tiny Morgan's Gap library. From the newsstand at the grocery store. No one stopped me from reading the news. No one punished me if they found a novel under my pillow. Mack was right. But he was also very, very wrong. I had plenty to fear.

I was alone at the orchard and would be for a while by the sound of things.

I looked straight ahead as we passed the circus tent. We cruised by like any other truck would. The door to a Lincoln Continental opened and a man in a dark suit got out. I didn't look directly at him. From the corner of my eye, I noted him shift with us as we moved by—turning, turning until we were gone. His tracking stare made me hot, then ice cold.

I risked a glance in the rearview mirror, but it was too dark to see if the man was anyone I recognized. Then again, the icy frisson along my spine told me everything I needed to know. For a few years he'd practically owned me. I could only hope the recognition hadn't gone both ways.

We rode the rest of the way in silence. It took forever to reach the refuge of the cottage, and once we had, the noise of the gear shifting into park made me jump. The windows glinted with flashes of the moon peeking in and out of a midnight-blue sky filled with the skitter of clouds.

The farm was quiet. The goats and chickens had put themselves to bed out of habit and fear of predators in the dark.

I understood them better than I wanted to.

"I'll walk you to the door," Mack offered, as if he sensed I didn't want to be alone.

And I was immediately more afraid of other things. Like wanting the big tinker to linger for a while.

"I'm fine. I have my flashlight," I said, opening the door and flicking the flashlight on to illustrate my point. "Thanks for the ride."

Climbing into the truck with a man I was unaccountably drawn to after all this time had been enough sudden intimacy for today.

Just as he'd stopped the truck when I asked out on the main road, he acknowledged my dismissal without argument.

"I'll be back to finish fixing the press," he said.

I nodded and swung the passenger-side door closed. Mary had asked him to do that. The cider was important. I'd carry on with her wishes. After all, the press was in the barn. Nothing intimate about the bleat of goats and the smell of hay.

He didn't pull away until I had made it to the stoop and unlocked the door, but as soon as I crossed the threshold he put his vehicle in gear. I closed the door behind me and slid the bolt in to place. Against a world that had far too many Ezekiels and not enough considerate tinkers.

I made it to a chair at the table before my watery knees gave out, but it was a long time later before I was able to stand up and walk to the cold fireplace. The embroidery hoop was on the chair where I always left it, covered by an extra piece of unbleached muslin to protect it from soot when the fire burned. Sketching was frivolous and forbidden by the Sect but sewing had been allowed. I'd become so accomplished at mending no one cared if I used a little thread to embroider—if the subjects were appropriate. I had no audience who understood if I turned one of the sisters into a scolding blue jay or Brother Tate into a strutting banty rooster. Stitchery had been an outlet for my feelings when no other outlet was allowed.

I'd run away with only a few belongings, but the applewood needle box had been one of them. Mary May had seemed to expect me to take the chair by the old embroidery stand and the snake spoon when I'd arrived back in Morgan's Gap.

*"Best put her back for now. There isn't time for all that. She's been hanging there for fifty years; another ten won't matter."*

Dear Mary May. She had known I would be back. Just as she always knew other things—when a nanny goat would give birth or when a storm was coming.

She'd pulled muslin and thread from a cupboard and I'd gladly taken up the stitchery that had always comforted me.

Tonight, though, it was late. My eyes were grainy and tired from my earlier tears and some rest might diminish the hollow ache in my chest. The moonlight filtering in through the wavy glass of the windows made shadows undulate around the walls of the kitchen. It barely illuminated the faint letters that spelled out HONEYWICK in the cornerstone of the hearth and the scratched-out date that was even less distinguishable from the soot stain than it had been years before. But it was my companions, the wooden snake spoon and the apple orchard hoop, that drew my attention. Once, I'd thought the hoop charmed, like something from a fairy tale. Tonight, a sudden shifting light made me see movement again, the same way I had years ago.

I blinked. It was only an illusion caused by passing clouds and my dry eyes, and yet, I still reached for the wooden spoon. I'd worn it slightly smooth around its edges these last few years as I'd worried it often by the fire when my fingers grew weary from needle and thread. But tonight was the first time I rose with it in my hand and carried it with me to my bedroom.

Another year gone. Now Mary was gone as well and I'd been given a charge. I would need to take the goat cheese to sell and trade for the things I'd need while Mary was gone, and she must have left me with the names of the other wisewomen for a reason.

Mavis Hall, Truvy Rey, and Jo Shively.

And that last scribbled bit…

*Granny Ross.*

Hermit or not, I'd heard whispers about Ross women. I'd been living with a woman I considered fay for years. I'd seen a lot of unexplainable happenings with my own two eyes. Mary May wasn't only an eccentric old woman. She could predict the rain in the turn of a leaf. She could time the birth of a baby—goat or human—almost to the second. She could take the fire out of a burn and a wart from the skin with a pass of one gnarled hand. What did I have to fear from "witches"? There were darker things. Still, the old house creaked around me as the night wind picked up and whistled over the vine-covered shingles. Boards settled in the rafters and on the turret stairs. Not footsteps. Only age and the change in temperature as evening deepened and cool mountain air permeated cracks and crevices of the old house. I shivered, although the rock walls around me had stood for a hundred years or more.

*Here be witches and wayward girls grown into lonely women spooked by the wind.*

But with the familiar snake against my palm, the old house didn't feel as empty as it had before. I crawled under the faded quilt on my bed and fell asleep thinking about Hansel and Gretel and the bread-crumbs they'd dropped behind them on the way to the witch's hut in the forest.

# Four

*S*iobhán knew where to *plant the apple seeds.* Perhaps they knew where they needed to be and simply whispered the knowledge to her while she slept. The Morgan thought her very clever to wish for an orchard of her own. He gave her the land with barely a bat of his eye, completely focused on the high rocky peaks under which coal had been found.

Siobhán told no one else. Asked for no help. She went all alone to plant the seeds. The first on a slight rise in the middle of a meadow that had been cleared for timber to build the settlement houses. She ignored the stumps that would rot to feed the seeds she planted. From the rise, she spiraled outward, planting as she went in concentric circles. From a crow's eye view the symbol she traced with seeds would have been recognizable to the folk she'd lost and the ones she'd left behind.

Always. Forever. Unending.

Eigríoch.

As she planted each seed, she sprinkled a few grains of the dirt she'd brought all the way from home. Blessed Celtic dirt, kissed by the fae long before man

*walked the earth. The tears she'd kept inside throughout her long journey now
scorched trails of salty acid down her cheeks. She gathered them on her fingertips, wasting not a drop, and watered each seed with her grief. Better to turn it
around and do some good. Her loss would be another's gain. And so on. Until
time forgot how many Wright wisewomen and woodsmen had ever been.*

*Her own babes would be half Morgan. And from what she could tell her
husband's power came wholly from subjugating the land, not working with
it. He stood in opposition to nature, not in partnership with it. Yet, the wind
had blown her to him. The seeds had whispered. She could but listen and do
her best.*

*The sun was setting when the orchard was finished.*

*Siobhán sat beneath the rise where she'd planted the first seed. The words
her mother had taught her to say were neither spell nor prayer, but rather
some glorious in-between. Her hair flew away from her moist face, blown
by a breeze that sprang up in response to the fay power she invoked.*

*There was a sudden quickening all around her—in the air, under the
ground, and in her own body. What the land willed would be. She could
only pray the orchard would take root and grow. That it would watch over
her and her children and protect them. That it would show her the way to
live even as The Morgan killed a little more of her soul every day.*

I woke to a world that was muffled and strange. I quickly brewed some
strong chicory and gulped it down, bitter and unsweetened, to dispel the dream-haze lingering at the edges of my perceptions. Siobhán
Wright *Morgan*. With each dream, she became more and more real. It
was hard to think of her as a figment of my imagination when I lived
and breathed as her night after night.

And I had to admit she'd buoyed my courage with her long journey
and her determination. My reaction to the faded circus tent was out of

proportion to the threat it actually posed. The Sect drew heavily from rural communities to increase its membership. Summer revivals were common. Depression-era thinking and living still permeated these mountains. It was a place that much of the world had moved on from and forgotten. The people were hungry for salvation from poverty and hardship, if not in this life, then in another, better one, waiting for them when they died.

No longer groggy, I fetched the spoon I'd slept with and placed it back on its hook by the hearth. I traced the tiny snake as I always did, once, twice, three times. Had my fingers smoothed the scales over the last months of constant use? Or had I only gotten used to the carved bumps and ridges so they felt less distinct from my skin than they had before? Like the young woman in my dream, the whimsical snake seemed as if she might understand my predicament.

I had more in common with Siobhán than I had with the people who had raised me. No wonder I needed to believe she was real. Better that a kindred spirit once existed than that I was only the wayward worthless woman the Sect believed me to be. Beneath my fingers the snake felt worn and I drew my hands away lest I should ruin the old carving with my constant worrying.

*I haven't been found.* Pearl wouldn't be discovered. With her community connections, Mary had helped me cover my tracks well. I was hidden. Safe.

I completed the morning chores Mary had assigned to me and all of hers that I could remember as well. I let the chickens out to scratch and retrieved the eggs from the laying hens. The small kitchen garden was already well established. We'd babied it through the lack of rain. I gathered in a few tomatoes and cucumbers and watered the greens that Mary had said would keep producing well into winter if the weather was mild.

The sun was high in the sky when I finally admitted I was stalling.

Throughout the morning, I'd noticed the orchard as I hadn't before. The sweet scent of apples that had ripened early and fallen to the ground carried on the breeze to permeate the air. My stomach gurgled, reminding me that the cold biscuit I'd had that morning hadn't been a proper breakfast.

Over a split-rail fence that divided the property between orchard and farmyard, I could see the heavily laden trees. Their squat, spreading canopy bathed the ground in cool, green shadow and I suddenly needed to walk the same spirals I'd dreamed about.

I needed to revisit the one tree on the rise.

*Eigríoch.*

Mary May always told me to listen. She lived her life in a constant state of active intuition, as if she heard directions from the world around her for each footfall, each breath, each day.

I'd been in the orchard a thousand times since I'd come back to Morgan's Gap, but I'd never paid particular attention to any one tree. That seemed strange to me now. As if an old friend had been patiently waiting for me to reclaim our acquaintance.

Once, I'd made my way to the center of the orchard as if I'd been pulled by an invisible string. I could well remember practically collapsing beneath craggy, sheltering boughs. Had I somehow seen when it was planted in my dream? Or had I only imagined it? Had I seen its life begin as a seed carried all the way from Northern Ireland in Siobhán Wright's petticoats? Or was I only desperate for direction now that Mary was gone?

Mary had said that apple trees don't normally bear fruit after their fiftieth year, but her trees were special. I'd thought she'd meant well tended, but now I wondered. I'd never seen her trim or prune. I'd never seen her spray. My lips trembled with the memory of Siobhán's prayerful spell. Forever.

Had her orchard watched over her and her children as she'd hoped?

I followed Siobhán's path, tree by tree. I allowed my hands to go where they would from bark to branches to shining dark green leaves. I didn't touch the apples themselves for fear I would make them fall too soon. I wondered that I'd never seen a variety before that was a deep honeydew green splashed with crimson around the swell of every globe. I avoided the apples on the ground and their attendant dancing honeybees, their buzzing furies of yellow jacket wasps.

But I breathed in their scent—sweet as honey, sharp as resin, lush and earthy as molasses.

I tried to speak Siobhán's word for always, but, awake, my mouth was unfamiliar with how to shape the foreign consonants and vowels. I hummed instead, the rhythm of the words she'd spoken coming to me more easily than the pronunciation. As I walked through the rings of trees, one after another, a swelling fullness came to me. I hadn't known how empty my chest had been, for how long. My heart, after all, resided in town behind a pretty picket fence, unreachable, beating far away, keeping me alive, but barely.

The unexpected fullness—was it awe? Or reverence?—brought tears to my eyes. I was shocked by their sting. Yesterday, I'd cried all I was allowed to cry for the year—that was the bargain I'd made with God, with fate, to let my baby live happy and free. So I didn't allow the moisture to fall. But my vision prismed, turning the orchard into a sparkling wonder by the time I reached my destination.

The one tree. The first. It was smaller than I remembered from my childhood, but it was much bigger than the tiny mound of dirt that had covered the seed in my dream. Was it my imagination or were the apples on its branches larger than all the others in the orchard? The queen tree sitting higher than the rest in the orchard on a mossy green rise that was for all the world like a throne.

"Eigríoch," I suddenly said. "Her prayer was for the orchard, but she also meant to name you." Of course, the tree didn't reply to my fancy.

This time I didn't collapse. I stepped up the rise and sat carefully against the gnarled trunk. The Market Day basket was self-explanatory. I was already gathering my courage for that task, but I wondered about the list of names. Did Mary want me to reach out to those women for help?

"I'll make the cider from your apples and only yours. That's right, isn't it? The rest will go for pies and sauce, for butter and jelly. But yours will create the golden-brown liquid Mary prizes above all else."

Wind rushed through the leaves above my head. I imagined it as a soft, permissive response. Were these the kind of whispers that helped Mary know what to do?

I couldn't tend Pearl, but in Mary's absence, I could tend the orchard. I could manage the harvest and make certain that none of Siobhán Wright's effort went to waste.

Here, in the shade of the tree she had planted, I no longer wondered if Siobhán was real. She was here with me, among the trees, in the breeze, the echoes of her long-ago footsteps still reverently held in the springy depths of the moss that cushioned my seat.

I allowed my head to rest back on the tree and looked up into the canopy. No hint of sky showed through the branches, only lush fruit and the rustle of leafy shadows, so when a bright, emerald slither detached itself from the darker shades of forest and fern gully, I gasped in surprise. I wasn't afraid. The harmless serpent zigzagging its way from tiny bark ledge to knot to ledge again meant no menace. In that serpentine way, it made no haste to reach me and I was able to stare in fascination at its velvety scales. Its lack of shine meant it was about to shed its skin. I'd read that somewhere, sometime, in some hoarded bit of ephemera I'd found.

The snake was no bigger than a pencil or pen. Very like the snake on my spoon I'd loved since I'd seen it as a child. It paused on a low branch to rest or to scratch its loosening skin.

How many times had my fingers traced the carved wooden snake? I had memorized her. And here she was, as if my constant attention had brought her to life.

"You can't be her," I said. The little snake flicked its tongue out and in and out again, so tiny and pink and quick.

I wasn't Mary May, a woman who saw portents in clouds and imagined prophesy in the yolks of the eggs she cracked for breakfast. A wooden carving couldn't transform into a living, breathing creature.

And yet, I'd seen the clay statue of Billy in Mary's bedroom after the goat had disappeared.

One spring when I was still at the home, I'd discovered a tiny windowed alcove kept warm enough by a nearby bricked chimney to allow a tolerable place to hide and read. I'd snatched moments there, only moments, but long enough to discover that an early robin was building a nest under the eaves. It had been March and still too icy for many bugs. I'd crept away from dinner with a pocket of crumbled biscuit. The bird began to wait for me every evening. She would peck on the windowsill and I would tilt it open and beckon for her to come closer. I could still hear the flutter of her wings. Could remember the satisfaction of giving her the bits of bread even as my own insides gurgled with hunger.

The snake made me think of the robin, now, so many years later.

The sisters had caught me. Worst of all, in their eyes, I'd brought several younger girls up to the attic to meet the bird as well. I could still remember each child by the mending I'd done for them. Esther had loved daisies and I'd covered her threadbare jumper with them. Ruth of the perpetual chapped cheeks had gotten cardinals on her frayed Peter Pan collar. And tiny Mary, older than she appeared but who never seemed to grow even when I managed to slip her my milk and porridge, had weakly petted the rabbits leaping around the tattered hem of her skirt.

When I finally managed to sneak to the attic again after punishment—no bread for so long I learned to appreciate and long for the dry drop biscuits that were simply flour mixed with water—I found only the remnants of the nest the sisters must have destroyed.

It was then, on that day, I realized the beliefs they were trying to instill in us were wrong—ugly and twisted in ways I hadn't understood before in spite of their harshness. That there may very well be a heaven and hell, but hell on earth was created by cruelty. That kindness and care about a whole wide world was the counter to the Sect's hate. That the persistent belief in wonders they refused to see or hear might save me.

The snake's eyes glittered like tiny jet jewels, but it came no closer. I was halfway expecting it to slither all the way down and crawl into my pocket, so I stood up and stepped away. A carved wooden spoon did not become real no matter how lonely a person was for companionship.

As I stood at the base of Eigríoch, an apple fell with a dull thud beside my sneaker. I bent to pick it up while the green snake watched. The fall had slightly bruised the fruit on one side. From the battered skin an earthy molasses scent rose so strongly my stomach growled in response.

"Is this a gift, then, Old Tree?" I asked. I polished the apple with the corner of my shirt and then bit into it, accepting the present with gratitude magnified by my empty stomach. Juice flooded my mouth as I chewed. "Thank you," I managed through sticky lips.

Since I'd arrived at Honeywick, Mary had given me apples in every way imaginable—pies, cider, sauce and butter. But I'd never had an apple straight from the tree. I ate the tart fruit there and then, wiping the juice from my chin with my sleeve. During those luscious bites I gave not one thought to any of my troubles or to Siobhán's.

Later, I would feel guilty, but constant vigilance had worn me down so that the fruit, watered by mountain dew and fed—if my dreams could be believed—by dirt carried all the way from Northern Ireland, transported me from fear for long, precious moments.

When I was finished, I placed the core in my pocket to carry back to the compost pile. The snake had disappeared sometime while I'd concentrated on chewing. I ignored the urge to run back to the cottage to check if my spoon was still hanging by the hearth.

# Five

Market Day began in Morgan's Gap during post-settlement times when farmers had learned to take advantage of the crowd that gathered for once-a-month court hearings. Produce, livestock and other goods were brought to be sold or traded and it became a social event as much as an economic venture. Eventually, the people spread from the courthouse lawn to the adjacent scrubby green space that some gave the lofty moniker of "park."

Mary had often told me tales of Market Day happenings to make me smile... or in the hope I would choose to attend.

Unlike me, I'd bet the sturdy willow basket hadn't missed a Market Day in many years. I couldn't let it miss one now.

Once the fairgrounds diminished to a speck in my rearview mirror, I was surprised that my nervousness was joined by something that felt a lot like excitement. The sun was shining, the sky was blue and the forest that covered almost the entire mountaintop was a thousand shades of green shifting and trembling and swaying as I drove through. Mary called the forest the wildwood, and the name was fitting for the twining, twisting greenery that barely opened up to allow town, orchard, farms and roads to exist, hugged and hidden by the wilderness all around them. I cranked down my window to breathe deeply of a breeze cooled by woodsy shadows, remembering the long-ago rush of forest-scented air that had shown me the way out of the revival tent.

I was soon on the narrow winding streets that had never been laid out in an organized grid the way a true city's streets were. Morgan's Gap was a quirky, hodgepodge place that had been built over time in between rock and hollow and ravine. The old false fronts of the first constructed buildings appeared when you reached the end of the main road as if the town had sprung up from a mining crevice, an enchanted place like Brigadoon.

Enchanted or not, the community was struggling economically. Known for frequent mining accidents and poor management, the last easily accessible coal seam had been extracted a couple of years ago. Morgans still owned a big ugly Colonial-era house in the middle of town. As I drove by, I noticed all the windows were shuttered, as usual. Judson Morgan had invested in contract mine interests in the surrounding areas that kept the family wealthy and influential. It also kept them mostly absent. I'd never seen the descendants of The Morgan I dreamed about. Thank goodness.

To find work, the Morgan's Gap miners had to travel all the way to Grundy now and many had relocated altogether. The people who were left scraped along in what most people in the suburbs of Richmond would consider substandard living—small farms weren't lucrative and much of the land on Sugarloaf Mountain was national forest land.

Mary's wildwood might not be profitable, but it sure persisted when crops and mines failed.

It was bluegrass music I heard and not Gene Kelly singing as I pulled the Rambler into one of the few remaining spots along the street that encircled the courthouse and the park. Along with the cloudless sky and the forest breeze, the quickly plucked banjo and whiny contralto singing about a fox on the run made a grin stretch, unfamiliar and wide, on my face.

Had it really been so long since I'd smiled?

Thin sheets of plywood had been laid out around the four-man band to form an impromptu dance floor and several children were mimicking the one old lone man who was flat footing all by himself as if it was the most natural thing to do on a sunny Saturday morning. I paused after I'd retrieved the basket from the passenger side until I caught myself tapping my toe and scanning the children for a familiar chubby face and sparkling eyes.

Across the street from the courthouse and the park there was an old stone church with a tall, black-shingled steeple that stretched high above my head against a backdrop of cloudless sky. Its cheery red doors were thrown open wide to catch the breeze, and both the sanctuary above and the fellowship hall in the basement were open to the public. As I walked by with Mary's basket, I saw parishioners trimming the grass and hedges and decorating the interior of the church with fresh flowers and greenery for Sunday. I paused to make way for a bustling group carrying their own baskets and bags onto the lower level, where chairs were being arranged in a circle by a few others.

A pang unexpectedly hit me and my smile grew strained at the casual camaraderie of the group—laughter, conversation, teasing and fussing—all familiar and strange to me at the same time. Sect groups were always more stilted. Everyone watching, judging, playacting or fanatically shining with belief and me always trying to determine which one.

But never this.

Men and women, young and old, children and teenagers all working in and around the church. Many—even the women—wearing jeans.

"Be careful with that frame, Ryan. It's an old rickety thing," an elderly Black woman instructed a teenager with impressively drastic sideburns on each side of his cherubic face and a bright scarlet letterman's jacket on his back.

"Not the only old rickety thing that's still got some life in it," a heavily powdered and rouged white woman with bright pink lipstick joked as she took painfully arthritic steps along the walk. The two women nodded at me in appreciation for my deference as I stepped a little farther aside to allow them to cross.

"You should stay with us and piece awhile," a younger woman who had been setting up chairs said by way of greeting them at the basement door. She was talking to the boy. His cheeks flushed to match his jacket and he stuttered a negative reply in a voice that broke, going from deep to a high squeak.

"His father is over there selling some chickens. Ryan won't be able to help us sew our quilt top together today," the first woman said with a grumpy look over her hunched back toward the makeshift market. Her friend with seemingly aching joints huffed to show the world and the boy what she thought of that.

"Got some good laying hens," Ryan said with a cough after clearing his throat.

"Football and farming is all well and good, but you've got a special talent for design. Your father just doesn't understand," the younger woman said.

"Don't worry about it. Just come by whenever you can," the arthritic woman interrupted. "You're always welcome whenever you can slip away."

My pang was nothing compared to the longing on the teenager's face after a couple of older men had taken the quilt frame from him. He lingered, fingering the colorful pieces of cloth in the Black woman's basket.

The last of the straggling quilters passed me on the sidewalk and I moved on, taking a glimpse of possibility with me. There was hope in the women's easy friendship and in their acceptance of the teenage boy's obvious interest in sewing. There was real love in the air around the little church as a faith community came together. Not to hate, but to tend and support and create.

So different from the Sect.

Across the street and a little way from the church, beyond where the band played, there were two lopsided rows of makeshift tables covered in bright clothes and filled with an assortment of wares. The variety dazzled my homebody senses—produce, yes, but also all manner of instruments, implements and food—canned goods, fresh-baked bread and smoked meats, pottery, handmade dulcimers and drums, and baskets like the one I carried looped on the crook of my arm.

Music, laughter and conversation formed a pleasant hum of friendly activity. I made my way through with less trepidation than I'd expected. Honeywick had been home for a while, but Morgan's Gap was also home, especially since it sheltered and nurtured my Pearl.

Almost four years, safe and sound.

But the Sect tent had risen on the outskirts of town like a ticking clock counting down to when my daughter might be discovered.

"Saw you over there thinking about dancing," a smooth voice rang out at me while the other people swirled away and around. I turned to see a large Black man wearing an apron that must have been specially made to fit him. A tall white cap perched on the top of the man's bald head, and I watched, fascinated, as it didn't fall even though he manned a giant outdoor grill with tongs and dexterous speed—flip, turn, flip, turn. Delectable smoke rose up from the pork ribs he tended and he made quite an appealing sight surrounded by copious clouds of fragrant fog. Nerves eased by his smile, my stomach now gurgled for better, sweet and tangy reasons.

"Maybe a bite to eat before you hit the dance floor," he teased. "Ribs won't be ready till dinnertime, but I've got some fried peach pies over here. Come and get you one."

The sticky sweetness in the air identified, I followed the scent, as hungry for the friendliness of the offer as I was the fried pie. But I had to wait. Several people were in front of me in a line that stretched from the booth beside his grill. While I waited, I watched him turning ribs, fishing fried pies from a vat of golden oil bubbling on propane flame, then wrapping each pie in wax paper before he exchanged it for coins.

"Thank you, Mr. Warren," a woman in front of me said.

"You bring Hank back for some ribs later," Mr. Warren replied, his hat still perched even though he tilted his head down to wink at the shorter lady.

My interest was piqued when I heard a couple of Mr. Warren's patrons talking about a name I recognized.

"Don't you go messing with anything that Ross woman gives you to drink. I don't care if you do want David Belcher to look your way. Trouble. My mama always said there was nothing but trouble to be found up in Crone's Hollow with them Rosses."

My heartbeat quickened at the thought of what trouble I might find with Granny Ross. Mary had written her name on the very bottom of the recipe card as if she almost decided not to write it at all.

*But maybe wayward women can't afford to be afraid of witches.*

Finally, it was my turn, and I stood with a watering mouth while Mr. Warren wrapped a fresh fried pie for me. Its crust was crisped brown around the edges and here and there the amber fruit filling oozed.

Like a child, I flicked my tongue to taste the peach as soon as I had the treat in my hands.

Mr. Warren laughed at my happy sigh.

"I'll give my wife your compliments. She canned those peaches last summer and I reckon she might have canned 'em just for you. Here. Have another on the house. You're peaky. Put some meat on those bones," he said. I did feel peaky in comparison to the hale and hearty cook with his smoke rolling fit to fill the entire park with goodness.

The coins I'd given him suddenly weren't enough. I stepped to the side to allow the people behind me in line to buy their pies. There was a chair nearby and I perched on it to root around the cheese in Mary's basket. I found the stack of white linen squares I was looking for and I took my needle box from my skirt's pocket.

It was only a moment's work. For maybe fifteen minutes I stitched. When I was finished, I stood to find the pies were all gone and there was a lull in the crowd. I'd eaten every last crumb of both pies in between stitches, but they had fueled the creation of a plump pig in the corner of one square. On a whim, I had given the pig a tall chef's hat perched crookedly between his ears.

"Thank you for the extra peach pie," I said. "I'm Rachel. I live out at the orchard with Mary May." I stood and offered the handkerchief to the man behind the grill.

"Well, look at that. I was wondering what you were up to," Mr. Warren exclaimed.

"I sew things," I explained, but I couldn't really explain how the ideas for sewing came out of the blue at times. *Like Mary's wildwood whispers.* The sudden thought made the tingle in my fingers more electric.

"My wife's been after me to put up a sign. I'm going to show her this pig of yours," he said. "And she'll be glad Mary May's girl liked that pie so much as this."

I didn't correct him. He probably meant tenant or boarder. Not daughter. The pang in my chest at the designation was too personal to air by correcting an innocent mistake. "Everyone seems to love them."

Mr. Warren carefully folded the embroidered handkerchief and tucked it into a pocket of his apron. Then he used a corner of the apron to wipe his forehead. Again, I stared in wonder while his cap stayed put on his smooth head.

"Oh, not everyone." He nodded out toward the crowd, and I looked, curious about his meaning. At first, I couldn't see what he was referring to, but then as I stared I could see some townspeople giving the barbeque grill and pie booth a wide berth. "But as many as I could want. Those that don't can get on by." He smiled at me when I turned back and I saw a glitter in his eyes that said he wasn't so easygoing that he didn't know what was what.

"Their loss," I said.

"You'd better take your basket to a table before these ribs are cooked or everyone's going to be too busy licking their fingers to buy your things," Mr. Warren warned me, dismissing me and anybody who thought he minded bigots at all.

The hope I'd carried away from the church expanded a little bit more in my chest.

I thanked him again and made my way to an empty table, where I spread out Mary's carefully packaged cheese. I had barely settled into the festive atmosphere, the delicious pies still sweet on my tongue, when I noticed some men and women who were obviously Sect standing at the edge of the market. All the women, even the younger ones, wore kerchiefs like the ones only the matrons used to wear and likewise their clothes were uniformly made of muted colors. The majority of men wore flat-brimmed black hats. They weren't mingling and they stood as far away from the music as possible, but they handed out fliers to everyone who walked by their solemn group. No doubt advertising for the revival. Back before I ran away, there was already talk about adopting modest dress and plainer living. A few people skirted around them without taking papers, but far too many of the market goers reached out for fliers and even handshakes. Too many of the male townsfolk stood to the side for earnest conversation with the Sect men.

I didn't recognize anyone, but my pulse kicked up anyway and I licked a sudden clammy sweat from my upper lip. I wouldn't let their presence chase me away. At least they weren't coming by any of the tables, and I had no intention of approaching them.

I had hoped maybe some of the women on the recipe card would come by, but after I'd met dozens of people and my pockets were filled with coins I knew it wasn't going to be that easy. My wariness of the people handing out fliers didn't ease, but they stayed where they had stationed themselves and gradually I was at least able to look away.

While I waited to sell the last of the cheese, I stitched on some more linen squares. The band had gotten tired and had been replaced by an elderly Black woman picking a guitar. She caused the crowd to stir and many people shifted toward her playing. She still played bluegrass, but blended with a bluesy spirit. I liked it but felt the unexpected prick of salty moisture at the corner of my eyes even though I couldn't hear the lyrics. The tone was enough.

Even on this sunny day in the mostly friendly crowd, hope was tinged with the specter of sadness.

"I like ladybugs," a little girl suddenly said at my elbow. I hadn't been conscious of the tiny red insects I'd been sewing on the cloth in my hands. They walked, flew and sat prettily as if they'd sprung to life on their own beneath my needle.

"Don't crowd her, Bug," a woman gently scolded. To me she continued, "Her father calls her Lady Bug."

I finished the last black spot, snipped the thread and handed the fascinated little girl the completed handkerchief.

"Then, this must be for you," I said.

The mother opened the butterfly clasp of her pocketbook with a click, but I shook my head. "It was only a small thing to pass the time. A gift." The woman hesitated, then rushed on with a request for me to add more ladybugs to a child's cotton blouse she pulled from a shopping bag at her side, but only if I would charge her a fair price. I was happy to oblige. The little girl was singing to the ladybugs on her handkerchief as we spoke, happy but disconnected from everything going on around her.

"Ladybugs are just about the only thing that brings her out of her own little world," the mother explained.

I took the blouse and folded it carefully and placed it in Mary's basket, promising to have it completed soon.

The woman smiled and thanked me, then took her daughter by the hand to lead her and her new ladybug friends away. My heart swelled again, this time with the warmth of a secret kinship, mother-to-mother. I couldn't walk hand in hand with Pearl, but I'd given her the duck tag-a-long as this mother wanted to give her daughter ladybugs to make her smile.

My attention was suddenly drawn to a commotion. Children from all directions were making a beeline to something on the opposite side of the park. The tall, the small and all ages in between converged around a man I easily recognized from here. The tinker had arrived. He must have scolded the kids not to push and shove because suddenly they were all quietly waiting and patiently holding out their hands.

He took something from his pocket and placed it in the first outstretched hand. Then another and another. Each child would exclaim over his or her small gift, then run away to show friends, siblings and parents.

"He must spend all his free time carving those toys. Always has pockets full to give to the children. My Patty has a whole box full of bits and bobbles he's made," a woman said. She picked up a round of cheese and handed me some coins. "I guess he has to have something to do with his time now that he…well…he isn't who he used to be." A teenager in a letterman's jacket exactly like the one I'd seen on the teen named Ryan straightened his shoulders and shoved his hands in his pockets as if to prove they were empty. No silly old carved toys on him. My jaw clenched against the wholly unnecessary defense of a person who probably didn't care what these two thought of him. I wasn't surprised when the two of them avoided the barbeque grill and pie stand on their way out of the park. Or that Mr. Warren didn't call out to them to come over for some pie.

I tried not to be obvious about watching Mack give out all the toys while I continued to stitch. He laughed. He teased. He made more of an effort with some children as if he had carved something special just for them. A small boy with thick glasses exclaimed over a jackrabbit. A lanky girl with scabs on both knees and roller skates tossed over her left shoulder was rapturous over a pony.

There hadn't been any toys at the Home for Wayward Girls. We were expected to work as soon as we were able and even the smallest toddlers were given chores. Thank goodness my sewing had been seen as useful. I mostly mended, but I learned to cover holes and frayed hems and seams with embroidery, brightening our old faded garments as I went without anyone giving me grief.

Rabbits, robins, a silly old goose.

Butterflies, morning glories and smiling sunflowers.

The Sect folks had finally handed out all their papers and left. The weight of my memories eased with their departure.

The boys and girls around Mack were loudly enjoying their hand-made toys. He smiled and laughed with them and the sun shone down on their shared happiness and I was suddenly, fiercely glad to be in town today to see the tinker this way. Some people might think he'd come home too damaged or too different, but had he always taken the time to brighten a child's day?

He was making a new place for himself and finding ways to make the world a little bit better following his ordeal.

And a little was something.

A peach pie here. An embroidered pig there. A carved pony. Or tag-a-long ducks. Some cider. New acquaintances...that might even become friends. Morgan's Gap wasn't perfect, but lots of folks were trying. Maybe I could be a part of that in spite of my past and my secrets.

"Teresa told me you were going to embroider a shirt for her Molly. I thought I'd see if you could add butterflies to this pinafore I made for my daughter." A group of several young women interrupted my stitching. The one that spoke first held up a ruffled dress that looked like it would fit a first grader. One of her friends held up a plain white apron. "And I wondered if you'd embroider this for my grandmother's birthday next month." The third woman laughed and held up a plain pink skirt that looked exactly her size.

"I have room in the basket. Leave them with me and I'll see what I can do," I said. My fingers were already tingling as I took the dress, apron and skirt from the ladies. We exchanged names—Tess, Linda and Cindy. The new people I'd met were whirling in my mind when I sat back down and remembered the tinker.

All the children had finally run away with their Market Day prizes and I was well and caught looking his way by the carver himself. He had slowly moved closer and closer to my table and I hadn't even noticed until he stood alone with his hands in his pockets...looking at me. I paused in my stitching, an idea coming on so strongly that my fingers twitched on the needle and I almost dropped it.

This idea would have to wait, though. I wanted—no, needed—to add the saw-whet owl to my special project and I'd left it in my embroidery hoop at home.

Mack didn't come any closer. He stood for a while without moving, as if we were sharing a quiet moment together in the crowd even yards apart without saying a word. Then, suddenly, he nodded a hello as if remembering where he was and what he should be doing. He turned and walked away almost before I could acknowledge the nod with one of my own.

Disappointment threatened to sour the good, sweet peaches settling in my stomach. He was only respecting the parameters I'd set. Cool friendliness was all I wanted to allow, wasn't it? I started stitching again, experience helping me place the needle as my attention stayed on the retreating figure of the former quarterback.

I'd come to Market Day. I'd eaten pie that had inspired me to improve my own. I hadn't found the wisewomen whose names Mary had scribbled on the recipe card she'd left me, but I had sold her goat cheese, given away some gifts, and taken on some work. I had also managed to control my panic when the Sect had made an appearance. All in all, my chin was a little higher and my feet firmer on the ground when I headed back to my car.

I might not know how to have an easy friendship with a man. I might never know. But today was something and I refused to let my awkwardness with the tinker spoil it.

I would seek out Truvy Rey, Jo Shively and Mavis Hall even though the very idea made my heart race again. Moreover, I would go see Granny Ross in spite of the rumors. Or maybe because of them. Crone's Hollow. I'd braved a busy Market Day in town. I would brave reaching out to Mary May's friends. She had left me their names for a reason. It was time for me to figure out why.

But it was the tinker I thought about on the drive all the way to the orchard. The sound of the relaxed laughter Mack had shared with the children lingered in my ears, more appealing than an impending visit to a woman some thought of as a bona fide witch.

*Ezekiel*

Ezekiel Gray had been directed to the tinker's shop by a local primitive Baptist preacher whose congregation was helping with the music for his services beginning next week. A Big Tent Revival was always an occasion in towns like these.

Morgan's Gap had boomed and busted more than once with signs of success and failure in every direction. Mayor Morgan lived in a sprawling colonial mansion in the heart of town. On lopsided streets caused by the irregular geography of mountain ridges, large Victorians lined up side by side with tiny saltbox farmhouses. There were no modern suburbs. No high-rise apartments. And the main street looked very like it had looked for a hundred years, with simple shops and faded false fronts painted in shades of red, blue and green gone to softer hues than they'd once been.

Reverend Gray had become accustomed to the privilege his position as the guest of honor afforded him in small rural communities. There were churches of every shape, size and denomination in Morgan's Gap, but a traveling preacher was welcomed like a celebrity. New! Fresh! People made way as he walked down the street in his purposefully austere and old-fashioned great coat. They tipped their caps and nodded and he graciously inclined his head in return. He didn't welcome conversation. He kept his expression severe and he knew from examining it in many different mirrors that the wide-brimmed hat shadowing his eyes and features increased the gravity of his demeanor.

Not long ago he'd been visited by the idea of growing his hair long. The longer brown locks that brushed his shoulders now were threaded through with silver as befitted a wise prophet. His parents had known. God had inspired them to name him after the Founder. Ezekiel Gray. He was the direct descendant of the prophet who had established the Sect and a walking example of a godly man. They had raised him to be the leader he was destined to become. They had not spared the rod. And now that they were gone, he held *himself* to the highest standards.

Twice widowed, his people said. A tragic figure who nevertheless bore his hardships as only a man and the head of the church could. God's mouthpiece on earth.

Only he knew that when his second wife had driven her brand-new Oldsmobile Vista Cruiser into the river she'd been farther from home than she was allowed. And only he knew that her body was never found. The authorities had posited that her body had washed away even though there had been no heavy rains to support the conclusion. But he hadn't shared his doubts with the police or with his followers. They might not understand he'd been fooled by his lust for a young girl, one he'd assumed would make a good wife. He had buried an empty coffin. The best money could buy. He himself had preached the eulogy.

His devout parents—God rest their souls—had taught him strictly with flame, flagellation and fasting. As a young boy, he'd cried when his stomach was so hollow it hurt as it tried to eat itself. He'd cried even harder when they'd applied the heated iron of a cross to his buttocks, to mark him, to make him, to brand him as God's own messenger come again to earth.

His cries had been ignored.

He'd learned to stoically pray through his suffering instead. Until, as a teenager, he'd achieved the grace of finding the Holy Spirit in the flames. By then, he barely needed fuel from food. Pain drove him, fed him, energized him—his pain and the pain of others. He shared his penance any time he could with insects, first, then animals.

His father used the fireplace to heat the iron cross whenever Ezekiel needed the firmest of lessons. How he had dreaded it, and yet, he almost missed it as well. The last time his father had lit the fire, Ezekiel had been entranced by the rattle of the matchbox. He'd been transfixed by his father's hands as they'd drawn a long, unlit match from the box. He'd almost swooned in anticipation when the match slid and crackled to life against the roughened paper on the side of the box.

The flame as it devoured the burning match was like looking into the very eyes of God.

After that, he hadn't needed his mother and father anymore. He had stepped forward into the position they had prepared for him.

It was better to look for Rachel in every crowd anyway. Much better than when he'd seen his parents' faces, here, there, everywhere. Now it was a pair of accusatory dark eyes and thick brown curls he watched for; a tall, thin figure who had somehow refused to bend to his will. On every street corner, in every shop, during every sermon and potluck dinner, he searched for a familiar obstinate brow and Rachel's tight smile, the one that had constantly mocked him no matter how bruised or bloodied.

It was her empty grave that haunted him and not her swollen lips.

Her disappearance only proved she'd deserved every lesson he'd ever tried to teach her. He had never been able to accept her death without a body to bury. It was as if she'd slipped through his fingers before he was done with her. Then again, unfinished business would haunt any man.

He found the tinker in an old building that had gone from carriage house to garage before being turned into a workshop. Boom. Bust. But always hanging on. Peeling paint on the front of the building still advertised "Gas" and "Oil," but the solitary gas pump out front was missing its hose and some sort of thorny vines had busted out the glass. A newer sign swayed from a rusted iron arm. On the dangling shingle, a flourish of recently painted letters spelled out "Repairs."

The inside of the shop made his nose crinkle with competing scents of sawdust and oil, but he was on a mission and wouldn't be deterred.

"You there. Brother Tatum said you're the man who built the lectern in the gazebo on the green in the middle of town. Made of cherry. Fine work. Impressive. I'll begin preaching this weekend. You might have heard. And I need a new pulpit. To better glorify the message of our Lord..." He found himself unable to get wound up with his usual enthusiasm because the tinker had barely glanced at him in spite of his coat and his hat, in spite of his crown of silver-shot hair and his glorious mission.

"Saw the tent going up," the man said. But his focus was entirely on a piece of greasy machinery in his hands. His calloused, dirty hands. "I don't have time for a rush job right now."

"...No time?" The tinker's disrespect shocked him. His fists clenched in response and his teeth ground together. "You are being called to do the Lord's work."

The man placed the junk he had been working with on a scarred bench filled with piles of other rubbish. He slowly rose from his perch on a stool and finally looked up. He was taller and broader than Reverend Gray had initially thought. Much taller. Much broader. His fists loosened in response to the revelation.

"I have no interest in pulpits," the tinker said. He moved over to retrieve a large screwdriver from a hook on the wall. For the first time, Reverend Gray noticed thousands of tools on the wall, some sharp, some pointed, some with large blunt heads for hammering and some with fine chiseled edges for cutting.

But he also noticed the tinker's limp and an entire corner of the garage filled with *toys*. His lips curled into a disparaging smirk.

"No interest in the Lord's work, but plenty of interest in insignificant bobbles and bits, in frippery and nonsense," he replied.

"Mr. Coombs, my ducks won't come along today!" a little girl shouted as she and her mother came into the garage. Reverend Gray frowned, prepared to admonish the curly-headed child for shouting, for her untamed hair, for interrupting men's business. Before he could, the tinker *welcomed* her.

His whole manner changed to one of deference. And, strangely, he glanced from the toddler to Reverend Gray as if Ezekiel was the one who shouldn't be there. With no regard for a visiting reverend's status, he dropped everything to repair the child's broken toy, adjusting a loosened wheel as if ridiculous wooden ducks were more important than enhancing the message of God.

The girl's mother apologized for bothering the tinker, but she didn't spare a glance for Reverend Gray. She didn't nod or half bow or even blush. She was an older woman. The sort who were often given to straying from their appropriate place.

When his own blessed mother had died, she had shrieked as if she was possessed by demons. He had closed her gaping mouth and staring eyes himself, afterward. He had arranged her features into graceful, quiet repose.

As the girl waited for the tinker to examine her toy, she skipped around his workbench singing a nonsense song. Gray watched her, his eyes narrowed to show disapproval, but neither she nor her mother cared. Their disregard for him was shocking, but there was something else about the child that bothered him. Something he couldn't pinpoint. She paused in her skipping and met his stare, boldly, and for several long seconds they were locked in mutual perusal. He deepened his frown and he was finally rewarded by a sudden nervousness in the girl. She raised a lock of her curly hair to her mouth and absentmindedly chewed the end of a curl in a disgusting gesture he'd always abhorred.

"There. No problem. All fixed," the tinker said.

The man had hurried to help the child and now he practically pushed her and her mother out the door, thankfully removing the hair from her lips in the process. Gray paused as something about the young girl's mop of chestnut curls nudged him. They should be combed and pulled back into braids. For neatness and cleanliness. She couldn't chew a curl that wasn't free. The floppy ribbons on her dress were also too wild. The red apples embroidered around its hem flagrantly bright. There were even green worms crawling on each piece of fruit. The flash of their black bead eyes mocked him.

Only the little girl's face was as it should be, scrubbed fresh and shiny until her cheeks glowed.

"God despises disarray," he said, his usually modulated voice too loud in the space.

The woman and the girl stopped in the doorway. The young child's eyes had gone wide with fear at his angry tone. She was tiny and her mother wasn't much bigger. He drew himself up to his full height to loom over them.

"Morgan's Gap obviously needs a revival," he continued.

"In my experience, it's usually the preacher who needs an audience, not the other way around," the older woman said with a tilted smile.

The tinker laughed. The little girl mimicked him, although she couldn't possibly understand. He'd been right. The woman didn't know her place. The tinker moved forward before Ezekiel could decide if he should put her in it.

"I'm afraid Tatum wasted your time, Reverend," the tinker said. "The other podium was a special favor for an old friend. I don't generally do such large pieces." All humor was gone from his voice.

Ezekiel would have had to look up to meet the other man's eyes. He chose to walk away instead. Around the disrespectful woman and the recalcitrant child, who still laughed like the devil's offspring, a gratingly chipper sound—songbirds pecking at his eyes between every chirp. He would be eternally grateful his parents had raised him correctly. He faced challenges to his mission at every turn, but he would not be overcome by them.

Gray marched back through the town with even greater purpose. More people stopped and stared and gave way. He wasn't angry at the child or her mother. It wasn't rage at the tinker that burned in his belly and blazed from his eyes, drawing people's attention. It was the Spirit. Firing him up for the Holy work that must be done. His hands shook and he buried them deep in his pockets where the familiar rattle of the matchbox he always carried helped him to focus.

It was Rachel. She was the real reason he hadn't ascended to prominence. Her empty grave was a secret that gnawed at his confidence. People could see it. His failing. Whether she had washed away or run away made no difference. She had escaped him and the fire she deserved.

He needed to pray.

Surely as the second coming of Ezekiel Gray he would be given the opportunity to rectify his mistake. The very idea of Rachel's body finally buried where she belonged made him smile.

# Six

Siobhán

The Morgan Settlement, 1882

The same compulsion that *drew her to the place where she'd planted the orchard kept drawing her back to the sprouting trees.*

*First she sang to the planted seeds. Then she sang to the first hints of green. Before long she was singing to saplings much bigger than ordinary plantings would have been after only a fortnight in the ground. No one asked where she went or what she did and soon she was known for walking into the wildwood and disappearing for hours at a time. As long as she was home when The Morgan demanded her time and attention—always at night, always fast and furious and finished with no talk beyond his curses at her inability to conceive.*

*It was the mines that received most of his attention, thank God. The mines and the new railroad being constructed that would carry the coal he stole from the pillaged mountain to Richmond and beyond. Wrong of her to be glad for such a reprieve, but the bruises on her wrists and thighs, on her buttocks and breasts, made her fiercely glad indeed.*

*There were blossoms on the saplings that spring. Impossible blossoms,* delicate and pink with snowy white around each ruffled edge. She sang to the blossoms as she walked the spirals that morning, her fingers trailing over the silken petals. Her song was a lullaby, although there was no sleep in this place, only a biding, a pause upon waking.

The Morgan cursed her empty womb, but she didn't feel barren. She felt expectant. Even her bruises didn't matter. The blossoms on the saplings seemed a promise of better things to come.

She saw him for the first time with apple blossom pollen dusting her hands and fallen petals crushed beneath her bare feet. The air was sweet and heavy, lush with life, and the man who came over the knoll from the hollow beneath the new orchard wasn't a surprise. A breeze stirred, carrying with it a blush of color from the trees in butterflies of pink petals, which landed on his hair and shoulders. His hands were in his pockets. His feet and head were also bare. The flowers tangled in his curls.

She'd approached him without fear even though they were all alone, drawn to him by the same impulse that had drawn her here weeks ago.

"I've heard your singing before in the babble of the brook and in the wind through the trees. When the bees first stir to fly out into the dawning day, I've heard your song in the whir of their wings," the man said by way of greeting. It was so different from what she was used to that she paused several paces away from him, struck by his strangeness. He was tall, almost gaunt, but while his body had sharp angles and calloused hands, his eyes were as soft as the petal-flecked hair on his head. "I'm sorry I startled you. You're welcome here. You and the trees," he continued.

"This land is yours?" she asked, embarrassed because it had been fully hers in her mind moments before.

"This land belongs to no one, although man says I own this patch of it. When I say you're welcome it's because both of us feel the rightness of you being here, me and the land…and the bees," he said.

*Only then did she notice the hum in the air and the bobbing, swooping bodies of honeybees flitting from sapling to sapling.*

*"An offering…" she whispered. Now she recognized the bees' buzzing as part of the hum that had been such a warm welcome on the day she had planted the seeds. The first honeybees to this new world had come from across the ocean as well. Just as she had. Tossed by waves and circumstance.*

*"Yes. Certainly that. But also a spiral of give and take, receive and reward, life and death and life again," the man said. "I'm known as the beekeeper in the settlement. But aren't I kept as well? The honey and the mead, they strengthen me. The wildwood sustains. You've felt it. I've heard the knowing in your song. It's merely an echo, after all. A voicing. Adding words to the wordless singing all around us," he said.*

*"The beekeeper," Siobhán repeated. Sure enough, the honeybees weren't only collecting pollen from the apple blossoms on the trees. They were landing on the petals that were caught in the man's hair. They were resting on his shoulders with haunches brightly powdered by their industry.*

*"Harry O'Connell, at your service," the beekeeper said. But the name wasn't his any more than Morgan was hers.*

*He was a woodland creature more sprite than man. His bare feet, like hers, were comfortable in the grass. His loosened collar allowed the sun to brown the exposed skin of his neck and chest. Freckles jigged across his cheeks and nose with every change of expression and sunlight danced in the amber flecks of his brown eyes. He talked out loud in a way she recognized from thoughts and instincts she'd never heard put to spoken word.*

*"I'm Siobhán," she replied. Leaving out The Morgan and the settlement. Leaving out steamships and famine. Not because she was hiding any of those things, but because none of them mattered. Only the trees and the bees mattered now. Only the song of the wildwood that had brought them together before either of them had known how to sing.*

I was damp with sweat when I woke, my cheeks flushed by heated dreams that had made me ache for the kind of touch I'd never had. Siobhán had known more passion than I'd ever experienced. The Reverend had hated his lust for me and deemed it a necessary sin. When I didn't become pregnant, he'd come to bed colder and colder, as if he was punishing himself for my failure and his poor choice of me as a wife.

The beekeeper seemed more fairy than man. I'd read too much in my life and fancy fueled by fiction had to be influencing everything I dreamed. But his easy sensuality left me blushing at the way my imagination continued after waking.

Mack had phoned the night before. He had fixed the part for the cider press. He would be coming today to finish the repair.

He'd called before I'd gone to sleep, no valerian tea to stop my dreams.

I might be a runaway wife with a hidden child, but I was still a woman. The tinker was an attractive man. He was also the only man I'd been close to in a very long time. In my dreams, the beekeeper had looked completely different from the tinker...at first. But it had been Mack's face nestled between Siobhán's breasts when I woke.

I ate honey with toast for breakfast. The thick golden liquid in the glass pot winked at me in the sun streaming through the front kitchen window. Mary had said her honey came from an apiary nearby. I would never be able to glimpse a honeybee without blushing again.

Wild, fay Siobhán. The dreams were a secret history revealing itself slowly, ever so slowly, whenever I closed my eyes. They were detailed and vivid. Siobhán was real, and I wanted her to have a happily ever after with her beekeeper, but I was uneasy. I knew those bruises. I wanted to believe that Siobhán would leave The Morgan and his temper, but I knew she wasn't the type of person to run away.

Besides, what good would running away do if I, if she, was found?

As always, stitchery soothed.

I carefully chose several shades of green thread guided by the tingling in my calloused fingers. *This. That.* The rightness of the chosen colors settled warmly in my hands and heart. First I outlined a ribbony serpent with a forest green so dark it was almost black, then I filled in her scales with the lightest, brightest hue of sun-kissed grass. The spoon had gone missing. It was as simple and oh-so-complicated as that.

It was easy to suppose Mary had created a likeness of the pet she adored. But was it more than that? Had she created the goat that adored her from a lump of clay?

Mary believed in folk magic. She often spoke of portents and possibilities, and she baked pies the same way a doctor wrote prescriptions: "Take two bites and call me in the morning." When we baked/cooked/worked around the farm, Mary would point out all the natural prescriptives for what ailed man or beast—birch bark for headaches, pine tar for hoof health, cinnamon sticks over every door and window.

I had been raised by superstitious women. Their beliefs were in a bound book with a tooled leather cover, but what was the Book of Ezekiel if not a recipe for salvation? It wasn't a stretch for me to be drawn into Mary May's kinder, more rational practices.

*A glint of emerald moving through shadowed leaves.*

As I sewed, I named her. Eve. The whimsical little creature hanging by herself outside of the garden depicted on the hoop had stirred my wayward heart years ago. I'd thought often of her and of how the promise of paradise could never be found in a home with people who hurt me, no matter that I was told and taught that I deserved the pain. I had known that even as a girl. I hoped to see the tiny serpent again. Until then, I would have her likeness with me. A reminder that away was a place I was still trying to claim.

As my fingers plied the needle, they were directed by something deep down inside of me, deeper than blood, deeper than bone. It was my soul sewing, and after the snake I'd loved for years took new shape on the cloth in front of me, I was well and truly spent. Only the sound of Mack's truck arriving in the farmyard made me perk up and rise to go outside.

The tinker was already lifting his wooden toolbox from the back of his truck.

"This contraption is probably older than Mary," Mack said by way of greeting as he led the way into the barn.

"The orchard is very old. The first tree was planted in the nineteenth century," I replied. Mack paused and looked up at me from his kneeling position by the press. My cheeks grew hot. I only knew that from a dream. Blushes. And bees. I didn't try to resume our old dance. One couldn't waltz alone. I met his eyes. I didn't look away.

"I wouldn't be surprised if this press is that old too." He turned back to his task and I exhaled, long and shaky and slow. Dreams. Too many dreams. Of how good it could be between a man and a woman who cared for each other.

"The revival preacher came to my workshop. Ezekiel Gray. Someone had told him I would build him a pulpit," Mack said.

I didn't crumple to the floor only because I locked my knees against the fall while I tried to draw air past what felt like a sudden cannon ball embedded in my chest. After I'd seen the revival tent going up, I'd been afraid. It hadn't been because I was alone that night. It had been because the wind in the eaves had been warning me that Ezekiel was in town. The worst thing about fighting fear is that sometimes fear is justified. The tinker wasn't a nosy man, but he was watching my reaction as if he cared what I thought about the preacher's request. He'd been with me when I'd seen the Sect tent. While I struggled to breathe, he depressed the button on a dented oil can to lubricate the mechanism he'd put back into place. The click, click, click of his thumb on the mechanism drove the iron lodged in my breast deeper and deeper.

"Pulpits can be dangerous things. More dangerous than guns in some men's hands," I choked out. A superstitious dread crept spider-like along my spine as I spoke, as if referring to my husband would conjure him out of the shadows reeking of sulfur and burnt photographs; but I had to try to warn Mack away from him.

"What kind of man threatens a little girl? Pearl came into the shop while he was there. One of the wheels on her mother duck had come loose. She was excited. Laughing. That preacher acted like her laughter was an abomination," Mack said. His distaste for Ezekiel was written in the frown on his face. He hadn't needed my warning after all.

I blinked and swallowed hard, trying to quell the sensation of spiders on my skin. There was no hope of dispelling the leaden weight in my chest. It was dread of this very thing and I'd carried it always. Pearl and her father. In the same room. Face-to-face. But she was hidden. Still hidden. He couldn't have known. Couldn't tell. Would never feel the tug I felt deep in my womb every time I saw her or heard her or remembered her yeasty baby scent.

I finally drew in just enough air to sustain life, hoping for cleansing, but we were in the barn and the fresh forest breeze I instinctively knew I needed was dulled by a century of hay dust and chicken fluff.

"Rachel?" Mack looked closely at my face and reached for my shoulders.

All the blood had rushed to my feet. I swayed in place like a sickly sapling wilted by drought.

"A sick man. A terrible one. With twisted beliefs." My voice was a hoarse whisper. I might be revealing I'd known Ezekiel Gray in another life, but I forced the words out hoping to ease the lead in my lungs.

"Some folks around here will automatically welcome him and even defer to him as a man of the cloth." Mack released my arms when I managed to find my balance and keep to my feet. "But Pearl's mother saw him for what he is."

"And you," I added. I didn't correct him about Pearl's parentage. The false assumption sent shards of glass through my heart, but I let it pass. For her. She needed to be known as Helen's daughter. The preacher would come and go. The tent would go up and come down. He would leave and I would stay. Pearl would stay. With Helen. Hidden with Helen. There was hope for us still.

But the same sort of dread I felt for Siobhán Wright in my dreams I now felt on my own behalf. Was escape even possible in a world where husbands held all the keys?

Mack turned the handle of the press and it whirred to life, lowering the platform that must have crushed thousands upon thousands of apples so red they were almost black in its lifetime. I couldn't force the thank-you I needed to say from my lips because the descending platform seemed to crush my chest as well, slowly, slowly, even from several feet away.

"I told him I wasn't interested in building him a pulpit. He wasn't happy with me when he left." Mack straightened to his full height and I suddenly imagined the lanky figure of Ezekiel standing beside the broad-shouldered war vet. A fierce joy filled me, not unlike the one I'd experienced when I'd seen Mack handing out toys from his pockets on Market Day. He saw through Ezekiel Gray. Really saw him. There was a rightness to Michael Coombs that tingled through me in the same way the soul sewing did, as if the world was a virgin piece of muslin and he had been created with all the perfect colors of thread at its center. Suddenly, I felt less awkward with the tinker. Maybe I was beginning to understand how I could be friends with a man…if the man was Mack.

I remembered the urge to sew his saw-whet owl that had come over me at the market. I needed to stitch the owl flying within my protective honeysuckle circle. Because Ezekiel wasn't big and brave, but that didn't make him harmless.

I had learned the hard way that cowardice and violence went hand in hand.

"He doesn't need a fancy pulpit to be dangerous. Morgan's Gap would be better off without him." I tried not to rush back outside, but I couldn't help hurrying to find the wildwood breeze. Mack followed me into the morning sun. We both turned our faces toward the soft wind blowing from the trees that surrounded Honeywick and the orchard. I almost imagined a difference between the rustle of apple tree leaves and the leaves in the forest—oak, maple, locust and birch. The ebb and flow of the mountain breeze was almost like a wordless conversation between the trees, punctuated by the sibilant murmur of the pines.

Mary's whispering wood. My spidery nerves settled, soothed as much by Mack's distrust of Ezekiel as by the fresh air.

"It's always trouble when hatred finds a hollow where it can multiply itself. He'll find some echoes here, but hopefully the good will drown out the bad." Mack spoke his hopes to a small nanny goat that had bumped his leg for attention. He leaned down to scratch behind her ears. I was fascinated by the gentle movement of his large, calloused fingers. "Don't let folks like him keep you away from town. I saw you at the market. Looked like you were getting on just fine without Mary."

"I took on some work from people who had embroidery requests. And I met Jeremiah Warren," I said. Inconsequential things to a man who regularly traveled all over town, but they loomed like large accomplishments in a life that had been very small for a long time.

"Mrs. Warren grows the best peaches on the mountain and Jeremiah knows how to put them to good use," Mack replied. He smiled down at me in such an easygoing gesture of good humor it made the fresh air I'd been enjoying catch in my throat. Not a gasp. Not quite. But the dazzle of sunshine in the curls on his head and the twinkle in his eyes suddenly put Ezekiel Gray and the Sect far from my mind.

Maybe I could learn how to be friends with a man like Mack. But this? I wasn't prepared for this.

I should have laughed to match his lightheartedness, but my fingers were on fire with tingles and I could only long for my needle and thread…among other impossible things. The little goat had leaned into his gentle touch without any fear.

The smile on his lips faded and the spark in his eyes turned into a different kind of light all together. I was left with a much more serious Mack and my awkwardness intensified.

We stood for a while, both leaning toward each other, but moving no closer together. Inches. Feet. Yards. Across town. Did distance matter with Mack? There was a crackle between us even when we didn't touch. I definitely wasn't prepared.

"Well, I better get on with my sewing then. Thank you for fixing the press."

I took several steps toward the cottage, equal parts relieved and disappointed when he didn't urge me to linger. He followed me, but only to climb into the cab of his truck and crank the engine to rumbling life.

Why should that rumble bother me? Because it proclaimed that Mack was here or because it meant he was about to drive away? I wasn't prepared to physically touch him. Finding myself even thinking about it was intimidating and I should be glad he tuned into my feelings and humored them so easily.

"You can count on me. Anytime," Mack shouted above his truck's roar. He drove away, but his perceptive evaluation of Ezekiel echoed in my heart.

## Seven

*I spent the rest of* the day with never-ending spirals whirling behind my eyelids every time I blinked. The thought of Pearl's safety—and even Mack's—settled heavily on my shoulders.

I plied my needle hurriedly with fingers that tingled until the tips of my thumb and forefinger were almost numb. I sewed the carving I'd seen dangling from Mack's rearview mirror, but I gave the owl true flight. His wings stretched wide, soaring onto the muslin held tightly by the birch hoop.

Eve and the owl. The owl and Eve.

But it wasn't enough.

When I finished, I waited for the impulse to sew something else, but my fingers had dulled. I couldn't think what to sew for Pearl. I tried to calm my nerves. To quiet myself while I listened. But there was no tingling to show me the way.

Siobhán had been so brave.

It was one thing to hide. It was another entirely to protect. Siobhán had ritualistically planted the orchard and prayed for it to protect her and her future children. I went out on the front stoop of Honeywick so that I could listen closer, as I'd seen Mary do from time to time. I closed my eyes. Something about the rustling leaves, from the apple trees in the orchard to the surrounding wildwood and back again, made me believe dreaming about Siobhán had been a message for me. There was an urgency in the breeze-stirred conversation.

Or did the conversation stir the breeze?

I had no earth lovingly carried all the way from an Irish mother's blessed herb garden, but I did have apple seeds.

I used a chair to reach a high shelf where I'd seen a dusty jar full of the tiny brown teardrops. It rattled as I set it beside the recipe tin, pride of place in the center of the worn farm table made from slabs of wormy chestnut, scuffed by decades if not centuries of meals served on the now-familiar earthenware pottery plates and mugs.

I had seeds aplenty, but did I really think surrounding Pearl's home with spirals of planted apple seeds was going to protect her?

And still the breeze whispered through the leaves, urging, nudging, freshening my hope. Better to believe in fairy-tale fancy than to give in to despair.

He was here. He was here. He was here.

I couldn't drag Pearl away from her happy life in Morgan's Gap, but every beat of my heart echoed the warning like a mantra of damage he'd managed to etch into my arteries. He'd left me with a murmur, a fluttering weakness between every thump. But I wouldn't let the defect stop me. Just as Siobhán hadn't let The Morgan stop her.

I picked up the jar and shook the seeds to drown out the swoosh in my chest. I hadn't only watched Siobhán in my dreams. I had *been* her. I had taken every step. I had planted every seed. Maybe I could re-create those steps around Pearl. Maybe I could let her belief and bravery be my own.

I had followed the breeze once, long ago. It hadn't led me astray. I had found Mary May. I had discovered the orchard. Or it had discovered me. I felt a similar pull now, a familiar urging carried in the fresh mountain breeze.

I needed to plant new trees that would grow in a protective circle of life around my daughter.

Mary May had been so good to me. She'd given me a home and a refuge when I needed it most. I remembered her walking in the orchard. Often. I'd thought she'd been taking fresh air and exercise, but now I wondered if there had been more to her walks. A meditation. A casting. Around and around to the heart of the spirals created by the apple trees.

As I made the decision, Eve slithered onto the tabletop. I hadn't seen her come up from the floor, but there she was in relief, bright and green against the aged wood. She coiled in the spot where the jar had been and lifted her head to look at me with her shiny jet eyes. More spirals in her body. One, two, three. She had grown since I found her. Since I had sewn her effigy in my mountain montage.

"And do you approve of a midnight visit to Morgan's Gap?" I asked. She stretched her head higher, so high her serpentine body swayed to and fro to maintain her balance, inspiring me to reach out a hand. She came into my outstretched palm easily and effortlessly. The strength of her sinewy muscles was pleasant as they expanded and contracted to wrap her body around my wrist. "An unconventional bracelet, to be sure," I teased. But I did turn my arm this way and that to admire the gleam of her against my skin.

I hugged the jar of seeds with my other hand against my breast.

I had been raised on prayers and portents, on signs and symbols. The Sect sisters thought strict sacrifice of all luxury gained favor from God's representative on earth. What was that if not a spell woven with rough fabrics and chilblained fingers? An incantation murmured by gnawing bellies and muffled sobs before "godly" men who were never moved to pity? My robin had taught me that the Sect way was cruel and flawed, but a sudden breeze and my first taste of apples at Honeywick had given me hope there was a better way. My dreams as Siobhán had found a corresponding niche in my heart. We were women. We were in danger. Something must be done. And, for now, there was only me to do it.

It was well after midnight when I drove into town. I'd accidentally fallen asleep, but I'd dreamed of Siobhán planting the orchard again; so even though it was predawn by the time I left my car at the edge of the park across from Pearl's house, I didn't regret the fresh spirals in my mind. I didn't know what people would think if the seeds actually started to grow. Maybe townspeople would simply pull up the seedlings and throw them away. But I only needed the protection around Pearl to last as long as her father was preaching in Morgan's Gap.

Eve had disappeared while I slept.

No Mary. No Pearl. No Eve.

Only me.

I walked to the Queen Anne Victorian that was my daughter's home. Morgan's Gap felt cooler around me than it had on Market Day. It wasn't the temperature of the air, but the clandestine nature of my task. I didn't think even the friendlier people I'd seen at the market would approve of me preparing to cast a spell. The white gingerbread trim of Helen's house looked less idyllic in the dark. More gleaming and toothy. The blank windows glinted strangely beneath a pale sliver of moonlight.

Pearl was sleeping inside, completely unaware of danger.

Daunted but undeterred, I began to follow in Siobhán's footsteps. I was too shy to try to claim the words she'd said with my own lips and tongue. I only thought them as I stooped to press each seed into the ground. The entire town was still. No dog barked. No cock crowed. My breathing sounded loud by the time I'd walked around Pearl's house three times. I paused after the third loop. Three was important somehow. I sensed something in the air. Ozone? Smoke? Nothing, really. I couldn't physically detect whatever caused the slightly heavier atmosphere. And it faded so soon that I doubted I had truly felt it in the first place.

I continued.

During each pass, I willed my daughter to have a better childhood than I had. One with shoes that fit, books to read, music that wasn't funereal and absolutely no one crushing, bruising, switching or break-ing her, day by day. Robins if she wanted them. A whole flock.

Strawberries.

My mother had been in labor with me when she'd shown up asking the Sect sisters for help. She'd died at midnight just as I'd drawn my first breath. They never failed to remind me that I had killed her. That she was nothing but a loose woman with the mark of the devil on her shoulder, which she'd passed on to me. It was only an innocent straw-berry birthmark. I refused to believe their lies.

Her name had been Anna.

I rose from the last seed. The house was the center of the last spi-ral. I had ended right beside a window. There was no way of knowing what room was behind the dark glass. I couldn't see inside. My imag-ination made it seem as if Pearl was just beyond the panes and my heartbeat rushed painfully behind my ribs as I strained to see her and feared doing so at the same time. Seven spirals had been laid and I held my breath in anticipation.

Nothing happened. I was only a hollowed-out shell of numbness, waiting and waiting some more.

In my dreams, Siobhán's spirals had made a difference. I'd felt life embrace her with possibilities. But here and now, the earth didn't stir beneath my feet. My body simply shivered as a hint of dawn pinked the horizon. A strange lightness, as if I'd gone insubstantial as dandelion fluff, almost threatened to lift me off the ground. I heard a truck in the distance starting and stopping, then starting again. The milkman was beginning his deliveries. The sudden reality of morning routine barely managed to anchor me back to the ground, in someone else's yard.

I stood, swaying, willing myself back to normal from whatever balloon state I had entered.

If I was spotted, it would cause speculation, if not outright concern. This wasn't midday, when a woman might walk for fresh air in between her ironing and sweeping. Besides, the milkman would know all the women on his route and recognize I was out of place. I hurried back to my car, stumbling several times. I climbed in and turned on the heat, full blast, trying to dispel a chill that had nothing to do with the weather. I didn't linger even though the bold irrationality of what I had done made me too light-headed to drive.

This had been harder than going to Market Day. In that I had listened to Mary. In this I had followed the breeze again, and it had led me closer to Pearl than I'd been since her birth. So dangerous in so many ways. Because I wanted to be near her with every fiber of my being, even though I shouldn't be.

I didn't want to see the lights come on in the dark house and the bustling beginning of another day in my daughter's life. Not when I couldn't be a part of it. All I wanted was for Pearl to be safe. And yet, I also wanted to kiss her forehead again.

I leaned my head against the steering wheel for as long as I dared, fighting the urge to stay. To never leave her window again. But, of course, I had to, and just as the sun peeked over the horizon my foot somehow found the accelerator and I forced myself to press it toward the floor.

I drove back to the orchard, avoiding my slumped shoulders and the dejected look on my face in the rearview mirror. My secret daughter was probably no more protected than she had been a couple of hours ago, but I had tried.

It had nearly destroyed me, but I had tried.

# Eight

*Siobhán*
*The Morgan Settlement, 1883*

The Morgan didn't like *Ross women*. *They'd ventured deep into the Virginian wilderness when most Europeans had been content to settle on the coast. They'd been on the mountain longer than he had and most of them looked it, gnarled hands permanently stained by dirt and dyes and the green living things they grew and gifted to those who needed help around town. That's how they'd lived peaceably with the Cherokee for generations. Ross women rarely took husbands. But there had been love and passion. Some with Ross blood had gone away with their brethren when the soldiers and settlement came. Others had stayed.*

To Siobhán, *the women were like the bees, part of the hum that had welcomed her to her new home. Once she'd met them, they were as "home" to her as the apple orchard that was beginning to unfurl its leaves to the sky. As home to her as the apiary with its semicircle of woven skeps tended by a beekeeper with mossy eyes and curly chestnut hair.*

*Her husband muttered about witches and warned her to stay away. Then he went back to his coal and his grand scheme to somehow bring the railroad up the winding pass to the settlement nestled in the gap between one craggy peak and another. Morgan's Gap, they had begun to call it. As if the wildwood that claimed the entire mountain would acknowledge any ownership and The Morgan's dominion.*

*Siobhán didn't try to obey. She was a Morgan only in name. The babe that grew in her belly and the heart that beat in her chest were both Wrights. They knew the wildwood from peat and bog and fairy fen. The original Ross women had also traveled with seeds and soil, with feather and twig, with dried flowers and dandelion fluff. As Siobhán had planted an orchard, they had planted a garden, deep in the wildwood, and when it grew the entire forest had quickened.*

*But the wild magic had always been there.*

*Nature abides and different folk tend and tap into its power in different ways.*

*So every day she left the fine plank-board house The Morgan had built for her in the center of the fledgling town and went a-wandering. She visited the orchard, speaking prayerful spells to every tree and napping near the First Tree to dream about a fay kingdom she could almost see in the dust motes that floated in sunbeams, but only from the corners of her eyes when waking. She visited the Ross women and their wildwood garden. She helped them pick, grind, brew and steep. In the absence of her granny, they became the women who nurtured her. In the absence of her mother and aunts, they became the women who surrounded her with knowledge and acceptance.*

*And she continued to visit the beekeeper.*

*Oh, the keeper of the bees, with honeyed lips and knowing smiles, informed of all the secrets on the mountain by the bees' dance on his arms. He was otherworldly. Like the visions Siobhán saw at the edges of things, except warm and real and in her arms whenever she wished.*

*The Morgan had coveted her and claimed her. The beekeeper knew her. Understood the whispers of seeds and the sanctity of trees. He honored the abiding wild. He respected the Ross women and their medicinal brews. He was a woodsman like her brothers, but his bees made him something more.*

*He knew about the baby before The Morgan did. Knew without her telling. Simply from the slight change in her abdomen and the way she placed her hands upon it when she didn't know he was there. Was it his or The Morgan's? He didn't seem to care. It was hers and that was sacred. Part of a cycle he worshipped without going to a church at all.*

*She began to pray that the baby wasn't a Morgan.*

*As the newness of their marriage wore off, he controlled his temper less in front of her. He was a cruel, unforgiving man. Striking the maids and even his beautiful wife when they displeased him. His work was her salvation. His roughness in their marriage bed was her burden to bear.*

*The beekeeper kissed her bruises. His bees tickled the skin of her cheeks and breasts and stomach and thighs as he brought her to wild ecstasy with his lips and tongue. He showed her what softness and joy could be had between a man and a woman, as well as all that was ferocious without cruelty.*

*"Be careful, child. Drink this. Take care," the oldest Ross would chide.*

*Even the orchard seemed to whisper warnings when she visited to pray. For her loosened dresses could no longer hide what her husband or her lover, please God, had done.*

It was easy to imagine a poor, naïve immigrant as the victim of a sweet-talking hippy. Did they have the equivalent of love children in those olden days? I imagined Harry O'Connell driving a van painted with peace symbols to lure young women to outdoor concerts and radical communes with his sparking amber eyes. But no matter how my brain tried to jade my dreams on waking I knew Siobhán hadn't been naïve. Even if she had been hungry for kindred companionship, she hadn't been "led astray," as the sisters would have said.

I'd been her in my dreams. I'd felt the flush of her physical response to Harry O'Connell. From my skin all the way to my toes. But there had been a deeper connection between them as well. The bees. The trees.

*The wildwood.*

Hadn't I heard the trees whispering in the breeze that had shown me the way out of the revival tent? I had felt the pull of the First Tree myself years ago. The hollow inside of me now didn't negate what had happened then. Nor did the damaged heart in my chest. I remembered that tug, that inexorable pull. It was the same compulsion that had led Siobhán to the place where she'd planted her seeds. That had led her to Harry. That had led me to plant the seeds around the Queen Anne Victorian Pearl called home.

And every time the tingling in my fingers showed me what to sew.

Siobhán was a kindred spirit and my dreams were no coincidence.

Both of us had been trapped, forced into marriage by murderers.

And we'd both been called by the wildwood.

There hadn't been a ring on my finger for years. I no longer gave any credence to the church elder who had placed it there in the first place. But there was no denying that to the state, to the world, I was Ezekiel Gray's wife.

Why hadn't he ever taken another?

I'd heard the revival preacher was single. News traveled fast in Morgan's Gap and news of a "pious" widower even faster. I shuddered to think of how mountain mothers unmoved by marches and ideas of liberation might line up their unmarried daughters to parade them in front of Gray.

There had been no storms for weeks after I'd left. Maybe Ezekiel hadn't believed I'd drowned and washed away.

Missing. Runaway. Always a Wayward Girl.

He had much uglier reasons to find me, to bring me home, to punish me for what I had done.

The doctor had known I was pregnant.

What if Gray had never remarried because he knew there was a child?

# Nine

The road to the Ross cabin was marked by a small circle of stones that only contributed to the tales about the mysticism of their mountain home. I rarely socialized and even I had heard others talk about strange creatures in the wood surrounding Ross land and even stranger happenings—floating orbs in the dead of night, plants with miraculous healing powers, elixir streams bubbling up from the ground. I figured a lot of those same people would find my pet snake just as strange, but I still had an elevated heart rate when I turned onto the driveway that was little more than an overgrown path.

If the orchard had called me with a tug of a string knotted in my heart, the Ross cabin and the wildwood around it seemed more likely to warn me away. The sun was still high in the sky, but the forest crowded close to the drive, so close that branches and vines trailed along the side of the Rambler, tangling its tires and screeching along its hubcaps. Was it me or was it the cut man had made into the wildwood to create a road that the forest objected to?

The undergrowth was too thick to see more than a foot or two into the trees. The rest of the forest floor was a mystery shrouded in verdant shadows, an almost solid mass of vegetation. A living, breathing fortification. I inched the Rambler brazenly forward.

"Mary May sent me," I murmured aloud. Eve was coiled on the passenger seat beside a fresh-baked apple pie. But I wasn't speaking to her.

It was only coincidence that the road curved and opened up then. Past a barn and through two fields of wildflowers. The cabin itself appeared on a rise in a small clearing with a massive forested mountain behind it.

Smoke puffed from the rock chimney that protruded from the cabin's tarred tin roof. There were no wires for electricity. Laundry hung on a long line stretched taut between two birch trees. Around the trees and the house was a colorful blanket of wildflowers—blue, gold, purple and pink. As vivid as the cabin was drab. A woman had come out on the covered porch at the sound of my car. She was dressed in a floral-patterned cotton dress with a pinched waist, long sleeves and a skirt down to her ankles. She was more like the cabin than the dress and the wildflowers. Gray hair pulled back from her face in a tight bun, no makeup, plain. As I parked, she puffed a corncob pipe she held between a full set of even teeth.

"Well, don't sit there and gawk. Kettle's been whistling for nigh on to quarter of hour," the woman who must be Granny Ross scolded with a frown. She took the pipe from her mouth and tapped it on a porch rail to knock the remnants of tobacco ash out and onto the ground where a mound of old ashes indicated the move was a long-standing habit. Without pausing, she reached beside the pile to pull up a tendril of what looked like honeysuckle vine just beginning to reach for the wood of the stoop. Quick and efficient, as if she'd done it a million times, she tossed the bit of vine into the woods.

"Damnable stuff. Constant nuisance. Won't have it attracting the bees around here. No, sirree," Granny cursed and spit right where the plant had grown. I was startled by her vehemence, but I'd come this far…

"Do you mind if Eve comes along?" I asked, exiting the car with the pie in my hands and the tiny green snake wound around my wrist.

"Well…well…no mind. Come inside," Granny Ross answered. Surprise sat strangely on a face wrinkled by time and experience and probably more used to expressing a no-nonsense, know-it-all attitude. Eve had been unexpected. But not in the same way the snake had surprised me. The old woman's eyes flashed with sudden excitement.

I followed her inside with something akin to trepidation, but I was pleasantly met by a neat and cozy, if cluttered, space. Acres of soft, colorful textiles were piled onto and hung from every available surface to offset the rough-hewn log walls and low-timbered ceiling— embroidered pillows, hand-tied quilts, knitted afghans and hanging macramé. Beside the fireplace was an impressive willow basket stuffed with skeins of yarn stabbed in the center with worn wooden needles. It was too warm for a fire, but sure enough the kettle was whistling over a small one responsible for the smoke I'd seen curling from the chimney.

"I brought pie," I said, although I was somewhat ashamed of my offering. I'd followed the recipe Mary had left for me, but the crust was too dark and smelled more of scorched flour than cinnamon.

"I see that you did." Granny Ross nodded at a small wooden table near the hearth and I placed the pie there.

"I'll open a window so the heat won't get to you. I'm used to it and by now my old bones creak if I don't keep 'em toasted even in summer," Granny Ross said. Placing her pipe on the mantel, the old woman gestured toward a rocking chair situated in a corner away from the fire. I accepted the seat and watched her go to a window and wrench it open a crack, arranging a loose piece of mosquito netting over the opening to keep flies out. "Keep it simple here. No 'lectric stoves. No fans 'cept what we power ourselves." She fanned her face with her hands to illustrate what she meant, then came back to the fire and swung the kettle from the flame. She poured boiling water into two waiting pottery mugs on the hearth, placing the kettle back on its hook once the mugs were steaming and full. Taking the chair nearest the fire, she picked up her knitting needles, as if sitting and picking up were always moves executed together. Along with the needles came a rectangle of deep forest green that she began to knit and purl without missing a beat of our conversation.

The pie sat ignominiously ignored, and I can't say I blamed her.

"She tagged along with me today," I explained as if Eve was a lap-dog who had come along for the ride.

"But she doesn't always. Not if she doesn't approve, I'll wager." Granny Ross chuckled. "Got a weasel myself. Ain't here today, is he? Slick as a whistle, gone this morning without a trace. Ornery old cuss. But sometimes wildwood creatures will vanish if you're working hard on something too. Takes energy to manifest a critter. And to hold 'em. Gotta learn to tell the difference."

*Not if she doesn't approve.*

I remembered the apple seeds and wondered about Eve disappearing before I left for town. Had she disapproved of my effort or had I used every ounce of energy I had to create Siobhán's spirals from my dreams? I wasn't sure if I'd needed to recover from effort or emotion or both.

"Your drive is overgrown. It almost felt like the briars and brambles didn't want the Rambler to get through," I said. In spite of the warmth from the fire and the coziness of the décor, a liquid shiver down my spine made me sit up straight. Suddenly, I noticed the bundles of dried herbs and flowers hanging from the ceiling and other tied bundles of twigs and *paler things* that shone stark in the flickering light. Not bleached bones. Surely. Cork-stoppered bottles lined several kitchen shelves—viscous fluid, dried leaves and seeds formed strange patterns in them.

People thought Ross women were witches. Centuries ago and even today. Maybe the superstitions weren't that far off the mark.

"I do what I will. Whenever. Wherever. Whatever," Granny Ross said. "The wildwood is wise, but it doesn't know all. Never has. Never will. Some folks are too trusting. Me myself? I'm suspicious. Some folks say clever. Some folks say canny. Some folks say *witch*. But say what you will, I'm uneasy these days. Restless. There's goings-on in town that don't bode well. Not for you. Not for me. Not for anyone with animal companions or a place in the wildwood. Some say a man has come to town, but I say a devil."

Her knitting continued completely without attention as if her hands had a life their own and were determined to finish the piece while they could, row upon row, quick as you can. I watched, mesmerized, as the mysterious knitting took shape, but also because I couldn't meet her eyes. They did glitter, and sharply, like moss seen through glass. I was breathing, but my lungs felt too porous when she looked at me like that. Ineffectual. As if the oxygen I drew in wasn't getting where it needed to go.

"I've been safe at the orchard for a while," I whispered, as if Ezekiel Gray would hear me if I spoke too loudly.

Granny's knuckles went white as she tightened her grip on suddenly stilled needles.

"But not now. You're not safe now, girl. Not at all," Granny Ross said. "And what's more, you know it. You hear it in the wind and feel it in your blood. Ain't age that chills you so you draw close to the fire even as the days grow longer and hotter."

Eve had moved from my wrist to my lap. I'd been rocking her gently to and fro as if she was just hatched from her leathery egg. Her audible hiss startled me and I looked down to see she'd risen up as if she would strike at an invisible foe. The tip of her tiny tail whipped back and forth in the air, and if she'd had a rattle, it would have whirred a warning.

"I'm not sure what to do," I said. "I've been tending the farm, but I'm not…"

"You're not an orchard keeper. That's Mary's calling, not yours. And how do you know this deep down to your bones?" Granny Ross asked. "Not because of a burnt crust." Her knuckles had relaxed. She knitted again, but this time in slow motion. Knit…one…purl…two.

I'd come to see Granny Ross because of Mary's scribbles. Had she ever visited the cabin for a conversation that was more like a fortune-telling? I found myself compelled to share, as if my words were colorful loops of yarn wrapped around my hands and slowly dwindling down, line by line, toward the work in hers.

"I've been dreaming about an orchard keeper. Or an orchard maker named Siobhán. She planted the first apple trees," I said. "There's a man too. Harry O'Connell."

Click…click…click.

She took the words I'd given her and added them to another row in her lap.

"The beekeeper." Granny Ross sighed. It was a tired exhalation as if the topic wasn't pleasant to her. She gave up on her knitting. She placed it back into the willow basket and stabbed the knitting through with her wooden needles as if she needed to keep her handwork from running away. "I've dreamt of him before. And his bees." She shivered, and even if I hadn't seen her curse the honeysuckle vine, I would have guessed from the tight set of her jaw that she didn't like the dreams or honeybees at all.

"I'm missing something. Something I need to protect...myself." I'd caught the slip in time. Granny Ross was wise, but she didn't need to know all my secrets. And neither did her weasel, who had nosed his way past the screen netting to flow into the room, all liquid brown fur and eyes that gleamed with mischief like his mistress's.

"You've made a good start. Finally. After all this time," Granny Ross said. "Hiding will only keep you safe for so long. True protection comes from strength. Now that requires more." She rose and scooted the weasel away with one foot as she went to retrieve our steeped tea. "You've been here for what? Four years? Mary was smart to finally leave you to it. Though I expect her advanced years and the wildwood had a say in her timing." The wrinkles around her eyes and mouth somehow didn't mock her reference to Mary's age. "Some people do their best when their backs are up against a wall. You're like that. I can tell. There's power in you, but most of the time it's dormant. Waiting. Watching. You've got to figure out how to bring it to life. I can help you with that."

The cup was steaming when she brought it to me. The liquid in it was a duller green than Eve. It swirled with unidentified additives. Brown bits of—leaves?—floated on the top. Suddenly I was reminded of Alice. Eat me. Drink me. Liquor and cake. But no pie. She still ignored the burnt pastry offering and it sat on the little table like a silent testimony against my cookery skills. I didn't really want to drink Granny Ross's tea. It seemed momentous somehow. An admittance that there was no way back to hiding and that I could only go forward into mysteries and magic and possibly even mayhem.

Power. My fingers tingled at the thought.

When I sipped, it felt exactly like lifting the stale flap of the big circus tent and stepping outside. Surprisingly sweet and rich, the tea soaked into my body spreading warmth and energy before it even reached my stomach.

I licked my lips when I came to the last of it. I had seen the dregs in the bottom of the cup and I was suddenly dizzy, afraid the white powder left on the leaves might be dust from the bones I'd imagined in the bundles above my head.

"Keep dreaming if you must, but to truly prepare yourself you need to wake up, reach out, learn from wiser women around you," Granny Ross said. "Don't fear the waking. Don't shy away from your own strength."

Her weasel was sitting at my feet. I hadn't noticed him there, but Eve had. Her tail no longer twitched, but her jet gaze was locked with his. Neither of them moved or made a sound.

"I dreamed of Siobhán planting the orchard. I tried to re-create it. It was ritualistic, like she was placing a powerful ward into the earth against the man who was hurting her," I said, quietly. The dying flame from across the room flickered in the weasel's eyes. "My mimicry didn't work. Nothing happened."

"Sometimes you can feel it when the wildwood wakes in you . . . like a wind in your hair or a whiff of an approaching storm," Granny Ross sipped her tea with both hands as if she needed the remaining warmth from the cooling liquid. "But not always. It takes practice to recognize the signs. The tiniest speck of pollen is more powerful than anything man-made, but most folks barely notice. You might have started something that'll need finishing one day. You might have bought yourself some time. Never know."

"Time for what?" I asked, as mesmerized as Eve by the flames in the weasel's bright eyes. The creature still hadn't moved. I didn't know if his stillness was predatory or playful.

"To find yourself, of course." She leaned over and sat her mug on the hearth. "Those touched by the fae grow into their power, but sometimes they grow away from it too. You've got a spark. Can see it even now in your eyes. I'd imagine you shine on your birthday, don't ya? They say a birth day is special. That on the day and hour of your birth the veil between this world and the land of the fae is a gossamer thing." She stood and held her hand out for my mug. I gave it to her, but she didn't carry our mugs to the washbasin that sat on a nearby slab table. Instead, she examined the dregs left in the bottom, tilting the mug this way and that and glaring with narrowed eyes. "He was always going to come for you. He's a hunter, that one. He likes the pursuit. Especially of a quarry that has damaged his pride. He's angrier now than he ever was. You escaped them, didn't you?" I started in my chair. "Maybe even escaped him, eh? And your escape revealed his weakness. To himself. To the world. You're the one he looks for, aren't you? He searches every crowd for your face. Wanders the streets. Looking, always looking."

Was I the one Ezekiel was looking for? Or did he somehow know about his daughter? *I'd imagine you shine on your birthday, don't ya?*

"Do you see all this in my mug?" I asked. Mary May wouldn't have betrayed my secrets, but how much did the wildwood breeze carry to every wisewoman willing to lend it her ear? The weasel had finally settled in front of the fireplace, where the flame had diminished to embers that still warmed the floor. His relaxation only highlighted my tension. Granny's warning had found its echo in what I already knew, and my entire body tingled as it braced for impact—once you've accustomed yourself to expecting fists and fury that expectation never goes away. You're always halfway to a tornado's coming position. Eve hissed again even though the weasel had left her alone and seemed to be sound asleep.

"Well, that, and I went to a revival meeting, didn't I? Walked right in and sat down to hear what he had to say," Granny said. Her eyes still shone with a dark light, but there was no humor in the pinched quirk of her lips. "Tent didn't fall. No flames licked at my feet. But damnation was there, all right. Bubbling up like a hot spring in many a person's belly. Ezekiel Gray ain't the only one who's mad. And he draws the angry to him like flies to spoilt milk."

I could remember sitting in church with my head full of passages I'd memorized from books to protect myself from the fury streaming from the pulpit. It had been years before I knew that was what drew me to reading materials—my own warding begun when I was small, a word at a time.

"Revival usually only goes for a week or two. That's when the money and enthusiasm seems to run out," I stammered. The hot air around us practically shimmered with Granny's warning or prediction or reading. Whatever had just happened made goose bumps rise on my skin. What if Ezekiel was still in town on Pearl's birthday? My shining fay girl.

"We'll see," Granny Ross said. But her eyes were narrowed, her lips pursed. "For now, you've got work to do. Eve will help. Pay attention to her. What she does. What she doesn't do. When she appears. When she disappears. It's a conversation she's helping along between you and the wildwood. She's no ordinary snake."

"There was a carved wooden embroidery hoop on a stand in Mary's kitchen," I whispered. "And a spoon." Crazy to think a carved snake had become real. But no crazier than an orchard calling to you or leaves whispering your name.

From birth, I'd been raised to believe in the miraculous. I had only ever been skeptical of my dull Sect teachers, not the existence of miracles themselves. What was the flash of a robin's wing outside the dirty window of a lonely attic? What was a still-steaming piece of apple pie fresh from the oven and placed before you when your stomach had never been full a day in your life? What was a needle and a fine length of bright scarlet thread?

Miraculous. All.

"A hoop and a spoon…" Granny's eyes narrowed thoughtfully and she rubbed both of her calloused thumbs into the palms of her hands, around and around, as if her thoughts would be helped by the ridges and lines life had left there. "Stitching and stirring. Stirring and stitching. Keeping an orchard is important. Harvesting and brewing? All important." Granny paused and closed her eyes. I leaned in to hear soft, whispered murmuring, but her words weren't distinct. She whispered to herself or to the wildwood, not to me. Then, her eyes popped open, and I jumped. "But, now, *stitching and stirring* is a whole other thing. Takes lots of practice to get it right. Some never do. You're going to need courage. The kind of courage that makes a young girl stand up and walk away. The kind of courage that makes a mother jump in harm's way, between the very devil and her child," Granny said. A faraway look had come into her eyes and I knew when she spoke of a mother she wasn't speaking of me. "Folks call it handwork or women's work and I figure it is. Only wisewomen can handle the magic that rises from a pair of busy hands."

She stopped swirling her thumbs and lifted one up to examine its tough pad closer to her face. I could see a white scar there, shining against the tanned skin of her hand. "Stitching is repairing what's torn. It's more than mending. It's creation. Bringing threads together to make something new. You'll find yourself stirring things up before you know what's what. You've lived a hushed life these last few years, but there's a lot in you. I can tell. I can feel the gumption sizzling beneath those sad eyes and the ideas roiling in your gut." Granny lowered her hand and placed both palms on her narrow hips. She raised her chin and met my eyes. "A spoon and a hoop? Those are challenges as well as a gifts."

Eve was no longer paying attention to the sleeping weasel. She had coiled herself around my wrist again, as if she was ready to go, so I stood. And Granny nodded as if I was doing what she had advised: listening to a tiny green snake.

"You should add some honey to your apples," Granny said, as if she'd had a sudden inspiration, but she shared it grudgingly. "Potent stuff, honey. Dangerous..." She paused, thoughtfully, chewing the pad of her thumb. "...But sometimes danger is necessary." She let out a huff like she was blowing away her uncertainty. "Practice that pie but guard your heart from the beekeeper. He's long gone. No good will come of falling in love with him now." At that she cackled and the hair rose on the back of my neck. "On the other hand, Michael Coombs is flesh and blood, isn't he? Complicated. But definitely flesh and blood."

"I have no intention of marrying, Granny Ross," I said sternly as I crossed to the door.

"Did I say anything about marriage?" Granny snorted.

The tiny fire in her hearth had nothing on the heat in my cheeks. I hadn't mentioned the tinker. Not once. What had she seen in those dregs? Gentle, calloused hands and children's laughter. The smallest of owls and the scent of sawdust, a surprisingly appealing cologne.

I carried Eve back to the car, pretty sure my hot cheeks meant they were twin beacons of red. Granny followed me out but stopped on the porch with her pipe back between her teeth. She lit it while I opened the car door, but I didn't see a lighter or a match. Only the quick snap of gnarled fingers and a sudden spark to the corncob bowl.

*Some dabble. A little of this. A little of that.*

I was uncertain of what the orchard or the greater wildwood wanted from me, but I knew I didn't have time to dabble. Pearl might be growing into her gifts, but she was still so young. If she was going to "shine" on her birthday while Ezekiel was in town, then I needed to protect her. Before I could get in the car, the sound of another vehicle broke the bubble of isolated wilderness I stood in with Granny. I turned to see a Volkswagen minibus resolutely chugging up the lane. More grass than dirt, the road didn't seem to bother the smiling Black woman behind the wheel who waved from her open window. Beside her, as if it was riding shotgun in the passenger seat, was a worn guitar case. Hand-painted on the side of the bus was a large sun with exaggerated sunbeams extending in all directions and "The Reys" spelled out in enthusiastic swirling letters.

"Well, now I see what that was all about," the woman said as she parked the yellow-and-white bus beside my Rambler. "I was busy, you know. No telling what I'll find when I get back, leaving laundry day to Primrose, alone."

"That girl is plenty old enough to hang the washing, Truvy," Granny scoffed, around the pipe in her mouth. A cloud of smoke fanned out around her wizened face. "Besides, she's probably got half a dozen cousins there to help. You worry too much."

"You're the one worrying, old woman. Or I wouldn't be here," Truvy replied. She opened the door of the VW and jumped to the ground. It was a big leap for her. She was tinier than Granny Ross, even with an impressive Afro that added six inches to her height, but she didn't seem one bit intimidated by the scowling woman on the porch. I towered over both of them, but their spirited banter made me feel small.

"Not a bit. Not a bit. No call for it. A little of this, a little of that, we'll soon have things right as rain," Granny insisted.

"Rain sure would be nice," Truvy said. She fanned the neck of her brightly colored minidress, making the geometric pattern dance. Then she walked around the Rambler and stretched out her hand. "I'm Gertrude Ivy Rey. Little brother couldn't get that mouthful out so I've been Truvy since he was in diapers."

"Truvy is your east-wise neighbor, give or take fifteen miles as the crow flies," Granny informed me.

"Partial to whip-poor-wills myself," Truvy added, extending her hand.

I liked the tiny woman's easy manner and the crinkled edges around warm brown eyes that said her smile was frequent. I didn't come from a background where women shook hands, but I reached for hers quickly. I might have been raised by bigots who didn't like that times were changing, but I didn't agree. Her hand was strong and warm. Where the pads of her fingers brushed the back of my hand, the hard ridge on the tip of each was noticeable. A musician's calluses from the guitar strings she must often pluck and strum. She squeezed my hand tight and I reciprocated. Eve went along for the ride, but Truvy didn't startle or jump back from the tiny green snake. She only blinked, slowly and thoughtfully. Her eyelashes weren't artificial. They lushly framed eyes shining with certainty and self-assurance I'd never experienced myself.

"Well, now I really do see," Truvy said. "That's how it is, huh?" She asked the last of Granny Ross and the old woman went so far as to take her pipe from her lips to reply, solemnly.

"Yes. The balance is off. Things are shifting. Trying to make up for it. But this lack of rain ain't right. The whole mountain is simmering. Some brewing to do, for sure," she said.

"And some stitching and stirring," I added, flexing my tingling fingers.

Both women looked at me. Truvy in surprise and Granny...was that appreciation in her eyes? I couldn't be sure.

"I'm Rachel...Smith," I said. I'd never had a last name of my own and I certainly had no intention of using Ezekiel's ever again.

She nodded, looking from Eve to me to Granny Ross, who still stood on the porch above us.

"Truvy plays the guitar. And sings like her grandmother. All the Reys do. The wildwood speaks through us in different ways, but certain ways tend to run in families. Singing, stitching, brewing," Granny said.

"I pick and pluck. Note by note. Sometimes the notes come together to make a pleasant sound. Sometimes they just tell me a thing or two when I listen. When I feel the vibrations," Truvy said. Granny Ross might be the witch, but Truvy Rey had her own share of unaccountable knowledge; it twinkled in her deep brown eyes like fairy lights in a shadowy forest at night.

"Always trying to play for me and tell me what she hears or feels. As if the leaves in the bottom of a cup don't tell me all I need to know," Granny grunted around her pipe.

"Stubborn old woman," Truvy said, but not unkindly. "Know-it-all." She sniffed to tell Granny and possibly me what she thought of that.

Our hands were still clasped. Truvy examined Granny, then me, suddenly more serious. My fingers tingled. It wasn't loss of circulation. It was the same kind of energy I felt when I sewed but intensified, as if the calluses on her fingers were compelling me to action. Come to think of it, I had calluses on my own fingers where years of needlework had left a soft ridge on my middle and pointer fingers and on the pad of my thumb.

"You come to see me soon, ya hear. I'll play for you," she whispered.

I looked down into big dark eyes that swirled with too many secrets.

Maybe the vibrations of her guitar strings had told her things about the whole darn town. But I had bigger secrets than most. Too big to trust to a woman I'd only just met.

Truvy smiled; her forehead softened and the secrets in her eyes lightened as sparkles of sunlight came through the trees to warm our heads.

"Don't mind me, girl," Granny advised. "If she offers to play for you, you should take her up on it. Folks always hounding her to play for them and she only does it when the strings call her to do it."

Another vehicle interrupted our introductions. This time it was an old motorcycle with a sidecar and I started in disbelief as it sped up the drive, kicking up dirt and grass beneath its rear wheel. A bright red scarf flowed behind the driver, and an old leather helmet, goggles and a bomber jacket completed the jaunty ensemble. The motorcycle spun to a stop with a flare of torn turf and a final rev of what had to be a World War II–era engine, judging from the black smoke and the rattling of the entire assembly.

"That girl always has to make an entrance," Granny grumbled.

I was suddenly charmed by the idea that we were all girls to Granny, whether we'd been many years women or not. To a woman of her advanced years, I supposed, we all did look young. With plenty of adventures...and mistakes...ahead of us.

"Don't start without me," the driver called as she kicked the stand of the cycle into place. She dismounted and pulled off her goggles and helmet, revealing a head full of rusty auburn curls and a movie star's face. How did a person not smear their lipstick while motorcycling through the wilderness? She tossed the protective equipment over the handle of the motorbike and unzipped her jacket. "Mavis sends her regards. Not too happy I was called away," the cyclist said. "And who is this?"

"Rachel, meet Jo. Jo Shively. The wildwood saw fit to saddle us with a young'un and I have complained ever since," Granny said. I was beginning to be able to tell when she was really grumpy and when she was only sparking. Her eyes told the tale, bright and twinkling when she was not actually in bad humor. She liked Jo (as well as she liked anyone) and was glad to see her.

"It's nice to meet you," I said.

"Oh, yes, I've heard all about the pretty neighbor with the sad eyes," Jo said.

"She's been dreaming about Harry," Granny said, for all the world as if she was sharing juicy gossip of a real tryst.

"Beekeeper dreams," Jo replied with a distant look. "I don't even like men and he's visited me a few times. Although I definitely prefer the current beekeeper by far."

"Don't shock her. She's adjusting to a lot already," Truvy scolded. Granny was the eldest, Jo was younger than me, and Truvy was someplace indeterminate in between. But she had a knowing, nurturing personality that softened and smoothed Granny's rough edges. Did the experience of keeping her guitar strings in tune help her keep friendships in tune as well? All three of them were strikingly otherworldly, standing there together in the beams of sunshine filtering through the canopy of forest that extended over Granny's cabin and drive. A fay trio in sunbeam spotlights made flickering by leafy shadows.

My face was warm again, but I felt a sense of belonging I'd never felt before. Belonging and accepting. Whatever color. Whatever partner. But I was still trying to process what was happening between the three women.

"Are you a coven?" I asked.

All three startled at the question and Granny Ross tossed her head back to cackle exactly like the witch I'd innocently accused her of being.

"The wildwood called us together. Same way you were called to the orchard. Invisible threads from heart to heart to heart. Doesn't always happen in threes, but it's special when it does. I brew. Truvy plucks and sings. Jo...well, Jo..." Granny paused.

"I solder metal junk into something new. Which accounts for this frizzy mop of oft-singed hair and my frequently hurt fingers," Jo said, illustrating by spreading her hands out so I could see several bandages.

"Intent, empathy and action," Truvy elaborated. "Those are our strengths. Granny sets things in motion. I understand. Or my guitar strings do. And Jo fuels. Got more energy than a body has a right to."

"Not as much energy as Mavis gets from the honeybees..." Jo began, but Granny interrupted.

"We three work together just fine," Granny said forcefully.

"I'm alone," I said. It wasn't a question. I knew it. Granny would say I felt it deep down to my bones.

"You don't know who you are yet. You are one. That's true. But on this mountain you'll never be alone," Truvy said. "Those born to the wildwood are all rooted together."

"I wasn't born to the wildwood. I was born in Richmond. Or at least that's where I was left as a baby at the Home for Wayward Girls. And the orchard was planted. It's grown wild, but I'm not really sure if it's a part of the wildwood," I said.

Jo had pushed both hands into the pockets of her faded jeans. "I'll never understand Mavis and the bees. I think the orchard might be the same way. It's a part of the wildwood, all right, but needs its own devotee. I help with the cider every year, but I never feel comfortable there. I'm out of place like I am at the apiary. The bees' hum is alien.

And I don't vibe with the old apple trees. Now, my junkyard in the woods? That's my place."

I thought about how the twisting tangle of forest around Granny's cabin made me nervous. Like the wind in these leaves was saying something I couldn't quite understand. Was the orchard home? Somewhere deep down I did seem to hear it. The First Tree had called me. Its mystery was somehow a part of me and had been since I'd left the circus tent all those years ago. But I still thought of the orchard as Mary's.

"The wildwood shows us the way. Always has. Always will," Granny Ross said. "Everything is connected, but there's a place for each and every one of us. Together or apart. Here or there. We're all connected. Make no mistake, that orchard is part of the wood. It's connected to the mountain laurel and the mushrooms, the sassafras and the ginger, the birch, the oak, the ash…"

"And the honeybees," Truvy murmured.

Granny Ross looked at her sharp and long, but closed her lips tight, making her mouth a thin, straight line.

"I've never been connected," I confessed.

"You weren't *aware* of your connections," Truvy corrected. "Not the same thing as being alone. You come see me. Soon as you can. I'll play for you."

"Seems to me you can't be alone if that tinker is always hovering around," Granny interjected over Truvy's repeated offer. Her mouth softened with wicked humor.

Oh, no. We were back on Mack and this time with an audience. The other two women perked at the possibility of a real-life affair.

"Well, I guess I'd better get back to Honeywick. I have some stitching to do," I hurriedly excused myself and finally sank down into the open car.

Truvy had gone serious again. Her smile had disappeared. "That's a name I haven't heard someone say out loud in a long time," she said.

"Long time past," Granny said around the pipe she'd placed back between her teeth. "No harm in saying it now." But the old woman's thumbs traced circles around and around in her palms.

I waited for several seconds, but no one clarified Truvy's concerns, so I filed the exchange away for later and turned the key in the ignition switch.

"Never said marriage!" Granny shouted as I backed the Rambler back into a yard that seemed even more riotous with wildflowers than it had been a half hour before. I pulled away to the sound of her laughing, as if she'd never seen a funnier sight than a grown woman blushing at the very idea of taking a lover.

Jo was laughing too, but Truvy was silent and watchful in my rearview mirror as I drove down the road.

*"Come to see me soon, ya hear. I'll play for you."*

*"To truly prepare yourself you need to wake up, reach out, learn from wiser women around you."*

At the girls' home, I'd kept my true self hidden. It was impossible to make friends that way. There might have been girls who initially felt as I did, but we all learned to keep our heads down and do as we were told.

*Wayward girls.*

I didn't want to keep my head down anymore. I wanted to be difficult to control. As unpredictable as I could be. The wildwood ways these women embraced called to me too in the tingling of my fingers, in the hugging coils of my serpent companion, in the swoop in my stomach that said I'd taken a leap.

Maybe any woman could be fay if she walked far enough away from the expectations of lesser men. Or maybe I was only fooling myself.

Mary May had written Truvy Rey at the very top of the recipe card she'd left on the kitchen table. I could hear her voice saying the names over and over again in my mind.

*They say a birth day is special. That on the day and hour of your birth the veil between this world and the land of the fae is a gossamer thing. I'd imagine you shine on your birthday, don't ya? You've got a spark. Can see it even now in your eyes.*

Pearl's real birthday was in August, and that was only a couple of months away.

I would take Truvy up on her offer even if I was nervous about what her strings had to say.

# Ten

Siobhán

The Morgan Settlement, 1883

The beekeeper's cottage was *built of river rock he'd carried to a perfect hilltop spot in a pony cart. The rock had been mortared with red clay mixed in a barrow with straw, and its roof was thatched, as her childhood home had been. On one side there was the beginning of a round room that had already been built high enough to reveal that it would one day be a small turret, as whimsical and charming as the man who stacked its stones.*

*The Morgan's house was a fancy monstrosity in the center of town, all square and squat and built from lumber and glass. Siobhán hated it—the polished mahogany floors and grand staircase, the wainscoting and the silk wallpaper filled with exotic flora and fauna she'd never seen. It was a house for show, a place where The Morgan could keep all his stolen treasure, including her, on display.*

*She ran away whenever she could. To the wildwood. To the orchard. To the beekeeper. The need to escape like a repetitive spell whispered in her heartbeats.*

*She tried to deny it at first, but she lingered in the orchard hoping he would appear, and when he didn't, she went to find him. The stone cottage felt like home the second she discovered it, led by a magnetic instinct that drew her as his bees were drawn to her apple blossoms. The scents of dried clay and sun-baked straw, the simple polished earth floor, the stone hearth that matched the exterior walls, filled with smoky ash from that morning's meal.*

*Siobhán knew it was his even though he wasn't home. There were woven skeps hanging on hooks beside the door. She could see the repairs he must have made in them in bright patches of yellow willow against the paler, aged reeds. And she blushed at the hastily made bed in the corner piled high with faded quilts sewn by some other woman's hand.*

*Was he married (like her) or was he alone (like her) or would he even want her to visit again, again, again?*

*There could be no harm in peeking in an unlocked door. She backed away and closed it. If he had wanted to see her again, he would have come to the orchard, wouldn't he? She forced herself to take several steps back toward the settlement that would be a town soon if The Morgan had his way. He would. He always did. He talked often of establishing the town so that his brother would come to America and join him in his mining venture.*

*Singing interrupted her footsteps.*

*A fine tenor carried on the breeze in a brogue she already knew well.*

*If she'd been drawn to the cottage like bees to flowers, she was even more drawn to the beekeeper's song. It was a familiar lullaby. One she'd always known. She sang accompaniment under her breath until she hunted down the source of the sound.*

*Her first glimpse of the apiary was bathed in sunlight. Pollen motes floated like sparkling dust in the beams and settled in a fine powdered sheen on the beekeeper's sun-burnished hair. And the honeybees themselves danced like busy wee fairies with swift swords at the ready to sacrifice for their queen. They didn't muster to defend their hives against her when she arrived. They merely widened their dance to include her within their dizzying circles.*

"You've come," Harry said, the honeybee dance reflected in his eyes. Or maybe it was mischief that danced there, kindled by her appearance.

"I cannot stay away," she replied. A confession of a truth he already knew. She saw the knowing in the curve of his gentle smile.

"The wildwood is where you belong. You came across the sea for me, for the bees. You were hummed here by the rhythm of their wings, did you know? Could you feel it?" Harry teased. But even though the quirk of his lips and the twinkle in his eyes were mischievous when he drew nearer to her, he spoke in a low whisper as if he said intimate, serious things. The manner of his body—from squared shoulders to the shaking hand he lifted to her cheek—was solemn.

"My mother said I'd know where to sew the apple seeds. And I did," Siobhán said. His fingers brushed her cheek so gently that only his calluses made her feel his touch at all, but the whisper of connection was enough to make blood rush to her skin. Her lips tingled. Her nipples peaked. She opened her mouth to draw quickened breaths.

"You and I are not incidental. We are here, together, now, because of the seeds and the bees. They have given us this gift," Harry said. He leaned in close, but she didn't close her eyes. She was dazzled by the sunlight that caused honey striations in his eyes and an aura of gold in the hair around his face. "This. Precious. Gift." He punctuated each word with the softest of kisses. She gasped. Thrice. Each time his lips lightly grazed hers. So very different from the cruel, punishing kisses she'd known from The Morgan.

And to different effect.

Her entire body hummed, picking up the vibrations of the hives all around them. As if Harry's lips had transferred their life force to her. She was no innocent. She was a married woman, bedded frequently, almost obsessively, by a man who wanted an heir. But, this, she had never felt. This thrumming from her heart to her womb. The flush of heat from lips to *legs. This shaking need centered between her legs, but throbbing outward in search… in search… of home.*

*Harry gathered her close and kissed her more deeply, still gentle, but with the added caress of his tongue. The scent of honey rose from Harry's sun-warmed skin. Its sweetness filled the air around them. And she tasted honey as their tongues danced. Wildwood honey. Apple blossom honey. Their forbidden kiss blessed by fairy mounds and standing stones and twining roots and bramble thorns.*

*What were the laws of men to this? Nothing. Less than nothing. The Morgan took and trampled and tore. The wildwood twined in its own sweet time, knitting together the souls that it would.*

*As they sank to the ground, loosening clothes with impatient hands, bees joined them. It wasn't only the beekeeper's touch that caused Siobhán to shiver and cry out. Bees danced across his back and her bare breasts. Their bodies, entwined, were soon dusted in yellow. Neither of them paused. They had nothing to fear. More and more bees landed on them as they coupled. With no inhibition. The warm grass the only bed they needed. The tickling sacrament of a thousand wings encased them in a living bower.*

*For the first time, Siobhán reached for and found pleasure as the beekeeper also found his. He collapsed beside her, whispering her name again and again as if it had become his prayer. The apiary was their church. And now they had supplanted the marriage The Morgan had forced upon her. She was the beekeeper's wife in the eyes of the wildwood. Of this she was certain. The bees left them as they lay side by side catching their breath. One by one each insect flew back to their usual work as if there had been no interruption.*

As soon as the sun rose, I rushed outside. I was still in the lightest cotton nightgown I could order from the Sears catalog and the morning air was cool enough to freshen away the heat of my dreams, which had left me perspiring at midnight.

I knew what I would find when I brushed away the honeysuckle vine to reveal the stone I'd been able to get a better look at as a child. In my dream, the cottage had been new. Still under construction. And the stones had all been shades of beige, gray and even white. As I pulled the thick vine aside, the sunrise illuminated the blackened stone I remembered from my first visit as a child.

The beekeeper had built Honeywick. I'd vaguely assumed the name had something to do with the flowering vine that covered it, but now I knew it had been named for the bees and the honey they made.

I placed both palms flat on the wall and pressed. When I brought them away they weren't stained. Whatever had blackened the stone had happened long ago, but my chest and throat felt tight and my lips had gone dry.

I'd seen the cottage under construction. I'd smelled the fresh scent of its thatched roof. I'd seen the damp clay of its mortar and felt Siobhán's longing to stay. What had happened to Honeywick in the intervening years between then and now? Sure, it had been added on to. Made bigger and modernized with electricity and plumbing. But why had the date on the hearthstone been scratched away and what had happened to the bees? The current apiary was on the other side of the orchard, far from where Harry O'Connell had so lovingly tended his woven skeps. I shivered. My sweat had gone clammy against my skin. All the things I didn't understand were as dark as the stones under my hands.

Reluctantly, I allowed the vines to fall back over the stone. Honeywick was mostly green now with speckles of sunny yellow blossoms that should soothe my amorphous fears.

*That's a name I haven't heard someone say out loud in a long time.*

I swallowed against the tightness of my throat and forced a deep breath into my squeezed lungs. Nothing was wrong. The panic that had rushed me outside eased slightly as I stepped away from the cottage and allowed the scent of honeysuckle to soothe me. Granny Ross had told Truvy that there was no harm in it now.

Of course, that did leave me wondering what the harm had been.

Honeybees were already humming from flower to flower as I made my way back inside to dress for the day. I'd never really noticed how much they loved the honeysuckle on the cottage's walls or how much their constant buzz had become a part of my waking moments, echoing my dreams. Unlike Granny, I enjoyed the bees. Their humming calmed me even better than the honeysuckle breeze. Whatever had happened in the past, the cottage had been my secret fairy-tale promise even before it became my refuge. I hoped Siobhán and her bee-keeper had the happy ending I'd never enjoyed myself.

But the blackened stone...

I paused outside the open front door. My bare feet were pleasantly cool on the stoop. I tilted my chin and squinted into the sun. The busy honeybees filled every sunbeam with pollen as they came and went. I imagined the golden dust drifting down to land on my upturned face. If the stained walls were a portent of doom for the people I dreamed about, I willfully pushed it from my mind.

# Eleven

*G*ranny Ross *hadn't cut* into the pie, but she had encouraged me to try again. Experimentation in the kitchen wasn't something I'd been allowed as a child, a teen or a wife. Was it any wonder I'd held back while Mary cooked, mainly jumping up only when it was time for the washing after she was finished?

The ancient little lady never measured ingredients. Her time in the kitchen was a whirl of sights and scents and sounds that overwhelmed with enthusiasm and mess. I was used to keeping a kitchen spotless—nay, sterile. I stayed out of the way, wondering why she even took recipes from the dented tin, because she rarely glanced at them.

It was only now that I understood why she had placed them on the table while I sat in a high-backed chair to watch her work. The recipes had been for me. At some point, she must have hoped I'd be inspired to stir something up.

But the lessons I'd learned over a lifetime were hard to overcome.

She must have despaired when I scrubbed and wiped and tidied up after her, entirely missing the point.

Mary had a joyful connection to food preparation that meant her feasts were for the nose and eyes as much as for the stomach. She had fed my soul more than once, and yet I'd been in such a haze of fear and grief, I hadn't learned a thing.

*Some people do their best when their backs are up against a wall.*

When I stepped into the kitchen with the intention of following Granny's advice, I looked around at the polished surfaces in dismay. Unconsciously, I had been tidying and organizing since Mary had disappeared and the silent kitchen seemed sullen at its sparkling best, as if the cold stove preferred to smoke and bubble and boil, as if the sink preferred to be piled high with spoons and pans and mixing bowls. Without thinking, I'd arranged the jars on the shelves by size and colors the way Ezekiel would have wanted.

I stood in the doorway and stared, my heart painfully stop-starting in my chest and my mouth gone dry.

I'd run away, but I'd brought him with me.

In a sudden rush, I went for the recipe box and dug out the apple pie recipe. I gathered all the ingredients, one after another, and without bothering about an apron, I measured the flour for the crust. Mary had a large butcher-block breadboard she used for working dough. I took it down from its place beside the stove and placed it on the table. When I'd made the pie for Granny's tea, I had cleaned as I went, tentative, unsure of myself.

Not today.

I liked cinnamon. There'd been donated candy at Christmas at the girls' home and we'd been allowed a handful on Christmas mornings. My favorite had always been the dark-burgundy-striped ones.

So I added more cinnamon to the jar of apples I opened, for the girl who had savored her few pieces of burgundy-striped candy a year. There was no honey left on Mary's shelves so I measured the sugar, the brown sugar and the butter and set the mixture to simmer on the stovetop. Granny had suggested honey, and I paused a moment over the omission, but I reasoned store-bought sugar wouldn't make that much of a difference. Soon, the entire kitchen smelled of Christmas, but not just any Christmas, a happy, better one than I'd ever known.

My fingers didn't tingle like they did when I was compelled to sew, but the kitchen was charged with energy nonetheless. My hope had become a tangible thing carried on waves of savory sweetness. All the love I had for Pearl radiated from me into my task, and maybe, just maybe, out into the world, all the way into town, molecules of fruity goodness carried on the wildwood breeze.

Flour motes floated around me, suspended on steamy, cinnamon-scented air. Dusty bowls and sticky spoons cluttered the sink. The shirtwaist dress I'd worn to visit Granny Ross was disheveled and no longer navy blue, but an avant-garde painting made of pie ingredients in splashes and puffs of white and yellow and red. Eve had appeared and she was coiled near the recipe card, looking from it to my efforts with a serpent's version of a Mona Lisa smile—tongue flickering in and out to taste Christmas in July.

It was hot outside. By the time I placed the pie in the oven, the entire kitchen was an oven itself. The pastry might have cooked on the counter given enough time. Perspiration had dampened my hair into a wild mass of curls and wilted the painting on my dress.

But I wasn't going to go wash up. Not yet. This time I wouldn't burn the crust.

I looked around at the glorious disaster I'd made of the kitchen. My heart was beating steadily and a big smile made my cheeks ache while my mouth watered in anticipation.

A knock at the door interrupted my silent revelry.

In hindsight, I can't believe how happy I was when I went to answer without one thought about my disheveled appearance or the wreck of the room around me. My expression went from joyous smile to rictus of pain in the seconds it took me to register that two Sect acolytes stood on Mary's stoop. Only shock interrupted the startled scream that bubbled up into my throat.

"We're here to invite you to revival, ma'am," the smaller acolyte said. "May we speak to the man of the house?" He appeared young and earnest. His eyes large in a freckled face. He should be in a Boy Scout uniform, I thought. Rescuing a kitten or helping a little old lady cross a busy street. Instead, he represented the Sect in a dark wool suit, a sheen of sweat on his brow from the heat.

The other acolyte was older. Probably still high school aged, but his eyes were sharper and harder than the smaller teen's. They narrowed quickly as he registered my fear and like a predator he stepped forward as I retreated out of instinct, habit and self-preservation. It was a mistake. He liked my fear.

He was tall, but his limbs were strangely out of proportion with his body. Even longer than they should be. His manner made such a reach threatening.

"He isn't home. I'll tell him you stopped by," I replied. My quick thinking was rewarded by a sudden uncertainty in the older acolyte's manner. His fists clenched and unclenched with a nervous energy that only heightened my fear. I could see his jaw working as he paused. He wouldn't push his way inside another man's house.

I hated the subterfuge. I wanted to tell them to leave, to go to hell, to get out of Morgan's Gap and never return. But I didn't have the power to back up those orders. Not on my own.

"You'll want to come tonight. Reverend Gray is helping us all find the path of righteousness that leads to the kingdom of heaven!" the freckle-faced acolyte gushed. The disconnect between his worship of the man and my lived experience with him was utter and complete. His naïveté made his adulation so much worse. It was as if Ezekiel himself had knocked on my door. My body went numb. I locked my knees against sudden weakness, refusing the sickening faintness that made the world go blurry at the edges of my vision.

"As you can see, I'm busy baking. Perhaps another time," I said through gritted teeth.

They were only misguided youth, but they would become like Gray and the other Sect men he shepherded toward abusive behavior nearly as bad as his own. The wrongness of it made my jaw clench. *Find someone better to follow*, I thought. It was too late for the older one. His brief uncertainty at the mention of a husband had already faded. I could feel his eyes tracking over my face and figure. With that sickening mix of scorn and lust I'd tried for years to forget.

"Thomas, why don't you go back to the car while I...pray...with this poor woman. She's obviously in great need of spiritual direction in her life," the older acolyte instructed, as if he was standing behind a pulpit and not on a stoop that needed sweeping.

His foot was suddenly in the door, preventing me from closing it in his face. I'd misjudged his feelings of importance and how far he would go to "minister" to me whether I was tied to another man or not.

A cold wash of adrenaline flooded my overheated body at the same time a sudden breeze flowed through my damp hair. The younger teen was already obeying. He sensed the anger, had probably borne the brunt of it himself, and was happy to run for the long, black Lincoln Continental parked in the gravel drive.

I was shaking but determined to block his trespass with every fiber of my being.

Pearl was safely hidden in town. There was no evidence of her existence in the cottage. I'd never allowed myself so much as a photograph. But my instinct to protect her still rose up, threatening to drown me with adrenaline.

The threshold of Honeywick was a line I wouldn't allow the Sect to cross.

He didn't bow his head or murmur bible verses. His hand erupted from his side and he grabbed my arm in a wrenching grip that would have pulled me off my feet if I hadn't been willing my body to be as immovable as stone.

"Keep your prayers and your hands off me," I said quietly.

I was more furious than I'd ever been. Because I'd been wrong. I hadn't brought Ezekiel or his oppressive expectations with me. Here they were on my stoop after years of freedom and an afternoon full of joyful abandon. I rejected him and his ideas once and for all. No one burning my photograph's lips away. No Sect prayers. Not ever again.

The sound of bees visiting the flowering vines on Honeywick's walls penetrated my fury. Or maybe they echoed it. Their humming was louder, closer than usual. In fact, their buzzing almost vibrated my skin as if I could feel the beating of thousands of wings nearby. The acolyte's hand loosened. His face went slack. He'd wanted more fear. He'd wanted tears. Maybe even blood. Only his lord, not in heaven, knew what else he'd wanted before the familiar rattle and roar of the tinker's truck interrupted. Mack drove up on the grass to leave room for them to leave, as if he belonged at the orchard and the Sect did not.

I didn't mind.

"We aren't finished," the acolyte ground out, tightening his hand again to cruelly pinch my arm before he jerked away. Just another Sect man who took a "no" from a woman as a personal affront.

But I had embraced my wayward self in the wildwood, and I wasn't going to cower.

"You are very wrong. I was finished with the Sect a long time ago," I replied. It was as much of a warning as his words had been for me. His tainted beliefs had no power over me here.

Mack climbed out of the truck with his usual grace, his leg no hindrance even though it should have been for a man of his height and girth. His athleticism would have contrasted drastically with that of most other men, but I was struck by how very different he was from the teenager who had threatened me. Mack had the confidence of movement that comes with experience and constant activity. The acolyte stomped down the steps. He was taller than his partner, but leaner and softer than Mack. If you didn't look into his eyes, he would seem all gawky angles and growing pains.

But I knew from experience meanness could make up where muscles left off.

"Sinners will burn," the acolyte shouted once he had the entire length of the Lincoln Continental between him and the muscular tinker.

To Mack's credit, the only aggression in his response was to shut the door of his truck, but that was enough for the teenager. Without another word, the older acolyte climbed behind the wheel and revved the engine he'd left running.

They didn't know me or who I was. They hadn't sought me out. I was only a stop on their rounds. But my rejection would cause the older acolyte to remember me. These weren't colonial times and I wasn't Hester Prynne with a scarlet *A* embroidered on my breast, but I had blatantly refused to honor their invitation to the hottest evangelical ticket in town. That marked me. Set me apart. The last thing I should do, but the only thing I could have done.

As black smoke began to pour from the kitchen filled with the sickening stench of burning pie, I could feel a more scorching heat from the acolytes' eyes. I stood my ground, smoke and all, until the Lincoln was gone.

Mack waited until they'd driven out of sight before he approached. I let him come closer without a greeting. I no longer felt the buzzing of the honeybees, and the strange energy I'd experienced had drained, leaving me shaken. He paused at the steps, looking up at me from the yard. I couldn't avoid the perusal so I pretended not to notice while he gave me the once over.

I was fine. The Sect finding *me* wasn't the worst that could happen. I was so fine that I couldn't unroot my feet to go turn off the oven and throw out the ruined apple pie. My eyes filled. They had interrupted the Christmas I had tried to claim.

"Can I help you, Rachel?" Mack asked. Deep and quiet. With every bit as much grace as his physical self. My tears dried before they fell. The tinker had been through enough in his life. He didn't need more war now that he was home.

"It's only a burnt pie. Not my first. Won't be my last," I said with a forced laugh. And finally, for Mack's peace, I was able to hurry inside. He followed me into the house and opened the kitchen window over the sink to let the smoke escape while I turned off the oven. I grabbed a couple of pot holders and held my breath as I carried the blackened pie outside. Relieved laughter gently shook my shoulders. Charcoal didn't matter. Only Pearl mattered. Only Pearl. I was no longer faint, but I was giddy. My head threatened to float off my shoulders.

In spite of my earlier fears, Ezekiel didn't know. Could never know. I'd been determined not to move in the doorway. And I hadn't. Not an inch. In the same way, I was as bound and determined to keep my daughter a secret. Forever. Even if the acolytes mentioned the run-in to their leader, he wouldn't know it was his runaway wife they had stumbled upon.

"I'm sorry about the apples," I said to the orchard when my laughter hiccupped to an end.

Mack had joined me outside after opening a few more windows. He leaned against the doorjamb and rubbed the hip of his bad leg as if it still pained him and I caught myself before I could shy away from his innocent movement. Not Sect. Not Ezekiel. Not here to push or shove or force me to do anything I didn't want to do.

"There'll be fresh ones before long. It's good there's a creek around the trees. Good, rich soil even during a heat wave. Lots of farmers hurting this season. If we don't soon get some rain," Mack noted. "Reckon there'll be lots of praying for a break in the weather up at that big tent tonight."

"Better to pray in the fields," I said. There was no god to be found in the circus tent unless you worshipped Ezekiel Gray. Unconsciously, I echoed Mack's movement, rubbing the place on my arm where the angry acolyte had grabbed me.

Mack's attention fell to my fingers and he straightened away from the doorjamb. Then his entire body went still. I wasn't sure if he even breathed.

"You don't have to pretend everything is rosy with me. I'm not broken, but I do have a better nose for bad news going down than I did… before," he said. He stayed motionless. As if any movement would startle me away. He wasn't exactly wrong. He was treating me like the broken one, as if I was an injured wild animal he wanted to help. "You aren't alone," he continued, softly.

Helen. Jeremiah Warren. The women who had asked me to sew for them. Granny Ross. Truvy Rey. Mavis Hall. Jo Shively. *And Mack*. My community was growing, but none of them knew all my secrets. That Gray was a murderer. That Pearl was our daughter. That I was so alone I ached with the isolation through the long dark hours of every night.

Nor that I was terrified my daughter's approaching birthday would reveal her to a monster.

"Sometimes alone is best," I replied. Mack moved out of my way when I stepped toward the door. He walked out on the porch and turned to face me, but I wasn't going to draw him further into the battle I was facing. "Have a good night, Mack," I continued as I slowly shut the door. He let me. Of course. Silly to imagine for even a split second that he wouldn't.

I don't know how long he stood on the porch beside the smoking pie. I only know the kitchen grew dark and cold around me while my cheek was pressed against the door.

I'd stirred all my hopes for Pearl into the pie I'd burned when Ezekiel's acolytes came to the door. But I couldn't give up. I wouldn't stop there. Would any Sect acolyte I'd known years ago in Richmond actually have tried to grab a woman and push their way into her house? Ezekiel was escalating their fanaticism. The Morgan's Gap I'd enjoyed on Market Day wouldn't be a good fit for him—not the integrated quilting circle or the artistic football player or the Black chef and his long line of customers—but there had been some who might be eager for Ezekiel's point of view. I remembered the ones who had shunned Mr. Warren's booth and disapproved of Ryan's interest in quilting. The ones who had been disrespectful over the changes in Mack, that he'd gone to war and come back "lesser" in their eyes.

Truvy Rey had offered to play for me and Granny Ross had advised me to take her up on it. It wasn't until I stood in that smoky kitchen smelling of ashes and trembling with fear that I decided I needed to do so as soon as possible.

Because it wasn't only fright and fury making me shake. It was determination to protect Pearl and hold her place in Morgan's Gap no matter the cost.

*Pearl*

Sometimes Pearl dreamed. Of bees. Of owls. Of birds. Not like the ducks she fed at the pond who waddled slower than the pull-along toy the tinker had given her for her birthday. The birds in her dreams swooped, quick as quick. Faster than she could run. And sometimes she woke up laughing because of the way they danced in the air of her mind.

She dreamed about a lady too. A crying lady. Had she fallen? Had she broken something? No. She had lost something important. Her Favorite Thing. When Pearl dreamed that, she woke up with tears stinging her own cheeks. She'd kept her duck and its ducklings close that day, not trusting the string to keep them all along behind her.

Mr. Mack the tinker, the *Toymaker*, had said the duck family was a gift from someone who loved her. Everyone loved her. But Pearl knew in the way she often knew things that the ducks came from the crying lady. She'd lost her Favorite Thing, so she'd given Pearl a gift. Poor lady. Kind lady. Lucky Pearl.

She took good care of the ducks. She fed them grass. She gave them names— Mary, Harry and May. She sang to them every night and tucked them under the covers before she went to the window.

Pearl could tie her shoes and count (further than most people thought she could count because there was always something else to do around twelve). She helped her mother in the garden and in the grocery. And she only cried a little when she fell. She was bigger than she used to be, but she still didn't know why she had to stand at the window each night for as long as she could. Her mother didn't like it. So she'd learned to wait until her mother had shut off the light and closed her door. She'd learned to wait until late, late in the night, sometimes dozing off and on before she finally slipped from bed in her dark bedroom and went to press her forehead against the cold glass.

Watching.

Waiting.

Outside at night was different than outside during the day. Shadows around things gave them different shapes. But Pearl wasn't afraid. She reminded herself: streetlight, trash can, birdbath, picnic table. It was during one night's long watch when she'd seen the Crying Lady looking for what she'd lost. She'd gone around and around, bending over and straightening, bending over and straightening. Pearl would have called to her if it had been during the day. She often said hello to people. Her mother said she'd never met a stranger. But the Crying Lady was very busy. And her mother also said busy adults shouldn't be interrupted.

So Pearl had watched the lady go around and around. Her circles had made Pearl sleepier than usual. Her watch hadn't been long that night. She'd gone back to bed before her legs were tired and her eyes were burning and heavy. Something about the Crying Lady's circles had caused Pearl to go to sleep and that night she hadn't dreamed at all.

# Twelve

*I wasn't looking for a* hundred-year-old beekeeper when I decided to visit the apiary on my way to Truvy's place. But my sensual dreams as Siobhán had done more than give me a restless sleep or an education into what had been lacking in my marriage bed. Just as I'd come to know deep down to my bones that the First Tree was important, that Eve was important, I was certain that the bees were important too. Folk magic was complicated, and ignoring Granny's sudden whim about adding honey to Mary's pie was probably more serious than I had initially imagined.

The Sect finding me. Burnt pie.

Who knew what my clumsy efforts might bring upon me, Pearl or the community?

On a shallower level, I'd developed a hankering for honey that would probably make Granny Ross cackle.

*What would it be like to taste honey on Mack's lips?*

Apropos of nothing.

I'd passed the turn off to the apiary dozens of times. Until my lucid dreams had gone *there* I hadn't thought anything about it. Or the plain shingle-style sign that hung from a post near an old dented mailbox. The shape of a honeybee had been burned into the shingle and I braked the Rambler at the sight of it, long enough to shake away the "memory" of bees crawling delicately all over my skin.

I had been around people more since Mary had disappeared than I had since I'd fled to Morgan's Gap, and even though Ezekiel hadn't found me yet, my heart still pounded as I followed a winding short drive to park beside a battered red Jeep Wagoneer.

The rear of the Wagoneer was open. It was more truck than wagon. Nothing like the fancy Oldsmobile I'd ditched in a lake to try to throw Ezekiel off my trail, but I still experienced a superstitious shiver. I'd watched the Oldsmobile disappear beneath the murky water that day. As water had bubbled up to suck the weight of it down, I'd imagined the first Mrs. Gray drowning, possibly held down, struggling. I gasped against the feeling of not being able to breathe.

I could see the hives in the distance. Some were the newer box hives, white and square. Some were old-fashioned skeps made from dried woven grass coated with mud. Among the hives a figure moved clothed in beekeeper's garb—a hat with netting, a long canvas coat, dungarees tucked into tall rubber boots. Harry had used no protective clothing to come between him and his bees.

"Hello," I shouted a welcome as I exited the Rambler. I wasn't sure how close was too close. I was no Harry. Or Siobhán, for that matter. I wouldn't be rolling around naked with these bees.

The keeper waved and walked toward me. Bees followed, but not too many. Several swirled around us. One, only one, landed on my arm and I stilled, but I didn't shoo it away.

"That's it. No sudden moves. They'll check you out, then fly away. Unless you smell like a flower. Always best to avoid flowery perfume around honeybees," the beekeeper said. "I'm Mavis Hall. You looking for some honey?"

The keeper removed her hat to reveal a riot of curly red hair. Siobhán was lifetimes ago and far away, but I suddenly felt like I was looking at her hair and Harry's freckles in this woman who was shedding the rest of her protective clothing to strip down to a macramé vest, polyester blouse and bell-bottom jeans.

"Yes. I'm Rachel. I live with Mary May at the orchard. We're all out," I managed to explain. Mavis Hall. One of the names Mary had left for me. I thought I'd been stopping on a whim, but now I wasn't so sure.

"Groovy…I have a jar in the wagon. Knew I needed to bring one from the house today," Mavis said.

She was the first person I'd met in Morgan's Gap who appeared to know the Summer of Love had happened. California was more alien than the moon to most of the people here, but Mavis was tuned in. Did she read as much as I did? Beneath her colorful blouse, her small breasts were free, and the belt that rode low on her hip-huggers had psychedelic stripes and a white enamel buckle. Instead of the expected peace sign, the buckle was shaped like a tree with a tangled network of roots that reflected the canopy above its branches. It made me think of Eigríoch. I liked her immediately.

Even if she did make me feel like my strange life had aged me well beyond my years.

"Hey, you okay?" Mavis asked.

My grief over the life I'd lost up till now must have shown on my face. "Sure. I've been having some crazy dreams is all. Left me groggy during the day." Considering the erotic nature of some of my dreams, it was an intimate confession.

"Let me guess. *Harry*. Sorry I don't have any of *that* to offer you, but I'm happily hooked." Mavis laughed.

It was a good-natured rebuff and it took me a minute to understand what she meant before my face burned. I had noticed her bra-free cleavage. I couldn't deny it. But I would have been lost if she had accepted it as an advance. My sexual experience was brief, traumatic and so far from enjoyable I had no idea what I would actually enjoy or *if* I ever would.

Somewhere south of my navel whispered "*Mack*," but I ignored it.

"I'm only here for honey, I promise," I assured her.

"Well, there's honey and then there's honey, am I right?" Mavis winked. But she really was only teasing and I relaxed. She liked me too, even though everything about me was more uptight and uncertain than her. "So you're Rachel. I've heard about you, but never seen you, and that's a real accomplishment in a town like this," Mavis continued. I tensed defensively and it must have shown. Either that or Mavis was more perceptive than her macramé let on. "Shhhh, don't worry. Drifters gonna drift. I feel ya. I'm tied to this place. My body. My blood. Like a redheaded Jesus. I ain't going anywhere. But being rooted ain't for everybody. I get that."

"I'm trying to root," I blurted out.

Mavis nodded like she understood me. Not like Harry had understood Siobhán, but almost better. No pressure. No romantic expectation. *Groovy.*

"Mountain soil a good place for that. Stuff roots quick around here. But be careful. Once you're rooted here you don't transplant well. I ran away when I was sixteen. Went all the way to Memphis. With a boy. A singer. So sexy you can't imagine, but he got me there and then what? I couldn't find my place. I missed the bees. His hum wasn't the same." Mavis had rested her hip on the hood of her station wagon. I could see her running, wild and free. But I wasn't surprised that she'd come back. She was as at home with the honeybees as Harry had been if not more so. Even as she spoke with me her head was constantly tilting this way and that like she was in a conversation with every bee as they flew around her head.

"I'm glad you came back," I said. And I was. I'd never had real family ties. The Sect women at the home in Richmond had been my jailers and my task masters. The Sect's religion had never spoken to my heart. But in my dreams I'd somehow been a woman with a tangle of red curls like Mavis.

"You'll find your place here, Rachel. I feel it. Do you hear the bees?" Mavis asked. She straightened away from the car and opened the passenger-side door to reach inside and retrieve the jar of honey. Far-fetched to imagine the bees had told her I was coming and that I needed more, but no more outlandish than planting apple seeds around Pearl.

I looked toward the hives. I could see tiny dots from here, swirling around and around. Circles. Always circles. Circles were everywhere I looked, awake or asleep. The spirals Siobhán had made with her apple seeds. The ones I had mimicked. The stones stacked around and around to form Honeywick's tower and its spiraling staircase. Around and around.

"Close your eyes and hold your breath," Mavis said. I obeyed, only flickering my eyelashes when I felt her press the sun-warmed jar of honey into my hands. I cradled it to my chest and closed my eyes again. She left both of her calloused hands over mine, over the jar. "This is a gift. From the bees. From me. From the wildwood. Like the apple blossoms are a gift from the orchard to the bees. To me. It's a cycle. A circle. We don't break the circle, we thrive. I had to learn that."

With my eyes closed and my breath held, I could hear the bees. I allowed their hum to fill my head and echo in my chest. The bees' vibration caused my heart to flutter.

"You are okay, Rachel Smith. You and me, the bees and the orchard. We are okay," Mavis continued. Her voice was closer, and in a stunning moment of clarity, I understood. I found Mavis as appealing as Harry. And she was trying to tell me it was all right to have unconventional feelings.

I opened my eyes and I met sparkling gold-flecked eyes in Mavis's face. Her nose was only inches from mine. The scent of sweet honeysuckle was suddenly strong in the air around us.

"That Harry was a potent soul, let me tell ya. He's been seducing folks around these parts for a century. But I've heard there's something brewing between you and a certain handyman. Blue eyes. Not brown. Shoulders *for miles*. Too footballer for me. I'm still all hum. Wait till you hear Jo's sculptures sing. She's gifted." Mavis touched her nose to mine to gentle the reminder that she was taken, then stepped back. I grinned. How could I not in response to the mischievous expression on her face? I hadn't known how much I needed some playfulness in my life until that exact moment. Some acceptance for being different. Together.

But my smile faded.

"Two broken pieces don't make a whole," I said, thinking of my scars and his.

"But a bunch of broken pieces make a mosaic, and damned if that isn't what some of us have made here on this mountain," Mavis said. "This one a bit of sky. That one a bit of moss. This one honey. That one tart apple pie."

"And that one shoulders for miles," I said.

Her laughter hummed deep in her chest and it reverberated in mine to join the humming of the bees.

"The bees always know." Mavis quieted as a honeybee landed on my left hand. We watched it wiggle from side to side. It left circles of pollen dust on my skin. Alien. I understood another comment Jo had made. I couldn't understand what the bee was trying to tell me, but I glanced up at the woman beside me and I could tell she knew and understood every nuance of the bees' dance. A place for everyone. "Granny Ross sent you, I bet. This was a test."

"She said I needed to add some honey to Mary's apple pie," I said. I raised my hand to the sky and the honeybee flew away.

"Huh. I'm surprised. Granny doesn't like honey much herself. But my nan used to say that Ross women were always brewing something. And she was right. Especially when it comes to Granny Ross. Mountain honey is potent. Harry's bees came from Ireland, but these here bees came from the wild. My family tended bees deep in the wildwood for several generations before we coaxed them into skeps. Some say they descended from the original hives. From Harry's queens." Mavis squinted and paused as if the bees buzzing around her hair would tell her if it was truth or an old wives' tale. "She must think you need to stir up an extraordinary pie. Granny never comes to the apiary herself. Won't get near the bees."

Mavis chewed on her bottom lip and her eyes narrowed in concern as she tried to imagine why the old woman would send me.

"I've been having some trouble with the recipe," I said. I looked down at the jar I held. I twisted it this way and that and a kaleidoscope of sunbeams prismed through the thick golden honey, making the glass shimmer.

"You've been having some trouble, I bet. And with more than baking," Mavis guessed. "Tomorrow or even sooner I'll run into Granny Ross. She'll want to know what the bees thought of you," she continued.

"What will you say?" I asked. The humming of the bees was a constant, steady drone in my head and my heart. It wasn't intrusive. I felt comforted, as if their busy energy had reached out to envelop me.

"I'll tell her you belong to the wildwood and the wildwood belongs to you," Mavis replied. "The bees are never wrong. They like you. And not just because you smell like honeysuckle."

I'd belonged to the Sect for a long time, but there had been no sacred circle of give and receive. There'd been no friendship. No love. I'd been a prisoner. Alone. The only free will I'd been allowed had been stolen in bits and pieces of reading material blown on the breeze, forgotten on the sidewalk, discarded in the trash. Or in rebellious stitches subtle enough to pass as nothing. Harmless. Powerless. But always, always whispering against my oppressors.

I must have blanched in fear at the thought that the wildwood might be as cruel a belief system as the one I'd fled.

"Relax. Your fate isn't dependent on honeybees or canny old wise-women. You decide where you're planted. It's always been up to you," Mavis said. Her temporary solemnity had disappeared and she was back to punctuating her remarks with laughter and twinkling eyes. "Just know that you don't have to be alone to claim your independence. And you don't have to keep running once you discover where you're meant to be."

I blinked back tears at Mavis's kindness. She couldn't know about Pearl's approaching birthday or what it might mean if Ezekiel was still in town. She couldn't know how much I needed the friendship she offered.

Morgan's Gap was my daughter's refuge and I didn't yet know how I was going to defend it with a jar of amber honey, but I would.

# Thirteen

*T* *he sprawling farmhouse was* alive with additions, from porches that had been closed in with mismatched wavy windows to rooms built off the attic roof and shored up with stilts that reached all the way to the ground. It didn't look ramshackle. It looked full. Of movement. Of children. Of music and merriment. Some untouched chamber of my heart constricted at other signs of a happy childhood in a large family—bikes parked in a jumbled row in a lean-to with a bright red metal roof that matched a red wagon filled with Tonka trucks and a felt cowboy hat crumpled at the crown.

When I exited the Rambler, the sound of a fiddle and children's laughter came around the house to greet me. Judging by the additional sound of bootheels on floorboards echoing back at me from the trees surrounding the farmhouse, the young "cowboy" who had deserted his hat was now dancing.

I couldn't help tapping my toes up the front porch stairs. The interior door was open so there was only the frame of the screen door to rap on. But I rapped. I wasn't confident enough to let myself in even though Truvy had told me to come "anytime."

A young woman came to the door wiping her hands on an apron

tied around her waist. She had braided hair and Truvy's eyes—
serious, but kind, above high cheekbones and below naturally upswept
eyebrows.

"I'm Rachel from the orchard? Truvy invited me," I explained.

I was interrupting. This lovely place was too full for an outsider. Not
because I was from Richmond or because I was white. But because I
was an alien. What did I know about joyous cowboy dancing? Or guitar strings that whispered secrets for that matter?

"Oh, hello, Rachel. I'm Truvy's daughter, Primrose. Some folks
call me Primmie," she said. "Come on inside. Mama will be glad. She
said you were coming today, but I could tell she wasn't sure. She had
Nana's guitar out strumming with her head tilted like it wasn't speaking clearly."

I walked through the screen door into a front room filled with
the scent of something savory roasting in the next room. I must have
stopped and breathed deeply with an appreciative sigh because Primmie suddenly lost her seriousness in a grin that brought dimples out
on either side of her mouth.

"Chicken and dumplings. Plenty. You should stay for dinner," she
said.

I wanted to tell her the guitar hadn't known I was coming because
I hadn't been sure myself. Not until I'd seen Eve on the steering wheel
of the Rambler lazily sunning herself while she waited for me to make
up my mind.

"You better stir that pot, child. You don't want that thicknin' to
scorch," Truvy said from a doorway my nose told me must lead back to
the kitchen. The fiddle still sang in the distance with a twanging whine
that wasn't unpleasant at all, especially when paired with the boot-
stomping that was as good as a drum if not better. Happiness. And yet,
Truvy's eyes were as serious as they'd been when I'd last seen her.

"Yes, Mama," Primmie said. She wasn't a child, but she always would be to her mother. I absorbed the ache of that all the way to my motherless bones.

Truvy patted her daughter's back and they leaned their foreheads together when she walked by, and that too made me ache. An unconsciously adoring salute. The homage of princess to queen and back again.

*May the circle be unbroken.*

Truvy's attention turned to me. The petite woman placed her hands on her hips and looked me up and down as if she was seeing me for the first time. Maybe I looked different in her big, magnificently alive house. I could hear running upstairs as a game of tag commenced. Shouts. Movement. The fullness of home.

"The girls' home had fifteen to twenty of us at any given time. We never ran. Or danced. Or...sang," I said. From the kitchen, someone, I assumed Primmie, had started to sing about rivers of prayer.

"About that many here. A houseful," Truvy said. "My cousin brings them up the mountain by the truckload when he comes to play with us. That's him you hear on the fiddle. Not much work around here now that the mine's shut down so most of our relatives have moved away, but the young'uns like it here in the summertime. They come back to stay at the Old House whenever they can." She smiled below her serious eyes. And just like that I felt welcome. Like I wasn't intruding at all. I didn't blame the kids for liking it here. Bikes to ride. Music to dance to. Lots of cousins to play with. And what smelled like excellent food. I wished Pearl was with me so she could run off and play with the other children. "Usually I'd bring you back to the kitchen and we'd keep Primmie company while she cooks, but it's hot in there today. Too hot even with the back door open, and we'd never be able to hear each other over the merriment."

Instead, she led me to a side door that opened out to a porch enclosed by screen. We were welcomed by a subtle cool breeze scented by moss and the minerals in damp rocks.

"It's always nice here. There's a spring on this side of the house. It helps cool the air," Truvy said. She walked over and took up an open book from where someone had left it facedown on a two-seated swing. "My mother used to complain of the damp, but it's a blessing right now. No rain. No break in the heat." The guitar I'd seen in the front seat of her van leaned against the wall nearby. Truvy placed the book on a small table, then she picked up the guitar before she sat down. Like Granny Ross with her knitting, Truvy's fingers started to pick the guitar's strings. She didn't look down at her hand. She wholly focused on me as I took the spot beside her on the swing. Once I was seated, she gave the swing a nudge. "Imagine the spring will dry to a trickle if this heat continues."

The random notes she plucked weren't coalescing into a song, but I felt each twang of the string as I heard it. My own fingers began to tingle and I reached into the pocket of my shirtwaist dress to hold the needle box I no longer needed to keep in a hidden petticoat pocket. I fidgeted with it, thinking about what I would sew that evening by the light of a lamp when the sun went down, with Eve across my shoulders like a vivid green stole.

She'd been asleep on the passenger seat and hadn't woken when I arrived. In Truvy's shady yard, with all the windows down, she would be able to crawl out whenever she wanted if she got too hot. Honestly, the way she appeared and disappeared I doubted I had to worry about her even if the windows had been closed.

"You have a lot of big oaks," I said. "The shade is nice."

"There's been Reys here since my granduncle Abram followed his lover here after World War II. They met in France. In the trenches.

Tobias Hall was his name. He owned this land. Folks say he was half Cherokee. 'Course everyone and their brother in these parts used to claim to be descended from a long-lost Cherokee princess. Anyway, my grandfather came up here too. From Louisiana. He helped to build their house. Made it bigger when he met and married a Winston girl from Alum Ridge. That was Nana." As she spun the tale Truvy continued to pluck the strings of the guitar on her knee. In fact, her contralto voice almost sang the Rey family history while my tingling fingers restlessly worried the needle box until its soft rattle joined her song. "Might have caused some scandal if Tobias wasn't already considered different. This hollow was out far enough from town and back then folks left well enough alone. They called them friends and that was that. When Tobias died, he left the place to Abram and none of the Halls made a fuss. No prime farmland. Just a craggy old hollow with a farmhouse full of kids and it's been that ever since."

As someone with no roots or heritage that I knew of, I was fascinated by a tale told so many times it had become almost poetry—free spoken and matter-of-fact—of ancestors from here, there, and everywhere. Of a place they had all converged. Of home.

Mavis was a Hall. Did she also have Cherokee ancestors? I'd thought she looked like Harry, but maybe her family ties to the wildwood went back even further than his.

Bare feet slapping on floorboards interrupted and a young girl exploded out the screen door. It closed behind her with that summer sound of rusted springs and the smack of wood against wood and she paused as if she was suddenly shy now that she'd found grownups. She was small. No older than seven or eight. And she held Eve proudly in the crook of her arm as if the tiny green snake was a baby.

"She wanted you," the girl said, and she solemnly approached to place Eve carefully on my lap. Of course, I knew that Eve could have easily found me herself and she must have had a reason for bringing the child with her, but I accepted the snake as carefully as she was offered.

"Ruby, say hello to Miss Rachel Smith," Truvy instructed.

Ruby placed her now empty hands behind her back and echoed "hello" as she'd been told. But there was a spark in her eye that said a girl who could understand a green snake's wishes knew there was more to life than misses and manners.

"Nice to meet you, Ruby," I replied.

Suddenly, she reached out to finger the edges of my skirt, where I had embroidered the cheery yellow trumpets of jaunty honeysuckle vine and the tangle of persistent and protective green that wrapped the cottage up in leafy camouflage.

"I'd like some vines on my dress too," Ruby said wistfully, but with a twinkle that said she found the swirls of vine on my hem jaunty too.

Her dress looked like all dresses do on little girls in July when their legs seemed to grow about an inch a day. It was simple red cotton and a ruffle had been attached, no doubt to lengthen the skirt and lengthen the amount of time Ruby could wear it. I could easily embroider vines on the thin material of the ruffle.

"Would you like some red rubies instead?" I suggested, wanting to do something special for the girl.

Truvy hadn't stopped playing, but now she tilted her head toward the strings as if she was hearing something besides notes from each twitch of her fingers. "No. Needs to be honeysuckle. Like yours," she said.

"That's what Eve says," Ruby agreed. Sure enough, Eve's head was raised high above her coils and her head swayed as if she was nodding up and down, up and down.

"Well, give her your dress and go get Primmie to find you something else to put on while she sews," Truvy said.

Ruby pulled the dress off, revealing a white cotton slip underneath.

I had already taken the needle box from my pocket, but my chest suddenly tightened. I couldn't draw a deep breath and the edges of my vision went dim and blurry. Ruby was a healthy little girl gone to gangly as she grew, her arms and legs seeming too long and thin for her torso. But that wasn't why I couldn't breathe. It was the sudden knowing that shocked me.

The vines were important. They were the reason my fingers had been tingling while Truvy played. They were the reason I'd come here today. Mary had told me honeysuckle protects. It was a ward a lot of wildwood folk planted near their doors. Her cottage was covered in the sweet-scented vines. Someone had planted it all around Honeywick's blackened walls many years before.

"Mary May gave me this applewood needle box. A long time ago," I said.

Her gift hadn't been random. Just like the invitation to come here today wasn't random. Ruby handed me the dress and ran back into the house and I drew a shaky breath. She ran on strong legs. Her eyes sparked with mischief. But somehow, some way she needed honeysuckle for protection.

"Granny says you stitch," Truvy said. "And stir." She was finally playing an actual song and the familiar chords soothed me. I was breathing easier now, in and out as I threaded the needle from the bobbins I also always carried in my pockets. I had the right shades of green and yellow, as if I'd known what I'd need when I got dressed that day.

"Mary May gave me an embroidery hoop. It's very old. Someone carved it up like a tiny Garden of Eden a long time ago with leaves and a big apple with one bite taken from it. And there was a wooden spoon that hung on the hearth of Honeywick. A carved snake coiled up its handle," I explained. "They belonged together. Like maybe they were both carved by the same person as matching pieces."

"And now the snake spoon is gone," Truvy guessed. She didn't react to the cottage's name. Not this time. The swing swayed beneath us. I hadn't seen her nudge it with her foot and I hadn't consciously nudged it with mine, but the movement flowed forward and back with my breathing, with her song.

"I am working on Mary May's apple pie," I said. "I guess that's the stirring." A recognizable blossom was already taking shape on the ruffle of the dress in my hands.

A breeze had picked up. It whistled softly through the hollow where the old Rey house was built, cooled by the trickle that flowed from the spring house. Hair I hadn't realized was damp lifted from my creased forehead.

"I reckon Mary May left you that recipe for a reason, but there's lots of different ways to stir things up," Truvy said. "You might have seen Granny knitting. If she would listen to my strings, she'd spend more time knitting and less time brewing. But she's stubborn. And she isn't content to let things take shape. She has to toil and trouble."

"You asked me to come so you could play for me," I replied. While I sewed, I pushed the idea of Ruby being vulnerable away from my mind. I eschewed the very idea. She was sparkling. She was fast. She was strong. She would be for a very long time. One day she would leave this world, but not before she passed on the Rey musical gift to a new generation. The vines grew and tangled all around the ruffle on her dress.

"There's danger, but you know about that. There's love, but you're resisting the vulnerability of that. You're strong. You've always been strong. But it's time for you to be strong and brave in different ways than you've ever been before," Truvy said. She'd hushed the volume of the song she played and her fingers danced lightly over the strings. She was playing an old, old folk song I'd heard as a child, but it sounded as if it had traveled to a land beneath a green Irish hill and back again before echoing out of the hole in her guitar.

Needing to be strong wasn't new to me, but I feared the unknown changes Truvy was predicting. A leaden weight of dreadful certainty settled in my limbs. My sewing slowed. Could Truvy really pluck knowledge of events and people from her strings? Granny believed she could do it. And she feared what the strings would say about her.

"Why did the name Honeywick startle you the other day? And why am I dreaming about Siobhán and Harry almost every night?" I whispered, hesitant to interrupt but plagued by unspoken truths Truvy seemed to know.

"Folks don't call the orchard that anymore. Not even the folks it was built for called it that. Not for years and years *and years*." Truvy continued to play as she spoke, so her answer came out lilting and low like a lullaby. "Brace yourself. Those dreams will become nightmares before you're finished. Some places are marked by tragedy and violence. By harsh lessons that just don't seem to get learned. Folks say Crone's Hollow is hainted. I reckon ghosts are only a lasting lesson endlessly repeating till people learn it. These secrets aren't mine to tell. Hush. Hush. These old strings rarely exercise discretion. But I do. Oh, yes, I do." There were tears in Truvy's eyes when she placed her palm over the fretboard to still the strings.

My breath caught and my needle paused as the reverberations of Truvy's playing faded. I could have sworn the last few notes were the beginnings of a familiar birthday song. The eeriness of the tune set against the constant worry of Granny's words about the thinning of the veil made my heartbeat stutter.

August was coming up fast.

"Someone is hunting. Someone is hiding. But you…you've got work to do. Granny was right about the stirring, but she's wrong about a good many things too. You go on and dream. Listen to the wild-wood. To your heart and to your hands. Listen and learn. And when the hunter finds the one who is hiding, you'll be prepared." Truvy spoke softly into the stillness and goose bumps rose on the back of my arms in response.

When not if. *When the hunter finds the one who is hiding.* Now, my heart slowed to almost a standstill as if my blood had thickened. I was haunted in so many ways. By my past and by Siobhán's. By my hopes for Pearl's future.

I didn't feel the usual satisfaction of a job well done when I bit off my thread and put my needle away. I'd done my best to help, but I still felt a tangible sense of Ruby's vulnerability in the air.

"Some things can't be helped. At times a wisewoman merely holds back the hands of fate. But we do what we can and that has to be enough." Truvy sighed and rose to place her guitar back in the corner.

She was tired. I could see it in the slump of her shoulder and the shuffle of her gate. I was tired too. As if I'd sewn the hem of a dozen dresses. I was beginning to recognize this particular tiredness. It came on whenever I sewed with tingling hands. Or baked with intent. I'd felt this way after I'd planted the apple seeds around Pearl's house in town. It was more than physical. It was a spiritual depletion. As if a wisewoman put more into her work than sugar and spice or chords or nicely sewn lines. Had we been working spells on the porch swing in the mossy-scented, damp-flavored breeze?

Only the wildwood knew for sure.

It was well into evening when I decided to head back to the orchard. Truvy's place was full, yet they'd all easily welcomed one more. I'd been absorbed into the happy gathering and I could understand why all the children wanted to visit often. They had family, friends and freedom to enjoy while also having the structure of loving adults who made sure they were safe and fed and loved.

Above all, loved.

How could I leave too soon? And wasn't any time too soon to go back to the quiet, lonely orchard?

Primmie and Truvy had insisted on packing up a big piece of lemon pound cake for me to take home "for later" even though I was already stuffed from dinner, afternoon cookies and tea, then supper. But they hadn't only fed me with delectable Southern delicacies. I'd been fed with friendship. Even with family. While I'd only been visiting and watching, I somehow felt as if I'd been adopted for a little while.

Truvy followed me out to the porch. It was dusk. The sun had set. Peepers sang from the puddles by the spring house and a slight breeze whispered through the trees. I heard the screen door smack behind us more than I saw it although a very soft glow from the kitchen followed us outside.

"Glad you came," Truvy said. Maybe it was a question. Or maybe it was only a statement. I answered anyway.

"Yes."

From somewhere out near the driveway a bird's call began—sudden and surprising.

*Whip o' whil—whip o' whil, whip, whip o' whil.*

"He loves that old fence post out there. Claims it as his perch every evenin'," Truvy said.

The call began hesitantly, but it became increasingly enthusiastic and clear.

Eve tightened on my arm, and in the glow of the inside light I could see her rise up and sway to and fro as if she was responding to the bird's call.

"Do y'all have whip-poor-wills in Richmond? A kind of nightjar. Squat and speckled. Don't be frightened. He'll come up here to see me now that I've stepped outside," Truvy said.

Sure enough, there was a ruckus of fluttering wings, and Eve hissed, but the bird only settled itself on Truvy's outstretched arm. She crooned to him and smoothed his crest. I couldn't see him well in this light, but the breathless wonder of a wild creature coming out of the night to be with us on the porch made me sway, slightly light-headed. It wasn't shock. It was recognition. Familiarity.

"Call him Wil," she chuckled. "First came to me when I was about Ruby's age."

I drew in a deep breath of evening air, but my chest expanded further, filled with more than oxygen. Eve was a comforting companion. Not a pet. More than that. How had I managed without her for so long? I remembered how reluctantly I'd walked away from the wooden spoon all those years ago. Had I somehow known the snake carving was more than a carving?

Just as Billy was more than a tiny goat figurine.

"It's always sound for me. My uncle gave me a wooden whistle. Rough carved. Nothing special. But I mimicked birdcalls with it. Was especially keen to talk with the whip-poor-wills at night. Whistle disappeared. Wil appeared. Uncle said I'd called him in. My mother knew better. And that was that." Truvy continued to absently smooth Wil's feathers as if she was rubbing down the rough edges of a hand-carved whistle.

"Eve just appeared too," I whispered hoarsely. I'd experienced a lot of love today. Too much. I ached with the overload from the bones out.

"You go home and rest. And don't worry about how this or why that. We're here to help. Together, we've got you. Intuition is your guide. A powerful guide. But you have to allow your heart to feel in order to follow it. Don't be afraid to feel," Truvy said.

I wanted to tell her I allowed myself to cry once a year, but I knew she'd not be impressed by that. What about the other three hundred and sixty-four, she'd say.

Granny said I needed to stitch and stir. Truvy said I needed to feel. What would Jo advise?

The more I connected with the women on the mountain, the more determined I was to preserve Pearl's place here. And, yes, even my own, though I hadn't discovered yet how exactly I belonged.

# *Fourteen*

*Ezekiel*

*E* zekiel Gray *had taken* to wandering around Morgan's Gap during the day. He called it Visitation. And he did visit with all the important men who ran the town—the mayor, the sheriff, deacons and ministers of other churches, bankers and merchants. He had big plans. To move the Sect away from the city. To take only the most faithful followers and form a separate community away from the influence and the interference of secular laws in Richmond.

He'd traveled to many outlying areas in summers past, but he'd yet to manage a solid foothold in any of them. Morgan's Gap was farther afield, but that made it even more appealing. It was already an insular community surrounded by acres and acres of undeveloped land and everywhere he was greeted and treated with respect. He wasn't seen as a prophet by all…yet. But all did see him as a representative of their savior on earth. Every word from his lips came directly from God. Their deference was his due, but it didn't make him forget where respect had been lacking.

He walked the sidewalks instead of driving because he was looking for the small girl with the wild hair and even wilder laugh. He kept an eye out for her and her mother, whose eyes had flashed far sharper and more judgmentally than they should have. Something about the two of them made the skin between his shoulder blades tight and left a permanent tickle in the back of his throat that no amount of clearing could banish. The girl hadn't left him with phlegm. She'd left him with fury. And it would only diminish if he could find her and her mother and admonish them without interference for their brazen behavior.

It was as if the child had vanished. And the more the thought of her hiding from him took hold, the more often he thought he heard the peal of her laughter floating on the breeze. He'd found himself at sunset looking toward a neighborhood of houses he hadn't visited. He rushed forward with the sudden thought that the neighborhood would disappear if he didn't hurry, but his toe encountered a small obstruction. Ezekiel cried out as he tripped and fell hard to one knee. He heard the telltale sound of polyester fabric tearing as the seams of his trousers were pulled apart at the seat.

Between the two hands he'd used to catch himself was a small sapling no more than a few inches high.

Surely it should have been crushed easily beneath his shoe. Was that lilting laughter again in the distance? He looked up and searched the sidewalks and streets to no avail. There was no one. The shimmer of heated air above the asphalt made him light-headed. He grabbed the little leafy plant and ripped it up with him as he stood. He took great pleasure in crushing the plant that had tripped him in his fist before throwing it as hard and as far as he could.

As he watched the crumpled sapling sail end over end, his car pulled up beside him at the curb. There was no hint of laughter now. The breeze had gone silent and still. One house in the neighborhood he hadn't visited was taller and more ornate than the rest. It suddenly drew his attention. He squinted at its gaudy gingerbread trim, but he'd given orders for his acolytes to fetch him when it was time to prepare for the evening service.

He could easily visit that neighborhood tomorrow. Especially that Queen Anne Victorian. Something about it. Maybe the glare of sunlight in its front window bothered him. The tickle in his throat increased. The skin between his shoulder blades turned to stone. He would come back. He wouldn't give up his search. The girl and her mother needed to be chastised. And they would be. Unlike his wife, they hadn't simply vanished between one day and the next. They were still within his reach. But townspeople were already heading for the revival tent and he had to get ready. Souls were on the line. And so was his hope for establishing a Sect community on this mountain.

A fresh dark blue suit had been laid out and brushed for him. Recently purchased, the trousers were wider than he was used to, but he'd eschewed flared legs or bold patterns. The blue was his only concession to modernity. The cloth accented his pale hazel eyes, heightening the intensity of his sternest expression. The matching blazer had wide lapels and his new tie was broader too, but he was successful in his God-given mission, in part because he utilized a certain amount of showmanship. The dais that raised him above the crowd was like a stage. When he stepped up onto it, the crowd in the tent would erupt into applause not unlike fans welcoming a rock star to perform.

His parents hadn't understood that part of his gift. They had attempted to hold him back, but he'd known ascendance was necessary to truly claim the legacy of his namesake.

He prayed as he dressed behind velvet curtains that had been hung on a makeshift frame of plywood outside the tent flap. He didn't pray to calm down. Oh no. He prayed knowing that the anger burning in his belly was the Spirit. He prayed it would use him to convict the townsfolk who had come out to the big tent tonight. He'd been a tool of the Spirit his entire life, but it wasn't until his parents were gone that his True Path had been cleared.

The crowd did roar as he entered the tent with his hands clasped piously around a soft, worn Bible. He'd had his acolytes break it in by rolling it as if it was dough, back and forth, back and forth. He didn't like the feel of it in his hands. He imagined the oil of their sweaty fingers had soaked into the leather cover. But it was perfect for thumping and waving and showing the world that he was intimately acquainted with its contents.

Of course, it wasn't the words that mattered. It was the special status those words granted to him—and, likewise, to a lesser extent, those who would follow him.

Oh, as always, there were plenty of backsliding folks who had come more out of curiosity than faith. But he never failed to make use of that fallow ground. Ezekiel stepped behind the pulpit, ignoring the slight disappointment that it was an ordinary portable one instead of the hand-carved beauty he'd wanted. He looked out over the assembled people. Boredom and hunger could be easily transplanted by faith and fervor at the right time and place, and there was no better time and place than a hot summer night in a dried-up town.

No bars. No theaters. Even the tiny bookmobile was an anemic thing filled only with old, worn-out books and driven in a route circumvented by low funding and low expectations.

He was the star attraction tonight.

A charismatic man of God with a devoted coterie and a thrilling ability to speak to the people's deepest and darkest fears and expectations could smoothly and easily step into that vacuum.

He wouldn't be held back by an empty grave.

Why, even now, with that bold child's defiance fresh in his mind's eye, he could easily see a dozen or more women—young, no doubt fertile women—in this crowd who would gladly wed him. He shifted as he thought of the bedding, but he pushed that Godly responsibility to the back of his mind and focused on the one at hand: education.

Besides the young women, he saw bankers and shopkeepers, teachers, a barber and the coach from the high school's football team. But he was most gratified to see the sheriff of Morgan's Gap, Bill Long, sitting with his hat on his lap and a stony-faced wife beside him.

He wanted to laugh aloud and he did. He laughed and welcomed everyone. If he also looked from face to face for a terrible tight smile, no one knew. She wasn't here. Of course she wasn't here. Maybe she *had* washed away.

It was only him and his purpose. Who better to lead the reformation than he? What better alternative to heresy than the Sect?

He'd discovered unacceptable decadence in Morgan's Gap. Although it was isolated on a mountaintop in rural Virginia, the current state of the world had infiltrated. Braless women prowled the streets with no check on their clothing, words or behavior. Children were allowed to be wild and disrespectful. And he'd even seen mixed-race socializing on more than one occasion. No one knew their place. Too many of the people in Morgan's Gap were dabbling in ungodly practices—counterculture hippies. Degenerates.

Morgan's Gap needed to be exposed and cleansed.

The people who filed in until every chair was filled, with even more folks left standing in the back, were hungry for what he would give them. He could see the wide, eager eyes trained on him, waiting for what he would say. Every man in this economically challenged community was looking to him for assurance that their beleaguered, dirt-digging subsistence was BLESSED. Their pride needed bolstering so they would keep putting one foot in front of the other—for him, for the Sect. Their reward for living right awaited them in heaven. But all HONOR and PRAISE was here on earth with HIM. The Sect raised up righteous brothers to their place as LEADERS by Ezekiel's side and these simple farm folk—already looking at him as if he had all the answers to their troubles—were ripe for the picking.

"You have all come here tonight because God has led you here. Your eyes have been clouded by sin! Your hearts have been closed to His Truth. The secular world has led you astray with the devil's music and loose women. Your wives and daughters leave their godly place at home, taking jobs meant for men, and you allow it. Your teenagers gyrate to rhythmic music, brainwashed by dark men and lusting for loose women, and you allow it," Ezekiel accused. "You know this isn't the way. You've come here tonight because you knew you needed to repent. Turn your back on the world's ways and follow God."

His sermon was the fieriest he'd ever preached. The blood of his followers boiled by the time he was finished. The walls expanded with the hot panting breaths of the men and women he worked into a frenzy of indignation at the sacrilege going on all around them, in their own schools, businesses and churches.

Anyone who didn't worship as they did was evil. Root them out. Anyone who didn't look like they did was evil. Root them out. Anyone who challenged or changed or strayed from their accepted beliefs? Root. Them. Out.

The devil was behind questions. The devil was behind marches and movements and newspapers and books, bell bottoms and most music and short skirts and…and…and…

A few on the fringes slipped away. They were unimportant shadows compared to the crowd who stayed. Every "amen" was like a cry for blood. Every "hallelujah" fueled by righteous fury. The high school football coach stood up and pulled his wife with him. He took out a handkerchief and wiped the lipstick from her mouth. She didn't protest even though his movements weren't gentle. She stood, tears streaming down her face, in front of a crowd of her neighbors who were cheering him on. She took off her own tacky plastic hoop earrings with shaking hands at his direction.

Ezekiel blessed him and shouted "amen" over his actions himself.

The wife sat back down as if her knees had given out underneath her. The coach sat back down like he had reclaimed his proper place as the head of his family. A little boy sitting beside the woman began to swing his legs so that with each arc his polished shoes kicked his mother in the shin. No one stopped him. The woman took her kicking with downcast eyes and tears tracking her cheeks.

Ezekiel's acolytes led the hymn he'd chosen for invitation. It was a discordant moment. From anger to penitence. From enjoying a show to becoming a part of it. Ezekiel was drenched with sweat and shaking from exertion. He had recruited an army, after all. The first steps down the aisle for each of them were only the beginning. He sat to receive every soul who walked up to repent and be saved, knowing they were committing to so much more. He shook the men's hands. He clasped their shoulders. He met their eyes. His new followers would take what they'd been taught into the community. They would leave the tent and go back to their homes, their jobs. And soon, the whole town of Morgan's Gap would be bound together in the unity of his purpose.

God's purpose.

He hadn't needed the tinker's pulpit, and the big limping loser would be just as useless when it came to protecting rebellious children from God's wrath. From *his* wrath. There was something about that

Victorian house in town. Why had he never noticed it before? Its turret. Its trim. The sudden flash of the sun in its front window. He didn't push away thoughts of the house or of punishing the little girl and her mother. He reveled in them even as he prayed.

The revival tent was miles away, but I could too well imagine what was happening there.

By the time darkness had fallen, the doors were definitely, most assuredly locked and every light in the house was on. I had enjoyed Mary's old Victrola more than once since I'd come to the orchard and tonight I was glad that I'd splurged on a new Motown album that brought a whole other world into focus. One of dance floors and heartbreak and women's brave, bold resilience. I liked the way the music floated down the tower staircase to fill the cottage with soft sound.

I made myself calmly prepare a piece of toast and poured a cup of milk, thinking of Mavis and her bees. *The bees always know.* I sat down at the table with the jar Mavis had given me. When I opened the lid, the scent enveloped me like a warm hug and my mouth watered. I dipped some up with a spoon and carefully spread its decadent thickness on my toast. I didn't want to waste a drop so I popped the spoon in my mouth to lick it clean. I was stunned by the flavor, alone at the table in my nightgown, and I closed my eyes as Mavis had instructed me to do at the apiary. The honey was sunshine on my lips and a flurry of apple blossoms against my skin and all the life and energy of spring. Did I imagine the visions that flashed behind my lids? Pink petals. Raindrops. A pair of green, twinkling eyes. Was the hum in my head and my heart only a memory of the hum I'd experienced at the apiary or a result of the record playing in Mary's room?

I savored every bite and every sip, every sweet melting taste against my tongue. The snack edified me more than I thought it would.

Then I sewed. I sat at the hearth even though it was far too warm for a fire. Driving home from Truvy's, I'd noticed the outer edges of the wildwood wilting, leaves baked and curling in on themselves, but even in the height of the drought I still found the scent of a century of happier baking captured in the blackened stone comforting. As was the dance of the honeybees I added to the muslin stretched in the embroidery hoop.

Mavis's bees.

One. Two. Three.

A baker's dozen.

Yellow and black with fuzzy edges to show the kiss of pollen on their legs.

A song about kissing from the album playing in the distance. Tinny. Haunting. But as I sewed Truvy's Wil, I didn't think about the cruel punishing kisses I'd actually known. Stitch…stitch…stitch… wings, beak and every speckled spot.

I imagined the kind of kiss I'd never had, gentle and soft. A taste. A touch. A step I didn't know how to take. But there was no denying whose lips I imagined. Mack was different from every other man I'd known—his quiet, his grace, his consideration of my every flinch and sigh. He didn't walk into a room like he owned it and me. He walked in where he was welcome. He only approached by invitation. He followed my lead and respected my feelings.

But what were my feelings where the tinker was concerned? My lips seemed to know better than I did.

I didn't check the door again when the needle started to scratch on the paper in the middle of the record. Mary's player only had a manual arm to lift the needle back to its stand. I rushed to do that before the record or the needle was ruined. I gently bussed the top of Billy's head with my finger to say good night.

Eve was coiled on the nightstand when I went to bed. I wasn't alone. *You don't have to be alone to claim your independence.*

But all of my trepidation found me again in my sleep. I didn't dream of the beekeeper or Siobhán. Or Mack. Instead, I was trapped in a nightmare. A spider was industriously weaving a web and everyone I knew was going about their lives, except a thousand invisible threads trailed and tangled from their feet and hands, from their hair and their hearts, until the whole town of Morgan's Gap was bound by sticky, silken floss.

I rushed from person to person, frantically clawing at nothing but air. I didn't know how to break the spider's threads. My hands couldn't find the webbing my mind knew was there. Mack was caught. And Mavis. Granny Ross and Helen. A terrible hum finally interrupted my efforts and drew my attention to a sickening tremble in the enormous web—bees, hundreds of bees—it was their struggle that caused the web to shake.

Pearl.

As I tried to tear the web away from each little bee I suddenly knew it was Pearl's face I was striving to uncover.

The spider laughed in the center of the web it had made. I recognized the laughter. I knew it well. I'd heard it peal at the sight of blood, as joyous as a child with a new toy.

The malevolent insect hadn't seen Pearl, although it had trapped her, but I couldn't leave her covered by the web. She had to see. She had to breathe. She had to be.

Just as I saw her precious eyes open and look at me, really look at me for the first time, I felt the sticky tangle of floss in my own hair, on my own hands and arms and feet. I fought. I tore at the threads even as they tightened all around me. My head was covered. My eyes and nose and mouth. I pressed my lips together because if I screamed the webbing would fill my mouth and even my lungs, but then I couldn't speak to my child, to reassure her, to cry out against the unfairness of it all.

It was the lack of air that woke me. I fought against the quilt on my bed as if it was the spider's web, but before I was fully awake I heard Pearl's voice as clear as a bell. Later I would realize her voice had a tinny sound because it came from the Victrola in Mary's room.

"Don't leave, Crying Lady. Don't leave. The apple trees are growing. Come back and see."

# Fifteen

*Pearl*

*G*rass. *Acorns. Dandelions.* A penny! Ants. Interesting. Watch for a while as the tiny insects march along with even tinier breadcrumbs in their mouths. Give them more crumbs. Cookie crumbs from the snack in her pocket she'd forgotten. Eat some herself. Yum.

Pearl was "enjoying the sun." Her mother was in the garden and she'd gotten distracted with her weeding. Her mother had said "not to stray far." Under the fence wasn't too far. Where the Crying Lady had been looking for whatever she'd lost wasn't too far. Pearl had gone—not far—to see if she might find it. She was closer to the ground. She was good at finding. The penny was a prize in her pocket. She'd turned it inside out for the ants, but she'd managed to poke it back into place and pick the penny up again.

That's when she saw the sprouts. She knew about growing things. Her mother grew things in her garden. Green things. Flower things. Things to eat and things to smell. Pearl followed the sprouts around and around but stopped when she heard her mother calling her name. She hadn't gone too far, but she almost had. With a last longing look at the sprouts in the distance, Pearl turned and ran back to crawl under the fence around her yard.

Now she knew that the Crying Lady had been planting seeds.

There was washing up and lunch to be eaten. Her mother was excited over fresh tomatoes. Pearl was more excited over the crackers, which would make more crumbs for her pocket. Maybe the sprouts would make the Crying Lady happy. But, no, as Pearl chewed her cheese, saving the crackers for the ants, she was sure that the Crying Lady was sad over something she'd lost. The seeds were nice. Sprouts were good. But finding lost things was even better.

She would watch again tonight. And tomorrow. And the next night. The Crying Lady would come back to see the sprouts she'd planted because Pearl had whispered above the new leaves, sending the news out and away to wherever the Crying Lady could be. But she wasn't the reason Pearl stood guard at her window every night.

Spiders. Pearl shivered as if a big spider had run down her hair. She wasn't afraid of bugs. She often played in the garden with her mother. If you left spiders alone, they wouldn't bother you. But that wasn't true of nightmare spiders. They spun and laughed and tangled and choked.

Nightmare spiders were bad. *And they must be rooted out.*

Sometimes Pearl knew things. And sometimes the words in her head were not her own. She didn't like the words that rang out in her mind, but she was sleepy, and when she was sleepy a lot of her thoughts came from others. After lunch would be nap time. She never minded. She and the ducks always slept well during the day.

Her mother smoothed her hair and placed a kiss on her forehead. She loved gardening and tomatoes and Pearl. She didn't know about the Crying Lady or the nightmare spider.

Or that the nightmare spider was real.

*Mack*

Mack didn't care for dreams. Not since his had gone from visions of running down a football field in the NFL to running for cover in a swampy foxhole filled with a fellow soldier's remains. He'd had a few good dreams recently, featuring a certain doe-eyed woman actually smiling at something he'd said. Actually, other things too, for which he was as out of practice as he was with a football.

But he still tended to medicate before bedtime with a little whiskey so that if the nightmares came he'd hardly remember them in the morning.

Tonight? He might not sleep at all. The anger he'd felt when he'd seen the slimy teenager grab Rachel, a quiet woman who floated around like she was afraid that if she fully put her feet on the ground it would be pulled out from under her, a magician's tablecloth, ta-da! That anger was still with him.

He got angry sometimes these days. It was never pretty. Before the war, he'd had an even temper. After? He kept busy. He kept to himself. And the sudden furies he felt against the government, against the world, against death and destruction and the unmitigated hopelessness of it all could be burned off by fixing things or making something.

Especially something out of wood. Wood calmed him.

He loved the scent of sawdust. He loved the way a piece would warm in his hands and almost tell him what it wanted to be—horse, duck, fox, snake. *Owl.* The first time it had happened he'd carved the saw-whet owl out of a piece of chestnut he'd carried to Vietnam. He'd held it like a child for comfort after his leg was shattered by a land mine. The owl had reminded him that home was waiting. For a while, he'd imagined other things would be waiting—the football, a girl he'd taken to prom, an office when he grew too old to run. But the war had changed things for him even before his leg had been messed up.

The football didn't matter anymore. He couldn't remember the Mack who had cared about scores and touchdowns and teams. He didn't care for the limelight or crowds. He didn't like to be inside. The girl he'd taken to prom had married a man too old for the draft and settled down in Charlottesville a hundred miles and another lifetime away.

The owl hadn't let him down, though. It had led him to pick up another piece of wood and another and another. Always deadfall. Never chopped. There was no killing in his creations. He sanded. He carved. He discovered within every piece the creature it would be.

And that was good.

Wanting to crush that Sect kid with his bare hands wasn't good. Knowing he could do it because he'd done it before was worse. He might have a bum leg, but he was still a big man. It wouldn't be a fair fight if he fought a couple of Sect teenagers just like it wasn't a fair fight when the biggest one had grabbed Rachel.

Mack hadn't knocked him into next week. But it had taken a supreme force of will not to. It took will and whiskey to stop him from getting in his truck, driving outside of town, and dragging the kid's master from his creepy repurposed circus tent tonight.

Why were people drawn to charlatans made large by smoke and mirrors, pulpits and prayers better sent toward a more spiritual destination? Mack's mother had taken him on a walk once, through the band of trees that lay behind the tiny farmhouse he still called home. She'd told him to wrap his arms around a large oak and press his cheek against its trunk. He'd done as she asked, about ten at the time, and he'd felt the presence of something much larger than glory-seeking preachers. He'd imagined the roots of the oak spreading deep beneath the ground under his feet. He'd looked up at its branches stretching high into the sky above his head. The wind had stirred through the leaves and his mother had smiled.

Shortly after that his mom had died. They said an aneurysm was a sudden death with no fear or pain. He'd gone back to the oak. He'd sat at its base and cried. Maybe his tears had soaked all the way to the tips of its root in the ground. He still had the paintings she'd left behind. Watercolors of leaves. Thousands of leaves. She'd kept them in a sunny attic room she used for painting. Eventually he'd brought them down. One at a time, he'd hung them. His father hadn't made him put them away. Pretty soon the farmhouse was filled with greenery his mother had painted.

Football had been more for his father after his mom was gone. They'd poured everything they had into the sport. It was still all the old man would talk about when he visited him in the nursing home in town. But Mack knew that the trees were more important.

His mother's leaves.

His wood. His carvings. The toys. The tinkering. Fixing what was broken was easier with things. Gizmos and gadgets. Tools and mechanisms.

People were trickier.

He didn't know what to do for Rachel. Something needed doing. He could tell. She was hurting. She didn't show it with a limp. But the pain was there in the slight then gone curve of her smile. In her eyes, too large for her face, like she was holding them open to keep tears from falling.

He knew Helen's girl, Pearl, had something to do with it. Everyone called her Helen's girl, but Helen had been seen as an old maid since before he'd picked up his first football. The baby had appeared one day. That was all. Folks tended not to ask too many questions about sudden babies in these parts. It was fairly common for grandmothers to become mothers when their daughters got in trouble by men who wouldn't step up and do the right thing.

But Mack saw more than most.

Rachel and Pearl. Pearl and Rachel. The bright-eyed little girl with a head full of chestnut curls. Rachel had curls. She kept them pulled back tight. Most of the time. But he'd seen a curl or two escape. He'd ached to catch one in his fingers.

Not that he would dare. He didn't know her story, but he understood every tiny flinch she made at sudden movements or loud sounds.

And now Ezekiel Gray. Looking too closely at Pearl. And his acolytes violent on Rachel's porch.

Rachel had simply appeared one day too. Mary hadn't asked him out to the orchard for a long time after that. Nine months or so. When he'd first seen Rachel, she'd been pale and gaunt. Sickly. He'd immediately recognized the appearance he'd had right after he'd come home from Vietnam—worn out, shell-shocked, broken.

No. Mack wouldn't sleep tonight. He was too tense with the energy necessary to keep himself from flying apart.

# Sixteen

*Truvy's suggestion about allowing* myself friendships and connections within the Morgan's Gap community had made me feel the weight of my separation and isolation more than ever. After visiting Granny Ross and Mavis, then spending all day at the Rey homeplace, Honeywick was too quiet. Mary May and I had kept to ourselves, but we'd had each other. The cottage was haunted with companionable memories of Mary May and me bustling around, and lately, it was even more haunted by Siobhán's memories.

Of her lost family.

Of her beekeeper.

And her fear.

I woke with an uneasy tightness between my shoulder blades that only increased as the morning progressed. The occasional bleat of a goat didn't dispel the sense of being all alone without friend or family, without support, should anything go wrong.

Or anyone.

I wasn't worried about the animals or the farm. I wasn't worried about my ability to be self-sufficient. My concern was more practical. What if Ezekiel found me? All alone with no one else around?

*There's nothing wrong with needing and being needed.*

*There's nothing wrong with reaching out a helping hand or grasping on to one that's held out to you when you need help.*

The Sect had sullied my understanding of relationships. And there was only one way to fix that. Eve was already on the Rambler's passenger seat when I placed a basket of cookies beside her. They were simple gingersnaps made from a recipe I'd pulled randomly from Mary May's tin. And I hadn't spent much time on my appearance. Powder. A ponytail. A shirtwaist dress. Loafers.

Truvy's advice had done what Granny's teasing didn't.

She made me acknowledge the urgings in my own heart.

And maybe it was because Mack wasn't pushy. He was as restrained as I was although we each had our different reasons.

There was only one road into town. Even with the cozy scent of ginger filling the car, I dreaded driving past the Sect circus tent. It sat silent at this time of day in the full sun that blazed hot in a sky that had been cloudless for far too long. There were no cars around it, and I let off the gas, drifting by very slowly only because I wanted to press the accelerator all the way to the floor and speed past as if the hounds of hell were nipping at the Rambler's tailpipe. The idea that the revival crowds had dissipated out into the community was more frightening than if they had all been gathered together here in one place.

Where was Ezekiel?

Where were his acolytes?

And all the men and women and children who were being taught to bow down to a mere man, an evil man, who had set himself up as God's voice here on earth? As if God would hate and hurt. As if God would torture and abuse.

I knew the answer.

They were running the shops and pumping the gas. They were

sitting behind desks at banks and schools. They were bullying on playgrounds. They were driving the squad cars and standing beneath flags and behind badges.

I didn't turn around. No matter what crowds the revival had drawn, surely there were plenty of people in town who wouldn't be influenced by what the Sect believed. And this circus tent, as contaminated as it was by all the musty sweat from the zealots it had sheltered for forty years, wasn't evil.

A damp sweat had broken out on my upper lip. I well-remembered Ezekiel in the pulpit, interpreting sacred text for men who could barely read for themselves. My former husband hadn't been highly educated or particularly well-read, but he was naturally cagey and clever. He was opportunistic and addicted to adulation.

In a culture that craved celebrity there was nothing as dangerous as an abuser who flourished under the limelight and who effortlessly used his popularity to create other abusers.

Morgan's Gap was sleepier than usual. The streets were very quiet compared to Market Day. There was where the makeshift dance floor had been. A paper cup blew across the patchy grass. There was where the band had played and where the old Black woman had picked the blues. Had she been a Rey? They all seemed to sing and play. Jeremiah Warren's booth was shuttered, but a new sign had been painted and hung on its roof. A chubby pig in a tall chef's hat. I smiled to see it, happy to know I'd inspired it with my silly stitches. I passed the quilting circle's church. Was it theirs? Did they all attend together? Ezekiel wasn't only diseased. He was contagious. How many sermons would it take before hate spilled over into the greater community?

Market Day had shown me how much potential Morgan's Gap had, but it had also revealed hairline cracks in a caring façade.

I'd driven by the tinker's workshop before, but I gripped the steering wheel tighter than necessary to pull the Rambler to the side of a mostly deserted street and parallel park near the curb.

Stopping was harder than going on by.

I was both nervous to barge into Mack's place and eager for refuge by the time I walked through the door. The town was sleepy and quiet, but I couldn't shake the idea that Ezekiel's ideas might be spreading over Morgan's Gap like an invisible smog.

The day was already hot. The air oppressively still and humid. Mack's shop greeted me with shadows, a high ceiling and a gentle breeze stirred by a corner fan. The not-unpleasant scent of sawdust and paint filled the space and I could hear a handsaw—back and forth, back and forth.

Mack didn't look up from his work. Perhaps in town he was interrupted too frequently to pause right away when the door opened and closed. He was intently focused on cutting the end off a weathered piece of wormy chestnut held in a vise grip on his rugged, well-used bench. I paused. And stared. Treated to a tableau of creative industry.

His muscled arms bulged. His calloused hands gripped. His broad shoulders and leaner hips were squared and his legs planted. Sawdust swirled around him like beige snow flurries, some of which had scattered into the curls on his head.

Why was I always struck by his size? Was it because it was in such contrast to his gentle manner? I tried to imagine him wielding a gun in the jungle. Aiming. Firing. Killing. Maiming. And I just couldn't. Maybe he hadn't always been a maker. But he was one now. Body and soul. He built. He crafted. He fixed. And maybe he'd become this man I saw before me in response to the man he'd had to be at war. Tears pricked my eyes at the thought. What he'd seen. What he'd done. What he'd suffered and the suffering he'd inflicted.

Mack suddenly stopped and looked up in surprise, as if he'd felt my presence before I'd said hello. I lifted the basket of cookies slightly and said, "Gingersnaps."

He released the saw and left it embedded in the board he'd been cutting. From nearby, he lifted a tarp and threw it over the other materials on his workbench. Then he smiled, as if he didn't mind being interrupted.

"They must be fresh baked," he said. He dusted his hands on the seat of his jeans. His movements disturbed the sawdust in his hair, so a flurry followed him as he stepped toward me.

"One of Mary May's easier recipes. And she had plenty of dried gingerroot," I said by way of explanation, even though the real explanation for why I'd arrived unannounced bearing cookies was infinitely more complicated, and less complicated, by far.

He had come very close in order to rummage through my basket, tossing aside the cheesecloth I'd spread over the cookies to keep flies away. The scent of sawdust was even more pleasant mixed with a hint of soap and sweat. I wanted to dust off his curls. My fingers actually tingled with the urge. I looked around instead. I'd seen some of his work in the back of his truck. I'd even purchased the tag-a-long for Pearl. But hanging from the rafters and lining the walls of his shop was an even more varied representation of his craft.

Every creature imaginable "flew" above our heads—raccoon, bobcat, opossum and bear. There was a life-sized great horned owl and a herd of miniature horses. There were geese and swans and white-tailed deer. Turkey and snakes. Quail and coyotes.

I looked back at Mack with eyes made wide by all the intricately detailed creatures I'd seen, but he simply bit into a gingersnap and chewed with a hum of appreciation as if the stunning display of his carvings was nothing. There were shelves along one wall filled with more mundane work—toasters and televisions, farm equipment and radios. All neatly sorted and lined up as if waiting for the next slot in his obviously full schedule.

"Can you smell the ginger?" I asked. It seemed rude to note his menagerie since he was so matter-of-fact about the collection.

"Maybe a little ginger. Mostly apples and cinnamon," Mack said quietly. "You always smell like cinnamon." He'd eaten two cookies back-to-back, but now he simply stood and looked into my eyes. I had to blink away my astonishment at a sudden, ferocious physical attraction that caused my body to go still. This was me. All me. No coercion. No demands. No intimidation or force. Just a pure, sweet longing in my body to be close to his.

Waiting... expecting... what?

I had never liked kissing or... any of those other things. With Ezekiel. Right now, surrounded by this man's industrious artistry, each creature so lifelike and delicately intricate, I thought maybe I would like kissing him. A lot.

He had eaten the cookies, but I was the one who licked my lips, nervously moistening a mouth gone dry. I shouldn't have come.

"I haven't perfected Mary's apple pie yet," I explained. Better cinnamon than burnt crust, I supposed, but I was flustered that he'd noticed at all.

"You went to see Granny Ross," Mack guessed. Or had he heard? Word traveled fast in Morgan's Gap.

"I visited Mavis at the apiary as well and yesterday I spent the day with Truvy Rey," I said. "She played for me."

Mack nodded as if he understood Truvy's all-too-knowing guitar. He offered me the only stool in the shop and leaned his uninjured hip against a sawhorse for himself. I perched, certain I shouldn't insist he take the seat.

"Were you ready for that? Folks around here are leery of Truvy's playing. She can be the bearer of bad tidings. Or hard truths. Of course, mountain people can be superstitious. But I don't know I'd have the courage to accept if she offered."

"I think Granny would say the time comes for things whether you're ready or not," I replied. I might not have been ready for Truvy to play for me, but I'd needed to visit her. To hear what she'd had to say.

Being raised by the Sect sisters had left me wary. But I was no longer going to let that stop me from reaching out and trying to forge friendships and connections with the women I needed to learn from. As for how nervous my past with Ezekiel made me around Michael Coombs... well, I couldn't overcome every weakness at once.

"I guess that's right," Mack said. He crossed his arms over his chest, but not in a defensive way. He was easy with me. And I was easy with him too. My body had relaxed as we nibbled cookies and chatted. I wasn't braced to flee or duck. I wasn't worried about saying too much or too little or the wrong thing altogether. "Reckon you'll be headed out to Jo's junkyard next," he continued thoughtfully. "She's usually involved with whatever Granny Ross and Truvy have going on in spite of how Granny Ross feels about Mavis's bees."

I hadn't thought beyond visiting Mack, but Mary had left me Jo Shively's name as well. Was this making friends? It had all happened so naturally. Going where I was invited. Where I was drawn. Like a thread pulled stitch by stitch until it became a flower or a leaf or a vine.

A whole tapestry takes lots of stitches, but they're assembled over time.

Mack's eyes tracked gently over my face. I didn't meet them. I was nervous again. The attraction that sparked between us gave small talk infinite complexities I wasn't experienced enough to navigate without butterflies in my stomach.

"Mary might not have explained to you about wildwood gifts. I owe you something for these cookies, Rachel," Mack said. He'd been light and easy over cookies, but he'd gone serious once more. The flutter in my gut set off an echo in my chest that made my stilled body begin to tremble. My eyes must have widened too because Mack sought to reassure me. "Let's keep it simple this time. I have some scrap metal I've been meaning to take out to Jo. I'll give it to you and you can take it to her. She likes interesting bits and pieces for her work. You'll see. She takes stuff that's useless to anyone else and turns it into something else. Amazing things."

He had straightened, gentle and easy again, and his eyes crinkled with the flash of a sudden smile. People crafting made him happy, as if we weren't surrounded by amazing things he'd made.

"Amazing things, huh?" I said. I stood and brushed the great horned owl that dangled near my head.

Mack chuckled in response, a deep, rich sound that resonated pleasantly through my body.

I took the warm memory of the slight flush that tinted his cheeks with me when I left. Reward enough for braving the awakening of possibilities between us.

Unlike Granny and Truvy, Jo Shively lived at the edge of town with only a few craggy forest acres between her and civilization. Mack had told me I'd know when I'd found the right place. He didn't say how, but as soon as I began to see the rusted-out frames of vehicles and farm equipment scattered on either side of the state highway I turned the Rambler into the first break in the trees. I found a long dirt track and I followed it and the practically archaeological refuse on either side of it to a big red workshop that had once been a barn.

There was no sign, but I'd definitely found Jo's wildwood junkyard. It wasn't an eyesore. In fact, the trees, vines and wildflowers that grew over, around and through everything that had been deposited made it look as if the greenery and brambles embraced the iron and steel. Around the barn the cluttered hulks of abandoned cars, trucks and miscellaneous parts of all manner of machinery coalesced to form a fantastical place—a riotous rusty village peopled by sculptures that appeared here, there and everywhere as my eyes became used to the jumble.

I parked and Eve wound around my arm, a routine I was becoming used to. We exited my car and I stood hesitantly beside it, not sure where to focus my attention. Many of the sculptures had parts that caught the breeze so that heads nodded, wings flapped and windmill-like pieces spun around and around. Clanks, squeaks, scratches and scrapes filled the air, but the noise was pleasant, not grating. The sounds from Jo's sculptures were melodious, a cheery welcome to this mad metal oasis in and of the forest.

Jo must have heard the Rambler's engine above the sounds of her art construction because she came out of the barn through a propped-open door, wiping her hands on a rag with scorched corners. The scent of solder was carried along with her, an almost ozone-like fragrance that tickled my nose nearly to the point of stinging.

"Mack called. Said you had some bits and pieces for me," Jo said by way of welcome. The interested gleam in her eyes might have been over what I'd brought with me or how I'd become a delivery driver for the shy veteran Granny had been teasing me about.

Her hair was frizzy and riotous around her face. Wisps of smoke even rose from several singed tips, no doubt attributing to the smell of something burnt in the air. Jo looked like a pinup girl who had climbed down from a garage calendar to pull some wrenches herself, then decided to thoroughly enjoy her stay in the less glamorous world of grease and scrap metal.

Her smile was dazzling white against a smudged face and she wore the workshop smears like some women wore makeup—with the nonchalant knowledge that she was a beauty and didn't care.

So very different than the women who had raised me. Jo was comfortable and confident and those qualities contributed more to her beauty than perfect skin and bone structure.

"He was busy and asked if I could bring you some scraps he couldn't use," I explained. "On my way back to the orchard."

Jo arched one auburn brow.

"I'm glad to see you. And I'm always happy to get more material," she said.

"I understand why Truvy said you were the action," I replied, changing the subject. It was easy with all the noise and motion going on around us. Jo grinned and hooked the rag in the back pocket of stained and ripped overalls she'd rolled at the ankles above her shiny motorcycle boots. Beneath the overalls only fastened at one shoulder, she wore a T-shirt with cut-off sleeves. Her muscular arms were smudged here and there with dirt, oil and rust.

"I don't like the world to be too still. I like to feel the wind. I like to catch it. Use it. Fly with it," Jo said.

"That's why you drive the motorcycle," I guessed. She had seen Eve on my arm at Granny's so she accepted her presence without comment. As for Eve, she paid Jo no mind and quickly fell asleep. I guess she approved of the junkyard.

"I guess so," Jo said. "I also don't like to sit still. Come on, let's see what Mack sent."

We unloaded my car and Jo exclaimed over metal gears and bars and broken chains as if each was a long-lost treasure she'd been waiting for. Then again, the quirky sculptures that kept catching my attention had somehow been created using pieces just like these. Method from madness. Or glorious cohesive madness from discombobulated madness at least.

"Movement is good, but Truvy says I need to work harder on harnessing my chaotic energy," Jo said. She'd fished an elastic from her pocket and was using it to sweep up her wild hair into a lopsided tail high on her head.

"You all work together," I said.

"Theoretically," Jo said with a smile that matched the cant of her crooked ponytail. "Granny does her own thing more often than not. And my place in the trio should have been Mavis's. I've got loads of natural energy, but her bees…they can be a force unlike anything you've seen. And she's so tuned in to them." Jo's face flushed and her eyes took on a faraway look. She tilted her chin in the direction of the apiary as if she could hear the hum from the hives even this far away.

"So a trio is three wisewomen who work together and your trio isn't as effective as you could be," I said. "Because Granny won't work with Mavis?"

Mary May had disappeared and I was a novice, clumsily trying to follow the hints she'd left me, but the women she'd wanted me to reach out to were less powerful than they should be. Right when Ezekiel had come to Morgan's Gap and Pearl's birthday was approaching.

My fear must have shown on my face because Jo slapped my back several times as if she could dislodge concern the same way she would loosen a piece of food caught in my throat.

"Granny is too nervous with Mavis because of her bees. And to be honest Mavis is too enraptured with the bees to work with wingless creatures like us! But don't worry. We manage. Truvy and Granny and me. We bless the babies. Welcome the harvest. Ward and wake, bake and brew. And Mack knows more about wildwood ways than he lets on. I'll tell you that. He knows all this was a gift from you to me." Jo gestured to the junk we'd piled on the ground. I stared, struck breathless by the image she represented. Her messy ponytail and stained overalls took nothing away from how much she looked like a smudged goddess of nature with a mound of offerings at her feet.

"All that stuff was from Mack," I explained.

"That he gave it to you first is something the wildwood will have to work out between you two," Jo said. Her eyes crinkled at the corners and I felt my cheeks grow warm. "Gifts can be tricky in Morgan's Gap. You should know that. There's give and take. But then there's promises made as well. There's binding. There's exchange. What I'm going to give you in exchange for this material is a sculpture I made before I even knew who the sculpture was for. But it's for you. I knew it as soon as we met."

Give. Take. Binding. Exchange. I suddenly remembered folktales warning about deals with the fae, but rather than increasing, my fear diminished in a rush of adrenaline that was more like excitement. Tricky wasn't impossible, and if it was a way of life for a woman like Jo, then I was inspired to learn these wildwood ways myself. I liked the way the gifts connected us all, like my embroidery thread connected all the elements of my wildwood tapestry.

I followed Jo through her junkyard, which reminded me of a monk's maze I'd once seen at a historic church in Richmond. The short meandering journey was meditative as well as magical. Past a rusted eagle with outstretched wings and feathers that tinkled in the breeze, around a spinning merry-go-round of fantastical horses with jiggling legs and quivering manes, by a fountain created with pieces of aluminum cut from soda cans and wired together into shimmering waves, until we came to the sculpture Jo had made for me.

I knew before we paused.

It was a doe with a fawn by her side. They'd both been crafted from wire, wound and knotted into perfect shape. You couldn't tell where the doe finished and the fawn began. They were one piece, curved in natural lines in spite of their mechanical composition.

"It's a quiet piece. Can you find the movement?" Jo asked. Her voice was low. Almost a whisper. A shimmer of aluminum was almost hidden by the wire composition, but when the wind blew it fluttered in the doe and in the fawn. It echoed in my own chest. Hearts beating together. Side by side.

Eve stirred and raised her head to look up at me. My eyes burned. My heartbeat sounded in my ears. But I didn't cry. I reached to touch the fawn's upturned nose, my familiar ache for Pearl giving the sculpture a resonance Jo couldn't have intended.

She didn't know. How could she know?

Eve had loosened as if she might slither up to my face. I drew my hand back from the doe and brushed the side of Eve's head to calm the tiny snake's apparent concern. She settled down beneath my touch and I released a ragged sigh. It was taking all I had to keep my tears from falling.

"Thank you," I said to Jo. I didn't try to refuse. The fawn had to come with me. And the devoted doe along with her.

"I can't promise a warding. I can only promise energy. That's my gift to you," Jo said. "I have so much of it, you see." She placed her hand on my shoulder and squeezed.

How had Mack known I needed to visit Jo?

Truvy had given me empathy and permission to feel. She seemed to understand things about me I didn't understand myself when her guitar strings sang to her. Likewise, Mack and Jo must think I needed some of Jo's seemingly boundless ability to harness wildwood energy and turn it into action.

Empathy. Action.

Feeling. Energy.

My heartbeat was no longer in my ears. Instead it pulsed through me as if every pore in my skin had become a drum. I'd come to Morgan's Gap to hide, but I wasn't hiding anymore. I was preparing to defend Pearl's home. And my own.

*Adam Moon*

They waited in the black Chevy Impala that belonged to the Sect. There were several identical sedans, but Adam still felt like this one was his. He kept it washed, waxed and ready to go wherever Reverend Gray might need them. Their wool suits had also been provided by the Sect and, in spite of the hot dry weather, he wore his with pride. He had even started growing his hair out in imitation of Reverend Gray. In the passenger seat, his fellow acolyte Thomas St. Clare fidgeted. He shifted in his seat time and time again. He drummed his fingers on the dashboard. Thomas's hair was still cut close and combed to the side, more Boy Scout than grown man. He even kept a comb in the breast pocket of his suit and used it frequently enough to annoy. They were parked out of sight of the road behind a stand of scrubby pines. Thomas had already combed his hair three times.

Adam had big plans. More and more he was supposing that Thomas wasn't going to fit in with them. He and he alone would be Reverend Gray's right-hand man. More than that, he would be responsible for the beginning of the Sect commune the prophet had preached about establishing in Morgan's Gap. Adam had the land. He'd inherited a large parcel of mountainside when his father died. He'd be hailed as a Savior himself if he offered it to the Sect.

When the time was right, he'd walk up during an altar call and he'd declare his intention.

They'd followed the heathen woman from the orchard to the junkyard just outside of town. It was an isolated place hidden away from neighbors and prying eyes and it held all sorts of possibilities. That hulk of a handyman stopped by the orchard nearly every day. Sometimes he wouldn't drive all the way to the house. Instead, he would circle the drive as if he was a sheriff on patrol.

Reverend Gray had been very clear on how wayward women should be handled and Adam figured he and Thomas would be able to dish out a few lessons to the old bitch who brazenly rode around with a motorcycle clamped between her thighs at the same time as the woman who had ordered them off her property. He thought maybe they'd even catch the women in the middle of unspeakable acts that the sordid recesses of his brain spelled out in Technicolor whenever he closed his eyes.

He'd practically had to drag Thomas away from the car and his comb. They'd crept through a graveyard of abandoned vehicles, fighting through an overgrown tangle of briars and vines that caught and held tight to pants, shirts and skin. Thomas had whined and complained with every prick and scratch, but Adam doggedly ignored the blood that oozed from his own torn skin. Up ahead would be glorious compensation worthy of Ezekiel Gray's right-hand man.

The sculpture was surprisingly light considering it was life-sized, but it was entirely hollow save for the fluttering aluminum hearts. Jo instructed me to take up one side while she lifted the other and we carried it back to where I'd parked my car. The trunk was empty now that I'd delivered the scrap and I figured the deer would fit although I was pretty certain we'd have to leave the lid open.

"I have some rope we can use to keep the trunk from flapping and so you can see in your rearview mirror," Jo offered after we'd situated the sculpture in place.

"The orchard isn't far," I murmured, whether to reassure myself, Jo or the now inanimate mother and child…I wasn't sure. The wind couldn't reach the sculpture's aluminum hearts and I didn't like their sudden stillness. I'd be glad to get them out and set up in Honey-wick's yard.

Jo vanished in search of rope inside the organized chaos of her workshop and I waited, kept company by the clicks, whirs and jingle-jangle of all the other sculptures that were still out in the breeze. I'd thought it was cheery when I'd arrived, but with no one else around the movement became eerie.

The creak-creak-creak of a child-sized rusty stick figure on a swing hanging from a scraggly oak tree sent skittering spider legs up my spine. The on-and-off breeze made it sporadic and discordant.

I rubbed the goose bumps that had sprung up on my arms and looked around. The encroaching wildwood made the animals in Jo's collection look lifelike, a metallic menagerie surrounding me, staring from every direction while vines, brambles and reaching limbs of bush and tree sought to reclaim the sculptures with twists and tendrils and roots climbing up from the ground.

*Ashes to ashes. Dust to rust.*

Maybe Jo was taking the most unnatural of materials and giving them back to nature once more. A sort of offering. I thought about how churches were often filled with sculptures. Of saints and angels. Of disciples and deities.

The breeze died.

The junkyard fell silent.

I held my breath, waiting for what, I didn't know—another gust of wind in the leaves, the continuation of the sculptures' strange song, a whisper, a sigh—until the pent-up air in my lungs exploded in a shaky exhalation that sounded weak in the stillness.

Something was wrong.

The hair on the back of my neck rose and I strained to see into the trees. There were too many shadows. Too many mysteriously overgrown pieces of junk that eerily resembled faces and figures between bushes and brambles and vines.

I froze, feeling akin to the deer sculpture with my head up, scenting the air as if to protect the fawn attached to its side.

Suddenly, a shadow shifted and detached itself from the undergrowth. Something stepped from the trees to swish through patches of tall grass toward me. A tawny speckled bobcat padded from one oasis of grass to another. Its ears perked toward me. Its eyes flashed in beams of sunlight. Appearing and disappearing in the greenery like a muscled mirage.

Swish-swish-swish.

The hushed sound of the approaching wildcat had replaced the sound of the creaking swing, but I wasn't creeped out anymore. The gooseflesh on my arms had another cause—reverence, and awe.

Jo's junkyard suddenly felt peaceful again, for all the world like a chapel. And the bobcat might as well have been in robes.

Eve had fallen back asleep on my arm. Now she tightened and raised her head. She swayed to and fro as if she heard a song I couldn't hear. Just as she had when we'd heard the whip-poor-will at Truvy's place.

I didn't say "Truvy's" whip-poor-will. I never called Eve mine either. I didn't own the bright green snake. Granny didn't own the weasel. They were our companions. And Granny had said the wildwood communicated with us through our companions.

As I watched the bobcat walk closer and closer to me, I could see its kinetic potential in the muscles of its back and haunches, in the curve of its neck and the twitch of its ears. Energy. Just like Jo's sculptures. Just like Jo herself.

Something in me responded with energy of my own. Like calling to like. An awakening.

"Rachel, this is Axel. Axel, this is Rachel. You've heard of junkyard dogs. Well, Axel watches over this place…and me," Jo said.

I'd known the bobcat was Jo's companion almost at first sight. But it wasn't until the introduction that I realized it was Axel's appearance that had dispelled the feeling that I was being surrounded and watched. Jo's place was unusual, but I liked it. Overall it had a good vibe. A breeze kicked up again while we tied off the trunk nice and tight, but the noise around us was joyful once more.

What had I been picking up on those moments alone before Axel had appeared?

*Adam*

By the time they got to the garage, they were both bleeding and breathless and Adam's enthusiasm had dimmed.

For one thing, the junkyard turned into a carnival freak show the closer they came to where they could hear the women talking. Monkeys made of bicycle rims spun at them from the trees. Spiky spiders welded from pipes scurried and snakes made from hoses hissed in the wind.

But it was the unnaturally large bobcat that made him grab Thomas's arm and pull him back the way they had come.

The junkyard didn't have possibility after all.

Better to wait until he was sure they had the bitch all alone at the orchard. It was farther from town. All they had to do was make sure the big tinker was kept busy elsewhere. All he needed was some uninterrupted time alone with the type of woman Reverend Gray said consorted with the devil. He'd gotten in trouble before for being too rough with his girlfriends. But there wasn't anything too rough for Satan's bride, was there?

Not anything at all.

# Seventeen

*S*he was pregnant. Overseeing *construction of the new railroad had frequently taken The Morgan away and she'd often gone to stay with Harry. Too often. People began to whisper behind her back, then, more boldly, even when she was around. When she began to throw up in the mornings, her maid responded with pursed lips and sly knowing eyes.*

*The Morgan had given up on having an heir with her. Rumor had it that he was trying with multiple girls around town, planning to set aside Siobhán and marry the one who could give him a child. Siobhán suspected no one could give The Morgan a child. Not the first wife he'd murdered. Not her. Not any number of other girls, willing or not for his crude, violent advances. It didn't matter. She wouldn't have claimed him as the father of the beekeeper's child. She wouldn't sully their beautiful wildwood-blessed union with such a lie.*

*The apple trees she'd planted had flourished. They now stood as tall as if they'd been growing for ten years. Their thriving proved the blessing. And the honeybees. The bees had produced so much honey this spring that Harry*

*had sent a cartload to a brewer. He'd promised the settlement—now offi-*
*cially a town named Morgan's Gap—honey mead for autumn, lush and*
*sweet.*

*But all Siobhán could think of was the babe in her womb.*

*The Morgan would kill the beekeeper when he found out. As much out of*
*envy that she had another lover as jealousy because he could not sire a child.*
*Of that she was certain. But what of the baby? Would he want to take it for*
*his own or would he seek to kill it too, the evidence of her fruitfulness and*
*his failure?*

*She had to protect Harry, the baby and herself.*

*Once her stomach had settled, Siobhán began to pack. She wouldn't take*
*any of the dresses The Morgan had forced her to wear. She packed the old*
*clothes she'd brought from Ireland. The petticoat with its ragged, untacked*
*hem, now empty. Her skirts that were harely fit for a lady's maid. The*
*wooden chest carved with swooping swallows, and in it the few coins she*
*hadn't spent. She would flee to the orchard and pray that the wildwood*
*would protect the baby.*

*"You dare to pack while I am gone," a voice sneered from the doorway.*

*Before she turned around to face her husband, Siobhán knew the sly maid*
*must be one of the girls The Morgan was bedding. She had rushed to tell him*
*about the morning sickness, evidence of his wife's betrayal.*

*"Let me go, you dinna want me," Siobhán said. Her voice shook like it*
*hadn't before she had more than herself to worry about. How many times*
*had she risen from abuse to wash and get on with her life, such that it was,*
*hattered but not broken. Trapped but not without hope.*

*"I want what is mine, and you are mine until death do us part. Or did*
*ya forget promises made?" The Morgan said. He was huge in the doorway.*
*Too big to get around even if she was fast enough to avoid his fists. Those he*
*had placed, clenched, against the frame of the door. His knuckles white as he*
*pressed his weight and might into the wood.*

"You'll kill me, then?" Siobhán challenged. The house was filled with his servants, but not all of them were bad. Some were God fearing. Some weren't unkind. Would they ignore her if she began to scream?

"You are a whore. A murderous whore. Who will blame me if I rid the town of ya?" The Morgan asked. He stepped into the room, maybe having rationalized to himself how he would excuse her death at his hands. Any excuse would do. The town was his. The world was his. A wife's life held no value on its own.

But the wildwood wasn't his.

Later, many folk in Morgan's Gap would swear that they felt the earth shake, that they heard the distant rumble of the mine collapse.

Siobhán sensed it in a different way. Never-ending spirals of infinite roots came to life beneath the earth of the mountain in defense of her and her unborn child, and the hand-cranked sirens began to scream.

# Eighteen

*The tiny creek that* meandered through the farm had slowed to
a trickle before Mary disappeared. Now, in July, after weeks of no
rain, it was nothing but a dry trail of polished stones broken occasionally by meager puddles. Desperate tadpoles squiggled like
oil slicks from pool to pool to survive. In order to keep the nanny
goats and chickens watered, I had to carry water twice a day, morning and night, to fill the long, low watering trough in the barnyard. I
rose early each morning to try to beat the heat, but as I carried water
from the rapidly diminishing pond at the spring house, I dripped
with perspiration. I'd made extra trips to try to save some of the pol-
lywogs, and my back and shoulders screamed even as the goats and
chickens moved in slow motion to take advantage of a fresh morning
drink.

Even with water and plenty of shade available for them in the barn,
the heat made the goats sluggish and the chickens irritable. Dust rose
around us, stirred beneath cloven hooves on the bare patches that
were spreading inexorably, day by day, throughout the yard. I coughed
as I hooked the empty buckets on the useless pump beside the wooden
trough, already dreading the same chore come evening. The pump

hadn't worked since I'd come to the farm. Mary had let the animals drink from the burbling creek when it was still flowing.

The pleasure of the goats as they slurped eased the pain in my shoulders.

The flutter of the aluminum hearts in Jo's deer, which I'd placed by the front of the cottage, cheered me.

I'd thought about asking Mack to take a look at the pump to see if it could be fixed. I really had, but there were other, less logical things I wished when it came to the tinker, and it was those things that kept me hauling water in buckets from a pond that mocked me with its gradually shrinking reservoir.

After I'd watered and fed the goats and chickens, I went inside and showered and changed. Luckily, the well that supplied the house with water was fine.

The one place in town I could probably go without worrying about bumping into Ezekiel or any of his followers was the library. I should have been used to driving by the Sect tent by now, but there always seemed to be something to shake me.

A lean-to booth of board and tin had been set up for refreshments with half a dozen picnic tables to the side. And an outhouse had been constructed on a slight rise behind the booth.

The town looked different after I'd seen the evidence of Ezekiel's popularity and his intention to linger. As if its Monday morning sleepiness was a façade. I had to remind myself that there were probably plenty of people who would never step foot in Ezekiel's tent or who would walk out once they heard what he had to say. It was only the heat and my personal experience with the Sect that made me suspect monsters behind every store front or picket fence.

The very idea of hate spreading from town to claim the wildwood of Sugarloaf Mountain made a cold knot form in the pit of my stomach.

It wouldn't. It couldn't. But the threat of it loomed over all the new friends I'd made.

By the time I arrived at the library, I was happy to lose myself in the stacks for a while.

I didn't visit the library often and I never visited on the same day as children's story hour, although I always lingered over bulletin board displays to search for Pearl's photograph. Helen Newbill had started bringing her adopted daughter before she could walk.

A good mom. A great mom. The best. There were plenty of good people in Morgan's Gap to offset hardship and the desperation it could cause in a community. Mary, Helen, Mack. Truvy, Jo, Mavis. Even Granny Ross. Witch? Possibly. But a good woman nonetheless.

Love of reading had saved me from the dark clutches of fanaticism and ignorance. Pearl had a better life than I had had, but I still wanted her to have a bigger life than she would have without opening herself to a world of ideas and stories and knowledge from outside her own sphere.

I had devoured everything on Mary's shelves while I was pregnant. From Malcolm X to E. B. White. But even Mary's extensive hoard couldn't keep up with me.

At the library I'd found so much my childhood had denied me.

What would the "good" sisters have thought of Agatha Christie? Considering I'd been beaten for a tiny truncated version of *The Scarlet Letter*, I thought not much. Each week, I chose a book from each section—mystery, science fiction, biography and history. A year into my enjoyment I started to understand why Mary had kept her own library of sorts—the library in Morgan's Gap was censored. There were books on women's suffrage but no books on the more current movement for equality. No Gloria Steinem. No Sylvia Plath. There were books about the Civil War, but none about civil rights. And certainly none by Gwendolyn Brooks or Ann Petry.

The Sect had tried to completely shut down my curiosity, but I thought censorship might be worse. Did the people who used the Morgan's Gap library know their reading materials were being curated in order to moderate their exposure to the changes happening in the wider world beyond the mountain? Cozy and quaint could be nice, but isolationism was dangerous. In many ways, the women and children in Morgan's Gap were being as kept and contained as the women and children in the Sect. And the men who had control of what the library allowed on its shelves? Were they very different from the men of the Sect?

Something told me they were the type of people who had been partly responsible for the worn-down grass around the revival tent.

I could have looked up the town's history, but I had grown too close to Siobhán. I was afraid of what I might discover. Real fear, as if I was the one who loved the beekeeper and longed for a future with him and our child, had settled deep in me, a hot knot of dread in my gut. It echoed my current fear of Ezekiel and his followers finding out about Pearl. It seemed impossible that Siobhán had managed a happily ever after once The Morgan confronted her about the affair. Had she survived? Had the beekeeper? Had their baby thrived? I needed to believe they had. I needed to believe Pearl could. Even if I would never be able to myself.

I had picked my selections for the day and I was headed for the counter with my card when I saw Mrs. Long, the librarian, taking down a current issue of a news magazine. The cover featured a group of teenagers at a music festival.

"May I check out that magazine?" I asked.

"We've had some complaints this morning. About the cover. I was told to take it out of circulation," she said.

"Are you going to throw it away? May I have it instead?" I asked.

I didn't have to ask why someone had complained. The long hair and peace signs would have been enough to draw complaints. I was afraid too that the man wearing a turban and playing a sitar at the edge of the frame would have been too much for a bigot to take. To me the photograph looked appealing. Young people from varied backgrounds coming together using music to connect, communicate and stand for human rights. Modern American music was a reflection of the world—its beauty, its injustices, its protests, its celebrations.

"You can have it, but don't tell anyone I gave it to you," Mrs. Long said. The librarian's blue eyes were rimmed with red as if she'd been crying. I also noticed her hair was in a severe bun and her usually made-up face had been scrubbed clean. Uneasiness swirled in my belly and I accepted the contraband with quiet thanks.

"Getting rid of a magazine won't stop progress," I said, tentatively reaching out to support a woman I thought might be a kindred spirit.

Mrs. Long looked around nervously as if someone might jump out and smack me for what I'd said.

"Morgan's Gap isn't big on 'progress.' Be careful. I didn't realize until this weekend how backward we could be," Mrs. Long whispered.

Behind her on the bulletin board were hundreds of photographs of children, Pearl included, enjoying books. As well as happy Polaroids of Mrs. Long herself, in makeup and bell-bottoms, in costumes and hairspray. I wasn't sure what had diminished her spark, but my skin crawled because her caution was familiar.

"For now. But times are changing," I nodded toward the bulletin board behind her and Mrs. Long turned. She scanned the board and unconsciously reached as if to check to see if the out-of-character bun was still tightly in place.

"I hope you're right," she said. "I hope they'll all grow up and move away," she suddenly added with a fervor that startled me.

*Away is a place.*

But for me and for Pearl, away was here. For Siobhán and her baby too. No matter how far you run, eventually you have to find *and claim* a home.

"If you ever need to get away—from town—you're welcome at the orchard," I said. Mrs. Long stilled. Her eyes were wide and swimming with unshed tears. I'd hidden for years. I was still hiding Pearl. I had carried fifty heavy buckets of water in the past week to avoid asking Mack to come to the orchard. But I had to invite the woman across the desk from me. When she'd turned her head to look at the bulletin board, the shifting light had revealed a powdered bruise high on her cheekbone. I didn't ask. She was clumsy. She'd tripped. She'd dropped a book from a high shelf.

Only I knew she would have done none of those things.

"Sheriff Long is my husband," the librarian said. She gripped the edge of the desk as if she needed the support. I placed my free hand over hers to share my warmth. She was probably always cold. Fear freezes you to the marrow in your bones. Heat wave or not.

For some reason I recalled that first morning at Honeywick when the long-ago deputy had been so dismissive of Mary May, as if she wasn't in charge in her own home. At one time, community had failed me. And the laws as they stood failed a lot of vulnerable people. But that didn't mean we couldn't make things better in the communities we built from here on out.

"Come and see me anytime," I said, firmly enunciating every word.

*Adam*

"There she is," Adam said, shifting the car into drive.

Morgan's Gap was quiet on a Monday morning, with only a few other cars coming and going on the street.

"Her arms are full. No wonder she was in there for such a long while," Thomas said. His voice sounded as jittery as his movements. It set Adam's teeth on edge.

"Trash. All of it is trash. Places like that should be burned to the ground. All they do is fill people with ideas," he said. Spittle flew from his lips and he wiped them with the back of his hand.

"I liked children's story hour when I was a kid. I don't think there was any harm in it?" Thomas said.

Adam gripped the steering wheel tightly to keep from backhanding the ignoramus beside him.

"Reverend Gray hates libraries. He says the only books we need are the Bible and *Ezekiel Gray's Prayer Book*," he replied instead. He'd begun to doubt that he'd been paired with the best person to carry out Sect business. The man beside him—who was now chewing on his thumbnail like a rabbit caught in a steel trap—was pining after heathen nursery rhymes and film strips.

"She seems pretty harmless," Thomas said in a voice now muffled by nervous nibbles.

The woman had placed her filthy haul in the passenger seat of her car as gently as she would have placed an innocent baby. Now she got behind the wheel.

"We are on Sect business. Reverend Gray wants us to keep an eye on people who aren't living right. On loose and uppity women like this one. The community is getting out of hand and he's working to save Morgan's Gap. It isn't up to us to pass judgment. We are his eyes, his ears and his fists if need be," Adam said. To illustrate he slammed his palms against the steering wheel.

His companion jerked as if he had been hit, and again he wondered if the jumpy man—no more than a boy, really—wasn't backsliding some.

"God's will be done," Adam intoned, as a promise and a test.

"God's will be done," Thomas repeated. With true fervor or with pretended piousness? *Doubting Thomas. Doubting Thomas. Doubting Thomas.* The thought repeated in his brain along with the remembered sound of Thomas's teeth on his fingernails: nip, nip, nip.

As they followed the woman's small car at a safe distance, Adam decided he would have to speak to Reverend Gray in private about his doubt in his fellow acolyte's worth. And about the troublesome women they'd encountered in Morgan's Gap as they were witnessing. He would reassure the prophet of his own willingness to do whatever he was called to do.

He'd been called to serve God, to serve Reverend Gray and to devote everything in his life to the Sect. His land. His fists. His entire body and soul.

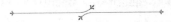

I took my usual long drive through town in order to pass Pearl's house. I let off on the gas and coasted by when I saw Helen gardening and Pearl playing in the yard. I had the window rolled down and I was able to hear her laughing joyfully at something she'd found on the ground. I almost pressed the brake. My foot lifted, but something stopped me.

It wasn't Helen. She looked up. She halfway lifted her hand in an almost wave of welcome. She'd always wanted me to visit. Not understanding why I stayed away. Eve hissed beside me and I glanced over to see something had roused her. She had stiffened and risen up. She swayed side to side. I looked in the rearview mirror and each side mirror as we slowly coasted. Not stopping, but not quite going either. I saw nothing.

The hair on the back of my neck had risen and my shoulder blades felt tight. Eve continued to sway. Pearl had noticed me. She ran toward the fence as if to greet me. The ache of wanting to stop and talk to her was so great it almost overwhelmed the feeling that I should be elsewhere. *Go. Go. Anywhere but here.* I pressed the accelerator to drive on. It wasn't safe for me to visit Pearl. It wasn't even safe for me to pause and wave while driving by. In my rearview mirror, Pearl waved and waved while Helen urged her to come away from the fence and the road.

The tightness eased the farther away I got. By the time I left town it was gone.

I wasn't as afraid when I drove back by the circus tent. In the midday sun, it looked shabbier. The beaten-down grass around it looked more sad than scary. There was a seat full of books beside me and Eve had appeared to coil happily on the sun-warmed magazine that lay on top.

Mrs. Long had asked me to call her Carol. I didn't know if she would ever gather the courage to come to the orchard for a visit or a longer stay. But my offer had eased her sadness. Whatever else, she knew that she wasn't alone.

Mack had told me I wasn't alone, and it was very hard to change the survival instincts of a lifetime, but how could I expect Carol to be brave like Siobhán if I couldn't be?

The pond at the spring house grew smaller each day. I would have to fill my large buckets a small pot at a time from the kitchen sink if I didn't call the tinker. As if I'd conjured him, Mack's truck was parked by the barn when I pulled up to the cottage. What's more, he had his caddy of tools by the watering trough and the hand pump dismantled into a thousand pieces all around his feet.

# Nineteen

*M*ack *didn't stop working* when I walked over to the trough to meet him. A fine, thin dusting of reddish-brown barnyard dirt covered him from head to foot. His hair was damp with sweat and his curls were spiky and stiff from the pomade the wet dust had made for each and every lock. A streak of grease check marked one cheek and across one eye and I followed the evidence to his hands to see, sure enough, grease on every digit and generously smeared into each palm.

He was so beautiful there, a giant of a man working away as peacefully as a deer in a field, that he stole my breath. Not at all also because in the heat he'd stripped down to a thin T-shirt so that on his bare, muscular skin the perspiration-dampened dust became a highlighting clay.

This was what it felt like to be a woman, unafraid.

"I saw you had a problem with your hand pump when I was out here the other day. Hope you don't mind me taking a look at it. Saw the buckets. Figured you'd be wearing yourself out with no help and the creek gone dry," Mack said. He glanced at me when he said it. Then he looked again, and his glance held for one long head-to-foot perusal.

I hadn't dressed fancy to go into town. I hadn't owned fancy since before I'd come to Morgan's Gap. But this was the first time he'd seen me in clothes that weren't baggy old borrowed rags from Mary. Sears catalog jeans. A poplin button-up shirt. Canvas sneakers. Nothing to catch anyone's eye. On purpose. But Mack's eye was caught. Just as mine had been caught by him—sweat, grease, dust and all.

"I was going to call you," I said.

Something had happened when I'd seen that bruise on Carol's face juxtaposed against the backdrop of all the children she was teaching to love books. Granny Ross had said stitching and stirring brought responsibility with it. If I was going to help my daughter, I was going to have to stir up some things in myself. I was following Mary May's breadcrumb trail, but I was also reaching out myself. Making friends. Learning from the women around me. And even extending invitations. Ezekiel's power had always been in keeping me beneath his heel. If I stayed down, even without his knowledge of it, then I risked being crushed by my fear forever.

"I thought you might," Mack replied. "Just thought I'd save you some trouble."

He reached to prime the brand-new red-handled pump he'd installed. It was larger than the one that had been there, but its movement was smooth with no squeaks of protest. After a few swift motions water began to pour from the spout into the trough. At first a reddish-brown gush, then as the silt cleared, a fresh, clear stream. Mack motioned for me to try it out and I stepped forward. It took two of my hands and my whole body weight to move the hand pump the same way that he had moved it with just one hand, but I kept the water going. Soon, the trough was filled and water sloshed out the sides.

My motions slowed when Mack reached to cup flowing water in his hands to splash on his face, hair, chest and arms. I was stunned to a standstill by the time he had taken an impromptu bath using the water I had pumped up from the ground for him.

"The spring that usually creates this creek bubbles up from deep in the ground at the spring house, but its source is high on the mountain. It might dry out on the surface, but there's plenty of water in the mountain and under this farm."

His face was shining and clean. His hair was rinsed and slicked back. His wet shirt clung to him like a second skin. Maybe I should splash some cold spring water on my face.

"I stirred up a lot of silt installing the new pump, but once it settles, you'll have all the water you need," Mack said.

I'd been waiting for the silt to settle for a long time. I'd been afraid to move. Scared of any disturbance that would muddy the waters of my life once more. But no matter how still I stayed, life happened— Mary disappeared. Pearl grew. The Sect showed up on my front porch.

Mack.

Well, Mack just *was* and that was enough.

I wasn't afraid.

He didn't act surprised when I reached to touch his face. He did stop. Completely stop. Talking. Breathing. Blinking. He held his breath while I traced the sharp angle of his square jaw. Then he sank down to half sit, half lean against the high end of the wooden trough. I could only assume he was giving me permission to do what I had to do next.

I stepped into him. Even propped, I had to go up on my toes to press my mouth to his, but the instant our lips touched his big hands gripped my waist and lifted me. He was the one who deepened the kiss. I wouldn't have even known how. All the kisses I'd had in my life had been violent and ugly. Except the ones I'd shared with the beekeeper in my dreams.

But that had been Siobhán.

*This was me. All me.*

And Mack was bigger and better and sweeter and more heartbreakingly gentle than any honeyed beekeeper could be.

# Twenty

*Ezekiel*

*Ezekiel liked to know* everything about the young men he admitted to his inner circle of acolytes. It was easy to learn from Scots-Irish country folk who had storytelling in their blood. Adam Moon was considered land rich in Morgan's Gap. At the ripe old age of eighteen, he was the sole owner of over a hundred acres that bordered the Jefferson National Forest to the west of the town. Fifty acres or so of it was too craggy and stabbed through by deep ravines to cultivate, but some of it was habitable and farmable, which in these parts meant Moon had it all.

He was the only child of a couple who were the last of the Moons, a family that had been listed on the original settlers' map. But his mother had been known for being a sickly thing prone to poor health and crippled by constant injuries. "Bad bones," some said. Others said, "Bad husband." Whatever the case, Ezekiel assumed the woman had simply been too weak for mountain life; the husband himself had passed soon after her as the result of a hunting accident fueled by carelessness and raw whiskey.

The second-best thing about Adam Moon was this: He was a true believer.

Ezekiel was taking his habitual turns around the outside of the revival tent, murmuring prayers, when Adam pulled up in the car he'd been given shortly after his usefulness to Ezekiel had been ascertained. He hated the interruption and was grateful for it at the same time. His feet were tired. His back continued to plague him with a strange stiffness between his shoulder blades.

He wasn't meditating with his laps and his prayers.

He simply couldn't seem to sit down or rest since the incident with that old bitch and her nasty daughter at the repair shop. His crowds grew night after night, but even after a whole week of services he didn't feel settled. When he wasn't looking for her on the sidewalks and streets of Morgan's Gap, he found himself driven to wander and occasionally even scan the empty field around the tent as if the jeering child would pop up to taunt him between one blink and the next.

Adam's arrival granted him a blessed reprieve. He turned toward his most faithful acolyte and the younger one who was so cowed by the presence of his prophet that he never quite met Ezekiel's eyes.

"How goes your witnessing, brothers?" he asked.

They had been charged with going door to door to encourage folks to come to meetings, but he'd found their neighborhood reports useful in other ways. There was a growing list of people who closed their doors in the brothers' faces. Or who outright disrespected them, as the old mother and her child had done to Ezekiel at the tinker's shop.

He was beginning to get a picture of who opposed him. And all those he could point out to his growing flock as representatives of the devil in this town.

"Father," Adam began, and the younger boy flinched slightly, as if the honorific was strange. To be sure, it was one used by heathen religions. Gray was more used to being called "preacher" or "reverend." Sometimes even "brother" by older Sect members. But he appreciated the deference Adam Moon conveyed with the title.

*The land.*

It might help the process of taking Moon's property for the Sect if he encouraged the boy to see him that way.

"Yes, my son," he responded. He'd been right. The tall, lanky boy squared his shoulders and his smile widened as if the designation had given him instant prestige.

"The woman who threw us off her porch? Well, she lied about having a husband. We've been keeping an eye on her like you said. Asked around. Ain't nobody's wife. She's strange. Awfully young to be living all alone now that the old woman who kept the orchard has gone and died or disappeared. And she's been meeting with other women. That junkyard whore. The one who rides the motorcycle and dresses like a man? And that old Ross witch. She even spent the day at the Rey place. And cozied up to Mack Coombs. He's a strange one too. Grown man with his pockets full of toys. She spent over an hour alone with him in his shop," Adam said.

Ezekiel got angrier with each woman his acolyte named, but at the mention of the tinker—that hulking blasphemer who deferred to misbehaving girls and uppity women—he froze. The tight spot between his stiffened shoulder blades itched. He'd been standing still too long. He needed to walk. If he couldn't find the girl and her mother from the tinker's shop, then perhaps this orchard woman would do. She needed to be informed of her proper place. Maybe she could serve as an example for all the loose women of the town with their motorcycles and witchery and mingling together without the leadership of men.

Each night when he lay down to sleep he saw a tombstone with his last name on it. Rachel Gray. Runaway wife. She'd left him. She had snuck out of the house while he was sleeping. He had woken up with a splitting headache and the bitter taste of bile in the back of his throat only to find her gone. Washed away? She might have drowned in the river. Or she might be somewhere out in the world living without him.

Her damned tight smile.

The more he thought about putting the orchard woman in her place, the more he determined that it was high time he did more than preach in Morgan's Gap. Rachel might have escaped his teachings, but others were within easy reach. He straightened the wedding ring he wore on the third finger of his left hand. It had been his mother's. He hadn't removed it since she died.

And it had been far too long since he'd had to wash blood off the gold.

*Pearl*

The Crying Lady had found what she'd lost. She was still sad, but her sadness didn't flow from her eyes. It was only a part of her, like the freckles on Pearl's nose or the dimple on her mother's cheek when she made a big grin.

No tears was nice.

Pearl was glad the Crying Lady had stopped crying. But her sadness still drew Pearl to the window. Pearl still watched. She still waited. She stood a silent vigil, night after night. She listened to the saplings whisper to each other. She felt their roots growing and reaching as they tried to make a circle around her house. The danger Pearl had been watching for was close. The saplings worried it was too close.

Pearl worried too, but it was the Crying Lady who was in trouble.

And Pearl loved the Crying Lady.

It was a deep-down love. One she didn't understand. It was different from the love she felt for her dimpled mother-who-was-not-her-mother. She loved Helen, but the love she felt for the Crying Lady was there too. Not in her tummy or in her heart. In her blood? Or in her bones? It was different than the love she felt for her wooden ducks or for gingersnap cookies.

It was more like apples, honey and dandelion fluff.

It was more like the brush of her fingers against apple tree sprouts rising up through the soil.

It was like the tinker's laugh. A surprise. Hardly anybody had heard.

In the middle of the daytime, if Pearl lay on her back and stared up at the sky, the birds would come. They always came. They made her laugh louder than the tinker, swooping and flipping and whirling in dizzying circles in the air. Her mother said they were swallows.

Her love for the Crying Lady was like the swallows coming to see her when she stared into the sky.

Dizzy. Dancing. Always.

Pearl stood at her window and imagined she had roots that grew like the saplings' roots, stretching, stretching. She needed to be part of a circle too, but no matter how hard she tried to stretch there were too many streets and houses in her way.

# Twenty-One

*I hadn't looked at my* wedding day photograph in a long time, but the day after I kissed Mack I retrieved it from the pocket of the apron that was now stained with apple pie ingredients and the soot from burning crust.

The young girl I'd been that horrible day no longer existed. She'd been an automaton stuck in a cycling system that gave her no choice but to marry a much older man she feared. I had held out hope that leaving the Home for Wayward Girls and the sisters would be a good thing, but I had been led, stumbling, out of one nightmare into another.

I was choosing my own steps now and my footing was becoming more certain every day.

My chest had loosened. My throat was no longer constricted. My pockets were my own and only I could choose how to fill them. I didn't need the photograph to remind me of anything anymore. I knew what it was like to feel trapped and hopeless. I would never allow myself to be in that position again.

One last time, I placed the photograph in the pocket of my borrowed dungarees beside the comforting rattle of the applewood needle box and headed out into the morning. But the nanny goats didn't come running to me, bleating their usual welcomes, as I primed the pump to freshen the water in their trough. They shuffled nervously around and around as if there was a fox or a coyote lurking nearby and the barnyard fence had them cornered. I straightened from my task, my hand pausing on the pump, and the trickle of water from the spout glugged to a stop. I strained to see what was making the nannies nervous, but there was nothing as far as my eyes could see in any direction. Several of the goats were showing the rounded bellies of pregnancy and I suddenly missed the vanished Billy. He could be a grump, but he also patrolled as well as a watchdog, always letting Mary know when anything was amiss. The lay of the land prohibited me from seeing very far into the orchard beyond the driveway and there was a tangle of wild woods between Honeywick and the main road.

A coyote could easily stalk the goats from that thick cover.

Several of the nannies had come forward to drink. They slurped hurriedly with wide frantic eyes that rolled this way and that and ears that twitched and twirled as if they were trying to get a fix on a threat. I looked all around again, from tree to tree to thorny brambles and all the dark nooks and crannies between. I couldn't see anything, no movement, no obviously out-of-place forms, but that didn't stop my pulse from kicking up in response to the goats' fear.

In a rush, I released the chickens from their coop and their nighttime roosts and they fluttered out in the usual feathery fuss to chase grasshoppers who no longer had much grass for protection.

They didn't seem to sense whatever had bothered the nannies. They immediately settled into scratching and pecking and chur-chur-churring, and their contented browsing made me scoff at myself. The nanny goats were only sensing impending motherhood and preparing to protect their babies. It caused a pang in my chest, but I could certainly sympathize. There weren't any predators stalking the barn-yard this morning. I rolled my shoulders and smacked the knees of my dungarees.

I was going to bake the perfect apple pie today.

I could already taste it. Sweet, tart, with a flaky, buttery, golden-brown crust. I'd been thinking about Jeremiah Warren's fried peach pies and I'd been inspired to try my hand at frying some apple ones.

But first, one hand brushing against my pocket had reminded me that I needed to visit the orchard.

Honeybees welcomed me. They buzzed around as I walked through the wildflowers, no doubt humming back and forth from their hives, pollen and water sources like the trough in the barnyard. Surely if the goats had sensed anything out of the ordinary the bees wouldn't seem so content in their work, busy and unbothered by my passage.

The Sect tent was miles away. I'd firmly sent the acolytes on their way, and even the tall, strange one who hadn't wanted to take no for an answer wouldn't be so willing to risk bothering a woman with a friend the size of Mack Coombs. They hadn't known I was Ezekiel's long-lost wife. There would be no reason for the reverend or any of his followers to connect those dots.

As I pushed away the lingering feeling that the goats had been able to sense something the rest of us couldn't, I had only one worry left: I hadn't dreamed of Siobhán since I'd dreamed about her (our) confron-tation with The Morgan.

In a way, it was a relief because I was afraid of what might have happened after the shaking ground had interrupted her husband's quiet fury.

In another way, it was torture because I needed to know. What had happened to the baby? To Siobhán? To the beekeeper and his bees? And it felt cowardly to simply ask someone like Truvy or Mavis if they knew what had happened, as if I was abandoning Siobhán. Some instinct told me I was meant to experience her fate along with her, side-by-side, step-by-step in a vivid dreamscape.

Usually, when I followed the spiraling circles of apple trees from the outside, inward, I had a meditative experience. My heartbeat would slow. My worries would ease. But not today. I couldn't relax. There was no evidence of drought here. The roots ran deep. Lush moss cushioned my every footfall. Verdant leaves freshened and cooled the summer air with every breeze that whispered through the treetops. There was a sweetness on the breeze that hadn't been there the last time I'd visited the First Tree. I paused to touch a low-hanging apple and noted a slight crimson glow around its stem that spread in faint threads of burnished pink to the roundest part of its globe.

The apples were ripening.

But instead of being delighted, I felt my heartbeat rush as if the discovery was a secret I needed to protect.

I looked over my shoulder. All I saw was the lazy swirl of the bees. I never felt alone in the orchard. I was in the company of the trees. But today, the usual calm welcome of wood, leaf and fruit didn't envelop me. The goats hadn't bothered the chickens, but they had ruffled my feathers for sure.

Mack had said we would know when it was time to make the cider. *Soon*, I thought. *Very soon.*

The alluring scent from the fruit I cupped gently in my palm rose up to fill my nose. My mouth watered and I licked my lips. A bee landed on the apple and I watched him explore. Yesterday I'd kissed Mack the same way the bee explored the apple. Seeking sweetness I wasn't sure I would find. Tentative. Searching. Mack had kissed me back with the same caution, mixed with curiosity. And we'd parted as slowly as the bee lifted off from the apple. Not disappointed. Only reluctant to admit that the apple wasn't quite ready.

On impulse, I rose on tiptoe and kissed the apple, my lips meeting not-quite-ripe fruit warmed by the sun and tickled by a bee's wings. The breeze came again to rustle the leaves around my face and to lift tendrils of my hair so they floated like a spiderling's webs across my cheeks.

Honeywick was more than a shelter. The orchard felt like home. And beyond the orchard the surrounding wildwood wasn't as strange as it had been.

It was also the perfect place to lay the old me to rest.

The First Tree waited on the rise. And Eve waited too. Which only served to confirm the instinct that had urged me out of my dreamless sleep at dawn. In the distance from the direction of the barnyard I heard the plaintive bleating of goats. Poor things. I would give them some extra feed. Spend some more time with them to calm them down before I started on the pie.

I listened for a few moments to make sure there were no distress calls, but I only heard more of what I'd heard before. Unsettled noises. Pregnant nannies safely enclosed but trotting around and around calling for no specific reason.

I sank to my knees on the orchard moss beneath the First Tree. Eve slithered back to give me room to turn the soil with my bare hands. I only needed a small hole. The ground should have been dusty and hard. It wasn't. Part of me thought moss retained moisture. Part of me knew the apple trees Siobhán had planted weren't ordinary trees. Maybe their roots had stretched deep into the water table beneath the earth by now, but something told me that they had also reached out to each other. I could sense the twining beneath my feet. The connection. Together, they would survive this drought.

As I had survived years of neglect and abuse to get to this moment.

I took the wedding photograph from my pocket and I placed it in the small hole I'd made. Just like that first secret pocket Mary had sewn into my petticoats had perfectly fit the tiny copy of *The Scarlet Letter*, the hole in the moss was perfectly big enough for Old Me.

When I tamped soil and moss back into place to cover up the photograph, a stronger breeze blew and I breathed it in, filling my lungs with apple-scented air as loose curls danced around my head and shoulders.

There. All done. Now I could get back and reassure the nannies.

Eve came to my outstretched hand. She slithered into my palm and coiled tightly there. She wasn't as relaxed as she should be. The hum of the honeybees had become a hush of settling leaves in the trees. Once they stilled, the orchard was silent. No birds called. No breeze blew. The bees had all vanished.

This had happened at the junkyard. I held my breath and went as still as the world around me. Only my heart made noise, pounding in my ears.

The pregnant goats had heightened protective instincts and they had all sensed evil approaching. I sensed it now as well. Not a fox. Not a coyote. Not a strange, pushy acolyte or Jo's protective bobcat. The air around me rushed in a sudden whirlwind that started and stopped with a whoosh that encouraged me to my feet.

*Stand up! Do not let him find you on your knees.*

I released my breath as I stood in the same instant I accepted that we knew—me and the wildwood, the wildwood and me. In me. The breeze I breathed in and held to strengthen myself.

"Daughter of Eve. Sinful whore. Witch. *Wayward wife*." Ezekiel stepped from behind a nearby tree. If he had taken a hatchet and embedded it in the tree's trunk, he couldn't have startled me or offended me more. His presence was jarring here. Blasphemy among the meditative trees.

Ezekiel had found me.

A cold flood coursed through my body. I wanted to run like the nanny goats, away from the predator that stalked me. But there was no fence. This was my away. This was the haven I had run to. There was nowhere else to go. Tension in my neck, arms, legs and back released at the thought like an arrow sent from the taut string of a bow.

"The woman you married is long gone. You won't find her here," I said. I'd been bracing for this confrontation since I'd left him. But I hadn't imagined the support of the orchard around me in any of those nightmare scenarios. The cadence of my words was strange even to my own ears. There was an echo as if my voice bounced off the returning breeze. Like Siobhán when she'd planted her seeds or like the beekeeper when he'd sung to his bees.

"You're mad! You belong in an asylum, under lock and key," Ezekiel said. "I gave you a home. A respected position. A chance to rise above your tainted beginnings." He came closer with fists clenched and it wasn't madness that glowed from his fevered eyes. It was corruption. It was evil.

"Is it mad to think for myself? Am I crazy to refuse your touch—fists or otherwise?"

Ezekiel had always been neat and clean. He looked nothing like I remembered. His hair was long and stringy with oil around his face. His chin and cheeks were covered in patchy stubble like his hands had been shaky or his razor dull when he had last shaved. His suit was smudged and rumpled and shiny at the elbows and knees.

But worst of all was the dull intensity of his bloodshot eyes.

This was a more dangerous Ezekiel Gray than I had known before. That certainty came to me, solid and sure.

All my new friends were far away at apiary, farmhouse, cabin and shop. Laughing in the library. Puttering in the garden. Carving a feather or a tail. Ezekiel had caught me all alone, far from phone or car. Terror froze me from marrow to skin and I quaked with the chills of my fear until the recently turned soil was unsettled beneath my feet.

It was the earth that brought me back from the cold. I'd only just dug a hole and the ground gave beneath me until the toe of my shoe was half buried too. I rejected the burrow. I shook off the dirt.

I placed my foot firmly on the ground over the spot where the Old Me was buried. Never again. No more. No early grave for this wayward woman. Mary May had shown me the way. Granny, Truvy, Jo. Mavis and Carol. I was learning from the wisewomen on the mountain. I was reading, stitching, *kissing*—and none of it was any of the Sect's concern.

I had so much still to learn, but some things I'd always known. I wasn't Sect. Never had been. Never would be. That wisdom had been with me since I'd first heard a robin's song. Since I'd shared my first biscuit. Since I'd read my first word.

"A man is the head of the household and the law unto his wife," Ezekiel replied. He sounded hesitant, as if he had expected me to crumple into tears and beg for clemency at his feet and now that I hadn't he wasn't as sure of himself. He seemed startled by my wide-legged stance, by my squared shoulders and set jaw.

"No man is the law here. Did you follow me here from Honeywick? Didn't you sense it as you skulked through the trees? Listen. Don't you hear the bees?"

The world had come to life again after its unnatural hush. The breeze had gotten stronger. I had to speak louder over creaking branches and whistling leaves. And the hum of the honeybees made my chest reverberate. I could almost feel the vibrations of a thousand wings in the air around me. Inside me. As if my heart took up their rhythm. As if we all resonated together—bee, tree, woman and wind.

"You'll pay for your disrespect. For your uselessness. You ran away from your responsibility but I've found you now," Ezekiel said. "They told me a wayward woman lived at the orchard. I came to chastise her. To lead her back to the path. To punish her if she refused even me. Instead, I find you. More than wayward. *Damned.*" He too had to raise his voice to be heard. His fervor caused spittle to fly out of his mouth and I struggled not to cringe as I had in the past. He was the abomination. The deterioration of his physical appearance only matched his soul. It was here, among the trees, that I'd found sanctity.

"You aren't prepared for what you've found. Not in this orchard. Not in Morgan's Gap. Not in me." Was it the honeybee hum in my chest that made my voice seem to echo? Me. Me. Me. Repeated by every leaf, every tree.

My embroidery flashed in my mind's eye. The honeysuckle had been for hiding. The apples for my hungry soul. Billy had been to hold Mary's place in my heart. Eve had been for companionship. But the bees had been for something else entirely.

Thunder rumbled in the distance, but there was no hint of rain in the atmosphere. No storm would bring relief to the mountain today. I glanced at the sky and it was a stark and cloudless blue. Not a cloud in sight.

"This town is tainted by heathen beliefs. No wonder you came here. But I'll set it right. My flock is growing. Godly men are seeing the light and bringing their women to heel. I'll make an example of you," Ezekiel said. "And even more will turn from their wicked ways."

"The apples and the bees are the only audience here, Ezekiel," I said. I'd planted my other foot on the ground near the recently turned earth. I imagined I could feel acres upon acres of roots as if tendrils had sprouted from my feet to join them. From the orchard to Granny Ross's wildwood, I thought I could sense the connection.

And the welcome.

I suddenly remembered the childhood friends I hadn't been allowed to have. Ruth with her collar of cardinals. Esther and the jumper I'd covered with daisies. Tiny Mary patting the rabbits on her hem until they were worn and gray. Poor Mary hadn't survived the need for another dress. Ruth had died at twelve from a persistent fever that was helped along by the damp and drafty dorm where we slept with a dozen others. And Esther. Poor, poor Esther. Like me, she had been married to a much older Sect man. She had died after her sixth child was born in as many years.

When I'd heard the news of her death, I'd hoped daisies grew on her grave.

Facing Ezekiel now with his brag about "bringing women to heel" caused acidic fury to bubble up in the back of my throat. That I'd ever had such a meager, useless hope for a girl who should have been able to live a long and joyous life.

Not my Pearl. Never my Pearl.

And never again for me.

The whole of creation responded to my fury, reaching out to firm my spine and square my shoulders.

"Leave the mountain," I said. "You aren't welcome here. You are an abomination to all that is and should be."

I'd been invited. Even before Mary May had told me to remember the orchard, Eigríoch had called. Disturbed by Ezekiel's shouting, Eve had uncoiled from my palm. She wrapped her bright green body backward up my arm, leaving her head alert and swaying a warning at my wrist. Instinctively, I raised my arm to give her movements a higher vantage point.

"You consort with the serpent," Ezekiel choked out. His bloodshot eyes bulged, and his face had gone a mottled bright red and sickly gray.

"You will never touch me again. You will never make me bleed. Nothing taints me. It never has. Not even the memory of you. The orchard has been my refuge, but it is so much more than that. You. Should. Leave," I said. The reverberation in my chest came up and out of my mouth so that the last words left my lips tingling.

"Thou shalt not s...s...suffer a witch to live," Ezekiel said. He had always prided himself on perfect elocution. His hissing stutter would have been a horror to him even if it hadn't resonated from my arm and the leaves and the undergrowth of wild bushes and brambles that mingled with the apple trees.

Black, copper, green and gray—snakes of every shape, size and color began to appear from their natural hiding places. A myriad of patterns—diamonds and stripes made a kaleidoscope of their scales that dazzled even as instinctive fear caused my pulse to race.

"Thou shall have no say in the matter," I proclaimed.

But he was no longer paying any attention to me. Whatever harmful intentions he'd had were forgotten as he backed away, ricocheting from each serpent he encountered with squeaks and squeals.

My raised arm trembled as the snakes began to coil, tails twitching as one strike after another antagonized the intruder in their midst.

"Morgan's Gap will be cleansed!" Ezekiel shrieked one last time before turning to run away.

I managed to keep my stance until he was out of sight. Then I collapsed against the trunk of the First Tree for support and Eve traded my trembling arm for the closest limb.

"Did you do that?" I asked my companion. She was completely calm now. As if nothing had happened. Her unblinking black eyes were unconcerned while I tried to catch my breath. My mouth tasted metallic. My ears were ringing. I saw only the tips of a few tails disappearing back the way they'd come and one shiny black snake gone for a lazy lay on a rock in the sun.

It wasn't only my arm that was trembling. My whole body shook. I leaned my forehead against the tree and filled my lungs with the rich scent of its bark. I wasn't afraid. Even though I knew Ezekiel wouldn't leave the mountain, it wasn't fear making me weak in the knees.

Once, I'd walked for hours in patent leather shoes that didn't fit until I'd collapsed in the very spot where I now stood. I felt the same, as if I'd physically exerted myself beyond normal boundaries. And yet, I'd done nothing but stand.

It would have been easier to surrender to the dirt. To allow myself to grovel all the way to the grave. Standing up to an invasion threatening violence and hate in this sacred place had taken everything I had, but there was a glorious euphoria in that.

An apple dropped and rolled to a stop against my foot. I dropped down on my knees to scoop it up and take a bite even though it wasn't quite ripe. It wasn't just the tartness that brought tears to my eyes—it was the reminder that I wasn't alone.

# Twenty-Two

*Ezekiel*

*E* *zekiel had stopped shaking,* but a sickly slosh of nausea still gurgled in his guts as if his revulsion was a brooding, unsettled thing barely contained by his flesh. He sat behind the steering wheel of his car and swallowed against the bile that rose sourly in the back of his throat.

He'd known it. All this time, he'd known. Rachel was not only alive, she was consorting with the beast. The devil had sent his serpents to her. Slithering, coiling, slick and slimy. She had even held one in her hand! She had raised it against him and he could still feel the penetration of its black beady stare. Perfectly natural for a man of God to feel fear when confronted by such evil. But the sickness in his belly now, hours later, was an embarrassment.

Her empty grave had plagued him and now he knew why.

He had gone to punish a woman Adam had accused of being strange. Instead, he had discovered even greater evidence of crimes against God. His own wife. Alive! Just as he had suspected. And worse, rebelliously standing against him. His horror was compounded by his disbelief.

The machinations she must have gone through to try to fool him. To not only run away, but to fake her demise. He could hardly accept that she'd calculated to such lengths to leave him. To abandon her duties as a pastor's wife and helpmeet. How had he not seen the signs of rebellion more clearly? He couldn't reconcile the girl he'd taken straight from the Sect sisters to his bed, to the blood-splattered floor on her knees before him, with the wild woman standing defiantly against him.

He'd heard the rumors about a society made up of healing women in Morgan's Gap. His acolytes had been keeping an eye on women who blatantly flaunted convention to seek each other's companionship outside of church and family. He'd seen some of them himself. One bold crone had even come to the revival. The old lady had challenged him during his sermon with a narrow-eyed stare and even a sardonic chuckle or two before she'd risen and walked out before the benediction, disgraceful as you please.

But to discover his wife was one of them! She'd been seen spending time with these women—the radical singer, the easy rider, THE TINKER.

Ezekiel's nausea was frozen away by the sudden shock of possibly being cuckolded, not by the devil but by a flesh-and-blood man.

All of them must be challenged. If that kind of disrespectful behavior wasn't stopped, the entire community would burn. He'd preached on it, night after night. About how women like that attracted other degenerates—hippies, artists, musicians. "Healing" herbs sounded suspiciously like drugs to him. False religions were gaining ground in popular culture. The Sect, his Sect, had to be sure God's true message was preserved. People, his people, and their leader had to be protected.

Daughters of Eve didn't heal. They lured. They seduced. They tainted.

No doubt the tinker had been weak to temptation. But what other men had been lured into the women's communion with evil?

Across the road from the revival tent was another large field. A tractor was currently dragging a mowing attachment around and around to cut the grass that had grown tall before the lack of rain had baked it brown. He'd heard the county fair would set up in that neighboring field in a few weeks. He'd initially thought it would be a good thing, drawing more crowds to hear his message.

Now he wasn't so sure.

Morgan's Gap was deeply contaminated.

*Witches.*

But the Sect was growing. His following was larger than it had ever been. The collection plates overflowed and their resources—including the mayor, the sheriff and many other men in powerful positions from Morgan's Gap to Richmond—were primed to wipe out any resistance to a proper way of life.

His wayward wife would be wiped out along with all the rest.

When he'd first seen her, she'd been a month shy of sixteen. The sisters had brought all the children from the Sect-funded orphanage to a summer Bible school. Ezekiel had just been tapped as the faith leader of the new church being constructed. He was only beginning to understand the newfound status he'd achieved following his parents' deaths. Rachel was no longer a child. She had been an assistant to the sisters, one so used to their orders that she followed them with barely a sound, enduring correction without protest. He'd seen smacks, pinches, and one of the younger sisters had purposefully stretched out a foot to trip Rachel at one point, making her fall to her knees.

He'd helped her to stand.

Even if he hadn't already decided she would be his, the moisture in her big, frightened eyes and the blood on the corner of her bitten lip would have sent him over the edge.

He should have known then that such intense desire was unnatural.

But he had been fooled by her supposed innocence. Now he'd seen the real Rachel. The brazen woman in the orchard bore no resemblance to the girl he'd married. He'd known that girl in every way he wished, driven to possess her. Now he knew the devil had tricked him with one of his own handmaidens.

But no more.

She hadn't died in the river, but she had chosen this wicked path and now she was as good as dead.

Ezekiel's chill left him at the thought and he got out of the car. He had to prepare for this evening's sermon. The heat wave hadn't kept the crowds away. His acolytes had opened the flaps of the tent wide to encourage air to circulate so the temperature wouldn't build throughout the day. But by the time the tent was packed they would all be soaked with sweat. He'd told them all that the perspiration was a sign of spontaneous baptism last night and the crowd had roared. He would expand upon the idea tonight.

Maybe he would even soak his shirt in water beforehand so he could take off his suit coat with a flourish and show them how favored he was. How powerful. How blessed. He'd be like a drenched rock star on a stage.

They would love it.

Love him.

A dead woman and her consorts were no challenge to his plans. Instead of going to read scripture as he'd intended, Ezekiel leapt up on the raised platform at the front of the tent and stretched out his hands. He closed his eyes and swayed to the imagined adulation of a make-believe crowd.

# Twenty-Three

*R*achel!"

The sound of my name roused me from nightmares very unlike the lucid dreams I'd grown used to. In a hazy hellscape of fire and brimstone, Ezekiel controlled everything around me. Ugly, gnarled roots burst up from the ground to coil around and around my body, and scratchy serpents, so unlike my own smooth Eve, bit deep into my skin. Actual snakes appeared answering Ezekiel's hissing call. I struggled against the roots to get away, but I was trapped. Dozens of snakes struck me until I was paralyzed by a thousand bleeding bites.

When I felt hands on my arms, I jerked awake and cried out, but as my eyes focused, I recognized my surroundings and the person who called my name.

"Take it easy. You bumped your head when you fell. Tuck was in a tizzy, let me tell you," Granny Ross said. The usual scold had left her voice, which was why I hadn't recognized her right away. "You're okay. Overdid it is all. Happens to the best of us."

"Tuck?" I asked. I sat up with her help and looked around. The floor was generously sprinkled with flour around a metal mixing bowl. Granny Ross dusted my dungarees as she lifted me to my feet. She paused when her dusting hand bumped the tiny needle box. The smooth cylinder that rattled slightly from several spare needles was usually imperceptible to anyone but me, yet Granny paused for several seconds with her hand over it. She looked up at me with a confusing sort of speculation in her eyes. Then she continued dusting as if the pause hadn't happened.

"Weasel. You met him. Name's Tuck. He came and found me. Brought me to you. Tempest in a teapot. Nothing to worry about. You just needed a rest," Granny explained.

"I was going to do it today. Bake the perfect pie," I said, remembering. "Or possibly fry some." Standing up to Ezekiel must have taken more out of me than I'd realized. I'd come back to Honeywick determined to get on with my day, but somewhere in between tying on an apron and mixing up the pie crust I'd decided to take a nap on the kitchen floor.

"I'd say you set your intention a little too hard," Granny Ross chuckled.

Only now, with the color coming back into her cheeks, did I notice she'd been deathly pale before. Finding me on the floor had frightened her more than she let on.

"I was going to bake the perfect pie for P...protection," I said.

"Well, now. That's a tall order for your first pie. The first pie that counts, anyway," Granny said. She dusted her hands together and flour *poof*ed in the air. "But you got an early start. You should have had plenty of energy. Some reason you weren't rested this morning?" The old woman's eyes twinkled and I got the crazy notion she knew Mack had been here. But she couldn't know about his visit or the kiss.

Not that anything had happened after.

We weren't ready. Like the apples. We needed more time.

Besides, my energy had been depleted by a much less pleasant encounter.

"Reverend Gray confronted me in the orchard this morning. I was...taking care of some old business. Burying the past. He followed me. Shouted insults like he was going to hurt me. Out by the First Tree," I said. I pulled a chair out from the table and sat down. My legs felt soft in the knees. My impromptu nightmare-filled nap hadn't recharged me at all.

"Oh. Well. That explains it," Granny Ross said. "Witch. Satan's handmaiden. Nothing but cowardice. I've heard it all before."

She pulled a chair out as well but she didn't sit. She dragged it over to the wall and used it as a step stool to reach for a green glass bottle on the highest shelf. She brought it down and set it on the counter, then went right to the cupboard that held the glasses. Granny Ross plonked a heavy glass beside the bottle, then she dusted the top of the bottle off with a clean kitchen towel before pulling out the cork with an audible "pop" that echoed around the room.

"You need some fortification. Dandelion wine will do the trick."

She poured the waiting glass to the brim with a faintly green beverage, and just as I was going to protest that such a big glassful was too much, she handed me the bottle and picked up the glass to daintily sip from herself.

I blinked and cautiously leaned closer to the opening of the bottle for a sniff. Sunshine. Grass. And children's laughter. All exploded behind eyelids that drifted suddenly closed as I breathed in the scent of the wine.

"Only the two of us. Go ahead and drink that down. You need it," Granny said.

I opened my eyes. Then I shrugged and complied. The scent was appealing. My nerves had certainly had a jolt that morning. My pulse still beat too quickly from being bound in my nightmare.

The liquid that flowed from the bottle was more bitter than sweet on the back of my throat. But I swallowed. Once. Twice. Three times.

"Good. Good. Three is good. But seven is even better," Granny said. She sipped from her own glass again. Delicate sips in contrast to my unladylike swigs.

Four. Five. Six. Seven.

I'd had stronger spirits before, but the dandelion wine sent its bubbling fermentation straight to my head. I hiccupped after the seventh swig and Granny Ross laughed.

"I don't know what happened in the orchard this morning, but it must have been something, I'll tell you that," she said. She leaned her hip against the kitchen table as if the wine might have made her a bit wobbly herself.

"Eve's friends came out to play. Dozens of them. A hundred snakes at least. They scared Ezekiel away. I didn't know she could do that!" I looked around, but the bright green snake was nowhere to be seen. I still didn't know how I felt about her having that much power, but she'd used it in defense of me and I couldn't afford to eschew that.

"You won't see Eve for the rest of today, I wager. They don't only vanish when the wildwood disapproves. There's a lot of energy used in their manifestation. After a happening like this, you need to rest. You drink up and then you sleep. Tomorrow will be a better day," Granny advised.

"Did she overdo it in the orchard? Was calling all those snakes too much for her?" I asked, my concern over her power switching to concern over the serpent's well-being. I'd grown awfully attached to the little snake in a short amount of time.

"Something like that." Granny's smirk said I knew nothing about anything at all.

Seven more swigs of the dandelion wine made my snaky morning and my Ezekiel nightmare seem very far away. When the bottle was empty, Granny helped me to place it on the table after I'd tried several times and missed on my own. She also provided me with a short, bony shoulder to lean on when I decided to take the rest of her advice to heart.

"Kissed him. You should have seen his face. So surprised," I rambled as Granny tucked me under the covers in the room where I'd first found *The Scarlet Letter*. The sisters had taken the tiny book away from me. They'd tossed it in the fire and then they'd thrashed me soundly for crying and burning my fingers when I'd tried to save it.

"Only surprised it took you so long. Poor boy's been mooning over you for years. And him more used to having to push girls away. Leastways before he went to war. Still plenty as would want him, mind you. Limp or not. But he's only had eyes for you since he got back. Not that his devotion has done him a bit of good," Granny said.

I mumbled something about his curls or his eyes or his broad shoulders. When I closed my eyes, it was a carved wooden owl I saw, captured in motion, mid-flight. A phantom, winging his way, alone, through the night.

"If you kissed him, there's hope for you yet. But there's a lot you'll have to get through first," Granny whispered. "A hundred snakes? I'd have liked to see that. And that phony preacher man dancing on his tiptoes, I bet. But he'll be madder than a rattlesnake himself now. We'll have to be ready. It'll take more than pie and dandelion wine to save the wildwood from the likes of him and those he leads."

I heard her talking from very far away. Somehow I'd shrunk small enough to climb onto the owl's back. As I buried my fingers in the feathers of his neck I felt more than heard a sort of crooning coming from his chest.

Then we were off, away from the cottage, through the orchard and plunging into the wildwood's shadows. I held on tight, more exhilarated than afraid. It was Mack's owl, come to life, and he took me exploring over hidden paths and winding trails. We swooped under vines and over briar patches until the mossy twilight damp clung to my skin and caught in the wild curls of my hair.

Soon I noticed the forest making way for us—green stretching tendrils curled back from the owl's wings, branches swayed purposefully away from my hair and thorns sheathed themselves in leaves as we swooped by.

And all the rustling movements along with the gurgle of streams that still managed to flow deep in the woods, protected from sun and heat, seemed to whisper welcome, welcome, welcome.

Finally, a velvet darkness deepened around us and all the movement ceased. The hush was a physical thing, and Mack's owl landed high on the branch of an oak tree rather than press on. I reluctantly climbed from his back, but he used his soft head to nudge me toward a hollow burl where several branches met. There I was startled to see the figure of a woman curled in a nest of moss that softly cushioned her body. Leafy vines provided her with a living blanket, woven more perfectly than hands could have achieved. Her eyes were closed and her chest rose and fell in deep, slow breaths that caused the tendrils around her face to quiver. It was Mary May with a honeysuckle pillow that was also like a sweet-scented crown that framed her wrinkled face. She was beloved. By me. By the wildwood. By this great oak tree that gave her a much-needed respite. Dream Me sank down beside Mary. The moss gave beneath my side as I stretched out to share Mary's nest. Sheltered by a lush canopy, with the night sky only showing off and on as an undetectable breeze brushed its curtain aside from time to time, I slept under peekaboo stars.

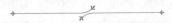

*Mack*

Every curve of every feather Mack had painstakingly carved out of wildwood chestnut had helped to bring him back home. Alive. Mostly. Not whole. Even if his body had been untouched, a man's mind wasn't made to see all that he'd seen. Whenever he had a chance to work on the small saw-whet owl carving, he figured he was putting some of what he saw into the cuts of the wood. A thousand cuts. Twice over.

And the burden of dark thoughts on his brain was slightly lifted.

No room for dark thoughts tonight, of course. He had Rachel to thank for that.

He had seen a real saw-whet owl once as a child. Before his mother died. He'd wandered too far into the woods and dusk had fallen faster than he'd expected. The barely there trail he'd taken had disappeared in the gloaming and he'd been terrified until the littlest owl he'd ever seen hovered over his head. Afterward, his dad said the owl was after insects that had been drawn to his body heat. But his mother had looked him straight in the eye while his father was talking in that way she always had of negating whatever his father said without saying a word.

His mother had known a thing or two about mountain magic.

The owl had led him home.

It had winged its way to his backdoor and he had followed the shush of its wings in the darkness.

He'd always watched for it after that. Especially after his mother died. But it wasn't until he came home from Vietnam that he'd finally seen the creature again. He'd heard the shush of wings and he'd known, deep down, he'd been listening for the sound since he'd been a boy.

The tiny owl had landed on an old forgotten fence post near where he stood at the edge of the woods. He hadn't been able to walk far. His injuries were still fresh and frightening, robbing him of the physical prowess he'd always known. By his welcome, the owl had flitted from the fence post to his shoulder. In that moment, his pain had been very far away. He'd used two fingers to smooth the feathers on the owl's head and he hadn't been a bit surprised to feel a ridge exactly where a knot in the chestnut had left a small ridge on the head of his wooden owl.

If he'd gone looking for his wooden owl, the worn T-shirt he'd wrapped it in would have been empty.

He'd been born and raised in Morgan's Gap. And his tour of duty had only confirmed what he'd learned growing up in the Appalachian wilderness: Ordinary was something you believed in if you didn't really believe in anything at all.

For the longest time, he'd listened for Rachel in the same way he listened for the saw-whet owl. She'd been silent. Almost not there. In a world that was often too loud for him to bear, he had ached to hear her. Her stillness had drawn him almost the same way wood drew him, full of what was meant to be if only someone would see it. He couldn't not see Rachel no matter how hard she tried to be invisible. He had been nonexistent to her. Not in the way he had been to a lot of women since he'd come back from Vietnam with scars, a bum leg and a tendency to get jumpy around loud noises or crowds. More like the way the world had been to him when he'd been in the thick of a bloody, battle-torn jungle.

He recognized when someone was fighting to survive. When just putting one foot in front of the other took everything they had.

Then, suddenly, one day he looked up and she was there. Really there. Looking at him like they had just met. He'd managed to keep working on the apple press even though that simple eye contact had wrecked him for the day.

Tonight, the owl carving hadn't been hanging from his rearview mirror.

He'd carefully walked out to the wood line. The sun was setting. Streaks of orange and pink lit the sky and the forest was painted black in relief. He listened for the hush of wings while he recalled every second of a kiss that had only lasted a few. He replayed the brush of her lips and the flutter of her lashes, her eyes at first open as if she wanted to memorize his reaction, then closed, as if she fully enjoyed his surprise. Sunny apple orchard had a flavor. He'd tasted it on her mouth. He craved it now like a man in a firefight craves whiskey to settle his nerves. He shook with the notion that he should have prolonged the contact in case it never happened again.

He waited for a long time. The sun went down. The moon rose, illuminating the black woods in soft, gray light. But the owl never came.

# Twenty-Four

$I$ woke on a day in late July before the rooster. It was still dark. I'd opened the bedroom windows after sunset yesterday to catch any hope of a breeze that would stir through the night. By midmorning, I would close them against the heat of the day, a summer ritual on the mountain I'd learned even before this particularly hot season.

Everyone was praying that the approach of August would finally bring rain, but each day dawned with a bright, clear sky and not a hint of moisture in the air.

Light, gauzy curtains hung on my bedroom windows and it was the soft swish of their undulations that had woken me. Not a breeze so much as a sigh of scent wafted into the room. Dry, but oh-so-sweet and heavy with what I knew was the honeyed ripeness of the First Tree's apples. I didn't even try to tell myself that the center of the orchard was too far away for me to smell when the apples were ready.

I knew.

The snakes had kept Ezekiel away, but the revival dragged on, and I no longer held out hope that the Sect would leave town before Pearl's birthday. It wasn't safe for me to watch over Pearl personally, but I had risked reaching out to Helen by telephone. I had suspected she was more than a simple midwife. Mary May wouldn't have asked anyone but a wisewoman to raise Pearl. Our conversation confirmed it. Helen would freshen the wards on her house and she would keep a wary eye on my daughter.

*"Our shining girl,"* she'd said. And I'd felt the truth of it. Of Pearl's shine. Of Helen's heart.

So day after hot, muggy day, I'd braced for further confrontation, but today held a more positive promise.

I dressed in a simple cotton skirt and blouse and I tied my hair back from my face with a red bandana. It was going to be a busy day. Filled with hot, hard work. But if Mack was right, Mary's friends would be here to help when the apples were ready. I wasn't sure who would come—Granny Ross? Truvy? Jo?—but I did know from years past, when I'd been nothing but an observer hidden away in the cottage, that harvest began at sunrise. With any luck we would have the apples in the cool shadows of the barn before the full heat of the day hit.

By the time I had prepared a pitcher of strong tea, freshened with mint leaves, and a platter of grilled-cheese sandwiches, toasted in a giant iron skillet, more than one vehicle was pulling into the driveway. I closed my eyes and took a deep breath. Never had the absence of Mary hit me so keenly. Not because I didn't know what to do. I'd seen the harvest from a distance several times. I'd kept to the house, but Mary had talked about the entire process. I could do it. Especially with experienced helpers. I was simply missing my friend, a woman whose bustle had brightened some of the darkest days of my life.

"It's that time again!" Truvy shouted as she hopped down from her van. She hurried around to help Granny Ross down, but I could tell from her overly casual movements that Granny Ross didn't want anyone to think she needed help.

Jo and Mavis roared up behind Truvy's van on Jo's motorcycle. Mavis was in a sidecar and I stared in wonder that an old-fashioned leather helmet had managed to squeeze over all that red hair.

"Ate the biggest, best apple in my dreams last night. Knew today was the day," Granny Ross said.

"The bees always let us know," Mavis said.

I warmed at the easy way Jo unbuckled Mavis's helmet, placing a quick, soft kiss on her lips in a way she probably wouldn't have if they hadn't been among friends.

Just then, Mack's truck pulled up with its usual rattle and roar. Granny Ross laughed. Jo arched a brow. Mavis grinned and Truvy nodded as if she wasn't at all surprised. Following Mack, several more vehicles arrived. I was surprised to recognize them all—Carol Long pulled up in a Volkswagen Beetle, two women I knew only as the twins climbed out of a shiny red pickup and a friend of Mary's I'd met named June got out of an old yellow-and-white Studebaker Wagonaire with a woman she introduced as her daughter.

"I'm Daphne, the football coach's wife," her daughter said.

"She's a painter. Forest scenes. Trees. Starry skies through a canopy of green," Jo amended. *Or corrected.* I liked it. A woman shouldn't only be identified by who she married. I'd been a pastor's wife. I hadn't been allowed to be much else.

"Come in and grab some tea and toast before we head to the orchard," I invited.

In the past, I had holed up in my room with a book or two on Cider Day and Mary hadn't tried to make me take part. Now I was hosting the helpers in the kitchen as if it was mine. Slathering toast with fresh butter, honey and persimmon or blackberry jam on request.

"Did you make this bread?" Carol asked. The librarian's eyes were clear today. Like me, her hair was tied back with a bandana. Hers was

Prussian blue. And she'd traded her fancier work dress for a cotton shirtwaist in a lighter shade of robin's egg. She'd asked for blackberry jam and she bit into the fruit and toast as if it was ambrosia.

"Yes. As hot as it's been, I've still been practicing my baking this summer. My bread is coming along, but I've still got work to do on my pie crust," I replied. Everyone in the room seemed to understand the undercurrent of what I was saying. They understood "stitchery." Men might deem a woman's place as the kitchen, but a woman's place—wherever she claimed it—was a place of power not servitude.

"This is very good," Carol said. She was relaxed and happy. A completely different person than she'd been the last time I'd seen her at the library. I was suddenly, fiercely glad some instinct had nudged me to make a couple of loaves the night before.

"Needs more salt," Granny Ross grunted, nevertheless eating the piece I'd prepared for her with extra butter and honey.

"It's fine. The honey is especially good this year. The bees are finding all the pollen they need in the wildwood in spite of the drought," Mavis said around her chewing.

"Will you have a booth at the fair this year?" Truvy asked. She ate her toast plain, thoughtfully, as if she was measuring the ingredients I'd used with her taste buds. More polite than Granny, her critique was in her eyes and her reach for a second piece.

"It wouldn't be a proper fair without mountain honey," Jo said.

"My first taste of honey was at the fair. I opened a jar right then and there and dipped a finger in," Mack said.

I sipped a long drink of cooling tea trying not to think of the honey-eyed lovemaking in my dreams.

Granny watched me like a hawk as if she was waiting for me to turn beet red and choke.

Looking around I thought every woman in the room must have

dreamed about the beekeeper at some point. Whatever had become of Siobhán and her lover, they didn't rest in peace. Mack had chosen plain honey for his toast and I couldn't help thinking how it would taste on his lips.

The twins, I heard Truvy calling them Fern and Fair, twittered between sips of tea without taking any bread. Mary had said they raised chickens on the other side of town and she'd even bought a carton or two of eggs at times when our supply was low.

"When is the fair?" I asked. I'd never braved the county fair before and even Mary May avoided such a crowd. I vaguely remembered her sending cider and pie last year, but not going herself.

"About two weeks from now. Always in August before school starts. They'll be getting it set up soon," Granny Ross said. "You need to perfect your apple pie before then."

The entire room paused in their nibbling and sipping. Granny's words were more than suggestion. They were portentous. "Need" seemed to echo from the far corners of the house.

Pearl's real birthday was also two weeks from now. It was only a coincidence, but for some reason my heart palpitated in my chest with a rushing series of whooshes that made me dizzy.

No one mentioned the faded Sect tent or the way it was filled night after night by their neighbors. Maybe it had been the snakes, but Ezekiel's fervor for evangelizing had only increased since our confrontation and the town had responded. I was sure that Carol and maybe even Daphne had been expected to attend at their husband's sides. No one talked about how we all feared the lingering revival and Ezekiel's nightly message of intolerance. How it might ratchet up tensions in a town already worn by the heat wave. Crops were failing. Livestock was suffering. Men and women were working harder to survive and being told that their neighbors were at fault. That the drought was God's judgment on the community for allowing everything from short skirts to Motown music.

No one mentioned that some folks still had plenty of water and there were a few special places like the orchard that were doing fine.

"I will," I promised Granny even though I still wasn't sure how the perfect pie would somehow stand in Ezekiel's way. Pearl would surely be at the fair. So would I. And I was more and more certain that it was important for all the wise folk and townspeople to come together. But there was no longer any doubt that her father would be there too.

"You're having trouble with the pie because your skill lies with a needle and thread," Truvy said. She'd flipped the muslin cover back to reveal my embroidery hoop to the room. My throat went tight, but I didn't protest. I only kept it covered to protect it from dust. It wasn't a secret by any means. Mary had watched as I placed every stitch to create the honeysuckle blossoms.

"Those bees look like they could fly away," Mavis sighed. Her appreciation colored her cheeks with a soft blush.

"Thank goodness your work doesn't hum," Jo said. She'd reached a hand out to lightly touch Billy's crooked horn and she winked at me to show she wasn't really jealous of her partner's admiration.

"And there's Tuck looking like he's up to mischief as ever," Granny Ross said.

"Like calls to like," Truvy said dryly.

Mack walked over and took the hoop up from the chair. Now I did protest, but it was nothing but a gasp that no one heard. Why did I mind more if it was Mack looking at my stitchery?

"It's the saw-whet owl," Mack said.

I'd added light stitches of silver to the owl's back, its eyes, and the tips of its wings so that it was kissed by moonlight like it had been the night I'd flown on its back. Mack looked from the owl to me. He searched my face, long and deep, and I didn't look away. But everyone in the room crowded around to see my work and interrupted our connection.

Suddenly all the notice and appreciation was too much for me. I wasn't used to it. I didn't know how to react. The powerful pull I'd always experienced from the tapestry was amplified by all the energy directed toward it. My fingertips tingled. My ears hummed. My lips went dry. A breeze tickled into the room through the screen door.

"All right. Put that down before all this praise goes to her head," Granny Ross fussed. She was looking at me with narrowed eyes. "I know what I know, Truvy Rey. She still needs to perfect that pie. And you all need to get to picking."

Granny went over and tossed the muslin back over the hoop that Mack had carefully placed back on its chair.

The breeze died and the tingling in my fingers eased off. I licked my lips to moisten them. Breakfast was done. We took turns washing the stickiness from our mouths and hands. Somehow I ended up at the kitchen sink at the same time as Mack. We jostled a little as we both reached for spigot, soap, towel at the same time, one after the other. Before I could step back and give way, Mack caught my hands in his to share the big bar of lavender soap between the two of us. I froze as he lathered us together. I shivered as his slick fingers slid over mine, feeling the pleasant sensation all the way to my... toes.

"I think you're clean," Jo teased. Mavis jabbed her elbow in her side and pulled her away.

"We'll be outside," Mavis said.

Granny, Mrs. Long, Truvy and even Fern and Fair had already disappeared. Daphne and her mother, June, followed Mavis out, but not before June winked in my direction.

Mack directed our hands under the cool water flowing from the faucet, but it didn't lower my body temperature at all. I glanced up and found him looking down at me, gauging my reaction to the unexpectedly seductive handwashing.

"You're distracting me." This was an understatement.

"I've been distracted by a thirty-second kiss for weeks," Mack said. It wasn't a complaint. There was a spark in his dark blue eyes. And the shadows I'd seen there were lightened and alleviated by his humor.

"I'm sorry." I wasn't.

"Don't be," he replied, leaning closer.

I didn't pull my hands out of his or try to step back. Maybe I should have. But I was too fascinated by the unguarded warmth in his eyes. I wondered if mine had that same wide, soft look, as if we were permanently startled by the feelings we caused in each other.

This time, Mack kissed me. Slow, soft, gentle. Such a big guy. And his lips against mine like a bee's wings on an apple. His eyes closed as if he savored the taste of my mouth. I kept my eyes open, savoring the look of him, so close, so softened, so sweet…just for me? I'd never seen him like this before, that's for sure. And I lifted my damp hands up to cradle his face because he needed cherishing.

But my touch undid the way he'd relaxed into the kiss.

He stiffened and pulled back. He wasn't used to hands on his face.

"Work to do," Mack said, gruffly.

How could I feel so powerful and like dandelion fluff at the same time? My whole body had gone to something hazy, too soft, too floaty, too dreamy. He was right. There was work to do. I needed to get both my feet back on the ground and head out with the others to pick apples. And yet, this newfound boldness was special.

"The First Tree is waiting," I agreed. I followed Mack outside, but not before I basked in the warmth of a confidence I'd never known before.

As Mack and I exited the cottage, a battered school bus pulled into the yard. The traditional yellow had been covered with red and white and an eagle had been painted on its side with more enthusiasm than skill. "Morgan's Gap, Home of the Eagles" was emblazoned in black on one side.

Daphne was shouting directions to a group of teenage boys as they piled off the bus. The coach's wife was perfectly capable of coaching herself. I was impressed with the number of volunteers she'd managed to assemble without her husband's help or, likely, approval.

"Welcome to Honeywick," I said. One of the bigger boys, nearly as big as Mack, stopped and stared at me. Another one, smaller, with a shock of nearly orange hair and a face full of freckles laughed and thumped the bigger boy on the back.

"Johnny was scared to come out to Crone's Hollow with us today. Don't mind his gawping. He didn't expect to see someone like you," the freckled boy said.

Johnny went red from his neck to his ears and pushed the freckled boy, but in a good-natured way as if they were all used to teasing each other.

"You've seen a pretty lady before, John Howard. Close your mouth and get to work," Mack said. His voice sounded gruffer than I was used to and I wasn't surprised when the teenagers hightailed it away.

"Crone's Hollow," I repeated. "I heard some women at the market call it that."

"People make up tall tales about things they don't understand," Mack said.

"And sometimes people hit pretty close to the truth," Jo interjected, passing by as if she'd already paused for conversation too long this morning. Her long legs ate the distance to the barn where she started directing the football team in what they should do.

"Nothing wrong with Honeywick. Nice to hear it again after all this time," Granny said. But Truvy's brow was knitted and I glanced behind all of them at the honeysuckle-covered cottage seeking a glimpse of blackened stone.

The football team worked well together, loading all the empty bushel baskets I'd carried down from the loft in the barn and stacked outside for the harvest into the back of Mack's truck. Once it was loaded with the baskets and the wooden ladders that lined the interior walls of the barn when not in use, I climbed into the cab and the teenagers climbed into the back. I didn't reach for the dangling wooden owl while Mack walked around to get behind the wheel, but I did whisper a soft hello.

The short trip overland to the orchard was accomplished to a fight song ringing out behind us sung by a myriad of breaking, off-key voices. Mack must have known it by heart, but he didn't sing along, and his profile was set into tight lines when I dared to glance his way.

The rest of the pickers rode with Truvy. She drove her van into the orchard as if it was an Army Jeep. Everyone piled out and Jo set up a makeshift throne made out of a faded quilt spread over a boulder with an apple crate for a footstool so that Granny Ross could comfortably watch the proceedings in the shade. I could tell they'd made her a similar perch many times before. I imagined the boulder itself had conformed to the shape of a wisewoman's bottom over the years. There must have been many before Granny Ross. Hopefully there would be many after.

"Only Rachel needs to see to the First Tree's apples. No one else," Granny proclaimed. She had picked up her knitting from the willow basket that seemed to appear at her feet. Her needles clicked and clacked with a speed that belied the obvious age of her hands, as gnarled as the First Tree's branches.

I felt the imperative of her direction in my gut.

Mack helped me carry a ladder to the base of the knotted trunk. And he settled the canvas sack around my neck and one shoulder. But he didn't reach for any of the fruit himself.

The sprawling branches above us were even more laden with fruit than I remembered. Sheltered beneath the seemingly timeless bower, we paused again. Neither of us moved to kiss the other, but for long seconds the desire shone from both of our eyes.

"Come on, Mack. Let her get to work before it's a hundred degrees," Jo fussed from several trees away.

I was already flushed even though the rooster still crowed in the distance, but up the ladder and deep into the First Tree's boughs I found respite even if it was only because the leaves hid my blushes.

I focused on moving from limb to limb and from apple to apple. Eve appeared on a branch above my head, and she followed my work as if she was a serpentine supervisor. When Truvy began to sing the beekeeper's lullaby in the distance, I didn't notice at first. I was already humming it beneath my breath. I hummed a little louder for a while until a deep tenor voice began to sing the words in a language I'd only heard in my dreams.

Mack was singing.

*In Gaelic.*

Truvy continued singing in English. Her voice was a clear contralto, rising and falling on the high and low notes until a body's heart was swept along. But I could hardly appreciate her unique gift because of Mack. His singing made more than my heart react.

How did he know the song? Had he dreamed about Siobhán and her beekeeper too? If I asked, would he explain the mystery of the blackened stone? My courage failed me. I was too connected to Siobhán. Too fearful of what had happened to her and the beekeeper and their unborn child.

The sack was full of apples. I had to climb down. But I hated to leave the shelter of the First Tree's leaves. Mack's melodious voice called to something aching and empty inside me. That warm hollow in my chest where family should be. Eve slithered to me and wound around my forearm as if she sensed my longing.

Jo had taken Mack's truck to fetch baskets and crates from the barn and now she was distributing them. I carried Eve down the ladder with me and emptied my sack carefully into one of the bushel baskets Jo had stacked under the First Tree.

"Good singing voice," Jo commented. Was her brow permanently arched, or did she only arch it often at me?

I nodded. I didn't trust myself to speak. My mouth felt dry, as if all the moisture from there had risen up to burn the back of my eyes. I was the one who had kissed Mack first. Why was I suddenly intimidated by the ache in my chest, as if it was something to turn away from, to hide, to tamp down and ignore?

"He's a good man. Always has been. His mother married away from the wildwood. His father wouldn't have known the difference between honeysuckle and dewberries, but Mack...he isn't like that," Jo said. "When Mack got back from Vietnam and started his tinkering, he heard about my sculptures. Next thing, he's bringing me material. Gifts. Every bolt. Every piece of busted tin." She unstacked the rest of the bushel baskets while she spoke. I counted six in all plus the one I'd already filled. "His mother would have raised him up to know the wildwood's ways if she hadn't died so young. But going away like he did and coming back hurt—and I mean on the inside—well, he's listening and learning about a lot of the things he missed."

"His mother was a wisewoman? Like Mary May? Like Granny Ross?" I asked. I placed the sack back over my neck and shoulder and prepared to climb the ladder to a different limb on the old, gnarled tree.

"Yes. And like Truvy and me," Jo said. "And Mavis, of course. Although her bees tend to drown out the trees."

"And what about Mrs. Long..." I began. The librarian was up a different ladder several trees away filling a sack similar to mine.

"Her mother has a miraculous green thumb. Makes a sunflower-ginger liniment the old-timers swear by. Lives not far from Granny's cabin in a place of her own. But Sheriff Long doesn't approve of homegrown remedies. Or of those of us who do." Jo frowned and the expression made freckles stand out on her furrowed brow. "She was young. And he was handsome. If you like the testosterone type. Pushy too. Wouldn't take no for an answer. Best her mother could do was to make sure she finished her schooling first. Carol used to write. I hope she still does even if it has to be in secret."

"But she's helping today," I noted. And looking happy about it too. She was flushed from exertion and heat, but I could see her smiling at something Mavis had said as they emptied her sack.

"I'll wager she's here because of you. It's good to have a young woman tending the orchard again. Maybe even trying to stir up a thing or two. Not that I'm ready to be declared over the hill yet!" Jo said.

"Young," I repeated, suddenly startled to be described that way. Between that and Johnny's gaping, not to mention Mack calling me pretty...no wonder I'd wanted to linger in the leaves. I wasn't used to gentle, complimentary attention. The Sect believed women should be humble.

"We're all young compared to Granny," Mavis said as she walked up carrying the bushel basket Mrs. Long had filled.

"I heard that!" Granny yelled from her makeshift throne. "Not a one of you can keep up with me. Best remember it."

"Rachel could. If she decides to," Mavis corrected, but quietly, as if she didn't want to hurt Granny's feelings or incur her wraith. But also with a faraway look in eyes she'd turned toward the distant apiary as if her belief in me came from the constant hum of her honeybees.

Jo stilled, watching Mavis and waiting for her to say more. When Mavis didn't expand upon what she'd said, Jo looked back toward me and shrugged. "She listens to the bees and the rest of us take what tidbits we can get."

Suddenly, Mavis was back with us. Her eyes focused and her smile…well, her smile was tremulous, as if she'd heard something sad. She lunged at me before I could climb the ladder and wrapped her arms around me.

"You may not have family, but you've got friends. All of us. Even Granny Ross. We aren't here because of the apples. Not really. We've always come to help Mary, but today, we came to help you," Mavis said.

"Sometimes those bees of hers talk too much," Jo explained when I gasped at how accurately Mavis had addressed my earlier ache. Only, my conversation with the women had eased away some of my pain, filling the hollow so it didn't echo quite so badly.

The Sect hadn't believed in friendship. Especially between women. We'd been kept working and worn without much chance for camaraderie. The brothers had encouraged competition, and among the women who vied for position, there could be no trust or empathy.

Was this how my apple pie would stand in the Sect's way? And not only the pie, but Daphne's painting and Mavis's bees. Jo's sculptures and Mack's carving. The toys he crafted for the local children. Everything crafted and made and shared. Our singing, and laughter, and the cider we would press from the First Tree's apples today.

*All together.* For some reason the thought caught and held and repeated in my brain—*together, together, together.* Like one stitch placed neatly after another and another.

I couldn't hear the click of Granny's knitting needles from where I stood, but I thought suddenly that her work was a reflection of what was happening when we all worked together. Making something out of nothing. Filling hollows so nothing bad could get in. Creating community with our creations and between each other.

*Wildwood ways.*

Laughter continued to ring out in the orchard from all around as I climbed the ladder to fill another sack and then another. The apples from the First Tree filled exactly three bushel baskets. No more. No less.

The other trees filled fewer baskets apiece, but Mack's truck was packed with baskets and crates full of apples by midday.

He had stayed busy carrying filled baskets all morning. Singing off and on until eventually I could enjoy the sound without the pain. When I emptied the last of the First Tree's apples into the final bushel basket, Mack was there to lift it onto the back of his truck. Our hands met on the wire handles and we both paused in our work.

Eve stirred to slither from my arm over to Mack's and for a few seconds we were tied together by a little serpentine coil of vivid green.

"Well, hello." Mack didn't startle or pull back. He didn't act as if the little snake bothered him in any way. Maybe that's why she continued up his muscular arm without pause.

"She does that," I explained, but I was surprised when Eve coiled around his biceps and closed her eyes.

"I've seen," he said, referring to how she often slept on my arms.

"You don't mind?"

I released my hold on the handles, and moving more carefully so as not to disturb the snake, Mack continued his task, but with care.

"She's small. I don't want to hurt her," he said.

"She's tougher than she looks," I assured him.

I wasn't sure if we were talking about Eve anymore.

"Size and toughness are two different things," Mack said. "I served with men half my size who weren't fazed by what they'd seen."

"Lack of empathy isn't strength," I said. He paused with his big hands on the tailgate.

"I guess not," he agreed.

His consideration of Eve made me think of the saw-whet owl. "I dreamed about your owl. He flew me through the wildwood. From sunset, through the gloaming, and into the soft hush of night. It felt real. Like he was showing me where the hidden streams curve through the trees."

I didn't mention seeing Mary May. It would have been like disturbing a quiet prayer in a mighty cathedral. It had all been nothing but a dream, but it had been sacred. Sacrosanct.

I followed him to the truck, unwilling to lose the excuse for closeness the basket had given us. The rest of the harvesters were strolling back to the barn and we were alone. Our nearness felt comfortable and filled with potential for greater intimacy.

Should I fear it, only because I'd never known the beauty of it personally?

My body had only known pain and humiliation from a man's touch.

Siobhán had known that. But she'd also discovered a better, more loving way.

"The saw-whet owl?" Mack didn't look surprised. If anything, he looked like he understood what I'd said. As if it hadn't been fanciful at all.

"I've never flown before. Nothing higher than a swing. And those not often. Where I come from doesn't have playgrounds. Or airplanes," I confessed.

"You left that place," Mack said.

"Yes. I ran away. But I didn't expect to find owl rides and apple pies," I said.

Mack's stomach audibly gurgled at the mention of pie and I laughed. I was hungry too. That morning's toast was a distant memory.

"Wouldn't even say no to charcoal pie right now," Mack said.

"I think we can rustle up something better than that at Honeywick," I assured him. But privately I promised myself that I would perfect Mary's recipe before the fair. If only to prove to myself and to Mack that I could.

The kitchen table was already covered with a waxed tablecloth and an array of Tupperware containers filled with food when Mack and I arrived back at the cottage. The savory aroma made my stomach growl. I glimpsed baked beans, potato salad, ham biscuits and coleslaw. A station wagon had been backed up to the stoop with its rear gate open and Truvy's oldest daughter was encouraging everyone to eat up. Granny Ross moved around the table sampling this and that with a long handled iced-tea spoon. Primmie must have been used to the old woman's critiques because she ignored them with a smile.

We had all washed our hands at the pump by the barn, then we'd filed into the house in a haphazard line. Mack joined the people filling paper plates and I retrieved lemonade from the refrigerator. Primrose had also brought a plastic pitcher of iced tea.

The twins exclaimed over the colorful ware with their clever sealing lids and Truvy told them she had a sales catalog in her VW if they wanted to order some of the newer colors for themselves. Memories assailed me. The "perfect" kitchen I'd left in Richmond had featured all the latest gizmos and gadgets. I'd been the first in the neighborhood to have a set of plastics that matched my orange kitchen. I'd had to keep the set in perfect order, stacked and sorted, never shared or loaned away.

Primrose's set was made up of opaque pastel colors: yellow, blue and pink. I liked it better but I never wanted any more of my own. I preferred Mary's copper and wood and glass.

Once everyone had eaten and sipped their fill, the twins stayed behind to clean up while the rest of us headed to the barn. The football team had carried the bushel baskets into the shade of the building after eating their lunch in the yard. The strains of Jefferson Airplane's "White Rabbit" came from a transistor radio one of them had brought out.

Fitting. I'd left the world I knew for another that was a strange wonderland of the unexpected—magic, not only in the mystical power of apple trees and honeybees, but also in the close ties between people who genuinely cared about each other. There was a high in that not unlike the high from the dried mushrooms that could probably be found in one of these teenager's pockets.

"You fellas can head on back to town now," Daphne said. "You don't want to miss the moon landing." She'd retrieved her purse from the Studebaker and gave each boy a half dollar coin as they thanked her, one after another. I had forgotten all about the men in the tiny Apollo 11 module so very far from Earth. We'd been as connected to the earth as we could be in the last few hours. Easy to forget all about men in space. Mary May didn't have a television.

"For their discretion," Daphne winked in my direction, distracting me from the moon.

What did people in town say about "Crone's Hollow"? Harvesting apples didn't seem like something that required secrecy. It had been a lovely morning of hard work the Sect would have considered almost wholesome. Even Jo's more ribald jokes had been carefully uttered away from teenagers who probably heard worse from each other.

"She's all oiled and ready to go," Mack said, leading us into the barn.

Sure enough, the press shone like new. The gears cranked smoothly and the wood gleamed.

"I've seen many a gallon jug filled from that tap," Granny said, pointing at the opening at the base of the trough that held two wooden drums made up of oaken slats. Over the drums was the grinding cylinder with its sharp teeth and above it was a large red funnel where the whole apples were to be fed.

"I'll go first," Mack said, with his hand on the crank that would spin the grinder.

While we'd been admiring the press, Jo and Mavis had washed the apples from the First Tree at the trough. Jo carried the first bushel of dripping apples to me and I fed them into the top funnel a few at a time.

"Three. Three. Three," Granny hummed.

Another throne had been made. This one of hay bales. Granny sat on her quilt like she was the Cider Queen. She needed to be there even though she wasn't able to do the physical labor anymore. Her presence was reassuring, a blessing on the proceedings. Every now and then a "do this" or "don't do that" guided us in the process. But I missed Mary keenly as the sweet sticky juice began to spray the air.

The pulped fruit fell into the slatted drums. Mack cranked tirelessly. I stooped, scooped and constantly fed the chewing cylinder, three by three. The air was soon heavy with the aroma of ground fresh fruit.

Jo and Mavis had help from Daphne and her mother. They rinsed and carried until all the apples from the First Tree had been ground.

When the drums were filled to overflowing, Mack wrestled the press lids onto them and threaded a big wrought-iron pike into the lids. On top of the pike he placed the four-pronged head used to screw the pressing lids tighter and tighter down onto the pulp so that the cider would flow into the glass gallon jugs I held, one after another beneath the tap.

Mack used a worn axe handle to spin the four-pronged top of the pressing pike. He repositioned the handle with every half turn. Apple cider was unfiltered so as the jugs sat and the liquid settled there would be a flavorful thick sediment of fruit fiber in the bottle. After a couple of hours, I'd lined up a row of jugs on the floor beside the press.

"Shake a jug and bring me a swig," Granny Ross ordered.

My back and arms screamed. My hands were sticky. My whole body was damp from perspiration and the spray of juice from the machine. I'd seen Mack start flexing his strong hands as if they were tired and sore too. Granny had done this for untold years. Mary too. As the oldest here, she definitely deserved the first drink.

I tilted the first jug we'd filled while Mack paused to flex his shoulders and stretch his back. The sediment flowed like a natural lava lamp then blended until the light gold juice at the top became a deep, rich amber liquid, thick with all the pulpy goodness the First Tree had shared. Granny didn't call for a cup. She took the jug from me with the ease of practice and used the crook of her elbow and her shoulder to balance its weight, and tilt it to her lips.

Swig she did. Then lowered the jug to close her eyes as she swallowed.

"Best ever," she declared with a definitive nod of her silver-crowned head.

"You always say that," Truvy scolded.

"Will be better hard and fizzy," Jo said from the barn's open door.

"Lush," Mavis teased.

"Like you don't enjoy your honey mead," Jo groused back. All good-natured. All light and happy in spite of tired backs and sticky faces. I was beginning to relax more around the playfulness. I'd never realized how tight my spine and shoulders had always been. Constantly braced for conflict and strife.

"Now Rachel," Mack said. He didn't wait for Granny to offer me the jug. He came over to her and she let him have it, her eyes narrowed and sparky. He brought the jug to me but not to my out-stretched hands. He lifted it to my lips and tilted it easily. I'd breathed its flavor all day, but the liquid was more potent—not with alcohol, it wouldn't be that kind of potent until it was allowed to ferment—but with the wildwood.

I'd tasted this dew on my lips when I'd flown over the forest on the back of Mack's owl. The richness that coated my tongue had graced the gloaming breeze and kissed my skin with the promise of sustenance, of fullness. The aching hollow I'd felt that morning had gradually filled through the day with work, with comradery and com-panionship. As I swallowed, the last of it was washed away with the taste of sunshine, fertile earth, forest streams, morning mist and the look in Mack's blue eyes. Even in the barn's shadows they were lighter now and filled with amber flecks like the mixed cider in the jug he took from my lips straight to his.

Another kind of kiss. Just as intimate.

I'd thought we were as close to the earth as we could be while we'd been picking apples, but this was closer. The cider soaked into my blood and bones before it even made it to my belly. Mack swigged from the jug as Granny had, but his strenuous exertions of the morn-ing made him thirstier. I was mesmerized by the movement of his throat as he swallowed again and again.

I pressed my fingers to my lips. I never wanted to forget. I hadn't truly understood that the orchard was a part of the wildwood and that they were both a part of the mountain. Morgan's Gap was held by roots twining, tangling, twisting together. By leaves breathing. By streams flowing. By every blossom, bud, fruit and fern.

And by the people who tended it all.

Granny asked for help to get to her feet and with Jo on one side and Mavis on the other she rose. It had been a long day. She was as tired as the rest of us. Daphne gathered Granny's dropped knitting and placed it in the willow basket. The piece Granny was working on was growing. It filled the basket, threatening to spill over its ample sides. Colors of moss, fern, bark and leaves were all blended together, but I couldn't guess what the finished project would be.

"Thank you, girl," Granny said to Daphne. "Find you a different man. One who would be here too. Now take my basket out to that ridiculous thing this one calls a car."

Daphne's eyes went wide and filled with tears. Truvy patted her shoulder.

"She's tired. Don't mind her manner," the kinder woman said.

"Tired, rude, but not wrong," Jo added. Mavis punched her arm.

"It was a mistake to involve the team. That money will spend fast and nothing is more valuable to a player than their coach's approval," Mack said, quietly, after the bus had gone.

"Will he really care that the boys helped harvest apples?"

Mack moved to take apart the press, hoisting the pulpy drums onto a wheelbarrow. It was a two-man job he handled with ease. Still strong. Even if his limp was more noticeable after the exertions of the day. Once the barrow was loaded, he paused to rub his hip and thigh.

"You tasted the cider. There's folks in Morgan's Gap who are afraid of that. The connection. The tending and all we get in return," Mack said. "Some men see nature as the enemy. They think farming is a war to wrest what you need from the ground. They don't understand the give that needs to go hand in hand with the take."

"The circles," I said softly.

"The cycles. The seasons. People used to be more in tune with the world's ebbing and flowing, the growing and dying. And that made them more in tune with each other. Now? They're out of touch with the land and ruled by their fears—drought, differences, greed. But what they most fear is people who are still in tune with the oldest ways."

"The wildwood ways," I said.

"My mother called it listening. A piece of wood whispers to me before I carve it. I hear what it is. What it will be," Mack said.

"The First Tree called me away from a Sect revival when I was only thirteen," I said. "I didn't *hear* but I *felt*. Like a tug in my chest." I'd never talked about that morning. Not even with Mary. Something loosed in me like dandelion fluff released to float on the breeze.

"Some have gotten it all twisted because they're only listening to what men say and there's always been men willing to say anything to get what they want. Troops on the ground. People under their control. Their face on a flag."

"Men on the moon," I added, tilting my face to the sky. The sun was still setting. The moon hadn't appeared yet.

"People can achieve fine things too. Seems to me exploration is more positive than war. Would be even better if the world came together rather than seeing it as another chance for competition," Mack said. "Why does it always have to come down to us versus them?"

"Divide and conquer and claim. Seems the opposite of what we're meant to do and be," I said. "The tent bothers me because it's a show. Not a faith."

"Too many people vying for position rather than being comfortable together. And when the man that leads them is evil, only bad things can happen."

Mack lifted the handles of the wheelbarrow to carry the drums outside. I pointed him toward the compost bin. Daphne. Mrs. Long. Their husbands weren't Sect...yet, but the two women weren't in very different positions from the one I'd been in. Married women didn't have much say. Their positions were totally dependent on their husbands. For better...or for worse. I hoped neither would face ugly consequences for living as wise, free women today.

*Crone's Hollow.*

Mary hadn't always been old, but I figured she'd always been different. Likely to grab your cup of tea and dump out the liquid to read the leaves before you were finished drinking. I thought of her as fay. Strange but only in the best way. Yet, it would be easy for others to think of her as a witch.

Had that caused problems in the past?

*Blackened stone.*

It was easy to imagine it had. Witch, fay, wisewoman. No matter the moniker, women who went their own way weren't allowed. Especially if those same women then taught others the ways that ran counter to the teachings of powerful men.

Mack didn't climb into his truck and drive away as everyone else did. I wasn't sure if anyone noticed. Granny Ross had to be helped into Truvy's Volkswagen. And even Jo's spark had faded. She climbed onto her motorcycle with less flare, slowly fastening the leather helmet over her wilted curls and under her chin. Mavis waved from the sidecar, but her farewell gesture was less energetic as well.

How many of us were tired from more than physical effort? We had put ourselves into those jugs along with the First Tree's fruit—our hearts, our souls, our spark. Magic? Yes. I thought so. That sip of cider had certainly been more than ordinary.

By the light of the setting sun, the harvesters drove away, the Studebaker's horn startlingly sharp and staccato among the other barnyard sounds gone sleepy and hushed—nanny goats bleated from their pen, chickens chirruped as they settled in their coop. The entire mountain had gone quiet with expectation, and I couldn't separate the two momentous occasions about to happen in my mind. Folks were probably in front of their television sets and radios already concentrating on what was happening on the moon. Meanwhile, my pulse thudded noticeably in my ears because Mack and I were alone and I suddenly knew I'd been waiting for *this* moment all day.

# Twenty-Five

"Would you like some supper?" I asked.

The offer was bigger than the kiss. And we both knew it. Mack went still beside me as if he would frighten me away if he replied. I wasn't afraid of him. I never had been. Nervous. Skittish. Flustered. All of those things, but not fearful.

"I'd like to stay awhile." Mack's voice was gruff, but not in the same way it had been with the football players. He cleared his throat as if he might be skittish too. But we'd both been through so much. If we wanted to be together for a little while, we should be, no matter what town gossips might say.

"I have a television in my truck. Fordham Jones got a new bigger one to watch the launch. Was gonna throw out the old one. I replaced the picture tube and it works fine," Mack said. His offer was matter-of-fact, but his tone was anything but. This was going to be a big step for us. Every bit as big as flying to the moon.

Suddenly, I was eager to watch the moon landing with him. Something to counteract our worries about the Sect and our nervousness about being alone together.

I washed up and changed clothes while Mack retrieved the tiny old-fashioned television. By the time I came out, freshened up and more nervous than before, he had found one of Mary's few electric outlets. He'd also found the tinfoil and used an exorbitant amount on a set of rabbit ears.

Through a haze of static snow, the broadcast was showing the Apollo 11 module on the surface of the moon. We sat in handcrafted rocking chairs in a hundred-year-old stone cottage and watched as they repeated the footage of the landing again and again. Each time was as thrilling as the one before.

Mack reached for my hand and I didn't shy away. Around us, the entire world seemed to be holding its breath. Together.

The whole universe was alive with possibilities that could take us wherever we wanted to go if only we could embrace our collective strengths and work together to get there. If only we could leave small-minded beliefs behind.

"I need air," I said. Mack followed me outside.

The wildwood breeze welcomed us out on the stoop, gently reminding me that love triumphing was sometimes as simple an individual choice to step away from hate. Eve had disappeared. I remembered Granny's advice. Was I making a mistake? Her disappearance might be discretion or disapproval. Or related to how much of my energy I'd given to the cider. Mack reached for my snake-free arm and I discovered that I didn't care.

The heat of the day dissipated around us. My skin chilled in the shadows of the stoop and I shivered as Mack gently enfolded me with his thick arms, but more than his muscles, it was his presence that held me. He was always so very here, with me, as if he didn't want to be anywhere else. The fragrance of apple pulp and sweat rose from his skin and clothes, along with the ever-present scents of sawdust and wood sap.

I pressed my face into his chest and stood there awhile, warming and gentling and settling my nerves. He was where I wanted to be too. It was luxury to allow it. Pure, sensual decadence.

For one night I wanted to rest from my constant vigil.

The flutter of wings made me pull back from what had become a tight hug as Mack held me close. On the stoop's railing a small saw-whet owl had landed beside us. The night wasn't yet too dark to see the gleam of two large saucer eyes turning this way and that.

"Your owl!"

"He does that sometimes," Mack replied, echoing what I had said earlier about Eve.

"Does he have a name?" I longed to reach out and touch the owl's head. To stroke down his back. I held Mack's upper arms instead, discreetly measuring their circumference, firsthand, for the first time. So strong and yet capable of such softness.

"I've never given him one. It seems like overstepping. Like trying to claim him," Mack said. "He really isn't 'mine' any more than Eve is 'yours.' Not a pet or a belonging. They're more like an extension of the wildwood. A tangible way to communicate with us."

"Companions and helpmeets. Forest Familiars," I said, only half joking.

He nodded into the top of my head and my heart stuttered as his nose nuzzled into my curls.

"I was one of those football boys, once. Not too long ago. It seems like forever. I grieve for him, sometimes. I came back from over there. He didn't," Mack said.

"Not lost. Changed, maybe. But…I like the Michael Coombs I know."

Now I did lift my head from his chest and look up at his face. The moon had risen, but even with a cloudless sky full of stars I couldn't make out the expression on Mack's face. I could only tell that he was looking down at me. Maybe trying to do the same thing.

We were on the moon. Moving forward into the future. The daring exhilaration of that thought matched the feelings Mack was causing in my body.

"You do," he said. It wasn't a question. He wasn't coy like that. He knew I liked him. I'd kissed him after all. I'd invited him to stay. There would leftovers in the refrigerator. Primrose and Truvy had insisted I could bring back the Tupperware when it was empty. But I was sure Mack wasn't lingering for the last of the deviled eggs or to watch the first moonwalk with me.

I nodded anyway, by way of answer, and even in the dark he must have been able to see the movement. The owl startled away, and I remembered in an instant the swooping thrill of flying on his back. Imagination. Probably. But was a dream ride any more outlandish than accepting the transformation of wood to living, breathing forest creature?

Even as I'd lived through a nightmare, I'd kept the idea of a fairy tale cottage close. Guarded in my heart. A possibility. A hope. Something told me Mack had done the same. If he hadn't fully believed in the owl and his mother's wildwood before he left for war, he'd needed them to get him home. He still needed them now.

And maybe me.

If only for tonight...

He didn't fumble for my lips in the dark. Instinctively our mouths came together with no need of starlight. He tasted of cider, and the sudden refreshing of that earlier connection with forest and earth, leaf and shadow, dew and spring water bubbling up from the ground made me gasp into him. Our breathes mingled as we panted—it was him and me along with our connection to the wildwood that made our pulses race and our bodies quicken with need.

I knew from my dreams what a kiss could be.

But those lucid dreams of a seductive beekeeper couldn't compare to Mack's tongue eagerly welcomed against mine. I had to hold on tight to his arms because my legs went weak. As if he knew, he cradled me closer, supporting me easily. Young. Pretty. I'd felt completely used up. Ancient. Alone. And then suddenly I wasn't.

But I was scarred.

Mack's hands were stroking my back and I stiffened beneath his fingers because I knew he'd feel the raised ridges left on my skin from years of beatings and injuries that had gone untreated. My back had been left with phantom pain, always tender from remembered abuse.

He pulled back from my lips. He brushed his mouth on my forehead and whispered into my hair.

"It's all right. I don't have to stay," he said, mistaking my reaction.

"My back isn't pretty, Mack. I have scars," I said. "I have a strawberry birthmark on my left shoulder the sisters always tried to stripe away."

He stiffened at my confession and reached to open the front door with one hand. He used the other he'd kept clasped around mine to pull me inside. The front room, the historic portion of the cottage, was dark, but in the later additions lights glowed—in the kitchen, in the hall, in my bedroom beyond.

By the light of the kitchen sconces, Mack stopped and let me go. He reached for the tail of his T-shirt and pulled it up and over his head. I'd seen some evidence of his trauma in his eyes. I'd caught glimpses of pale, white marks around his collar. Now he showed me the puckered streaks that trailed down the side of his torso and out of sight, where no doubt more scars were covered by his pants.

"My leg is even worse," he said. "Hurts every step I take. But the pain isn't half as bad as knowing the same men who pity me on the street will turn right around and send those laughing, singing, joking teenagers to the same godforsaken jungles. Or some other ones. Doesn't matter. Tundra. Desert. Forest. Beach. Sometimes, war is necessary. I know that. There are evil people in this world. But far too often war is an excuse to build power and make more money, never mind the consequences to ordinary men."

"And women," I added.

I stroked his scars in the same reverent way I'd wanted to touch the saw-whet owl. Tentative. As if he would push me away. But I didn't pity him, and I was definitely not repulsed. Mack's scars didn't make him less attractive. He was the man whose kisses I was beginning to crave. Scars and all.

And there was wonder in that every bit as miraculous as any other magic I'd discovered on the mountain.

"I called you pretty because I couldn't share with a whole busload of teenagers what I really see when I look at you. For the same reason I can't name the owl. You're as miraculous to me as he is. Someone who appeared one day and just like that I wanted to live. Not exist. Not cope from one numbed night to another. But *live*. Like I was a thinking, breathing man again. I'd found reasons to get up every morning since I made it home. But you...you make me feel alive. Like living is worth the risk of putting one foot in front of the other even if every step hurts. Completely worth it," Mack said. "Scars? You're so beautiful it makes me ache. That someone scarred you makes me fucking furious, but I want to see your back. I want to hold you and taste you and show you that we're good together even though there's evil in the world. *Because* there's evil. It's even more important to acknowledge what's precious."

I couldn't reply. I could only nod. My cheeks were wet and I finally understood why Siobhán cried more than I did. Scars could be beautiful. Hurting didn't have to be hidden. Not from everyone. Not from someone who understood your pain.

I saw a flicker of movement over Mack's shoulder. Eve had found a warm spot on top of the television set. Beneath her, the screen glowed as the world waited for Neil Armstrong to climb outside. The call of the saw-whet owl began in the distance, loud for such a small bird, a repeated short *hoop-hoop-hoop-hoop*.

If the owl and the snake were our familiars, we had their blessing. And if a man could walk on the moon, then we could certainly take another kind of risk.

I leaned against his bare chest. Not as brave as other things I've done, but just as desperate. If wildwood magic was real, if we were blessed by it after all we'd been through, it was also an elusive thing— dandelion fluff, apple blossoms, that first perfect swig of fresh-pressed cider—and we had to catch hold of the magic before it was gone, whenever we could, even if it seemed like we were chasing fairy lights floating through the forest at midnight.

The trick had to be to wish quickly, to turn your face up to the butterfly kisses of petals, to swallow deeply and taste that glorious first taste of cider on your tongue. Mack bent to kiss me again as if he understood the urgency of accepting what might be a will-o'-the-wisp whim of forest fancy.

I wrapped my arms around his neck and closed my eyes, certain that it was all Mack and not the cider or the moon landing that had gone to my head.

# Twenty-Six

*Granny Ross*

$C$*rone's Hollow. Weren't many* folks who would have said it in front of her just ten years ago, but time passed and so did any semblance of sense in modern youngsters who believed more in record players and fast cars than they believed in things they couldn't taste, or touch, or see.

Of course, Granny Ross could taste and touch and see a whole lot that others couldn't. For instance, her first sip of the cider had tasted like love's first kiss. Her heart had raced and her stomach had swooped and her head had gone dizzy and light as if she wasn't nigh unto eighty years old.

But when the taste had faded she'd been left with fear that had weakened her knees and made her hands shake. They still shook now. So much so that she had to leave her knitting in its basket and retrieve a bottle of dandelion wine from her special emergency stores reserved for those times when an old woman needed a sunny tonic against encroaching shadows.

A body got to be a certain age and the losses piled on till your shoulders ached with 'em. She'd lost her daughters to the city as soon as they were old enough to run away. Only Deborah had come back to Morgan's Gap.

But neither of her girls had come back home. Not really. The Ross cabin was too quiet these days. The silence only softened by a bubbling pot and miles upon miles of twisted yarn.

A crone was nothing but a wisewoman who had a special connection to the wildwood heightened by advanced years and fruitful practices. Not every wisewoman lived long enough to become a crone. And great age didn't guarantee you'd learn enough to become a part of the wilderness you tended.

Granny Ross wasn't a crone, although there were plenty of people in town who would cross the street to avoid the possibility of passing her. Meanwhile, Mary May was a gentle old soul who preferred baking to cursing. Mary was just about the only person on the mountain Granny acknowledged as wiser than herself. The silly ol' goose had been a hippy back when nobody else was and she was so much a part of the woods she practically had roots for fingers and toes.

Granny was too impatient to wait for roots.

She had enough energy to let out a scoffing chuckle.

Trouble came and went like cicadas. They scrabbled up from the ground and climbed high in the trees to screech incessantly for mates. Eggs were laid that killed off a slew of branches before they fell to the ground to hatch into grubs that burrowed and went dormant. But there. Always there.

Until the next emergence.

That boy, John Howard, had been scared to come to "Crone's Hollow." The other boy—looked like a Royce; always red, the Royces—he hadn't been scared at all. But he'd heard the tales too. And some dark enough to shake up a big strapping farm-boy athlete.

The cider had told her that too. Once it made it to her gut. It still bubbled there now, refusing to settle. Rachel had found her way to where she was meant to be. She and the tinker had found each other, but there were always those who wouldn't let the wildwood be.

Truth was she'd always been amused that folks were a little bit afraid of her, but she was beginning to wonder if her amusement was a luxury she couldn't afford. She wasn't getting any younger and she lived all alone. There were others that lived alone too. People she loved who might be in danger if folks got too scared.

The false preacher was succeeding. Helped along by turbulent times, he was amassing strength in numbers. Didn't matter if it was only the gullible, the insecure and the ignorant that flocked to him. There were enough of those types to threaten an otherwise peaceful community. And there were always folks who would want to use Gray's influence even if they didn't believe in his lies.

He wanted to hurt Rachel.

But she wasn't his only target.

Anyone who didn't follow him would be seen as a threat by him, by his flock, by the men who wanted to use him to remain in power themselves.

It was a tangle of human machinations that rivaled the natural complexity of the wildwood itself.

Granny found herself wishing Mary May hadn't disappeared. If the crone was around, maybe they could talk about things over a soothing cup of tea or three and maybe the old hippy would speak some wisdom that would calm the gnawing dread that wouldn't allow the potent cider to settle in Granny's stomach.

She tried not to think about her nightmares or how the feeling in her gut was one of recognition, as if the trouble brewing between the townsfolk and the wildwood was part of a cycle they'd all been through before. Mary would know—and maybe it was high time Granny knew too.

Strange now that she'd ever laughed at rumors of witchery.

But Mary was gone and Granny Ross was left with only the memory of bees. Buzzing in her head, in her gut, on her skin and forever on her mind.

# Twenty-Seven

*B*efore *I lost my* nerve, I headed out to visit Carol Long's mother. Mack knew more about the mountain and its people than I did, but Jo had said folks swore by the woman's liniment, and maybe Mack was too proud to admit how much his leg pained him.

He hadn't been able to hide it from me that first evening we spent together. Not during a long night of intimacy where we'd explored each other's bodies, scars and all. My face and neck heated when I remembered the "and all." We'd watched Armstrong take his "giant leap for mankind" wrapped in quilts on the floor in the glow of the tiny screen. Since then, Mack had visited me at night several times and I always noticed when his leg seemed to bother him.

If the liniment would ease the ache in his leg, then I wanted to buy some for him.

It was that simple.

He'd refused to accept payment for fixing the broken cider press. And the jugs of cider he'd accepted had already been his after all his work pressing apples. But I drove out to find Carol's mother for more complicated reasons than a favor owed.

Wildwood gifts. He'd told me that bartering on the mountain was complex and special. I felt that now. That this drive to make something for him was more than empathy or debt.

I kept seeing Mack's face as he placed the cider jug to my lips and tilted it so the fresh, tart liquid could rush over my tongue and down my throat. That had been our first true connection. More intimate than kisses. In some ways a preview of the night that came after. The amber flecks of warmth in his blue eyes had seemed a reflection of the lush apple pulp that had swirled in the jug as I'd swallowed.

But the sparkling striations hadn't disappeared.

I saw hints of them every time I looked at him after.

He had gifted me that sip of cider. And my acceptance of the gift had solidified the flighty attraction happening between us into something more solid and real. I needed courage to seek out the liniment because I sensed every wildwood gift was a pledge.

Some promises needed to be broken. I'd vowed before God to bind myself to Ezekiel Gray, but he had also promised to love me. There was no love in violence. There could be no binding without trust.

I was no longer a frightened young girl being forced into a life of pain and fear. I was a grown woman who knew her own mind. And the wildwood knew it as well as I did. I needed to claim my place in Morgan's Gap, beside Mack and my new friends, before I could possibly defend it and Pearl against the Sect.

I'd heard talk of Ezekiel roaming around town pausing and mumbling and moving along as if he was confounded by a puzzle no one else could see. Children had started to follow him on his daily tramp around the sidewalks of Morgan's Gap, but unlike the Pied Piper he would often stop and shout to chase them away.

I hadn't let his wandering frighten me away from Market Days. Once I'd even seen him in the distance, a black-clad form who always, somehow, missed a neighborhood with a certain Queen Anne Victorian and apple tree saplings that danced in the breeze.

And still, the revival continued on, a threatening blight on my newfound pleasure in Mack's company. Why couldn't the people who attended see that there was something very wrong with their leader?

Jo had told me where I could find Carol's mother. "Near Granny Ross" might describe half a dozen cabins and shacks on the mountainside around her. Luckily, a brightly painted mailbox stood out at the end of a driveway a half mile beyond the standing stones that marked the road to the Ross place. There was no name on the box and I didn't know Carol's maiden name anyway, but I felt a familiar tug and decided to follow the rainbow.

I found the driveway graveled well and easy for the Rambler to navigate. There were two tracks down the middle of the road, but they were smooth and the few potholes had been filled. By the time I came to a large circular turnaround, I wasn't surprised to find an old camping trailer instead of a cabin. Like the mailbox, it had been hand-painted in rainbow hues. The kind of paint job you would expect to see on a van like Truvy's.

I parked and got out of my car, but I stood hesitant beside the open door because I still wasn't sure if this was the place in spite of the tug in my gut. Obviously a permanent residence, the trailer had a large stoop lined with flowerpots and plant boxes. A profusion of green growing things softened the colorful backdrop, their gentle blossoms softly echoing the rainbow paint, but with a lighter, more natural touch.

The sound of wind chimes in every pitch and tone filled the air and my attention was called to bits of glass and metal flickering and tinkling together on strings in the nearby trees.

Color and chaos, but neatly kept was my first impression. The small lawn and the walk from the drive to the door were trimmed. I could

see the handle of an old reel mower sticking out from a small pot-
ting shed—also painted with rainbows beneath a vivid red metal roof.
Several rows of giant sunflowers grew on a sun-bathed bank along the
edge of the forest. They were only slightly wilted and another quick
look around revealed a hand pump like the one in Honeywick's farmyard and a couple of buckets. There was also a wooden yoke used to
tote the buckets to the plants that must have needed watering frequently in this rainless heat.

There was no sign or shingle advertising herbal remedies, but there
wouldn't need to be, would there? In Morgan's Gap, everyone knew
where to find cider or liniment. Or possibly more dangerous things.
I thought about the women discussing Crone's Hollow at Market
Day. *Bones*. A shiver ran down my spine when I thought of Granny
Ross's dried bundles hanging from the rafters of her ceiling. Roots not
bones. Surely. Roots.

The trailer door opened while I continued to hesitate and an indeter-
minately middle-aged woman stepped out onto the stoop. An uncom-
monly pretty face was surrounded by brown hair shot through with
silver that glinted in the sun. Unbound, it fell to her waist in simple,
riotous waves. She wore Levi's cinched in with a large leather belt and
a blue peasant blouse tucked into her jeans.

Her feet were bare, her toenails pink, and I couldn't help staring
because I could see the glint of a gold ring around her left big toe.

"You look like someone who's found their way, but you're second-
guessing yourself."

Her smile was big, but gentle. She wasn't mocking. The warmth in
her eyes and her dimpled cheek said she'd been in exactly the same
predicament before.

"I'm looking for ginger liniment for a friend. Jo sent me," I
explained. Jo hadn't really sent me. She'd only mentioned the liniment

in passing. But I'd been in Morgan's Gap long enough to understand how important it was to present your bona fides to people when you met them for the first time. "I live at Honeywick. With Mary May."

"Simple. Straightforward," the woman said, nodding. "I like you. Figured I would when Granny didn't."

I must have started because the woman laughed and this time her humor was at my expense.

"Don't look so surprised. Granny Ross doesn't like anyone. Even me. And she's my mother."

I thought maybe she was being too hard on a grumpy senior. Granny might be impatient with "youngsters," but I thought she secretly liked many of the people she scolded and I was willing to bet she'd fight for family whether she liked them or not. Carol's mother was Granny's daughter! Jo hadn't said a thing. Sheriff Long had married a *Ross*.

"I'm Deborah. Close that car door and stay awhile. I woke up this morning with a powerful need to infuse another batch of liniment. I ground and dried fresh gingerroot yesterday. And my nose was itching. Always someone coming by to visit when you wake up with your nose itching."

Was it Deborah Ross? She didn't have a ring on her finger. Only the gold ring on her big toe. As I closed the Rambler's door and stepped over to the stoop, I saw the ring looked every bit like a wedding band. Was the ring a memento or a trophy? Or a pirate's plunder? I was beginning to understand that the wisewomen of Morgan's Gap were more than unconventional. They were a gloriously unbound, unpredictable force, fueled by nature. Whatever the ring represented, I loved the way it glinted in the sun when she walked.

"I'm Rachel. It's nice to meet you," I said. And it was. The tug that had brought me here had settled into a warm, soft sense of belonging.

It wasn't only Deborah's welcome or her good-natured humor. A bright green ribbon of snake sunned herself on the rail of Deborah's stoop near a pot of what looked like wild daisies.

"Rachel," Deborah repeated my name as if she wanted to say the syllables herself. Her eyes took on a faraway look and I waited patiently. I was becoming used to wildwood ways. Mavis listened to her bees. Mack carved what each piece of wood told him it should be. Perhaps Deborah listened to something as well. The breeze punctuated that thought with an increased rustling of the wind chimes around us. The random music was as physical as it was auditory. I felt the waves of sound sink into my skin and penetrate all the way to my bones. My heart stuttered. My breath caught. The same breeze that made the wind chimes sing ruffled the loose curls around my face. "Rachel," she said again.

"Mary's been gone for a while, but I'm tending the orchard while she's away," I continued a little breathlessly.

Deborah blinked and her eyes refocused. Her attention, once regained, tracked over my face as if she would memorize my features. Mack had called me pretty. At best, I was ordinary, but the anything-but woman on the stoop looked at me more closely than ordinary warranted. What did she see? That morning, I'd thrown on a yellow skirt fresh from the clothesline and a striped green shirt. I'd slipped into my usual canvas shoes that were becoming smudged from being worn so frequently. I hadn't tied back my hair. It fell to my shoulders in a curly brown bob. No lipstick. No powder. Freckles across my nose.

Whisker burn on my cheeks.

Lips still swollen from Mack's kisses.

"You'll help me make the liniment for this friend," Deborah decided after her close perusal. "I have some shelled sunflower seeds from last year. I'll show you how to press the oil from them with your own two hands. That's the oil we'll use for the ginger infusion."

"Yes. Yes, I think that's right," I replied. I remembered how we'd all worked to make the cider and how tired we'd been afterward. We'd put ourselves into those jars. I'd seen Mack rub his old injury as if he was in constant pain. I wanted to put my heart and soul into the making of his liniment as well. To help ease those aches.

"This one showed up with the sun this morning. Slithered from pot to planter as if she was inspecting the inventory," Deborah said when I joined her on the porch. She went over to Eve and picked her up without hesitation. "Nose itching. Sudden serpent. Dreamed of bees last night. It's a wonder Granny didn't show up before you did to poke me out of bed."

"Your mother," I repeated as if to convince myself of their relationship.

It was impossible to imagine Granny Ross as anything so soft as motherly.

Deborah snorted. "I set myself up in this place when I was sixteen. No room in Granny's house for me and her both. But we're amiable. I mean, as amiable as anyone can be with a witch."

"Crone's Hollow," I said.

Deborah looked from Eve to me, quick, as if I'd startled her.

"Mary is a crone. The oldest and wisest of us all. All light and love and life even after all this time," Deborah said. "Granny Ross isn't a crone. Never will be. She can't settle into wisdom. I'll probably be like her although I've tried hard to take a different course. There's darkness in trying to bend the wildwood to *your* will. Granny is stubborn. Too determined. She can hear more than most, but she doesn't *listen* like she should. A crone listens and follows the wildwood way rather than trying to make her own will be done. Now, mind you, Granny's got reasons for being like she is. She's had to be tough as nails to survive. But a lot of troubles she's faced have been of her own brewing."

I thought about how the clicking of Granny's knitting needles made me nervous while the wind chimes calmed me down.

"I learned my lesson a long time ago. Be careful with Granny. And with her trio. Jo and Truvy have been a good influence on her since the wildwood brought them all together. But Granny still goes her own way more often than not and they've been known to get carried along," Deborah said. "Trust me."

I wasn't sure if it was Eve wound up her arm as comfortable as could be or if it was something subliminal the chimes were singing in my head, but I had trusted Deborah almost immediately. And yet, her troubled relationship with Granny Ross made my fingers itch and burn as if there was an obvious hole that needed mending.

I was still following the breadcrumb trail Mary May had left me. From the names she'd written there were trails to others. Some meandering. Some hidden. But as I followed them from person to person, I couldn't help feeling that the loose and strained connections I discovered were all wrong. Wisefolk were meant to stand together.

I had to lower my head to enter the painted trailer, but once I was inside I found a cozy, wood-paneled room lined with jar-filled shelves, a tiny dining table big enough for two and a miniature kitchen. In the back, there was a bed made up neatly with a patchwork quilt and a dozen crocheted pillows. There was a small door beside the bed that seemed to lead to some sort of a bathroom.

Shoved between the bed and the door was a small handloom with a half-finished weaving created from amethyst, gold and avocado yarn. The skeins were dusty and the colors had faded. Unlike the rest of the contents of the trailer, which hummed with business and life, the loom looked neglected and forgotten. My embroidery never had the chance to get dusty. The tingles in my fingers would never allow it.

The scent of ginger was strong in the air. Gone beyond the strength used for cookies to the point that tears rose up in the corners of my eyes.

"Before we start the infusion, I'll open the roof vents," Deborah assured me as I wiped my eyes and sniffed. "But first you'll grind the seeds and press the oil. Sit." She indicated a spot at the table where a clean mortar and pestle sat as if waiting for me to arrive.

Deborah propped the door open behind me and untied a rolled screen, allowing it to fall over the opening to keep flies out. The trailer was sheltered by the canopy of an immense oak. It was surprisingly comfortable, especially when she reached up to crank a ceiling vent open and the mountain air began to circulate around us.

Next, Deborah reached up to a shelf above the kitchenette and brought down a mason jar of sunflower kernels. She only had to take one step to bring it to the table, unscrewing the lid so she could tilt the kernels into the stone mortar in front of me. I intuited what needed to be done, but she placed her calloused hands over mine to guide me in the movements necessary to grind the seeds into paste. Tamp, tamp, around. Tamp, tamp, around. The repetition was as appealing as the singing of the chimes above our heads.

"I like the chimes," I said. Tamp, tamp, around.

"I love the sound the wind makes when it's given things to play with." Deborah stirred yellowish powder on a speckled enamel baking pan with a wooden spoon, nodding as she did so.

"I thought maybe the chimes were like Mavis and her bees."

Tamp, tamp, around. A nutty, rich scent was rising up from the paste in the mortar as it almost turned to cream. Deborah reached for it and spooned the paste into a stoneware bowl. Then she dumped more seeds into the emptied mortar so I could begin again. Tamp, tamp, around.

I looked up when she didn't reply and I paused in my tamping. Deborah had gone pale. Against her hair and blue top, her face was stark white.

"Nothing is like the bees," she finally said, nudging my hands back to work with hers.

So, Granny Ross wasn't the only one afraid of the wildwood bees. Out of respect for Deborah's sheet-white cheeks, I focused on our task.

Once I'd ground all the seeds in the mason jar and the stoneware bowl was full of paste, Deborah sent me to the miniature sink to wash my hands. I used a bar of plain, unscented soap and scrubbed my knuckles and nails clean. I dried my hands on a white hand towel that looked even more plain because of its colorful surroundings.

"It isn't hard, but you'll have to use all your strength." Deborah spooned several teaspoons of water over the sunflower-seed paste in the bowl. "You'll use the sides of the bowl. You'll roll and press almost like you're kneading dough and the oil will extrude into the bottom of the bowl. Keep the ball of sunflower paste out of the extruded oil as you work. Around and around. Press. Around and around. Press. Like this." Deborah illustrated the motions once, then twice around. Oil trickled into the bottom of the bowl.

I stood beside Deborah and took the ball of sunflower paste from her hands.

This was for Mack. To ease his pain. I strained, using the weight of my body behind my stiffened arm to turn my palm into a press. Tiny droplets of sunflower oil were my reward. I tried again and again until I was finally able to achieve a strong trickle of oil like Deborah had.

"From the wildwood is always best—sunflowers, ginger. Fresh is better, but I harvested these seeds myself last year. There's still plenty of goodness in them. And I dug those gingerroots two days ago. There's a ridge above Granny's wildwood garden that's always good for gingerroot, but you can find it all over the mountain. I'll show you the leaves to watch for. I'll tell you how to find it, dig it, wash it, grind it, dry it. You have to use dried gingerroot for the liniment or else it will mold," Deborah said.

Her instructions had a rhythm too. As if she was repeating a verse or song. I found myself humming the words beneath her breath, the sound of Deborah's voice linked to the sound of the chimes outside.

Finally, when no more oil came from the paste that had gone almost dry in my hands, Deborah reached for the ball of paste. She placed it to the side in a butter crock she'd taken from a child-sized refrigerator.

"I eat the sunflower butter on fresh bread. It's delicious," she explained.

The stove top only had one burner. Its flame was dialed low. On it, Deborah placed an open teakettle she obviously used for making liniment. With a gesture, she encouraged me to pour the sunflower oil into the kettle.

"Now, the ground ginger," she said.

I tapped the yellow dust into the oil. Deborah stirred a couple of times, then handed me the long-handled wooden spoon. All this time, Eve had been sleeping, coiled around Deborah's arm. She roused as the ginger was stirred into the oil and transferred herself from Deborah's arm to mine.

"Madame, inspector general," Deborah teased.

But, like me, she appeared to find Eve's curiosity endearing.

From outside, a crow's call joined in with our laughter, and as I continued to stir Deborah pushed the hanging screen aside to meet a gleaming black bird on the stoop. The other woman held out her hand and the crow dropped a broken piece of glass into her palm, shimmering and purple in the sunlight.

"He might as well be a magpie," Deborah explained through the open door. "He's as taken with color as I am."

She placed the fetched glass in a bowl filled with similar pieces on the rail beside the door, then she petted the crow's head as he tilted it this way and that to take a better look at the stranger inside.

Purple. Gold. Green. The glass the crow had brought to Deborah matched the yarn on her neglected loom.

"It will need to steep on low heat for a couple of hours," Deborah said. "No, you stay outside," she instructed the crow, who had hopped toward the door on the rail. She came back to my side and retrieved a lid for the pot. "The sun has moved beyond its zenith, so the sunflowers are in the shade and the porch will be shaded soon. If you'd like to help, we can do the watering while we wait."

I nodded, enthusiastically, because the trailer was slightly claustrophobic and it would be nice to be outside helping the person who had so willingly helped me. Plus I felt the urge to give back something to sunflowers as well. Cycles. I'd encountered what could only be considered mysticism on this mountain, but the wisewomen's beliefs were also practical. The fragrant liniment warming on the stove wouldn't have happened without watering the sunflowers that had provided the oil from their seeds.

With the screen settled behind us, I followed Deborah out to the well pump I'd seen earlier.

"You can water in full sun despite what old-timers say. The leaves won't scorch. But a lot of the water will evaporate, and during a dry spell like this, I avoid the waste," Deborah explained.

While she arranged a bucket under the spigot, I took a firm grip on the hand pump and put my back into drawing the water we needed up from the ground. Once the first bucket was filled, Deborah tugged it aside, being careful not to slosh out any of its contents. Then she placed the other bucket and I filled it as well.

"We should take turns with the yoke," I suggested as she settled it on top of both buckets, one on each end, and hooked their handles in place.

"It's very heavy. I'm used to it, but I'll appreciate the help," she replied. She bent at the knees and leaned over to position the curved part of the yoke on the back of her neck, then tilted so that the weight immediately went to her shoulders. With her arms, she helped to balance and hold the yoke in place as she rose to stand.

Only a little of the water splashed out as she took up the yoke and, after, as she walked toward the sunflowers, none at all. I watched her carefully so I could mimic the way she moved when it was my turn.

Once we reached the sunflower bank, I helped steady the buckets as Deborah lowered them to the ground. Then, we each took one and moved from flower to flower until the buckets were empty.

We repeated the process to refill the buckets and this time Deborah helped me settle the yoke on my shoulders. Helping Mary at the orchard had made me a lot stronger over the last few years, but it was still a challenge for me to stand and move with the full weight of the yoke on my shoulders and back.

"I warned you," Deborah laughed. I grunted in reply.

The walk to the bank felt much longer with the water buckets sloshing on either side of me. I spilt more than Deborah had, but I still felt triumphant when I'd delivered the buckets more than half-full to their destination.

It took several more trips for both of us before the ground beneath the sunflowers was saturated. By that time, the rest of Deborah's plantings around the yard and on her large stoop were in shadow. We watered all of those as well.

While we worked, I noticed my companion giving a wide berth to the honeybees attracted to her flowering plants. Why would she seem to fear creatures that must be her constant companions? I didn't know if these were Mavis's bees. Would they fly this far into the woods from their apiary? Or were the bees that visited the sunflowers, the daisies, the honeysuckle and all else wild?

If so, they didn't seem to shy away from us in the same way Deborah shied away from them. When I'd watered the final pot on the side of the stoop I'd been given, I made my way back to the pump to set my bucket down. Sweat dripped into my eyes, so I used a one-handed method to manage a trickle of enough water to wash my face and to cup several drinks of water in the palm of my hand. A thirsty bee landed on my pinky finger to drink from the moisture left after I'd drunk my fill. I watched, unafraid and fascinated.

But when the bee flew away and my attention was released I noticed Deborah had stopped several feet away, staring, her face white and the empty bucket dropped at her feet.

"It's okay. I'm not allergic or anything," I assured her. In fact, my vivid dreams had created an affinity in me for the insects Harry and Siobhán had cared for and loved. "Do you have a honeybee allergy?" I asked, thinking that would explain her obvious fear.

"No. But my older sister was allergic. She almost died once as a child. Granny always warned me to stay away from them," Deborah replied. "Near as I can tell, they're the one thing on earth she's afraid of."

"I didn't know you had a sister. Does she still live on the mountain?" I asked.

"No. She left Morgan's Gap and didn't return," Deborah said. She had that faraway look again. Like she was looking through me all the way to foreign lands. No wonder Granny wasn't a happy woman. Estranged from both daughters and all but ostracized by a community that feared her.

Estranged or not, Granny had certainly managed to pass on her fear of bees to this daughter. So strange for a wisewoman who obviously loved gardening to fear honeybees.

"I've heard everyone around here dreams of the beekeeper," I mentioned.

Deborah bent to pick up her bucket and brought it over to the pump. This time I pumped water for her while she splashed her face and drank from her washed hands.

"I have, but I don't encourage them," she said, simply.

I released the hand pump and looked at the other woman in surprise.

"I didn't know there was a way to make them happen," I said. "I stopped dreaming and I don't know why."

Deborah put her arm around my waist to companionably urge me back to the house and away from a buzzy trio of bees that had found the puddle at the base of the hand pump. I walked along appreciating the afterglow of hard work in good company. Sect women missed out on so much when they were discouraged from open, friendly relationships.

"Some beekeeper dreams aren't pleasant. Maybe you don't want to dream anymore," Deborah said. "The wildwood connects us. And part of that connection ties us to everything that's happened in the past. But how much we're comfortable with connecting is always a part of what transpires."

"Siobhán Morgan was in trouble in my last dream. I'm afraid of what might have happened to her. Too afraid to look up the history of the town at the library. And I haven't asked anyone what might have happened to her and to her beekeeper," I said. *And to their unborn child.*

"Your fear is blocking the dreams, then."

"But what if I want to know more? And not from a book or a tale. I miss Siobhán," I confessed, to Deborah and to myself. "Truvy said Honeywick is a restless place and that we're meant to learn from that, from the past. I shouldn't turn away from the dreams if they're trying to tell me something I need to know."

To help Pearl. Or even to help the whole of Morgan's Gap.

The scent of the warming liniment filled the air as we approached the stoop. Deborah sniffed deeply and we looked at each other and smiled. It had been a good, productive day.

"Sit here on the steps. I'll bring you a fried apple pie and some iced tea," Deborah said. "Then we'll talk about what you need to do if you want to dream again."

# Twenty-Eight

*I carried a tote of* fried apple pies and a mason jar filled with golden liniment when I left Deborah's place. My head was full of the morning. Why hadn't Mary May mentioned Deborah Ross years ago? And what about Carol Long? Now that I'd met her mother I was even more certain that we should be friends, although it might not matter how much we had in common if Sheriff Long stood in the way.

"You sleep in a cottage built from the stone and earth of the mountain. But if your dreams have stopped and you want them to continue, you're going to have to turn to living earth and roots. That's where you'll dream again. Outside. Go to the trees," Deborah had said. "But be prepared. The dreams you'll have under the stars will be real. Like traveling in time. Take Eve with you. Don't go to sleep without her."

She'd whispered the advice close to my ear and then she'd changed the subject to pie.

It was Jo's motorcycle at the curb more than the promise of a Cherry Coke that made me stop at the diner on my way home after a quick trip to return library books. Or maybe it was the call of the air-conditioning they'd installed to keep their kitchen cool. Jeremiah Warren's need for a cooler kitchen was the town's gain this summer with the heat wave wilting fields and the folks who tended them.

Unlike the town around it, the diner was modern and sleek, all chrome and glass with a shiny silver tin roof. The rectangular building looked like it should be on wheels cruising down the street but instead had parked at an angle to the corner barbershop where the businesses on Main Street had previously ended abruptly because of a jutting mountain ridge. The diner, narrow and long, had cozied up to the ridge just right, its windows facing out with a panoramic view of the town, to become one of the few local gathering places that didn't have a steeple.

Everyone called it simply "the Diner."

I paused in front of a newly painted sign that featured a pink pig in a chef's hat exactly like the one I had embroidered on a handkerchief for Mr. Warren at Market Day. The obvious appreciation for my simple gift caused warmth to swell in my chest.

But then noise swelled from inside the diner and the warmth turned tight and itchy.

I was stalling; my nervousness about joining the crowd I could hear laughing and talking and escaping the heat together was threatening to hold me back.

I slipped inside and the bell above the diner's door jingled to announce my arrival, but I quickly ascertained it was too crowded for most people to notice me. The anonymity was comforting even as I liked the idea that many of them might have enjoyed the cheerful new sign. The air that immediately enveloped me was conditioned as much by savory scents as the whirring appliance in one of the end windows.

Jo, Mavis and Truvy were seated on chrome stools at the Formica lunch counter. Long after the bell quieted, Mavis turned toward me as if someone or something had whispered in her ear to alert her to my arrival. She waved me over and Truvy patted the red vinyl seat to indicate I should sit beside her. I would have taken a table to the side instead, but they were all packed with people. Carol hadn't been at the library. I saw why. She was seated with her husband and his deputy at one of the booths. I recognized several other townspeople, including a booth filled with Morgans. I was pretty sure Mary had told me they owned the diner. I looked away from them, quickly, not wanting to see any similarities to The Morgan from my dreams.

There wasn't anyone I recognized as Sect. I walked toward the wisewomen. Mavis absentmindedly fiddled with a honeybee earring on her right earlobe as if it tickled, but her smile was welcoming at my approach, easing the tightness in my chest. I couldn't regret stopping. Not when they all seemed happy to see me. Rekindled warmth burgeoned inside me. Friends. These women were my friends. I had every right to come into town. To have a cold drink with folks who were glad to see me. Mr. Warren nodded at me from his command post over an impressive array of short order items on a sizzling griddle. His smile and his wink toward the direction of the sign out front made me smile and nod in return.

"Looks like everyone in town had the same idea," Jo said.

Sure enough. The bell jangled again and again. My stool was out of the way at the end of the counter. The icy soda I ordered was fizzy and refreshing. Through the opening from the kitchen to the counter, Jeremiah's graceful manipulations of his long spatula made him seem like a conductor in front of an orchestra. He went from griddle to deep fryer to barbeque oven lightly and easily in spite of his size. The savory scent of perfectly roasted pork, fried potatoes and bubbling greens filled the air. And the sweet scent of peaches made my mouth water.

I enjoyed the happy hum, sipping soda occasionally in place of conversation. The diner wasn't only a pleasant reprieve because of cool air and good food. There was something about being among people with common needs and pleasures. We weren't only in the diner together. We were hungry and thirsty together. We were savoring and sipping together. We were surviving a drought and troubled times...together.

The warmth inside of me transformed to a kind of wonder. There was magic in Morgan's Gap—friendly snakes and vivid dreams and plucked strings that could see into your future and your soul. But wildwood magic was ephemeral and fleeting and the harmony I'd found in the diner was just as delicate. Before long I noticed murmurs and sideways glances toward the counter where the most unconventional women in town sat in comfort and ease—one of them Black, a same-sex couple, at least one who consorted with serpents and a Crone's Hollow witch.

These were stolen moments, huddled together in peace while the wider, warring world pressed oppressively against the glass. But there were some customers in the diner who carried more war than peace with them wherever they went.

My last sip of soda had gone to water in the melting ice at the bottom of my glass. Not nearly as refreshing. The constantly opened and closed door had let in too much heat or my counter seat was too close to the kitchen. Beads of sweat had popped out on my forehead and when I shifted on the stool my clammy skin stuck to my shirt and skirt.

My chest had gone unaccountably tight again. The crowd took all the oxygen in the room for talk that went from pleasant to loud and jarring between one second and the next. There was a hissing sibilance of *sh...sh...sh.* Many conversations were featuring "she" in accusatory tones. About Mavis or Jo? About Truvy Rey? Or me?

Jo's laughter suddenly stood out as all the other conversation in the room died.

The beads of salty perspiration on my forehead dried instantly on my skin in a gust of outside air.

I knew before I turned what I would see. My lips went numb. My stomach clenched. Beside me, Truvy went tense and her knuckles turned white on the fork she was using to sample the piece of rhubarb pie we'd ordered together

"Is this a diner or the devil's own den?" Reverend Gray said in what I considered his Calm Before the Storm voice. Bile rose up and burned in the back of my throat. Many, many times that voice had been followed by pain. My fists clenched and my chin went up. The opposite of how I would have reacted not so long ago.

Sheriff Long jumped up from his seat and shoved his deputy to his feet as well, indicating that he should walk around and get in the booth beside Carol.

"Welcome, Reverend. Won't you come have a seat with me?" He motioned toward the seat he'd forced his deputy to vacate. His ousted deputy was looking at Carol for permission to sit before he scooted in beside her.

"I won't join you until those that don't belong here leave," Reverend Gray proclaimed.

Jeremiah Warren closed his giant barbeque oven. He twisted its wrought-iron handle with a screech and a clang. Then he turned to face the dining room. His smile was gone. There was thunder on his face. His hold on his spatula turned his knuckles pale.

"Do you mean us? Or Mr. Warren? What will we all eat if Jeremiah leaves?" Jo asked with a deceptively good-natured tone. The fury in every polite syllable felt tight like the dried sweat on my skin. Mavis hooked her arm with Jo's. They faced him together as a couple. *Here be witches*. I was proud to be their friend.

We were Truvy's friends too. We didn't care about what people like Ezekiel Gray thought friendship should and shouldn't be. An entire diner full of neighbors eating the delicious food Jeremiah Warren had prepared could all be friends in spite of our differences. No matter our sex or skin color or religion. We'd been talking about football, school, church and pies. We'd been laughing, enjoying the air-conditioning, the soda and Mr. Warren's graceful symphony. There had been peace. Tenuous harmony could become more stable over time. Stronger as we embraced it together. But now, because of Ezekiel, forks were going down. People grumbled and looked to the sheriff. A couple of men had risen from their seats and gravitated toward Ezekiel. One woman rose and pulled a small boy out of the diner, and the jaunty jangle of the bell over the door sounded far less welcoming than it had before.

All the Morgans left, save for a single middle-aged woman who sipped a mug of coffee as if she hadn't noticed a thing untoward going on.

The threat of dissonance that had been pressing against the glass was on the inside now. Closed within a small, crowded space. I could almost see it finding its way to this person and that, puckering brows, hardening jaws. The diner was suddenly a powder keg. Its potential for explosion exponentially increased.

I thought of Ezekiel's match and how fascinated he was with flame.

"Reckon I'll stay. Haven't finished my pie," Truvy said. She smiled grimly.

I wondered if her guitar strings had warned her about this moment. Or if they had played her here to this particular stool at this particular time. So she could stay. So she could eat pie while Ezekiel fomented hatred.

"I've warned you all about the degenerate behavior that's been allowed to go unchecked in Morgan's Gap. Will you or won't you do anything about it?" Gray intoned.

He hadn't seen me yet. My fingers had startled tingling. The hair on my scalp had risen to attention. I thought I sensed—something—I could reach out to if I needed to. Truvy's empathy. Jo's energy. Granny's intention. All there within my reach as if all their gifts somehow converged in me.

In my mind's eye, I saw myself sewing threads together from each of the women to create a kaleidoscope of tricolored rose. I felt the flower blooming in my chest where my heart should be.

I stood. My motion drew Ezekiel's attention and his face blanched. His eyes went wide. They were bloodshot as if he hadn't been sleeping.

"Witches," he uttered hoarsely.

*Ezekiel Gray's Prayer Book* was in his hands. Worn from use. As a trusted tome and a battering ram. I was certain I could see bloodstains on its faded leather cover, some of it mine.

"Sit and have some barbeque or leave, Ezekiel. The rest of us are fine with or without your blessing."

"Now, listen," Sheriff Long began.

Before he could intervene, Carol slid out of the booth. The deputy had been hovering indecisively. He stepped back with deference to allow Carol to stand. She looked up at him, gratefully, then shot one look at her husband. Two bright spots of red developed on the sheriff's cheeks and his lips pursed into a thin white line.

Had her look dared him to try to stop the granddaughter of Granny Ross from doing whatever the hell she wanted to do?

Carol walked past Ezekiel. The look she directed at him was one of disgust. One everyone in the room could easily interpret as a respected member of the community dismissing the ravening fanatic in their midst.

A look that said a Ross woman didn't suffer fools.

The entire room seemed to draw in a collective gasp. A drip of fat from the roasting pork in the oven sizzled loudly. No one said a word as Carol approached the empty stool beside Truvy. Then she sat down beside her grandmother's best friend.

I placed my hand on Carol's shoulder, tingling fingers and all, and her spine straightened as if she felt a jolt of electricity from my fingers. But before any of us could speak, the bell above the door rang again and a little girl ran inside.

It was Ruby. And she was wearing the dress I'd embroidered with honeysuckle vines. She looked around until she saw us at the counter, then she ran forward, paying no mind to Reverend Gray or the murmuring that rose up in the rest of the diner. Surrounded by sibilant whispers, Ruby made a beeline for us. Truvy turned, caught the leaping girl and lifted her onto the counter itself.

She sat and arranged her ruffle, then looked over at me, swinging her legs to and fro.

Like a princess on a throne, and my stitchery had never been worn so well.

"What are you doin' here?" Truvy asked. "Where's Primmie?"

"She said for me to come on. She was movin' too slow and I had to get here right quick."

I wondered if a bee had told her to come. Or Eve. Or a whip-poor-will. Or the wind in the leaves. However she'd been sent, the wildwood had been right. Forks were picked back up. Here. There. Someone coughed. Another person called the waitress over for another cola. The sheriff had sat down across from his deputy, although he didn't look a bit happy about it. Mr. Warren opened his oven back up and the familiar clang only made a few people start. Truvy slowly and methodically used the edge of her fork to cut away another bite of rhubarb pie.

It wasn't a conscious decision to release whatever I'd gathered in from my friends. It was more like I'd taken a deep breath and exhalation was inevitable. From the imagined rose in my chest an almost perceptible pulse seemed to expand the dining room. It was no longer close and crowded. The air was cool and conditioned again. Freshened by a wildwood breeze only a few actually saw and felt. Loose hair fluttered softly around my face, then settled back into normal waves at my neck.

The bell above the closed door tinkled lightly, as if fairies tapped its brass with their toes.

Explosion averted.

Ezekiel was a master orator and he knew when the opportunity was past. Whether it was Carol defecting from her place with the sheriff to sit with us or whether it was Ruby and her innocent leap to reinforce Truvy Rey, the crowd of longtime neighbors chose to continue eating or leave.

Too many left.

I was sad to see them go. Not because we would miss their company, but because it was evidence of an ugliness hidden in their hearts. A stain on the community itself. Morgan's Gap might appear idyllic as a whole, but it was only truly peaceful in places and parts. I remembered the folks at Market Day who had avoided Jeremiah's booth and the ones who had whispered about Crone's Hollow. I remembered the football player who wasn't free to sew and the jokes about Mack.

Community was like wildwood magic, a precious gossamer thing, light and fleeting, which could easily slip from your grasp.

The two men who had risen to stand with Reverend Gray walked out with him, one spitting to the side of the front door in a way that barely missed the linoleum of the diner's floor. The sheriff left shortly after, but I noticed that his deputy stayed, glancing in Carol's direction more than once.

She was shivering beneath my hand when I removed it to give her some privacy. What would she face when she went home at the end of the day? Sheriff Long had been angry and embarrassed. If he was anything like Ezekiel, he wouldn't react well.

"Knew it needed to be honeysuckle vine," Truvy said, fingering the embroidery on Ruby's skirt.

"Best kind of ward there is," Mavis added. "Except against bees."

I could have sworn the glass honeybee earrings in her ears shimmered on lobes that barely peeked from her red hair. The slightest of movements, as if the earrings could crawl around her ears if they wanted to.

The atmosphere was subdued. Everyone who had remained had taken note of all their friends and neighbors who had left in Gray's wake. It had been a close call. The ugly scene Ezekiel had caused could have turned uglier. As it was, the tension in the town had been revealed. The soda, pie, barbeque and air-conditioning had brought us together, but a man who could capitalize on our differences—in race, creed and nature—could so easily tear us apart.

Exhaustion slumped my shoulders. Whatever I had tapped into and released might have defused tension and cleared the potential for violence in the room, but it had left me drained. And there was a throbbing ache lingering in my fingertips that said honeysuckle would not be enough to ward against what was coming.

Ezekiel burned. And it was only a matter of time before his fuse ignited others. We'd only postponed the explosion to another day.

# Twenty-Nine

*I wrote down exactly what* Deborah had told me about pie crust when I made it back to Honeywick. Then I added Mary May's apple filling instructions from the worn recipe card I'd managed to add sooty fingerprints to last time I'd returned it to the box.

The new recipe was untried and pristine. Yet, I could already taste it. There were several bushels of apples left in the shed. The rest had been carried away by the harvesters for their own family's recipes. I wished I had saved some of the First Tree's apples for my pie. Especially for the one I would enter in the fair.

I bathed while the sun was setting, baking in my mind. I didn't wash my hair. I didn't have time to dry it before dark and I couldn't sleep in the orchard with wet hair. Back in Richmond, I'd had a portable hair dryer with a plastic cap and hose. Here, Mary May and I had brushed each other's hair by the fire on washing days. It had been slow but peaceful and I hadn't missed the portable dryer until today. There was usually a breeze on the mountain even during this heat wave. It might get cool before dawn.

What had almost happened at the diner had solidified my determination to learn from Siobhán and her orchard. Community was precious. In a way, Morgan's Gap was a kind of wildwood magic. I could feel its potential sparking around me, but I could also feel the possibility of it slipping through my fingers. Our fingers. If we didn't grab it tight and hold on fast.

But first, I needed to follow the fairy lights into the forest at midnight.

I'd spoken to Mack that morning when he'd left at the crack of dawn so no one would see him driving away from Honeywick. Since the moon landing, we'd shared several nights together. As I rolled two quilts around the feather pillow from my bed, my cheeks warmed with heated memories from the night before, but I tried to focus on the task at hand. I would use one quilt to protect me from the damp of the orchard moss and the other for warmth if I needed it. The pillow would be softer than the First Tree's exposed roots, gnarled at the base of its aged trunk.

I dressed in dungaree coveralls and a long-sleeve flannel shirt. Loose, comfortable and yet still protective. I would be walking to the orchard in the gloaming. There might be briars or branches I didn't see. I placed the applewood needle box in my pocket. It had always been a lucky talisman. Tonight, it was a necessity.

The jar of liniment sat waiting on the kitchen table. I would give it to him soon. But when the phone rang as I was headed out the door for the night, I didn't pick it up. It was Mack. I was sure. He wouldn't assume he was welcome for another evening without an invitation. Not only that, he'd want to check on me. Hear my voice. I wanted to hear his too, but this felt like something I'd put off for too long already.

The blackened stone.

The scratched hearth.

Deborah's fear of honeybees.

Crone's Hollow.

The sculpture Jo had given me stood in front of the cottage. Most of the grass had died, but I wasn't surprised to see new shoots springing up around the doe and the little fawn. Even in the dying light, the flutter from their aluminum hearts flashed continuously. I placed my hands on the metal, which was still warm from the sun. Maybe it was only the heat of the day lingering, but my whole body warmed as I stood there. Energy. I didn't reject the idea. I welcomed it. I was certain tonight would take everything I had and some of Jo's energy to supplement my own was a blessing.

I saw the whole hot summer stretching out behind me—Market Days and embroidery for neighbors, new friendships and lessons learned, courage and connection, meditative spirals and baking, kisses and the touch of calloused hands. All of it had been preparation for the fair on Pearl's birthday. The event loomed large and portentous with every tickle of wildwood breeze like a countdown on my face. I had come out of hiding. I was stronger. But there was more I needed to do.

Only when the metal began to cool beneath my touch did I release the sculpture and move away. The flutter had stopped. It was time I found out what had happened the day The Morgan discovered the woman he'd thought he had completely under his control had been living a secret life with her beekeeper in the wildwood.

*Mack*

Rachel didn't answer her phone. Not in the morning when it had only been an hour since they'd been together. Not at lunchtime or at the end of the day. Mack had only allowed himself three calls because he didn't want to harass a woman who had already been through enough. But when Rachel didn't answer her phone after dark, his desire to talk with her became real concern.

He'd only run into Ezekiel Gray a couple of times, but both

encounters had been more than enough to show that the man was still
a threat. What would prevent him from going to the orchard after one
too many evenings of frenzied adulation had gone to his head?

Maybe he wouldn't assume Rachel was alone. Folks talked. Word
got around. A whole bus full of teenagers had seen him and Rachel
together and he didn't fool himself for a minute that he'd been able
to keep his eyes off her. Since then, they'd been discreet, but anyone
could have seen his truck driving back into town in the early morning hours. Gray was the kind of man who needed false courage from
a crowd or from the certainty that he was stronger than the person
he tormented. Two to one wouldn't appeal to him, especially if he was
intimidated by the size and strength of one of those two.

Mack climbed into his truck and fired up the engine. The saw-whet
owl swung wildly on the rearview mirror as he whipped the wheel
and spun gravel out of the farmhouse's drive. Gray wasn't the type who
would see or be intimidated by the kind of strength Rachel had—deep
and abiding. The kind of power only found in survivors. Mack was
more than happy to lend his bulk to be sure Gray got the message:

He wasn't welcome.

Mack hadn't run into the preacher since that day he'd discovered
Rachel at the orchard. But he'd seen his influence all around town. There
were more fights between neighbors. More fallings-out between friends.
People who had grown up together and cohabitated for years were turning on each other. Suddenly, there was acceptable music and appropriate dress. There was Our Kind and Not Our Kind. Men in power had
become puffed up on it and those who weren't in power were on edge.

Ezekiel Gray didn't cause men to go bad. He simply watered the
seeds of badness that were already there—jealousy, ignorance, intolerance, hate.

When Mack arrived at the end of the orchard road, he was almost relieved to see Gray's black Continental pulled to the side of the lane. The headlights of his truck illuminated the man hunched behind the wheel—his long hair, his wide-brimmed black hat, his even wider eyes as he was blinded by the beams. The luxury car he'd no doubt purchased with money from collection plates was looking neglected. Dust coated the windows. The white walls on the tires were dingy. The black paint gone dull. Mack didn't pull to the side. He drove ahead, blocking the way and showing the preacher that some folks didn't have to lurk.

He stopped some distance from the house, not wanting to disturb Rachel's sleep. The cottage was dark. Her Rambler was parked in the drive. The goats and chickens all snug and buttoned up for the night.

She hadn't answered her phone because she didn't want to talk. That was her decision. He would abide by it. But he did reach for the saw-whet owl and take him down. Without fuss, he left the truck long enough to place the carving on a nearby fence post.

"Keep an eye on the place for me?"

It didn't feel crazy to talk to the little carving. And it felt right to leave him there to guard the driveway. Rachel had said she loved the owl. He wasn't a trespasser. Mack, on the other hand, was pushing the boundaries of what felt okay. Offering support and staring at a woman's house at midnight were two different things.

He turned the truck around and headed back out to the main road. Gray was gone. He took the long way around to get back home to avoid the revival tent. It was a long, lonely trip without even the sway of the owl carving on his rearview mirror for company, but he endured it. He had endured more difficult journeys. At least he was free to roll down his window and breathe in the same wildwood air that might be freshening Rachel's fears away in the exact same way only miles away.

And if Gray thought he was at Rachel's place, maybe he would leave her in peace.

# Thirty

Siobhán
Morgan's Gap, 1883

After the ground shook, *the rumbling continued for a solid minute. The Morgan had been stepping toward her with his fists clenched, but he stopped with one foot in front of the other. Somewhere else in the house a woman screamed and another started to cry. Men began to shout and doors slammed.*

*Siobhán pressed both hands over her abdomen, instinctively sheltering the babe from the chaos, but the move was a telling mistake. The Morgan saw her and the protective pose caused him to clench his teeth. A primitive growl came from deep in his gut.*

*He grimaced. "I will take that child. He will be mine. And once he's born I'll kill you. Not with laudanum. Nothing so easy and quick. You will suffer, woman. You will beg to die."*

*There was a banging from downstairs at the front door. Someone must have opened it. Seconds later, one of The Morgan's men shouted up the stairs. "There's been a collapse!"*

*She imagined being crushed deep in the mountain under dirt and rock.*

*Claustrophobic horror briefly distracted Siobhán from The Morgan's movements. She rushed forward when she understood what he was about.*

*"No time for you now." He shut the heavy door in her face. The sound of the key in the lock made nausea rise in her throat. She was a prisoner. He would keep her here until the baby was born and then he would kill her. There was no telling what he would do to Harry. The mine disaster wouldn't distract a man like The Morgan for long.*

*Siobhán tried the doorknob, knowing it was no use. It rattled but the door didn't budge. She crouched down to try to peer through the keyhole, but it was blocked. The Morgan had left the key! If one of the friendlier maids passed, they might take pity on her. Siobhán called out for help. No one replied. After the initial chaos, the house was silent. Everyone had gone. Whether they could help or not, they would go to the mine—to cry, to pray, to mourn.*

*Siobhán paced. If Harry went to the mine, he would die too. No matter the tragedy, The Morgan wouldn't be too distracted to kill him. She had been too lost in the perfect union of their love to be cautious. It would have been bad enough for her to frequently visit the Ross women. They were seen as wayward, too witchy and strange for normal converse. Only the most desperate souls braved the thorn-lined trail to their cabin in the wildwood for medicinal tea and tisanes, for herbal sachets said to ward and influence.*

*But what had Siobhán been but desperate?*

*She'd gone to the wildwood as often as she could. And too many people had seen her frequent detours in the direction of the apiary and the beekeeper's cottage.*

*Another strange one, fay and flighty, more comfortable with bee than man, and prone to sing his (or the bees') stinging observances whenever he did come to town. How did he always know more than he should about everyone's business? And didn't the honey he sold bring with it indecent dreams and occasionally a wild euphoria like drunkenness?*

She needed to warn Harry.

Siobhán dropped down to her knees in front of the locked door and felt along the bottom edge to gauge the gap. Her heart fell when there was none. She had thought to dislodge the key onto the floor and fish it into the room through the crack under the door.

She stood and paced some more. After a couple of circuits around the room, she opened the casement window. The ground was two stories below without so much as a trellis to climb or bushes to break her fall. The whole settlement had gone silent. The streets were deserted.

On the window seat, the chest her father had carved sat in a place of honor. She used much of the dirt to plant the orchard, but she opened it and felt what was left—the dust of home. So far away. She'd written her parents, but the letters had never been answered. She couldn't know if they were still alive. Her grandmother's ring had been transferred into the hem of her new petticoats. That and several pieces of silver. She kept them with her, always, as comfort and reassurance.

If she somehow escaped the locked room and The Morgan's clutches, she would convince Harry to run away. Even if it meant they had to leave the orchard and the apiary. She could take some seeds. And perhaps he could take a queen.

As she desperately planned, Siobhán traced the carvings on the chest. Each swallow from beak to tail. Each feather on each outstretched wing. She would take the small trunk too. It would hold the queen and the seeds.

A sudden flutter of real wings startled her. As if it had come to life beneath her fingers, a barn swallow had landed on the windowsill. Its sapphire back and ruby throat were vivid against the white plaster.

"Fly away. The sky is a better place to be," Siobhán urged, waving her hands to shoo the bird from the sill. The swallow leapt into space and swooped out of sight around the house as if it understood her words.

She would climb down. It was her only choice. She was strong. She'd worked hard every day of her short life. Her arms were muscled. Her back sturdy. She was more than The Morgan's wife. In fact, she had never been his. She was Siobhán. The Orchard Maker. The Beekeeper's Mate. Her parents might be long dead, but she was the Wildwood's Daughter and mother to the heir of her grandmother's ring.

She spoke to give herself courage. Calling the First Tree by name before she reached to pull herself up on the ledge. But before she could climb out the window another swallow dived to land beside her. Then another. And a whole flock of swallows formed a small murmuration around the open casement's glass.

One seemed troubled. It couldn't quite keep up with its brethren. Siobhán could see the reason why. A scarlet tassel dangled from its beak.

A key.

The key.

The weighted-down bird flew into the room, but it couldn't execute a graceful landing like the others had. It fell on the bed instead, dropping the key and staggering away shaking its little head.

"It can't be."

Siobhán picked up the key as the swallow smoothed its ruffled feathers in the middle of the bed. She rushed over to the locked door and bent to eye the keyhole once more. This time she found she could look down the long hall at the top of the stairs.

With shaking hands, she scrapped the key into the lock. As she turned it, the impossibly light, fidgety weight of a bird landed on her neck near her check.

"Thank you," Siobhán whispered. "Thank you, Eigríoch."

Once the door was open, she retrieved the chest her father had carved. She was already wearing the petticoat with the ring and the silver pieces in its hem. She closed the door behind her and locked it again, leaving the key in the keyhole as The Morgan had. If he thought she was still locked inside when he returned, it would give her more time to warn Harry.

*And escape.*

*She barely allowed that thought. It was merely a whisper in the rush of blood that flowed with every beat of her heart.*

*Escape . . . escape . . . escape.*

*Or maybe it was a prayer she was too afraid to voice because she already knew that she and Harry were as trapped by The Morgan's power as those poor men were trapped by the entire weight of the mountain.*

A night breeze blew through the apple trees. A small saw-whet owl landed in the tippy top of the First Tree and cried out *heep, heep, heep.* But the sleeping woman on the ground didn't wake. She'd rolled off her quilt. Her cheek was cushioned by moss. Her lips murmured words in an accent that wasn't her own. Another woman speaking, planning, desperately escaping. An emerald ribbon loosened from around the sleeping woman's arm and slithered to her other cheek to flick it with a tongue that could taste when there was danger in the air. It was a worried movement.

The sleeping woman dreamed on.

# Thirty-One

Siobhán
Morgan's Gap, 1883

*S*iobhán hurried up an *eerily quiet Main Street, the shimmer of newly installed glass in the General Store, overlapping wagon ruts and a cart full of the shovel boy's horse dung giving testament to the fact that Morgan's Gap had become more than a settlement.*

*Over the last months, she'd managed to purchase without notice a sturdy pair of boots, a plain woolen dress with a skirt that fell above her ankles for uninhibited walking and a broad men's hat. She wore them all now for the first time.*

*The weight of hidden silver bumped reassuringly against her lower legs and the hammered copper of her grandmother's ring flashed on her hand. She'd left the band that had bound her to The Morgan in the middle of the bed he'd forced her to share.*

*After the earlier earthquake the silence around her was absolute. No people was good. She wanted to flee into the wildwood without anyone marking her passing. But the lack of birdsong and insect whir was frightening. No dogs barked. No squirrels chattered or whistled in distress as she walked by.*

*She tried not to think of the miners who might be trapped in darkness deep in the bowels of the mountain. Had they been crushed? Or were they desperately waiting to be freed, a hundred men digging from inside and out as those within slowly ran out of air?*

*Her heart grieved, but there was nothing she could do for them.*

*Siobhán hooked the chest under one arm as her walk turned into a steep hike toward the orchard's high meadow and the stone cottage's hollow. She was fit from months of long walks into the wildwood to meet her love, but her desperate hurry had left her unusually winded. Her heavy breathing was the only sound in her ears for so long she doubted when she finally heard another noise.*

*Siobhán stopped and strained to identify the sonorous drone in the distance.*

*It was the bees.*

*Their humming was pitched high and frenzied. The vibrations of their distress hummed along the hair that had risen on her arms even though she was still far away from the hives. All of them, every last honeybee, had to be a part of the furor. It was hard to breathe, hard to think, hard to keep moving forward. Yet, she did.*

*Winded or not, Siobhán ran. Only the greatest reverence for her father kept her from dropping the swallow chest. She carried its precious burden to the cottage's stoop before she continued on to the apiary unweighted and flying with the bee's angry hum caught in her chest.*

*When the hives were in sight she finally heard Harry's singing. In spite of the swarms of bees murmurating in the sky above his upturned face or maybe because of them, he sang the lullaby he always used to calm them.*

*Siobhán stumbled to a halt and leaned to rest her palms on her knees as she tried to catch her breath. Harry was here. He hadn't gone to the mine. But before she could enjoy relief, Harry saw her and his singing stopped.*

*"Do not come closer. More than the quake has upset them. I cannot get them to settle."*

*His usually calm and confident voice quivered. That's when Siobhán understood. The hum in her chest was a warning. Not only the hair on her arms but her entire body from skin to blood to bone knew something was wrong. She'd felt the pull to the place where she was meant to plant the apple seeds. This was the opposite. She was being repelled.*

*Siobhán stepped back. Once. Twice. But it was too late. Whatever had upset them—the earth shaking or her intention to beg their keeper to leave the mountain—the swarms had detected an intruder. Her.*

*"No!" Harry bellowed, but they were no longer his. They were fully free and wild and furious.*

*The swarms massed into one undulating black cloud and a thousand honeybees flew against Siobhán.*

*She didn't have time to cover her face. There was no chance to run. They were on her in seconds and all she could do was fight the scream that would allow them to crawl inside and attack her very core.*

*But there was no pain. Not a single stinger pierced her skin. Although insects crawled over her from head to foot, not a single one harmed her.*

*"It's all right, my love. It isn't you that's upset them," Harry said from nearby. She stood, frozen, eyes closed, somehow able to draw breath as the bees that blanketed her allowed space around her nose and mouth. "I'm going to scoop them away."*

*She felt gentle swiping movements as Harry encouraged the bees to leave her. But as hundreds took back to the air the remaining honeybees moved to center their swarm around the slight swell of her stomach.*

*"It's the baby," Harry said. "She... she calmed them."*

*"He knows, Harry. We must take her and run. Far and fast. Or he'll kill you and take her for his own."*

*The last of the bees burst away from her skin as she spoke, their fury rekindled. Not because she would dare to take their keeper, but because their keeper was in danger.*

*"Leave the apiary? Leave the wildwood and the mountain?" Harry whispered. His face had gone gray. His freckles stood out starkly on his skin.*

*"And the orchard." The words caused bile to rise in the back of her throat. "We must. For her." She reached for Harry's hands and pressed his palms beneath hers where the bees had clustered.*

*"Honeywick is her home. I built it for her and for you," Harry said, his voice gruff with emotion.*

*"Honeywick," Siobhán breathed. The babe had been conceived the day the tower had been completed. She and Harry had moved the bed to the top of the stairs, where it felt they slept in the sky and made love beneath a quilt of stars.*

*"I've seen her in my dreams. I've carved her name in the last laid hearthstone. How can we leave when I've seen her here, living and loving and thriving among your apple trees?"*

*"He will kill you, Harry. He'll imprison me and the baby. He'll hurt us to punish me for loving you. He'll claim her and hate her at the same time. Deep down he's always known the fault lies with him. That he cannot father a child."*

*Harry raised his hands from her abdomen to her face. He cupped her cheeks between his honey-scented palms and leaned to kiss her. Once, twice, three times. His eyes sparkled with unshed tears instead of his usual humor.*

*"Then flee we must."*

The air was still, but Eigríoch's leaves moved as if there was a great wind. Gnarled limbs trembled and shook and the weight of the lush canopy they supported threatened to break the ancient branches tossed by some internal maelstrom.

The saw-whet owl flew up and circled the top of the First Tree whenever his perch was disturbed, but again and again he settled back to *heep, heep, heep* over the sleeping woman beneath the tree. She was restless like the old apple tree, tossed by some storm only she could see. The infinitesimal rattle of needles in her pocket was lost in the rustling of leaves.

She didn't wake.

The rough green snake—sometimes a carved wooden spoon, sometimes a bit of emerald thread—had given up on scenting the woman's aura. There was a blending. Someone who had stirred a century ago was also here now. Too here. Once faded and almost forgotten, the other's emotions were what caused Eigríoch to thrash. She had loved. She had lost. She had sacrificed everything for her child. And the sleeping woman was caught. Because she had also loved and lost and sacrificed. Two souls connected by place and circumstance and by the orchard itself.

The snake, who was more than a snake, slithered up to coil over the sleeping woman's lips and nose. She would wake if she couldn't breathe. She would come back to her own time and leave the troubled past behind.

She was needed here.

But the visions the wildwood fueled were much harder for the wildwood to end when the dreamer was determined to pursue the answers she sought regardless of what she might find. Too deep. Too far gone. Too much to come.

The saw-whet owl finally exploded high into the air, higher than before. He didn't circle this time. He flew. Eigríoch sent him away.

*Siobhán*
*Morgan's Gap, 1883*

*There was no time to pack. They only retrieved the swallow chest and a pouch of coins Harry had hidden high in a corner of a ceiling beam.*

*"Wait for me here. I have to tell the bees. Maybe the queen will come. Maybe she won't. But I have to try," Harry said.*

*While she waited Siobhán visited the hearthstone. She crouched down and ran her fingers along the letters Harry had carved there. He had dreamed of their daughter. He had carved her name along with the name of the cottage in the last laid stone.*

*But it wasn't the step she waited for that interrupted her reverie and dreams weren't carved in stone.*

*"Knew I'd find you here. Good a place as any for you to hear him scream." The Morgan laughed as he slammed the heavy oaken door.*

*Siobhán leapt up and ran, but she wasn't fast enough. She heard the scrape of the large mortar stone. Harry had built the cottage beside the massive boulder rather than try to move it alone. He used it for sharpening and grinding. The Morgan hadn't come alone. It would take several men at least to move the rock. Once it was wedged against the leading edge of the door she had no hope of making it budge.*

*Still, she tried.*

*As she pushed with all her might, she called a warning to the beekeeper.*

*Cries of "witch" and "adulteress" were shouted back and Siobhán fell away from the door. Slowly, filled with a new dread, she made her way over to the lone window and nudged the heavy shutters apart. Harry had been so proud of the fixed glass. Now through its thick, wavy extravagance Siobhán stared as dozens of people walked by.*

*The Morgan hadn't brought a few men. He'd brought half the town. No one should have been spared from the efforts to rescue the miners, but her husband wasn't driven by reason any longer . . . or he never had been, and there was no one in his settlement who would refuse a call to lash out at strange denizens of the wildwood who may have caused the wrath of God to fall on them.*

*A shopkeeper saw her peeking from the window and bellowed an accusation that chilled her to the bone.*

*"You done it. You and 'im and them Ross women with yer unnatural ways. Yer witchery shook the earth and buried the mine," the shopkeeper yelled.*

*Stones and mud clods and sticks plinked angrily off the precious glass as some took the opportunity to throw things at her as they passed. Thankfully, it was thick and paned with sturdy oak beams.*

*Her assurances that they hadn't had anything to do with the cave-in only riled the townsfolk more, but she continued to try, pleading for reason and compassion from people who saw The Morgan as infallible. They were simple, hardworking, backwoods people and he was their king. The gold in his pockets was as good as a crown. Whatever he proclaimed was truth. She had no hope of convincing them otherwise.*

*Some of the men carried clubs in their hands.*

*Siobhán searched the room for something she could use to break the glass. There was no axe. Only two wooden chairs, made from woven birch branches sturdy enough for sitting but too flimsy for creating her own club. She tried to use the swallow chest as a battering ram. Several panes of glass cracked, but the oaken slats wouldn't give way no matter how she tried. The chest began to splinter and her fingers were shredded on the shattered wood her father had so lovingly carved. No sparrows could help her now.*

*A sudden blast of wind blew through the laggers in the crowd, interrupting Siobhán's desperate effort. Hats flew off heads and skirts tangled around women's legs. Not a storm. There wasn't a cloud in the sky. She could hear their startled exclamations through the cracks in the glass. She dropped the chest, now smeared with her blood. It fell to the floor at her feet with a hollow thud. The force behind the wind vibrated on her skin and hummed in her ears and chest.*

*She felt no surprise.*

*The bees would not allow Harry to be attacked.*

*She'd seen their black clouds earlier. How many more honeybees would swarm to protect their apiary and their keeper?*

*Then she heard the screams.*

*Not Harry.*

*The Morgan had threatened to make him scream, but she would have felt his terror and pain if that had been the case. Instead, she felt the wild-wood's fury. The bees had known what was coming and Harry was no lon-ger soothing them with lullabies. The Morgan held no part of their beloved keeper inside him. He was an intruder, a destroyer. Someone who threat-ened their queens, their hives, their home.*

*Every bee from flower, from hollow tree, from creek and crevice, from skep, even from deep within the wildwood where man had never trod—all came. She felt them. Through Harry's child in her womb she felt them. Ris-ing, massing, swarming.*

*Stinging.*

*More screams joined the first, on and on until they were suddenly, hor-ribly muffled and choked off.*

*The Morgan hadn't closed his mouth or covered his eyes. He wasn't a wise man. He would have thrashed and fought against whatever tried to stand in his way until he was smothered and stung to death.*

*Silence fell. The hum was still there, but it had diminished. Honeybees died when they stung. Poor Harry's beloved bees. Thank you, thank you, thank you, her heart sang between beats.*

*The bees were a part of Harry. They had died for him. No doubt taking a part of him with them, but he lived! Witchery? The Wise Way was more than that. The settlers-turned-townspeople, so removed from the wildwood, would never understand.*

*The silence was broken again. Her heartbeat stuttered.*

*Shouting and a woman's scream—high and long and filled with fear.*

*The crowd had reached the apiary.*

*Had they found The Morgan, dead, covered by hundreds of writhing bees? Her answer came in the sound of running, screeching and the sud-den appearance of townspeople—some fleeing for their lives, flailing against the bees that chased and landed like arrows embedded in exposed scalps and necks and faces.*

Siobhán watched more and more people fall. There were still so many bees left and so many willing to die to defend their queens. She was distracted by the terrible tableau. It took her long moments to understand the flicker of fire as some of the men lit the torches they'd carried all the way from the mines. She'd thought they were clubs. She'd feared they intended to beat Harry.

She hadn't known to fear the flames.

# Thirty-Two

The roof caught as *soon as the first torch was tossed. There had been no recent rains and the thatch was dry. Siobhán ran for the tower stairs. A leap from that height would be deadly, but still better than burning alive. Black smoke roiled from the stairwell, driving her back into the front room. Another torch must have landed on the tower roof, taking that desperate option from her. The stone wouldn't burn, but everything inside would, including the rafters that supported the roof. If she wasn't crushed and burned by the ceiling's collapse she would die choking for breath.*

*Siobhán dropped to her knees to crawl beneath the smoke. But she had nowhere to go. She was trapped with no way to break the window or open the door.*

*Burning thatch was already starting to fall from above her head. She avoided the embers and sparks and the clumps of burning debris. She crawled to the door, hoping to find fresh air where the door met the floor. She was rewarded by a sweet breeze and she pressed her face to it. The conflagration at her back was almost unbearable. Soon, very soon, the flames would lick at her clothes and skin.*

*No sparrows or honeybees could help her now. And in the distant orchard the saplings already heavy with fruit could also do nothing at all. She prayed to the First Tree. To protect her unborn child. To protect her always. To give her a chance to know her name. To know she was loved. To know that she'd been conceived by joy and wildwood magic. By seeds and bees. By swallows and honey. By woven skeps and honeysuckle vine.*

"I sailed across the world to find you," Siobhán murmured as her head grew light and the heat behind her somehow turned icy cold.

She spoke to the babe inside her, but she also spoke to Harry and to the great wildwood. She spoke to Honeywick as it burned. She spoke to the sparrows and the bees. The Ross women had already been here, tending their wildwood garden. She spoke to them too.

Wise folk found each other. A spark in the eye. A tug to a place. The hum of a bee. A sparrow's cry.

There was a scraping at the door, but breathing smoke had left her confused to time and place. Siobhán heard the scrape as the ocean parting around a great steamship. Her new mistress was sleeping. A thing she did too much, aided by the laudanum never far from her hand. The husband was cruel and he watched Siobhán too closely, always boring twin holes into the small of her back with his eyes. More scraping. Only a month to endure before she would have grass beneath her feet again and the trees of a New World to meet.

Suddenly, she was lifted. She couldn't breathe. She struggled, kicking and punching out at the husband who was no longer content to merely stare. She gasped and coughed and hot tears stung her eyes and ran down her face. They stung her skin harshly and she cried out at the pain.

"They're both burned up, Granny," a voice said. Not her mistress. No. Her mistress was dead. Murdered. And she'd finally defied the murderer only to have him try to kill her too.

"Harry," Siobhán murmured, in spite of the pain.

She remembered. Thousands of bees dying. Honeywick in flames.

"She'll live. He saved her. His clothes on fire and he still got her out," Granny Ross said.

*They'd come to help.*

*Siobhán opened her eyes and rolled her head to the side. Other people were lying in the distance. She remembered. She'd seen them fall. The ground was thick with dead and dying honeybees.*

*"Not a one left alive for fifty miles, I bet," Granny Ross said. "He's gone too. Died with the bees. Joined, they were. Deep at the soul. He only lasted long enough to get her out."*

*"And the baby," the younger Ross said. Deborah. Her name was Deborah.*

*Siobhán could see him. Smoldering clothes. Skin burnt like hers. His face hidden in the grass, but his golden hair still bright in the sun. He was too far away to touch. She tried anyway, throwing out a hand in spite of the agony of movement. She encountered a tickle, a sigh, the soft flutter of wings. A honeybee crawled slowly onto her palm.*

*She couldn't reach Harry, but she cupped the bee gently and it was almost the same.*

Someone called my name. At first I didn't respond. It was wrong. Not the name I needed or expected to hear. But then a sharp pain in my palm made me gasp and cry out and the sound of my name came again, this time more familiar and said by a voice I hadn't known I was longing to hear.

"Rachel!" Mack said.

His weight dropped down on the moss beside me and I opened my eyes. We were illuminated only by a flashlight, and by its glow I could see the urgent worry on his face.

"The saw-whet owl woke me. He attacked my bedroom window. I followed him into the night," Mack explained.

I held my hand to the light. Blood oozed from half a dozen pin-pricks. I had jerked my hand when I woke up. I looked around and

Mack helped me, redirecting the flashlight beam until we found Eve coiled on the moss beside us. Unharmed.

"She bit you?" Mack dug for a handkerchief from his pocket and wound it around my palm.

"She saved me. I was lost in a vision. I...forgot where I belonged," I explained. "Her bite and you calling my name woke me."

# Thirty-Three

*M*ack *carried me back* to the Honeywick. I still felt as if I had one foot in the present and one in the past. I took deep gulps of the pre-dawn air and appreciated the support of strong arms around me. He had scooped me up without pausing to let me retrieve Eve, but I wasn't worried. She would find her way back to the house. Might even be there before we arrived.

Honeywick welcomed us home. It was startling to see the current house juxtaposed over a thatched roof engulfed by flames and black smoke rolling up to the sky.

There were no dead bodies on the grass. And there were thousands of honeybees alive and well only a mile or two away.

"I'm going to fetch Granny Ross. I'm guessing you don't have previous experience with visions that try to keep you."

Mack squeezed me tight as he spoke, suddenly giving me an idea of how much of his strength he kept in check when he was holding a woman half his size. I wasn't afraid. He relaxed his fierce hold too quickly to cause me discomfort.

"Call her and let her know I'm coming so she won't be alarmed," Mack said. He allowed me to slide down and find my footing before he backed away. He looked me over from head to foot at the door.

"She'll probably answer the phone before it rings," I replied.

Eve was waiting on the kitchen table. I picked her up before I went for the rarely used Depression-era phone hanging on the wall. Mack's engine roared and gravel spun as I dialed the Ross cabin's number, directed by a small book Mary had nearby.

I hadn't been wrong. Granny picked up the phone before the first ring echoed in the distance.

"I'm waitin' for 'im," she said, before I'd even said a word.

We rang off together.

I couldn't pretend to myself that I was fine. I still smelled smoke, and when I raised Eve to my face to thank her for saving me I could see soot marks on my clothes and skin. No wonder Mack had raced away. Had my clothes still been smoking when he arrived?

By the time I heard Mack's truck return, I'd managed to shakily light a small fire and I'd swung one of Mary's old fireplace kettles into place over it. The moves were more familiar somehow than the copper kettle on the electric stove. Probably not a good thing, but I needed some fortifying tea.

I ran my fingers over the letters on the hearth's cornerstone and over the scratches that obscured what had been carved beneath the cottage's name. It hadn't only been a date. It had been another name. I'd seen it. I'd read it. But now that part of my vision was hazy and I couldn't recall.

Only Granny Ross came inside. I wasn't disappointed. I felt vulnerable and out of place. Too much like another woman to feel as comfortable with Mack as I should. My hands trembled and I was smudged and shaking. Would I ever feel as if 1969 was my time again?

"Well, did you at least find the answers you sought?" Granny Ross said when she flung open the door. She stood with her hands on her hips and her mysterious knitting in the basket in the crook of her arm.

"I know what happened to Siobhán and her beekeeper now."

I didn't get up from the rocking chair by the tiny fire. Outside a rooster crowed. It was too hot and dry for the flames, but in spite of having almost died in a fire that had happened a hundred years ago, I needed the comfort of the fireplace right now. That, the applewood needle box in my pocket and the steaming mug in my hands.

"I brought valerian for that cup," Granny continued, quieter, now that she had assessed my weakness. She closed the door behind her and crossed the room.

"I know I need to extricate myself."

The old woman looked me over. I'd washed my face and hands. I'd smoothed my hair with a brush, but I hadn't changed clothes. There was still evidence of soot and scorch marks. I'd even found frizzled burnt ends in my hair.

"Never seen this. Not in all my years. Not even in people who've tried hard to see and hear and touch things they shouldn't."

"I've been clumsy since Mary left. Stirring up trouble. Stirring up the past. And I do believe it can be dangerous when we're not careful with our intentions. The wildwood is powerful and we're only human. Touched by the fae or not. I've felt the depletion. The fatigue. After cider making. Or baking. After my very soul is driving me to sew something. I'm certain we could work ourselves to death. Literally. But, Granny, the honeybees were only protecting Harry and his family. Their home. The hives," I said softly. I sat my empty cup down on the hearth at my feet near the scratches. What had Harry carved into the stone beneath "Honeywick"?

"The more powerful the wisewoman, the more she feels it when she's finished working. We all have our tonics. Dandelion wine, peach brandy, honey mead. But I've warned Jo about those bees. Their power is wild.

I'm certain it comes from beyond the veil. Closer to fairy than anything else on this mountain. Dangerous even without a wildwood connection. With it? No thank you. Don't want their honey or their stings."

Granny Ross bent to pick up my cup and took a twist of paper from one of her pockets. *Pockets are power.* She deftly dumped the contents of the paper into my mug and poured boiling water from the kettle into it. As soon as the water hit, the strong scent of the tisane filled the kitchen. I recognized the smell of valerian—slightly tangy, somewhat bitter, but there were other things I didn't recognize. Toad warts? Beetle powder?

I sipped it without question when she handed it to me. If it took a little of Granny's darkness dabbling to dispel the past, so be it.

"Been having nightmares about those killer bees my whole life," Granny admitted. She grunted and shrugged as she hung the kettle back on its wrought iron arm.

"They died for Harry." Tears filled my eyes. I had been so deeply asleep that I couldn't wake, but I hadn't been resting. I'd been fighting for my life and losing my soul's mate. More Siobhán than myself.

"She lived out her days here. First with my great-granny and then in this cottage. She was scarred. Kept her face hooded like a ghost at first, but later when people stayed away they said she didn't care. Not sure when it became Crone's Hollow. Then or later. Not sure when she became an actual ghost. Folks still see her sometimes in the fox fire or the evening mists. Pretty sure I did once or twice as a child in those early years of life when the veil is thin."

"Did the baby survive?" I asked, afraid of the answer.

"You need to rest," Granny proclaimed, taking my second emptied cup.

I looked up, but she wouldn't meet my eyes, and her caginess held my need to know at bay. I couldn't bear another loss tonight. Maybe Granny had shouldered all the loss she could endure as well.

"You still baking pie?" Granny asked.

The recipe box was on the kitchen table where Mary had left it and where I had studied through it time after time. She brushed the pie recipe with one finger, touching each name in turn, but she didn't pick it up, as if it wasn't hers to touch.

"Yes."

The compost was full of failed crusts. Clumsy attempts to stir that had done no one any good. I reached for the embroidery hoop in the nearby chair. I thoughtfully fingered the threaded needle I'd placed in the muslin for safekeeping until I needed to stitch again. Hadn't my embroidery been less clumsy? Surely I'd at least brought warmth and cheer to people.

Granny looked at me now that I'd let my question about the baby slide. Her eyes narrowed as if she could see all the pies I'd failed in my expression.

"We, all of us, stir and brew, plant and tend. We care for what the wildwood places in our charge. Most of us are drawn more strongly to one thing or another. The pie kept you busy so you could relax into your stitchery. Never met a young'un who didn't need to get out of their own way. Instinct, girl. Follow where it leads. You mend. Knew it soon as I laid eyes on you. You see where the stitches need to be. You see the whole. You've been stitching a spell since you got here. Thread by thread. Knot by knot. We've all been encircled by Mary's birch hoop. It will be your life's work, a never-ending tapestry, and no telling how long that will be with Mary as your guide."

How could someone broken years ago be a mender?

I looked at the embroidery in my hands. The old birch hoop was darker now from the oils in my fingers and constant use. My needle was waiting for the next inspiration. My eyes tracked over the yellow of the honeysuckle and the bees, the brown of the saw-whet owl, the sinuous green coils of Eve. Every prick, every stitch, and I suddenly understood. I wasn't broken. I never had been. I'd stitched myself whole with needle and thread, with books and friends, with everyone I'd ever created something for and everything I'd ever seen translated into chain stitch, French knot and whirlybird in my mind.

Granny wasn't wrong. I had sewn the entire wildwood and all the folks and creatures in it within a honeysuckle ward. Maybe that helped to mend. Holding us all together when the Ezekiels of the world threatened to tear us apart. *Community is wildwood magic.* I sat down, knees gone weak beneath the enormous responsibility of the spell in my hands. Because it was a spell. One I had stitched with fingers that tingled with a strange energy I'd simply accepted over time.

Granny Ross untied the twine around her mystery bundle of knitting and shook out what she had made. It was a shawl. Waves of brown, gold, blue and green were revealed. All the colors of the wildwood.

"Started in on it before you came to town. Now I know it was to keep you warm when you're called out at night."

She settled the shawl over my shoulders and it draped as if she'd measured the breadth and width of me with more than her eyes. I thought of all the times I'd seen her clicking away. I thought of how my fingers sometimes went for needle and thread without any direction from me.

"Thank you," I said, without protest. Some might say it was dangerous to accept a gift from Granny Ross. Deborah had told me that Granny didn't like me. Or anyone. Even though the sunflower woman was older and wiser than I was, I thought she might be wrong. I thought Granny might love more than she let on. Maybe more than she could handle.

"Looks the image of him. You've managed the mischief in his eyes," Granny said by way of you're welcome. She was pointing at the slinky figure of Tuck in the tapestry. I didn't tell her that Tuck's kind of "mischief," like hers, was a little bit worrisome, all wily and willful and determined to have his own way. I noted Granny kept her fingers away from the honeybees. Her nightmares must have been bad. I had been Siobhán in my visions, locked away from the horror of the swarming bees. I'd seen only the aftermath, as tragic for the honeybees as it had been for the villagers.

What if Granny Ross had dreamed as one of the villagers suffering hundreds of stings before a horrific anaphylactic death?

I wasn't sure how old Granny was, but she had kept the fear of the bees that the original settlers had developed because of the terrible way The Morgan had died. "Crone's Hollow" had probably been feared as much for deadly bees as for witches. That's why the apiary was no longer at Honeywick. After Harry's hives were decimated, it hadn't been safe to begin again near the cottage and apiary the townspeople had torched. Mavis had said her family had originally kept wild hives hidden deep in the wildwood. Maybe that had been until enough time had passed and it was safe to establish an apiary people knew about once more.

"Show more folks when you get the chance. At the fair. Don't keep it hidden away," Granny ordered. "The pie was never your most important task."

I nodded. I'd almost lost myself tonight. Siobhán's love and pain still lingered in this place and they compelled me to relive her trauma. Truvy had said a haint was a lesson that hadn't been learned. I'd needed to see what had happened. Siobhán and Harry had been isolated and alone. The villagers had been too frightened to accept the strange wildwood beliefs of the Ross women and their like, and the fledgling community of the Morgan Settlement had been too fragile to resist The Morgan's intolerant lead. So many years had passed, and yet, the stigma of Crone's Hollow remained in Morgan's Gap as a reminder. There was a lesson that hadn't been learned.

Witches.

Fay folk.

Wayward women.

I'd already experienced what a roomful of people could add to my embroidered spell. There would be all sorts of wise wares on display this weekend. Mine would only be one among many. We lived and worked apart, but I was finally beginning to understand how important it was for us to come together.

Harry had sacrificed the honeybees and himself trying to save his wife and daughter. This should be a more enlightened age, but people still faced persecution—for their skin color, their sex, their identity and beliefs.

"Don't take it from the hoop. The birch binding is part of it now," Granny warned. "I reckon Mary knew as soon as she saw you place the first knot."

I had worked on the honeysuckle vine for years. We had sat, easy in each other's company, beside the fire. Mary had often organized her recipes while I sewed. Each of us happily mumbling over our work. Granny knew a lot, but not everything. Mary had left two recipes outside of her box for me to find, the pie and the cider, and both had helped lead me to friendship and love and a connection with neighbors I'd never had. Both would be carried to the fair for everyone to share. I also still had the liniment I'd made with Deborah for Mack.

Everything around us, especially all the things we put the wildwood and ourselves into, was important. There was magic in ordinary things, empowering a community that could stand together against whatever troubles and turmoil tried to tear us apart.

I had to believe that Siobhán and her baby had lived.

But I knew now that Harry and all his bees had died.

*Please.* His magic had been enough to save his child. *Please.* Our magic had to be enough to save Pearl and our Morgan's Gap home.

# Thirty-Four

*P*earl's birthday dawned hot and breezeless.

While the pie baked, I took out the applewood needle box. I retrieved one of the needles that had survived the night with me. I carefully threaded it with calloused fingers that had finally stopped shaking. Then I added swallows to the tapestry. I put all my love for her into the sharp and quick wings of the birds. The chest had burned along with everything but the stone walls and hearth of Honeywick. In my stitchery, the cottage was peaceful, barely a hint of blackened stone peeking from beneath a profusion of honeysuckle vine. The vines also formed the frame of the tapestry all around the edges where cloth met birch hoop.

*They say a birth day is special. That on the day and hour of your birth the veil between this world and the land of the fae is a gossamer thing.*

I sang Harry's lullaby while the scent of brown sugar and cinnamon filled the steamy-apple air. The fair would be even hotter than Honeywick's pre-sunrise kitchen. I had a yellow gingham sundress ready to wear. I'd added apples to the neckline and hemline, bright with scarlet red thread. The remembered Gaelic from my dreams didn't feel unnatural on my lips and tongue. In fact, the words tickled with familiarity and nostalgia. Maybe the dreams would fade with time, but for now Siobhán and Harry felt close by. *Please keep my birthday girl safe on her special day.* I usually spent this day alone, but today I was going to be more connected with others than ever before.

Mending wasn't a goal. It was an ongoing process—stitch by stitch, tear by tear, smile by smile.

The bite on the back of my hand was still tender as I plied my needle, but I would always be grateful to Eve for waking me. When the last swallow soared with a glimmer of blue and blush above the Honeywick I'd sewn months ago and all the other wildwood creatures I'd added this summer, the pie was ready. The ginger liniment was already on the table in Mary May's Market Day basket. I placed the embroidery hoop, covered with its muslin cloth, in the basket too. Once the pie was cooled, there would be a place for it in the basket as well.

I donned two mitts and brought the pie out of the oven. The evenly browned crust thrilled me, all golden and savory. Bubbling, cinnamon-specked sauce rose tantalizingly from each latticed square. I had learned from Mary and my own trial and error. I had learned from watching Primmie and from enjoying Jeremiah Warren's fried peach pies. Jugs of cider were already in the car.

I was going to the fair to celebrate my daughter's birthday. And I wasn't going empty-handed.

I had made a gift for Mack. The pie and the cider, also gifts, would be shared around. And my embroidery would be shown with other handwork.

Women's work. Powerful work. Made by two ordinary calloused hands.

Not hidden.

Proudly displayed.

Every stitch that had helped me hold on to life when I'd had to give Pearl away.

The pie cooled while the sun rose, and I washed up before getting dressed. I placed the applewood needle box in a front pocket that I had embroidered boldly with a replica of Eve on the front of my skirt. I tied my curls back from my face with a red bandana and even powdered my nose. I didn't regret the hot roller set I'd abandoned in Richmond or the cloying Wind Song perfume. I was discovering how to be myself in Morgan's Gap, inspired by the women I was coming to know and admire.

Granny said Siobhán had lived out her days as a mourning recluse. No wonder I'd dreamed so vividly of her life. I'd been living much the same. I used to use makeup to hide cuts and bruises. This morning I used it without a heavy heart. I didn't have to hide anymore. My daughter and I could shine.

It was time. Pearl would be safe. There was no way for Ezekiel to know she was mine. And the only way to stop the Sect from gaining influence in Morgan's Gap was to stand against them.

To live openly and courageously in another way. The wildwood way.

Granny had said more people should see my tapestry. They would today. There had been some talk about putting the fair off until the weather turned, but it had been held in August for as long as the town could remember, so heat wave or not, folks had determined to carry on. There were other traditions later in the year—apple butter making and a Gathering at the Ross cabin that drew more than wise folk for fresh-baked rye bread and a communion with the trees. Mary May had always scoffed at the apple butter made from lesser fruit than what grew in the orchard she tended. But she had brought me rye bread wrapped in cheesecloth each year as if it was a precious taste my isolation couldn't allow me to miss.

This year I would go to the Gathering. And maybe even help with the bread making.

It was early when I arrived at the fairgrounds, but crowds were already beginning to form. My chest was tight and my pulse fluttered at my temples. I took a deep breath and got out of the car. Tents, booths and awnings had been set up this week. Now people brought wagons, baskets and boxes filled with items to sell and display. There would even be judging in different categories—from canned goods to giant squash and all sorts of arts and crafts. With basket in hand, I searched for and found a long picnic table set up for complimentary refreshments beneath a cheerful blue awning. I placed the pie there and asked two of the football players I recognized from Cider Day to fetch the jugs from the car.

"You're that girl from the orchard," a busy woman said. She glanced sideways at my boldly embroidered pocket. "Take a place card and label your pie so people know where it came from."

I automatically took the card she offered. I saw a few other place cards so I wrote my first name without protest. I added Mary's last name on a sudden whim. I hadn't been a Gray for a long time. In my heart, never. And I was no longer the invisible "Smith." The woman paid no attention and only rushed away to make sure, I thought, that everyone else was doing as they should.

I took my lighter basket and went in search of where I should place the embroidery hoop for the show. In the distance, the faded circus tent loomed. I was braving it too. I would never forget its musty canvas smelling of dry rot and trampled earth and sweat. But it had no power over me. Not anymore. Not the tent nor the man who filled it with fear. I had finally walked far enough away.

As I made my way around the fairgrounds, I noticed that one of the canopied displays was set off to the side, away from the other booths and displays set up by churches, businesses and Boy Scouts. There was no sign to indicate what was to be on the tables beneath its red-and-white canopy but I noticed Deborah Ross in its cool shadows and I headed that way. Sure enough, by the time I made it to the unlabeled tent, Mavis and Jo had arrived with a large wagon filled with jars of honey.

"So we're to have our own tent this year," Jo noted with a high curved brow.

"And Susan Morgan made me label my sassafras pound cake. As if everyone in town wouldn't know my recipe the second they took a bite," Deborah replied.

"Gray has them thinking we're goin' to hex their laying hens and sour their milk cows," Granny Ross said. She came into the tent with a newly begun knitting project in a basket on her arm.

"As if you would never do such things," Deborah commented wryly. Her mother scoffed but I noticed she didn't plead innocence.

Truvy arrived with a group of women carrying a large bundle rolled like a carpet between them. "They wouldn't let us near the quilters tent. Said ours is too big to display there and to bring it here instead."

The women unrolled and spread out a pieced quilt that revealed a landscape of sky, mountains, trees and streams.

"Oh! It's the mountain," I sighed, experiencing the tingling in my fingertips that was becoming almost common place. As if I was slightly electrified by something in the air.

"It's Morgan's Gap," Deborah said.

"No. It's the mountain before the settlers came. Before the first mine. Or road. Or railroad track. Before electricity or artificial light," Granny said. "A fair bit of singing went into this piece, didn't it?" she asked Truvy, quietly.

The younger woman nodded. The creases at the edge of her eyes looked deeper than the last time I'd seen her. Not from laughter. From effort and concern.

We gathered around the quilt. I clasped my basket behind my back to keep my tingling fingers from tracing the stitches of the fine work in front of me. Pieces of fabric in blue, green, brown and gold had been cut and placed like a fine painting. Except sewn into place instead of applied with a brush. But all the subtle shadings and textures were there. The front of the quilt had been backed and batted and knotted with a thousand little threads to create a useful blanket. Craft, but for shelter. Art, but for warmth.

This is what the elderly ladies I'd seen on my first Market Day had been gathering to piece together. Ryan had slipped away to help them. I could sense the young man's energy emanating from the fabric.

"Wouldn't allow us to meet and finish it in the Presbyterian church basement either. Suddenly, the walls needed painting and the bathroom was out of order. Been meeting there, all together, with no fuss about it for years. Friendly like," Truvy said.

I'd seen them. Been buoyed by the church's communal spirit.

The women of her sewing circle stopped smoothing the quilt and looked from one to the other around their circle—some white, some Black—most wise in practice if not in belief. Episcopal. Baptist. Backslider. Saint. All coming together to sew, to celebrate the mountain's elusive but ever-present magic in their lives. Community. I could almost hear Truvy singing as they worked, sweet and low. None of us had to say Ezekiel's name. The cloud he'd brought to town hung over us all, shadowing our eyes.

"I told you he's trouble. Doesn't want folks connected to each other, or the mountain, or the land," Granny said.

"He wants people to look to him and only him," I said. "He wants to keep people off balance. Isolated and afraid. People like that are easier to manipulate and control."

I didn't add that I knew from personal experience how far Ezekiel would go to ensure he wasn't challenged in any way. Or how much further I thought he'd gone.

The quilt was the finest sewing I'd ever seen, but I stepped back and brought the basket around to pull out my embroidery anyway. It was time. In a small way, the tapestry I'd sewn was also the mountain.

Honeywick. The vines. The apples and bees. Every creature representing the heart of the wise folk. I used a chair like an easel to prop the birch hoop the way I did at home. Then, I removed the cloth cover.

"Mavis," Jo softly exclaimed. "The bees."

If people had been too intimidated by its grandeur to touch the incredible quilt, my tapestry had the opposite effect. Dozens of fingers brushed bee, blossom, vine and serpent. Saw-whet owl and sky. The tingling in the tips of my fingers spread to my palms, up my bare arms, to my face and between my shoulder blades. I bit my electric lips and tried to ignore my fluttering heart. I'd felt the tingling this strongly only once before. I glanced around, half expecting Eve's friends to slither from field and flower but found Eve herself coiled around the liniment left in my basket.

I'd given her credit for summoning the snakes that frightened Ezekiel away. But she was completely at rest right now while I struggled to keep the strange energy coursing through me from causing me to fly apart.

I slowly backed away from the wonder and attention my handwork was receiving, but I couldn't escape the strange electrified feeling in my body.

"I have some liniment for Mack. I'll be back soon," I managed in an odd vibrato whisper.

No one appeared to notice the change in my voice or my retreat.

"She made it." Jo told Deborah. But I had already whirled around to rush out of the tent and I didn't pause to hear the reply.

I saw the truck before I saw the man. It sat on the road at the edge of the fairgrounds, tailgate dropped, tools spread out in readiness. Mack didn't need a tent or a booth. His truck displayed his purpose and his wares. Perhaps it was his utilitarian work that made his toys and carving more acceptable to the town than the wisewomen's wares. Or perhaps in his truck with his scars he was an island unto himself already, set apart from ordinary folk who were untouched by both war and wildwood.

He was certainly separate to me. He stood out, not only head and shoulders above the rest, but with a particular shine that said he'd survived the shadows, that he continued to survive them, every day and night.

He came around the corner of his truck to place more tools on the gate and I stopped. The morning sun glinted on his hair and I thought of poor Harry. I swallowed and quickly rejected the comparison with sweaty palms and pounding heart, all the strange electricity I'd felt frightened away.

Not like Harry. At all.

But images of a burnt and lifeless body on the grass surrounded by dead and dying bees haunted me.

Mack saw me then too and he forgot the tools. He watched and waited for me to begin toward him again. For me, the ever-growing crowd disappeared. The circus tent across the road receded into insignificance.

"You might have trouble with baking but not with sewing."

Mack touched the apples I'd embroidered on the neckline of my dress. One after another. Lightly. And even with his big hands and thick fingers, he didn't so much as brush my bare skin. He didn't have to. I'd felt his touch now. My mouth went dry and my eyelids closed. I drew a shaking breath. Apple after apple, he traced as if he was counting every single stitch. I was tingling again. More electricity filled the air. My aura practically crackled. I wasn't afraid. We'd explored this particular energy before. I hoped we would again.

"I baked a fine pie for sharing today. No charcoal this time."

I opened my eyes to meet his. My confident claim sounded slightly breathless. I tried to cool my cheeks by willing my flush away.

"And what's this?" Mack asked, but only after his attention had lingered over my eyes, my cheeks, my lips. He soaked up the blushes I couldn't control. But he did it gently, respectfully, still only touching cloth not skin. Tingles everywhere.

"Liniment I made for you. Deborah taught me. We used ginger and sunflower oil."

I took the bottle from Eve's coils and handed it to Mack. Our fingers met, both of us grasped around the glass.

"I'm fine," Mack protested, even as he reached out.

"Old injuries can cause lingering pain. I've seen you rub your hip when you think no one is looking. This will help."

Mack's hand closed more firmly on the gift, accepting, admitting, but more than that. A wildwood gift bound the giver and receiver together. There was magic infused in the making and magic dispersed in the sharing. Who knew? Maybe Morgan's Gap was enchanted like Brigadoon, built on the edge of Fairy, and maybe a lot of folks on the mountain had ancestral ties to the fae. I could certainly see a glimmer of magic in the amber striations of Mack's eyes.

I released the bottle. I tingled all over now and a distant hum murmured in my ear. Maybe attraction was a bit like magic too.

Combined, attraction and the wildwood together packed a powerful punch. The hum sounded like wings. It felt like apple blossoms floating in sunbeams. Or sunflowers waving in the breeze.

"I have something for you too." Mack went to the back of his truck and returned with a box in his hands.

My breath caught. The swallow chest. Mack offered it, outstretched, in the palms of his calloused hands.

Every feather. Every quill. Every wing. Every bird. As lovingly rendered as they had been in my dreams.

I'd sewn swallows for Pearl. Mack didn't know today was Pearl's birthday.

"Came to me while I was sleeping. Happens that way sometimes. My mother used to say the best ideas come from beyond the veil. I started making it months ago. Before we...got to know each other. I didn't know it was for today until now."

I accepted the gift. Of course I did. For me. For Pearl. For Siobhán. All her lovely, clever swallows re-created from a hundred years ago. I'd embroidered them only that morning and here they were again, risen from ash to live in wood once more.

"Thank you," I breathed. Maybe one day I would tell him all about Pearl and how we'd escaped to the wildwood. Maybe one day we'd all celebrate her birthday together.

"I'm going to kiss you, Rachel. In front of everybody."

I didn't say no.

# Thirty-Five

*Pearl*

*S*ometimes *she knew which* way a day was going to go. It was strange to her that grown-ups couldn't taste the bad that was coming on the back of their tongues. Or feel the rush of goodness coming like butterflies in their stomach.

This morning she'd poured extra syrup on her pancake when her mother had turned away to wash the skillet in the kitchen sink, but she'd still only managed to eat a few bites because her mouth was filled with bitterness.

They were going to the fair.

It was supposed to be a good day, but when Pearl got dressed she tucked her tag-a-long ducks back into bed.

She wished she could crawl in with them and pull the quilt over her head against the bad and the bitter. Her quilt was special. Always good no matter the turn of the day. Her mother's friends had made it. It was covered in wildflowers—buttercup, daisy, honeysuckle and dandelion. When she touched the fabric petals and closed her eyes, she could see their faces. They'd sewn the quilt for her before she had even been born.

But she had to leave it and her house and go to the fair today.

Her stomach hurt. No butterflies today. Only heavy, scratchy rocks. It was hard to get dressed. It was even harder to walk out to the station wagon. Helen was loading the back of the twins' car with tomato juice she'd canned the week before. Those had been hot, busy days. Good days. Pearl had helped. She'd pressed the steaming stewed tomatoes with a wooden pestle in a cone-shaped metal colander that kept the skins and seeds out of the juice. They'd collected the juice in jars so big her mother had to use an outside fire to heat the canner to seal them in boiling water. Pearl couldn't help with the fire or the boiling pot. She was only allowed to sit on the grass at a "safe distance" and stare at the flames.

Something about the flames had been bad.

She didn't know it then, but the rock-feeling in her stomach had started when she'd watched them dance beneath the speckled blue canner.

Helen didn't drive, but there were always friends when the load was too big for her bicycle's basket. Fern and Fair helped carry the tomato juice to a tent through a crowd so thick Pearl could only see legs every which way she turned.

"Stay close. Don't go far," Helen said. But she said it in her busy voice, which meant Pearl could wander if she wanted.

She didn't want to wander today. The fair was where the badness was. The scent of fried apple pies and popcorn didn't help. The sound of laughter was sharp and hurt her ears. The sun was too bright. The air too thick. It was hard to breathe.

"Doesn't make sense. None of these things are where they belong," she heard one of her mother's friend's say.

Pearl looked around. The tent held canned goods and garden vegetables piled on tables. There were also tables filled with things people had made. It was all a whirl of colors and patterns. She didn't know how to name them. Except the giant quilt, of course. Good, like hers.

But bigger. So big it covered the picnic table under it and fell down to make cloth puddles on the grass all around. The same women who had sewn hers had sewn the giant quilt too. Pearl could see their faces every time she blinked even though she wasn't touching the quilt.

"Judging won't be right this year. Mark my words," another friend of her mother's said.

"Never been right. Only they aren't pretending this time," the oldest woman said. Granny Ross. Pearl knew her name. Knew her grumpy voice didn't match the mournful sad in her eyes.

The women in the tent weren't happy. The badness was so strong now that maybe even some of them could taste it. Pearl swallowed against the rising bitter. She crept over to the giant quilt and dropped down to crawl underneath it. No one noticed her. Knees don't have eyes.

She found a shadowy place, cooled by the grass and filled with the smell of soap and sunshine that came from the quilt itself. All the noises of the fair got quieter. The unripe persimmon flavor in her mouth faded. Maybe it would go away if she hid long enough beneath the fabric mountain.

Blades of grass tickled her bare legs. Helen was teaching her how to braid. She plucked several blades of grass and knotted the ends together. Then, she started to plait. She would make a grass crown while she waited. She would become the fairy queen. No one could hurt a fairy they couldn't see.

And a queen could order the badness to go away.

*Ezekiel*

Blatant sacrilege directly across from God's house. The revival tent might not be a permanent structure, but it had been sanctified by his presence and prayers, by the nightly praise and penance since it had been erected.

Even from a distance, he could see short skirts and fraternization between men and women, Black and white, Christian and...He marched across the road with his Bible in his hand. He would speak. He would put a stop to this. What he found among the sinning horde was even worse than he'd perceived.

A makeshift booth had been erected and a man who had probably never seen the inside of a church, neither wood nor canvas, was dispensing a home-brewed intoxicate from wooden barrels. But it was the townsfolk lining up to fill and refill their glasses that shocked him to his core. He saw many familiar faces. Men—and women!—who had been to his revivals were now publicly drinking a disheveled devil's beer. The man had a braided beard tipped with rainbow-colored beads and he wore jeans with legs so flared it looked like a skirt when he walked. And his feet were bare in the grass.

Ezekiel opened his Bible and began to read all the passages about temperance. He was rewarded by some of the people gravitating away from the beer barrels. But the man dispensing the beer began to sing a sea shanty with ribald lyrics. His voice was a pleasant, deep bass that drowned out the scriptures. Some of the men in line joined in until an impromptu quartet was formed.

The familiar words of the passage Ezekiel was reading swam before his eyes as his heart pounded in his ears. Fury? Fear? It had been a long time since he'd been so disrespected. Suddenly, he was seventeen again. His parents had named him after the founder of the Sect. They had told him he was born to be a prophet. Then his father had found the mound of burnt animal corpses in the woods. He hadn't understood. The sacrifices God required of his messenger. They had lost their faith. He'd lived through that betrayal. Their horror and disbelief. The necessity of the even greater sacrifice that had followed. They had jeopardized his calling, but even as a young man, he hadn't allowed them to stand in his way. At this transcendent point of his ministry, he refused to be intimidated by a crowd of heathens brazenly mocking him and the word of God.

He would find a better place to speak. One where he could gather his people to him so that they could stand together against the decadence of this "fair." Ezekiel closed his Bible and walked away. He ignored several cheers that were probably not aimed at his back anyway. But his face burned hot beneath the unrelenting sun.

He blinked against the sweat that trickled into his eyes and a bright sunbeam detached itself from the midmorning rays in his path. Not a sunbeam, but a woman in a butter-yellow dress. A familiar woman. One he had lain with. One who had constantly failed him. One he had disciplined. One he had lost before God had shown him what he should do with her.

He had allowed the serpents to drive him away from her orchard refuge and here was the result.

Rachel stopped in her tracks. The wide smile faded from her sunbrowned face. Her dark hair was wild around her cheeks. If the crowd was brazen, then she was the queen of them all. A pagan queen with short skirts, bare knees and loose curls. He'd seen her plying needle and thread often enough to know she had been the one to sew the crimson red apples above the swell of her breasts and along the edge of the skirt to highlight her thighs. Snakes. Apples. Something about the design jogged another elusive memory. Ezekiel's hands clenched the Bible in front of him like a shield against how badly he wanted to make this impossibly happy version of his rebellious wife cry. She'd fooled him, playing at being obedient and meek. Pretending to be filled with true faith. Like his parents had pretended.

He crushed his Bible beneath his fingers.

"You will burn," he managed to speak, but his jaw creaked as if it needed oiling.

Anger made him shake. Only the fairground filled with people kept him from knocking Rachel to the ground. His most effective punishment had always been to knock her down and lift her skirts. To prove his dominion over her as lord husband. He swelled in his pants with the memory. Her, helpless. Him, in control. Never mind that he'd felt less and less in control as their time together as man and wife had gone on. She'd been so young at first. It had been easier then. Later, she had cowered less. Stared him in the eyes more. He should have known she would eventually come to this. Challenging him in front of the world.

He took another step toward her, but slowly. *Snakes*. He wasn't afraid. He didn't shake out of fear. His trembling was only righteous indignation.

"You don't belong here," Rachel replied, so calmly and confidently, he was startled to stillness. What had she done with the quaking, cringing woman who had cried and bled at his feet? She had once begged for mercy. Now, she stood tall and faced him, squarely, as if he should be the one to bend and bleed. "The wildwood has been since the dawn of time. The wise ways were here long before Morgan's Gap. Wise folk have tended what was sown. They've created and kept. They've endured ignorance, intolerance and hate. They've welcomed all who respect the connection with the wildwood. They've stood against those who don't. You should leave. Now."

It was *this place*. It had emboldened her wickedness. All his grand plans for the mountain distorted in an instant like reflections in a funhouse mirror. His feet shifted as if the ground beneath him had rolled and he swallowed hard. Ice settled in his guts in spite of the heat as her emerald-green serpent twined up her bare arm. Its beady black eyes met Ezekiel's and he found himself swaying along with its tiny head, to and fro, to and fro.

"Get thee behind me, Satan," Ezekiel groaned. He backed away from the witch, his privates shriveling to nothing. He had lain with her. He had given her his seed. Again and again. His stomach curdled and bile rose in the back of his throat.

"Too late for that." Her smile had returned, tight and cold. "You are his man, through and through."

Ezekiel fled Rachel and her snake and the jeering crowd, only looking back from time to time to make sure he wasn't chased. He didn't stop until he came to a creek and even then he continued until he was up to his knees. He dropped his Bible on the bank so he could wash his hands and face.

But the cold mountain water didn't soothe him no matter how vigorously he splashed. His movements dislodged his hat from his head and he paid no mind as it plopped into the water and began to bob away because bright sunshine suddenly blasted the top of his head with heat. Blessed heat. Like fire. It hadn't been the water he needed. He froze with his hands outstretched, like a vulture at dawn trying to warm its feathers in the rising sun. Water dripped from his sleeves and he turned his face up to the sky. How many of these townspeople had been baptized in these heathen rivers and streams? They were all praying for rain, but it wasn't water they needed. As his skin and jacket baked dry, an aura of heat surrounded his face, much like the glow of righteous fires he'd once basked in.

At times, he had been called to burn the bad away.

He calmed. The crowd in the distance laughed and played and sinned, but he was reassured of his supremacy as he swayed back and forth. He began to hum a beloved hymn, but in his mind the old familiar song was accompanied by the crackle and pop of cleansing flames.

*Carol Long*

She had already set up for storytelling in a booth near a platform erected for evening music. She had dressed for work, which wasn't ideal for the weather—sandals with kitten heels and a tailored button-up shirtwaist dress with a nipped waist and sailor collar. Her tote overflowed with puppets that had drawn children as if she was the Pied Piper through the crowd. She had secret notebooks filled with novels and essays that would never see the light of day, but the puppets and telling stories to children was a creative outlet she enjoyed.

If occasionally she strained at the confines of what was appropriate for the sheriff's wife it was her own fault. She had chosen respectability over freedom. Bill had already been a deputy with aspirations when he asked her to marry. That Ross girl from Crone's Hollow with a mother back from some failed commune up north and no daddy to speak of.

Bill nodded at her as he made another circuit around the fairgrounds. His uniform as starched and crisp as the day it was made. How she hated that duty—the hand-washing, the wringing, the hanging out to dry. Watching over the brown pants and shirt to be sure no bird left a mark. Then the pressing, every crease, every seam, the patches kept stitched in order.

In every way the showiness of Bill's uniform mocked her hidden notebooks filled with messy ink and even messier ideas. She wrote all the things she wasn't allowed to say. Whenever she could slip away. Whenever her Ross blood bubbled up and she couldn't tamp down her temper. This long hot summer had been interminable.

The never-ending revival had done nothing to bring people closer to their faith. Instead, it had stirred up animosity, setting neighbor against neighbor, rekindling fears and feuds, turning friends and acquaintances into enemies. She'd refused to go after her first night.

It had been the first time Bill had raised a hand against her. She'd backed away, quick, from his gesture even as he caught himself before actually striking her. Too late. She'd bumped her cheek on an open closet door.

He had apologized. He had disapproved of her boycott, but they hadn't argued again. He had gone out every night since without her. Only to come home angrier and more dissatisfied with her and the world.

He nodded, but he didn't smile when he walked by. It was his deputy, Cass, who paused and tipped his hat. His smile was fleeting, cautious, but there. Carol didn't dare respond.

Had Bill stopped himself because he was a good man or because he was afraid of Granny Ross? Did it matter? She'd never forget the raised fist. The resentful apology afterward. The continued disapproval and attendance of a revival that basically preached against what her family believed—that nature was sacred. That wise folk were supposed to bridge the gap between the wildwood and the townspeople. She may have gone off to school, but she hadn't completely turned her back on her childhood.

"You need to go over there and look at that quilt. It's amazing. The finest handwork I've seen," Midge, the first-grade teacher said. Carol and Midge had gone to school together. Unlike Carol's eccentric upbringing, Midge's parents were teachers too. Still taught at the high school. And none of them had gone to the revival since it had come to town.

Midge was speaking to Julie Holcomb, the mother of one of the children who had followed Carol through the crowd. A dozen boys and girls were waiting for the puppet show on the grass. Julie was younger than Midge and Carol. She had been at the revival every night. In the front row.

"You won't catch me near that quilt or anything else in that tent," Julie said.

Midge pointedly looked at Carol and Julie blushed beet red. That's when Carol understood they were talking about wise wares. Everyone knew she was Deborah's daughter. A Ross with a ring on the third finger of her left hand was still a Ross through and through in these parts. No matter how conservatively she dressed or worked or spoke.

"I'm glad they're keeping them away from the rest of us," Julie said. Not embarrassed. Her cheeks were red with contrariness and temper, not shame.

Carol met the woman's accusing eyes with utter calm. It was her chilling stare, the one she used to ensure quiet in the stacks. No bubblegum. No jacks. No loud talking. No roughhousing. To her credit, Midge continued gamely on. "You should go see it, Carol. Everyone thinks it will win the blue ribbon." Julie huffed and straightened her skirt as if the very idea was offensive.

"I'll go. And the puppets go with me," Carol said. "My grandmother helped to sew them after all."

Julie blanched stark white at the mention of Granny Ross. Horrified at the very idea of her little Billy being exposed to puppets sewn by a witch. Carol grinned and Midge laughed out loud while Carol shrugged out of her stifling wife-of-the-sheriff overdress. Underneath she had a perfectly respectable sleeveless sheath in pale green that would have made Jackie Kennedy proud. Why should she suffer in layers?

She kicked off her shoes too and went barefoot back through the crowd, leading all the children by the shine of her fire-engine-red toes.

*Rachel*

I'll admit to humming the beekeeper's lullaby more than once after the ugly encounter with Ezekiel. He had looked messy and strange with greasy unkempt hair and wild rolling eyes. As if his true nature was finally manifesting in his appearance. Pearl was with Helen and they were both *among friends*. We weren't alone. The tightness in my chest was only old, leftover fear. I didn't have to be afraid anymore.

At one time I would have run. I would have grabbed Pearl up and taken her away from the fair to hide her from her father. But she belonged here more than he did and this time we weren't going anywhere.

Word of the quilt had spread. Most of the fairgoers came by to see. Some to gawk and whisper about the potential for wickedness in the pickles and the devil's dandelion wine. But many to stare and appreciate in wonder. Quite a few touched my embroidery. Every brush of fingers gifted me with energy that built to near exhilaration by the end of the day. Honeysuckle. Serpent. Saw-whet owl and bee.

Granny Ross watched from another makeshift throne, her needles constantly clicking. Her stares were intense. And interested. Folks came for the quilt, but lingered over embroidery, crochet, macramé and tomato juice. Trades were made. A few bills and coins passed hands.

Wise wares were carried away. Some were bold: "What's the harm in lavender soap or a mint balm for my sciatica?" Some secretive: "I'll take this crocheted charm stuffed with lemongrass for friendship. "Or "I'll take this jar of dried herbs to rejuvenate my love life." The last whispered from woman to wisewoman with a hopefulness as old as time.

The worst heat of the afternoon had passed when the judges finally made their way to the wisewomen's tent. Not all came inside.

"Told ya. Never gonna change," Granny Ross mumbled from her corner.

But I saw two of the judges touch the quilt with careful fingers, not because they were afraid or condescending, but rather, they were appreciative of the work—the perfect stitching, the artistic piecing.

The overall effect of mountain, sky, grass and trees.

I hadn't brought my embroidery for competition. I'd only brought it to share. But one judge I recognized as a local postman touched the saw-whet owl and sighed as if he'd touched a feather of the actual little owl itself.

When it was time for the evening music, we all left the tent for cooler night air. Lanterns had been lit all over the grounds and children chased fireflies in the shadows. I looked up at the moon, thinking about a man's footsteps being all the way up there. Maybe the quilt would win a blue ribbon, no matter what Granny Ross said. It was 1969. Anything was possible. Anything at all.

As fiddle, banjo and dulcimer music floated across the fairgrounds, I almost believed the jaunty mountain music could counteract the moldering madness of Ezekiel and his circus tent. It had developed a sad sort of sagging lean, I noted. Its silhouette in the dark was a strange hulking blob. No longer formidable. As old and rotten as the ideas it had sheltered. And as rejected. The grass around it was empty. All the townsfolk were gathered together at the stage—Black and white, old and young, men and women and children.

Community might be an ethereal sort of magic, but we'd conjured it tonight with our art and music, with laughter and shared food and drink.

Were the Ross women really witches? Maybe. Eve had found her way back to my arm. Wisewomen. Woodsmen. Wise folk, no longer separated, all mingled with the crowd.

# Thirty-Six

*Pearl*

*S*he *wasn't sad when* her hiding place was found. She had plaited a crown for her head and several bracelets for her arm. She was thirsty and hungry. The bitter taste on the back of her tongue didn't keep her stomach from rumbling.

Helen's smile lit the shadows as much as the sunbeams when she lifted the corner of the mountain quilt.

"Time for lunch. Folks are filling their plates and picnicking over by the woods to get out of the noonday heat," she said. "Even fairy princesses need a little cold lemonade in the middle of a hot summer day."

Pearl crawled out from under the table and stood patiently while Helen dusted her favorite sundress off and straightened her skirts down over her shorts. She spent so much time on the ground that her mother let her wear shorts instead of petticoats. While she was "put to rights," she noticed a wooden circle holding what looked like a page from a storybook. Except all the animals and plants and the tiny house had been sewn with thread. She could see the strands of red and green, yellow and blue.

She didn't know she had taken several steps toward the page until Helen complained and sat back on her heels.

"Well, that's fine for now, I guess. Fairies are going to have grass-stained knees. It's inevitable."

Helen laughed, so Pearl continued over to the circle. There were flowers and vines. A weasel. A snake. An owl. And honeybees. But it was the birds above the vine-covered house that Pearl wanted, no, needed to touch.

She traced each bird, softly and carefully. The same way she'd touch glass or her Sunday school teacher's cross necklace.

Helen came to stand beside her. Her voice was strange when she spoke this time. She wasn't laughing and she sounded almost sad.

"Those are barn swallows. Rachel May stitched them."

"The Crying Lady. She doesn't cry anymore. She's happy now."

Her mother hadn't said not to touch, so she pressed her finger against the highest-flying bird. Barn swallow. Then she drew her hand back in surprise because the bird seemed to flutter.

"A little happier, I think. You're right. She would be very happy to know you like the swallows," Helen said.

"I love them," Pearl said. And she did. More than her tag-a-long ducks. More than pie. More than the swing that hung from the old willow tree in her backyard.

"Th...that's nice," Helen said.

But something was wrong. Pearl looked up from the embroidery to see her mother wipe the corner of her eye. And her smile was slippery like it was when they sang "In the Sweet By and By" at church.

"I think you need some lemonade," Pearl said, forgetting about the birds. She reached for her mother's hand and squeezed.

"Yes. We'd better hurry. It's getting too hot and everyone is making for the shade."

This time when they walked across the fairgrounds there were fewer knees. Pearl could see better and mainly what she could see was trampled grass and empty booths.

"I hope Mavis saved us some honey," Helen said. She pulled Pearl faster along.

At the potluck tent, they found honey and homemade biscuits. Two fried chicken legs and a slice of apple pie to share. All the lemonade was gone, but there were jugs of cider that some big boys had carried down to the creek. When Helen asked, the boys fetched two cups full and it was the coldest, best thing Pearl had ever tasted. She gulped the cup empty and one of the boys brought her another.

The fresh cider chased the bitter taste on her tongue right away.

"Let's take our plates to the shade," Helen said.

Pearl saw, then, where the knees had gone. The whole crowd had made for the shade beneath the trees that lined the fairground. Near the creek, where the forest began, the air was cooler. People had brought quilts to spread out and eat on.

"We'll wait out the judging and the heat of the afternoon here," Helen said. There were lots of children running and playing. Some of the bigger ones splashed in the creek, lifting up rocks in search of crawdads or water lizards. "Eat first," her mother said. She put Pearl on the edge of Primrose's quilt and sank down beside her to talk with friends.

"Labeled our food like it was poisoned," someone was saying.

"Their loss. That's the best apple pie I've ever tasted," her mother replied.

It was good. Pearl had eaten one bite of chicken and most of her honey biscuit, but she'd still wiped up the juice of her half of pie with a finger. It tasted like the cider, but sweeter, and it made her think of swinging and barn swallows... and rain.

Pearl remembered rain.

The way the damp air felt on her skin. The way it was like breathing moss and leaves and all the green growing things in until she didn't know where she stopped and they began. She remembered splashing in puddles and tilting her face up so that the drops plopped like kisses from the sky on her cheeks.

Why wouldn't people want to remember that?

"That man is over there preaching. But it doesn't look like he's gathering much of a crowd," Primrose said.

"Hate not taking hold today. Some of 'em are trying, but the fair has been going on too long. Too many years of folks coming together," Helen said.

Pearl stood and gave her plate to her mother. She had rested enough. The creek was gurgling and there was a path along it just right for a fairy princess to run.

"Stay where I can see you," her mother said.

Pearl knew. And she knew not to get in the creek. Maybe later, when her mother was finished visiting, she would help to unbuckle the white summer sandals on Pearl's feet. Then she might wade with Helen holding her hand.

The path was cool. The sunlight danced around her racing feet, the leaves over her head only allowing some beams to get through to the ground. She found other running children who weren't allowed in the water. They ran together, dodging water thrown at them or stopping only to see whatever creatures the older boys and girls had found in the pools.

Pearl was in sight. She was sure of it. Every step, every skip, every leap landed within Helen's view. But running was harder to control, and too soon, caught up in racing, she did wander far.

Too far.

She was catching her breath against a big old tree when she heard a voice that made her freeze. It was the revival preacher. Reverend Gray. He was different from the other pastors Pearl knew. He wasn't gentle or kindly or helpful. Or wise. He was scary with a strange light in his eyes.

"Only burning will purify the sin and the sinners. There's no hope for Morgan's Gap without the flame!" the preacher shouted.

And suddenly the bitter was back so strong that Pearl doubled over, gagging into the grass.

"You there. What do you think you're doing?" Reverend Gray came around the tree, pointing at her. Pearl backed away too quickly and fell, hard, landing flat on her bottom. Her breath started to hitch in her chest. She tried to gulp air, but she couldn't.

"The fall knocked the breath out of her," one of the people said. But no one came to help her up or dust her off the way Helen and her friends would have done. Worst of all, she'd dropped out of sight. She couldn't see Helen in the distance, and if she couldn't see her mother, then her mother couldn't see her.

All the other children had disappeared.

Pearl reached for her hair and soothed herself by brushing a long brown curl along her cheek and into her mouth to suck.

The revival preacher stopped and stared.

"Who does this child belong to?" he said as if he had a mouth full of rocks.

"That's Helen's daughter," someone said.

"No, she's not. She's a foundling. Helen took her in," someone else said.

"That dress," the preacher said. His face was red. He took another step toward her and Pearl panicked. She tried to scoot away. Her dress was yellow gingham. It was covered with bright red apples like polka dots all over. Embroidered. Like the barn swallows. Rachel May had sewn her favorite dress. She hadn't known her mother had gotten the dress from the Crying Lady, but suddenly she did know.

And the bad preacher knew too.

*Bad bad bad bad.*

"Hers. You're hers," the preacher hissed. "Those were green *snakes* on the dress I saw you wearing at the tinker's shop. Not worms. She covered you in *serpents*. Her sewing was always *wrong*. Always disrespectful. She only pretended to do women's work. It was always a silent abomination. Evil, unrepentant bitch."

Pearl cried. Not because the fall had hurt, but because the bitterness in her mouth and the light in the preacher's eyes made her feel exactly like the Crying Lady had felt before she got happier.

The strange preacher had gone still. Like something had caught his eye in the grass. Not a penny. Not a sprout. Not a ladybug or ant.

Her.

She was trapped by his stare, too afraid to scramble up and run away.

"She took you from me," the preacher said, quietly. He'd dropped down to his knees beside her. His quiet was worse than his loud. He raised one hand to smooth her hair and pull it from her mouth. "Mine," he said. And his gentle touch was worse than a smack would have been. "You can be cleansed. You will be cleansed." Above their heads there was a whisper of wind through the leaves and the sunshine came through. It lit the bad preacher's eyes like flames. Suddenly, one of his hands reached out to jerk the grass bracelet she'd made from her arm. It startled, snapped and stung, but before she could cry out—

"Pearl, there you are," the tinker said. "Your mom sent me to fetch you."

The biggest man she'd ever met scooped her up. Her fear was gone.

Mack was good. The same way rain was good. Like apple pie and cider. The bad preacher didn't try to keep her. He couldn't. Mack was too big. Too good.

"I fell."

Anywhere near the revival preacher was a bad place she would never go again. The tinker didn't speak to the preacher. Pearl hugged around his neck and watched over his shoulder to make sure the bad man didn't follow them. He didn't, but he was still scary, kneeling and staring. The light in his eyes was brighter than before and he was saying her name again and again.

She could see his mouth moving, but he didn't make a sound.

# Thirty-Seven

*I'd seen Pearl several* times and she did shine, but only as she always did in my eyes. Helen hugged me once and it had been as if she was trying to share a hug from Pearl in the safest way she could, carried and passed on by her. The love and care and consideration of the gesture had sent me to the creek, where some splashes of cold water had washed the tears away before they could redden my eyes or make track marks on my powdered cheeks.

Pearl was wearing a sundress I'd made from the same material I'd used to make my dress. Both dresses had embroidered apples, but the ones I'd sewn into Pearl's dress were so tiny they looked like red polka dots from a distance. I only had a brief moment of worry that we were dressed alike before pushing it away. I'd embroidered for other women and children in town and I'd seen more of my work here and there throughout the day.

That the women still wore my stitchery felt like a positive sign.

All around the fair, apples, honeybees, snakes and honeysuckle were jaunty signs of hopeful connection.

I remembered Ruby that day at the diner. Truvy had said it had to be honeysuckle not rubies on her dress. The strings on her guitar had said so. Eve had concurred. Had Siobhán planted the honeysuckle around Honeywick's foundation or had a fortunate wind carried the seeds from the wildwood? Honeysuckle for binding, for warding, for protection. Some would call it an old wives' tale, but a wisewoman knew old wives and old maids alike spoke from a place of knowing what was what.

The stubborn little girl had only been taking her customary place at the counter and maybe the embroidery I'd sewn into her skirts while Truvy played and sang hadn't made a difference at all. Maybe the town folk would have realized they were being hateful and ignorant with only Ruby's strength and innocence to guide them.

But the honeysuckle didn't hurt.

And today the home-brewed beer, the cider, the music and merriment hadn't hurt either.

Ezekiel's hate wouldn't spread. His sort of revival was over in Morgan's Gap and maybe a new sort of revival had begun.

I had almost allowed Ezekiel's presence and the confrontation that morning to spoil the day, but as the gloaming turned into night the reprieve of cooler air noticeably diminished my tension. In fact, the late summer evening settled over the entire crowd and we all fell sleepily under a convivial spell of twinkling fireflies and bluegrass music. All except Mack. He was a quiet man, but tonight his silence wasn't easy and peaceful. I could feel a stiffness in the big, warm body beside me. As if he was holding himself still. I'd noticed this sort of stillness in him whenever he didn't want to frighten me.

Something was bothering him. And he was trying to keep it from bothering me.

By the time the Reys took to the stage, the moon had risen. Truvy's grandmother began to pick her gnarled fingers across her five-string guitar more nimbly than I expected for someone her age, and when

Truvy began to sing a familiar mountain spiritual, several anonymous "amens" spontaneously rang out in appreciation. *Take that, Ezekiel.* Truvy's voice lifted us all to the moon. Man, woman, child. Black and white. Shopkeepers, teachers, farmers and vets.

One small step.

There was something about the music—Nana Josephine Rey's quick but melancholy picking sent out a compelling thrum that surrounded the crowd and brought them along for the will-o'-the-wisp ride of fleet fingers against string after string. And Truvy's lilting contralto made tears prick at the corners of my eyes. Together. We were all in this life together. Through drought and abundance. Through feast and famine. Through birth and death.

Planting. Harvesting. Hungering. Celebrating. Grieving. Exalting.

After Truvy's song, Mack exhaled and softened. He took my hand while Mrs. Rey played one last song. I recognized the beekeeper's lullaby. No one protested. It merged seamlessly with the hymns that had come before. Soon, the winners of the show would be revealed. Even if Granny Ross was right about the wisewomen's quilt being snubbed, it was the winner. Everyone knew it. And the wise folk would be sure to recognize the win if no one else did. I would make sure of it. The fair was a success because we hadn't let Ezekiel stop us from coming together. My pie had been eaten to the last crumbs. Only by friends, but there was nothing wrong with that. The cider jugs had also been emptied. And several people had asked if I had any apples to sell. The fair. Market Day and fall Gathering. Cider and apple butter making. Football and barbeque and fried peach pies. Music and dancing.

We would not be ruled by ugliness and fear. We would *be*. Singer, stirrer, sculptor, keeper. We would continue our tinkering and our stitchery. Our baking and our brewing. We would love each other. We would find harmony in the day as well as the night. The wildwood showed us the way, made up of a spectacular variety, growing this way and that, but all with roots twining side by side, around and around, in the same soil.

The orchard was part of the wildwood. Just as the wisewomen were a part of this community. Always had been. Always would be. And the wise folk way wasn't one that tolerated division or hatefulness.

The judges were to the side of the stage, setting up a table with red, yellow and the prized blue ribbons. But a restless murmur began to roll over the crowd. Before the final chords of the last song could be played, the fiddle's bow screeched across the violin and one of Truvy's many cousins shouted, "Fire!"

He pointed with his bow and the entire crowd turned toward the opposite end of the fairgrounds.

Only the torches near the stage had kept us all from seeing the beginnings of the flickering flames. Now an inferno raged behind us, consuming dry canvas and sending a tornadic flume high into the night sky.

"It's too dry," Mack said, the horror clear in his voice.

In the dark, people called for their children, shepherding their families together.

"It's the wisewomen's tent," I said. The mountain quilt. All the handwork and wares. Destroyed. Nothing would be left. "Was anyone left inside?"

Earlier in the day, I'd seen Pearl playing under the quilt. I'd seen Helen fetch her for lunch. I'd ached to be the one to dust off her dress. I'd smiled at the grass crown on her head and the Eve-like bracelet of braided grass on her arm. My birthday girl. My fairy princess.

Had she gone back to the tent? Had she been innocently playing there when the fire began? I'd been lulled by the convivial atmosphere around me. I'd lost track of her only a few times that day, but this time...

"Pearl." My voice choked with emotion.

Mack caught my shoulders, standing between me and the fire when I would have run toward the flames. In the dark, I couldn't see his eyes clearly, but I looked up at his face anyway.

"She'll be with Helen. She had a scare earlier in the day. I doubt she would have gone far from Helen's side after that."

Mack meant to reassure me, but I was suddenly more afraid.

"What happened?"

He hadn't told me. I had known something was bothering him, but he had been too silent for me to bring up the change between morning and evening.

"We'll mount a bucket brigade from the creek. To stop it from spreading," Sheriff Long shouted above the furor.

"I'll explain later. Find Helen and you'll find Pearl."

Mack gave my shoulders a squeeze before he hurried away to help put out the fire. Pearl under the table in a fairy castle with a quilt roof. Granny Ross on her hay-bale throne. I had spent years embroidering the wildwood montage in the antique birch hoop, but in those moments I only thought of Pearl, Helen, Granny Ross and all the other wise folk I'd come to love.

*Granny Ross*

Tired as tired could be, she sat outside the tent away from the crowd. She'd asked the girls to bring her hay bales outside under the stars and they'd done as they were told before they'd slipped away to be with all the rest of the town near the lighted stage. Josephine Rey was up there. She couldn't see her, but she could hear her guitar's twangy notes. Woodsmen had gifts too. She could hear the violin, the bass and the banjo—all played by Truvy's cousins, Paul, Raymond and Leon. But Granny believed it was the women who had the greatest bond to seed and earth, to tree and bone. You could feel the wildwood's power in Josephine's picking. It had been like that since she was a child.

But men found the magic where they could.

Music. Or carving like that tinker boy, Mack. Then she remembered he could sing too. A lullaby as pretty as the beekeeper himself. Granny quaked with that thought. She could hear Harry's song, but if she tried too long and hard to hear it, his singing turned easily into screams.

Those old nightmares.

Her nightly companions all these long years.

Anna had been allergic to bees and Granny had been too hard on her eldest daughter, keeping her close, dosing her with protective tisanes. Never allowing her to run and play after that first horrible reaction to one tiny sting. Her nightmares hadn't given her a choice. The wildwood had been warning her about the honeybees for as long as she could remember. But back then she'd also been lonely, susceptible to a sweet-talking stranger passing through. Deborah had been born. And two babies strained her protective abilities beyond all measure. She'd been almost relieved when the girls had run away, hadn't she? It shamed her now, but she couldn't deny it.

Then Deborah had come back with a baby of her own.

Folks thought she was hard, the quintessential Appalachian woman, iron-willed with a spine of stone, but she hadn't been able to make Deborah leave the mountain or give Carol up. Maybe she'd seen something in Deborah's older eyes that had told her it would be useless to try.

Done her best. Always done her best. But times like this when she was so tired the ache of her constant battle seeped way down to settle in the marrow of her bones, she wondered. Maybe she was nothing but an evil witch, after all.

The child came out of the darkness, quick, like a fox. *Or like a bird flitting across the sky.* That thought was nothing but a flash of barn swallows behind a blink before it was gone. It took Granny a minute to focus her blurry eyes and identify the young'un. She couldn't remember her name.

"Bad trouble's coming. I can taste it," the little girl said, wild curls all around her face and shoulders. Her face was suddenly as bright as if it was broad daylight. She stopped in front of Granny and looked up and for all the world Granny felt like she'd been transported back in time. She'd seen that very face look up at her before, wise beyond her years and telling her what for, and that hair. She'd seen it back then, but she'd seen it since. Rachel had those same chestnut curls.

"Well. Well," she said in reply, trying to gather her wits about her. A pang had stabbed her and now her heart felt like it was gripped in someone's hand.

Anna had disappeared. Deborah had never been able to find her. But the wildwood knew its own, didn't it? This child was the wildwood's through and through. Rachel had been called by the orchard, the wildwood's heart, because she belonged back on the mountain *with her own blood kin.*

And she surely wasn't a May.

"Do you ever taste trouble? It's bitter," the little girl said. *Pearl.* The girl's name was Pearl. And she was far too young to be asking Granny Ross such questions, bold as brass and not one bit afraid.

"Worse than a green persimmon," Granny agreed. "Don't always taste it, but I have before." She'd tasted nothing but green persimmons on the back of her tongue the day Carol married Sheriff Long.

"I've got to get the storybook page before it happens," Pearl said.

"It's important." The little girl darted into the tent and came out with Rachel's embroidery hoop in her arms. The stitchery clutched to her chest like a baby. "You should come with me too. It's bad here. Helen will take you home."

Granny Ross stood up. You didn't question when a Ross knew things. You just listened. Sometimes they were wrong. But most times they were right. And she was too old and tired to handle bitter bad tonight.

*Rachel*

My eyes watered against the thick, acrid smog that blanketed the fairgrounds. It clung to my eyelashes and the back of my throat as I called for Helen. People rushed by me and around me, but their faces were obscured by the black haze, made worse by the shaky beams of their frantic flashlights. Now and then someone would try to tell me where they had last seen the woman I was frantically searching for, but most people were as lost as I was, separated from their friends and families.

The blessed moments of community we'd managed had been taken from us. Or had it?

"She was by the stage last I saw her," someone offered between coughs. The flashlight in their hands glared in my eyes, leaving my vision dazzled.

"Over by the tinker's truck," another shouted, voice as hoarse as mine.

Finally, my throat raw and burning, I began to shout for Pearl without caring what anyone might think. I stumbled and fell to one knee and waited with my eyes closed for torturous seconds while I tried to restore my vision.

"Pearl is with Helen by the road where the cars are parked," Carol Long said near my ear. She'd heard me calling my daughter's name even though my voice had gone to nothing more than a croak. "Helen sent me to find you."

Carol had a flashlight in one hand, but she directed it to the ground, not into my face. I gladly took the other hand Carol offered to help me to my feet.

"Here. You take this light. I've got my bearings. I'm going to go check on Cass," Carol said.

There would be no scolding from me that it was the kind deputy she was worried about and not her husband. She disappeared into the smoke. All was dark in that direction now. I hoped that meant the flames had been extinguished.

With the borrowed flashlight, I made my way toward where Helen had been seen. I didn't feel relieved when the air around me began to clear. Not yet. Not until I'd seen my daughter safe and sound. Not even when the first vehicle materialized out of the fog.

But then I saw Helen.

She was waiting for me. She'd known I would come looking for Pearl. We understood each other as only mothers could. I stumbled into her outstretched arms and we held each other in shared relief.

"Go ahead. Give her a hug if she doesn't mind. It's dark and no one is paying us a bit of attention," Helen urged.

Before I could step forward to gather Pearl to me, she came of her own accord. She grabbed me around the legs and squeezed. I hugged her back, accepting the surprise gesture with relief. She hadn't been in the tent. Her face was smudged and her hair was tangled, but she was safe. And Granny Ross was already in the twins' station wagon. They were getting ready to take her home.

The fire had been extinguished. It had only spread a few hundred yards around the tent, and its distance from the rest of the fair exhibits had saved them, the field and possibly even the forest in the distance. Men passed buckets along a chain of people lined up from the creek to the smoldering remains of ash and canvas and burnt grass. Some women and children had even joined the line.

"I thought she might still be in the tent," I said.

"Don't have to worry about that girl. She knows," Granny Ross said from the open window. "Such a shine on her today. Such a shine."

I looked down to see Pearl looking up at me. There were headlights glowing all around us but her precious face was in shadow. Safe. I placed my palms on her warm little cheeks for the first time, to reassure myself, to take the measure of her well-being. She was always shining to my eyes.

"Mack made us a present," she said out of the blue.

"She knows things sometimes," Helen said. "And she's so sharp for her age. I've never seen the like."

"He carved a chest," I said to Pearl. I reluctantly released her face before my intensity frightened her.

"It's a box for special things like dirt," she replied.

I looked at Helen. Had Pearl seen the chest in a dream? I hoped she hadn't seen more gruesome things. The honeybees had only been protecting Siobhán and the baby. But poor dead Harry, the burns and the screams of the townspeople overcome by the swarm... I hoped she would never have to live through visions of that.

"There are barn swallows on it. Like the ones on your storybook page," Pearl said.

Storybook page?

"She shouldn't have taken it and I'll talk to her about that, but I think she knew something was going to happen."

Helen walked over to the car and reached through the window.

Granny Ross handed her a familiar object. A beloved thing. Pearl slipped from my hug and moved back so Helen could hand me the birch embroidery hoop.

I suddenly understood why Pearl would think it was like a storybook page. It did tell a story about Morgan's Gap. From blackened stone to honeybee. From seeds to apple trees.

I couldn't be certain, but I didn't think it was so much as singed or soot-stained.

"I tasted the bad all morning. I knew it was coming," Pearl said.

"Like green persimmons," Granny Ross added from the station wagon. "A Ross woman knows."

The poor old woman's head nodded as she spoke and her eyelids drooped.

"Long day for old bones," Pearl said, seriously. As if she knew. As if she felt Granny Ross's aches.

Granny chuckled. "Was thinking that. Rapscallion. Saw that face in the hand glass a million times. Y'all are in for trouble, let me tell you."

"You'd better get her home," I told Helen. Her words were slurred from tiredness and she wasn't making a lot of sense.

"Will you be all right?" Helen asked.

"Thank you," I replied. "Thank you for everything. I haven't said it before. Too big for thanks, but I want you to know how grateful I am." I didn't answer her question. I didn't know what right felt like. I never had. "I'll wait to make sure Mack is okay before I head home."

"He isn't okay," Pearl said, matter-of-factly. "His leg hurts. Something terrible."

"I made him some liniment. I'll remind him to use it," I promised. Helen helped Pearl into the backseat, then she climbed in beside her and Fair. Fern started the car.

Impulsively, I stepped up, bent over and placed a brief kiss on Granny Ross's wrinkled cheek. Her skin was cool to my lips and she didn't react. Only murmured something about her daughter.

"Deborah's helping with the bucket brigade. I'll check on her too," I promised.

"She's fine," Pearl piped up from the backseat. "Mad 'bout the mountain quilt, though."

We all should be mad. Once the smoke dissipated and before the ash grew cold, we all should be furious. Because there had been no lit torches near the wisewomen's tent. The fire could only have been started by one that had been carried with evil intent.

# Thirty-Eight

*M*ack *was covered in* soot, but he insisted on following me home. I knew Pearl had been right about his leg when he didn't get out of his truck. I went to his window and we kissed, a gentle sort of kiss I'd never experienced before. Our lips lingered together, intimately sharing our vulnerability and relief, but not having the energy for more.

"Use the liniment. It will help," I said.

"I'll watch until you're safely inside," Mack replied.

"The fire…" I began. My embroidery was clutched to my breast. I was filled with wonder that Pearl had known she should retrieve it, but the possible danger she had brushed against chilled me to the bone. Granny was right. She did shine. But she was still so young and vulnerable.

"Even the sheriff knows it couldn't have been an accident. I saw people passing buckets who had refused to come to the tent during the day," Mack said. "But someone carried a torch all the way out there. And there was kerosene. We all smelled it. Someone doused the mountain quilt before they threw the flame."

I closed my eyes. Only to see Ezekiel twisting the Bible in his hands and telling me that I would burn. Someone. Someone. Someone. I didn't utter his name. I didn't have to. I saw the knowledge of Gray's evil in Mack's eyes and those scorched holes in photographs where eyes had been.

"Go inside. Get some rest. I'll go home and use the liniment, and when daylight comes tomorrow we'll see if anything can be salvaged," Mack said.

I went to the backseat of my car and fetched the barn swallow chest so I could take the birch hoop and the chest inside with me. Everything seemed extra precious right now. Besides Ezekiel, when I closed my eyes I saw all the lovely things my friends had made. The destruction of all the love and care that had gone into the wise wares was worse than losing the items themselves. How heartbroken all the artists and artisans must be. Of course, I would rather have lost a tent full of embroidery than risk Pearl. I was certain they all felt the same.

Still, my remarkable little sprite had saved the wildwood tapestry.

True to his word, Mack only backed up and drove away after I'd gone inside and shut the door. I locked it for good measure, sliding the heavy old-fashioned iron bolt into place. Movement caught my eye as I prepared to turn from the door and I peeked out the front window. The saw-whet owl was on the porch rail. I wasn't surprised. Mack was in pain. He needed to rest and treat his leg, but the saw-whet owl had come in his stead. To keep me company and watch over me through the night.

Eve was already by the hearth. Instead of going straight to bed, I turned on a lamp and sat down to stare at the birch hoop for a while. I was tired, but a strange energy pulsed in my fingers. One that I never ignored. This time it was stronger and more compelling.

While Eve moved to doze on my warm feet, I took out a needle from the smooth applewood needle box. As I often did, I ran my calloused fingers over the age-polished wood. From the First Tree. A branch that had fallen *like a gift*. Next, I chose the thread. Blue, white and silver. I rarely outlined what I would stitch. My mind placed the shapes on the fabric and I simply stitched where they should be. This time, I saw the rain droplets—one, two, three. Dozens. And as I sewed the air around me grew heavy with moisture. My cheeks dampened. My eyelashes became spiky. I licked the dew off my lips and tasted the heavens.

It was well after midnight when I finally finished. I collapsed back in my chair, my hands limp, my shoulders slumped. The rain I'd embroidered sparkled in the lamplight as if it had fallen from unseen clouds above the honeysuckle vines. The scent of rain-soaked flowers filled the cottage around me.

Eve had disappeared. I'd been so consumed with the raindrops that I hadn't noticed her go. This time I knew it was because all my energy had gone into creating the rain. I left the embroidery hoop on the chair near the hearth and placed the swallow chest on the window ledge in my bedroom. Then, after one last look to see that the saw-whet owl had also disappeared, I stumbled to bed alone, save for the applewood box never far from my fingers.

*Mack*

Mack's leg throbbed with every footstep, but he had no intention of going home to apply Rachel's liniment. The stench of kerosene smoke had tainted his clothes, but he wasn't going to waste time changing either. There was an arsonist on the loose in Morgan's Gap. One bold enough to strike under the whole town's nose.

But not brave.

They had waited for the town to be distracted on the other side of the fairgrounds.

Anyone could have done it. Even the folks who had joined the bucket brigade to help put out the fire. But Mack had gotten a close look into Reverend Gray's eyes today. He'd seen that look in Vietnam. The kind of man who would frighten a child and not care. The kind of man who would watch a baby fall and not reach to pick her up. It had been all he could do not to give Gray the thrashing he deserved when Helen had asked him to go for Pearl.

But it had been the way Gray had pulled the braided grass bracelet off the little girl's arm that had brought Mack up short. The preacher hadn't been rational. He'd thrown the bracelet to the ground and the way it had coiled there had reminded Mack of Eve. Rachel's Eve. That's when he'd looked from Gray to Pearl and back again and his guts had frozen as hard as his fists had clenched.

Ezekiel Gray knew that Pearl was Rachel's daughter. Worse, he'd called her "mine."

Mack had seen Rachel's scars. He knew she'd had a terrible childhood. What's more, he had wept angry tears after they'd been together because of how jumpy and frightened she'd been. He was patient. He was careful. He made very sure he hadn't done anything she didn't want him to do, but he could tell that was the first time a man had shown her tenderness and care.

Gray was a monster.

He had beaten Rachel and when she found out she was carrying his child she had run away. To the wildwood. To the wise folk. To Mary May. And to Granny Ross and her trio. To Deborah and Carol. *And to him.* Didn't Mack listen for what each piece of wood was supposed to be? Didn't he believe in the healing strength of the forest and the mountain? In maintaining the sacred connection between humans and nature?

He'd never been comfortable in a brick-and-mortar church, but he'd found his faith in the clearing where the saw-whet owl had first come to him. Many of the wisewomen and woodsmen went to other churches as well, but Mack didn't. He was a man of the wood. It was enough for him. Still, one thing Mack knew for certain—Ezekiel Gray wasn't a man of God. He stood against love and unity. He was someone who hurt and destroyed, not someone who tended and created.

He was war. He was violence. He was *flame.*

Mack wasn't surprised when he found an almost empty can of kerosene behind the sagging Sect tent. What startled him was the kid in a worsted wool suit on the ground. He stirred, beginning to regain consciousness, obviously having been knocked clean out before. He rushed to the boy's side and helped him to sit up. The stink of spilled kerosene made him gag.

"I asked about the cans weeks ago. What they were for. He said I'd know when the time was right," the young man said. His words were slurred but rushed as if Mack was a priest and he had been longing for confession. "After we put out the fire, I came back here. I found him loading the cans into the back of our car. I tried to stop him. I knew he must have started the fire at the fair."

Mack stood up. He no longer felt his leg. His whole body had gone numb. What else would Gray want to burn? *Who* else? He ran for his truck. Every stride should have been agony, but he only felt fear.

*Thomas St. Clare*

"He said *snakes* over and over again," Thomas said. But the motor was running in the truck and the big man was already slamming the door behind him. He ground gears and spun gravel as he pulled away. "Snakes."

He rubbed the back of his head where an empty kerosene can had bludgeoned him. He had begun to have his doubts about Gray and the Sect weeks ago. But by then he'd been too intimidated to leave. There had been whispers of other "backsliders" who had disappeared after expressing their concerns. Ones who had left only to later disappear. There was a painful knot the size of a baseball on the back of Thomas's head. His parents had warned him. They'd said Ezekiel Gray was trouble. Now his new suit was dirty and torn and his ears were still ringing.

Gray was more than trouble. And some of his followers had no doubts at all. Thomas felt sick when he thought of Adam. His fellow acolyte had wanted to hurt the woman they'd been told to follow. He'd been obsessed with reporting her movements to Gray himself as if he'd been eager for orders to do more than just follow her.

When the police cruiser came down the road with its lights flashing and turned into the field where he lay, Thomas resolved to call his parents as soon as he made it to a telephone.

# Thirty-Nine

*Mack*

*He pushed the truck* as fast as it would go down long and twisting country roads. It was late. He was exhausted. Adrenaline no longer kept the pain in his leg at bay. The forest on either side of the lane pressed close. Through the open window, he could hear the wind whistling through the leaves and he could see the silhouette of the rustling canopy against the starry sky. If he didn't know better, he would swear a storm was coming, although there wasn't a hint of a cloud above him.

The saw-whet owl wasn't on his rearview mirror. Somewhere, out in the night, the owl flew. Mack felt his absence keenly. He needed wings to get to Rachel and warn her about Ezekiel Gray. The rattle and clank of the old Depression-era Chevy he'd rescued from the junkyard mocked him now. He'd been the fastest kid on the football field, but since then, there'd been so many times he hadn't been fast enough. The pain in his leg throbbed and reminded him with every heartbeat of a time when he'd been too late. Too late to save his fellow soldiers. Too late to save a village full of women and children. Too late to save himself.

He'd burned then. And it had been agonizing. Not only his own pain but the screams of others. He'd been the only one found alive not far from the smoldering ashes...and bodies. He'd managed to drag himself into the jungle, where he'd found shelter among the perpetually damp gum trees.

Rachel. So tough beneath her kind, watchful ways. So determined and resilient. Only a madman would want to hurt her. Mack's hands gripped the steering wheel tightly and his good foot let off on the gas only enough to keep the truck in the drive up to Mary May's farm. When it came into sight around the last curve, for a horrible instant, Mack thought he saw flames leaping from the roof into the sky. But as he slammed on the brakes and slid to a stop, the flames disappeared. He turned off the truck and sat staring at the peaceful scene. No fire. No sign of Gray's Lincoln. Stars twinkled above the cottage. Honeysuckle danced in the wind. Its fragrance traveled all the way to him through the truck's open window.

If not to hurt Rachel, where had Gray been planning to go with the kerosene he'd loaded into the trunk of his car?

Pearl?

"Hell, no," Mack growled and reached for the ignition. Even without wings, he would fly back to town. No way was that evil man going to burn up his own daughter while Mack still had breath in his body.

He cranked the engine and whirled the truck around in the grass, but a scent caught his attention and he hit the brake again. The orchard always held the fragrance of sunshine and moss and the rich scent of a few rotted apples that had fallen to feed the ground. Tonight, Mack smelled something sharp and sickening. He'd smelled it earlier in the evening. There was only a hint, but a hint was enough.

Kerosene carried on the breeze.

He turned his truck off again and jumped down, hissing as his bad leg took his weight. He couldn't drive into the orchard at night. There wasn't a reliable track. He would have to hurry on foot in spite of his pain. He took off in a limping run that became faster as the kerosene smell grew stronger.

He found the Lincoln by the side of a ridge where it had run into a naturally formed ditch. Unlike him, Gray had tried to drive into the orchard's hollow at night. Even with its powerful V-8 engine, the Continental wasn't built for off-road. The trunk of the car was open and empty. Maybe a madman, but a determined one. The ditch hadn't stopped him.

Now Mack could easily follow the stench of kerosene. Gray had started splashing it onto trees as soon as he came to the outer spirals of the orchard. Maybe he wanted to burn them all, but Mack knew where he was headed. What would draw him the most.

The tree where Rachel always sat. The one in the center of the orchard that she called the First Tree.

Mack tried to keep most of his weight on his good leg, which left him unbalanced and awkward. Too slow. Too slow. He no longer only smelled kerosene. Now, he smelled smoke. The thick black smoke of oil burning. Not trees yet. He could still stop Gray before wood began to burn.

But when he came to the rise where the First Tree grew, he didn't see the arsonist preacher anywhere. He should have remembered how Gray had attacked his acolyte at the circus tent. The first blow knocked him to his knees. The second blow sent him prone to the ground.

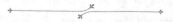

I woke to the frenzied flapping of wings. Eve was back, wrapped tightly around my upper right arm. At first I looked for the saw-whet owl, but the flapping was coming from multiple sources inside my bedroom.

I reached for the lamp. The sudden light illuminated dozens of birds frantically swooping and soaring around the tiny confines of my room. Barn swallows! I jumped from the bed and threw open the casement window. The swallows followed me and flew out into the night like living arrows shot from an invisible bow. I stood at the window, but my heartbeat didn't return to normal. The swallows were silhouetted against a smudged black sky. I couldn't see any stars. It wasn't clouds blocking the starlight that provided a dark backdrop for the birds.

It was smoke.

Billows of black. I followed the trail back to where it rose *from the center of the orchard* in the distance.

I stopped only for the shawl Granny had knitted for me. It wasn't cold, but I donned the shawl like armor. I didn't search for shoes or reach for the phone. My urgency was sharp and immediate—get to the First Tree. Granny Ross would know. Truvy. Jo. Mavis. They all had to know. The saw-whet owl was nowhere to be seen. Maybe he had gone for help?

No bucket brigade would be fast enough here, from hand pump in the farmyard all the way out to the First Tree.

I had to stop Ezekiel before he set the entire orchard alight.

I ran past the doe and fawn, barely noticing that their hearts were fluttering fast even though the air was still.

Mack's truck brought me up short, but I only paused for a second. Mack. Here. But nowhere to be seen. His truck door was hanging open. His headlights were on, but they glowed dimly as if they'd been on awhile and the battery was going dead.

*Honeywick in flames. All the honeybees writhing on the ground.*

I rejected the nightmare even as my bare feet sprang on dry moss, *nothing but tinder*, everywhere. The only moisture came from the angry, desperate tears tracking down my face. Ezekiel was a coward. *The long, stringy hair that hadn't been washed. His untucked shirt and unpressed suit.* I should have known this morning that his hold on sanity was loosening. Appearances had always been so important to him. And matches. His damned matches. He must have burned the wise-wares tent while everyone was at the concert.

And now, this. Out after midnight to try to burn something more powerful than his delusions of grandeur.

His parents. Oh, God. His parents' house had burned with them inside. They must have seen his instability. Didn't I know by now that no fires around Ezekiel were accidental? Then, afterward, so perfect, so pious. So *cleaned up.* No one had known. But had there come a time when his first wife had suspected?

She'd died in a boating accident, but there'd also been a fire. The boat had been nothing but a burnt-out hull when Ezekiel had been pulled from the water.

I stumbled over something in the dark. I fell onto—a person!—big, hard, warm and familiar. Thank God.

"Mack. Mack, it's me. You'll be all right," I said. He stirred beneath me and mumbled my name. "Help will be coming. I'm sure."

But was I? How would any of our friends know what was happening? I hadn't made a phone call. Not one. An injured Mack shook my confidence in intangible things. Magical apple cider wouldn't save us. I suddenly realized I'd left the applewood needle box on my bed. Why hadn't I grabbed it? Why hadn't I made a call? Somehow the two things in my panicked mind were of equal importance.

"W...watch out," Mack murmured into the moss.

It was no longer dark. Mack's prone body was lit by a flickering light from over the rise. I stood, knowing what I would see, but dreading it all the same.

Eigríoch was ablaze.

Its lower branches were completely covered with orange flames. They lit the darkness and the man who stood beneath their blazing canopy. Ezekiel stared at me. The shadows cast by the firelight danced eerily on his cheeks and the flames were reflected in his eyes, leaping and gamboling like his demons come to life.

"You will burn!" he shrieked.

I helped Mack to stand. He was much bigger and heavier than I was. It took a while, but I didn't give up. As if we had all the time in the world.

While I'd stitched the raindrops, I'd felt the energy of the entire community that had flowed through the tent that day. Every finger that had brushed every thread had imparted its strength to me. And some of the folks who had touched weasel, snake, owl and swallow had been very powerful wise folk indeed.

"We won't go away, Ezekiel. It's not that simple. You have exposed yourself for what you truly are. There is no pulpit to hide behind here. No applause. No approval. And we have seeds. So many seeds. Saved from this harvest all the way back to the first," I said. Mack was on his feet. Shaky, but upright. My voice echoed off the still-untouched leaves as if their trembling reverberated it back a thousandfold.

I looked up into the precious branches of Eigríoch. I remembered how the tree had called me and welcomed me. How I had been sheltered. The First Tree wasn't only a part of the wildwood. This tree was at the heart of the wildwood. I could feel that connection threatened as the flames began to devour the bark beneath. The seeds, no matter how sacred, would never replace all that Eigríoch had witnessed, all it had seen and felt and heard. And if the entire orchard burned...or if the wildwood caught...

It wasn't only my fingers that tingled now as I stood with Mack by the light of the First Tree burning. It was my entire body and soul. I hadn't paused to call for help with Mary's old telephone because I'd been calling all the wise folk together since I'd arrived at Honeywick. Maybe even before then, with the needles and thread Mary had gifted me all those years ago. With every stitch—chain, back, stem and knot—I had called. I hadn't known, at first, that I was weaving a spell with every strand of thread. But now I stood and raised my hands to defend Siobhán's orchard against a man who threatened me and my child and the community that had given us welcome and safe haven. Home.

Granny's intent. Truvy's empathy. Jo's energy.

Ruby's courage and all the Reys' music.

Mavis and the hum of her bees as they flew through the wildwood, drawing its magic from a million blossoms kissed by the mountain breeze.

Mack listening to what each piece of wood should be. Feeling and revealing with each flick of the knife in his hand.

Carol's storytelling. The brittle, brilliant flash of Deborah's bits of glass. Helen's nurturing. Primmie's dumplings. The stunning mountain quilt gone but not forgotten. Not if we held the truth of it in our hearts.

Community is wildwood magic.

"Don't," Mack said. His big hands closed around my waist to stop me from walking toward the First Tree. I had taken the step without thinking. I was compelled in the same way I had always been compelled to translate my thoughts and feelings into stitches. My embroidery had said all the things I hadn't been able to say when I'd been silenced by the Sect. It had voiced my frustrations, fear and hope while I'd been in hiding.

"I'm not afraid. Not anymore," I assured him. His hands didn't loosen. His fear of flames strong enough to keep both of us safe.

Granny had told me I needed to discover my strength. And I had. By celebrating and cherishing all the strengths I found in others.

"You killed your first wife. Didn't you? Had she seen through your perfect suits and shiny lies? Did you suspect you'd killed your parents?"

The crackling flames had licked up to higher branches. Embers floated into the air like soft, gentle, terrifying fireflies toward other trees. The stench of kerosene was heavy. It burned my eyes and made my tears oily and thick in my eyes. In patches around the First Tree the dry moss glowed and smoked like failed matches. If anyone should strike...

"I am Ezekiel Gray. I walk in the footsteps of the prophet. No one shall stand against me," he replied. "They used the flame to teach me Holy scriptures. Burned me with a match from the fireplace whenever I got it wrong. By the age of six, I could recite every word of the Prophet's book with no mistake. The flames speak to me. They reveal the will of God. The fire cleansed me of my first wife. How the boat burned! And God's flame devoured my parents when they became doubters. Their last screams were blasphemies, but the fire cleansed those away too."

"You devil," Mack said.

I could see his disgust that I had been in this madman's grip. Under his control. A Home for Wayward Girls had been a lie. We had been raised into horror, not home.

"No. Not a devil. Just a sorry excuse of a man," I said.

"My followers will help me cleanse this whole town," Gray continued.

But he didn't run to meet the people who began to arrive in the orchard, drawn by the fire. It wasn't Sheriff Long leading the way. It was his deputy Cass with a giant flashlight. Gray looked startled when the deputy rushed toward him. He was hemmed in by flames, but even if he'd had somewhere to go, I didn't think he would have run. Who would dare to arrest a prophet? He'd gotten away with so much, for so long.

Sheriff Long came after, dragging behind Carol as if he didn't want to be anywhere near the kerosene-soaked orchard. Carol paid him no mind. She looked different. Her hair was loose. Her lips were red. She was wearing a vivid pantsuit worthy of Mavis and her feet were bare like her mother's. But there was no ring to be seen. Not on her finger or her toe. After she checked on us and we nodded that we were okay, she only had eyes for Cass.

He had handcuffs in his hands.

A shriek called my attention from Cass back to Ezekiel. The fall of glowing embers from the First Tree's burning branches had found their maker. They fell like vengeful snow on Ezekiel's upturned face. He had raised his hands to cover his eyes. *His kerosene-soaked hands.* An ember had caught on the sleeve of his once-fine coat. It had blazed up and his frantic waving had only served to oxygenate the flames.

He was on fire.

He'd accused me of consorting with the devil. Now his face was strangely contorted between fear and ecstasy. He was only a man, but his inner demons had come out to play, and he was both terrified and fascinated by the fire that was only seconds from eating his flesh.

Cass leapt forward. He started to remove Ezekiel's coat, but he met resistance. The self-proclaimed prophet wanted to burn. As they struggled, Granny Ross and Deborah came from the opposite side of the orchard. Not from Honeywick. It was a long way through the wildwood from Granny's cabin and Deborah's trailer. Granny leaned hard on Deborah's right arm.

They must have headed this way long before everyone else.

Sometimes Ross women knew things.

Cass resorted to a punch. No one even gasped. Ezekiel slumped, stunned and limp long enough for the deputy to peel the coat from his back. The roar of a motor heralded Jo's arrival. Dark or not, she had come by motorbike. This time, the sidecar had been removed. Mavis rode behind her, holding on for dear life over bumpy terrain.

Truvy came alone. Primrose must have been left to mind a house that was always full of relatives. Mavis and Truvy made their way to Granny's side, and once there, I could see how their presence and power rejuvenated the old woman. She straightened and Deborah let her go. Mavis and Truvy took Deborah's place, one on either side.

"The young man you left for dead at the fairgrounds has filed charges against you," Sheriff Long informed Ezekiel, almost apologetically. Cass handcuffed the singed preacher. He ignored us all to stare at the burning coat Cass had thrown on the ground. The light from the flames leapt on the shadows of his face.

"All of this could have been avoided if people like you had rejected his hate on the first night of the revival," Granny Ross said.

"Morgan's Gap has been like dried moss for too long. Waiting for someone to kindle the tinder of fear and distrust," Jo added. She stepped forward to stomp on the coat as if to illustrate what she thought of that.

"Mending—healing—isn't a goal. It's an ongoing process," I said.

Half a dozen football players came running into the halo of light created by poor First Tree with buckets full of water from the farmyard. They dumped and turned to run for more, but it wouldn't be enough. No matter how fast they flew it wouldn't be enough.

I became aware of movement at the edges of the orchard, where the wildwood began. Likewise in the sky above our heads. The smoke didn't stop the saw-whet owl from finding Mack. It landed on his shoulder as if it often found a convenient spot on that broad perch.

Barn swallows swooped above us and other creatures crept below—Granny's weasel, Carol's library cat, Truvy's whip-poor-will.

The bobcat I'd met at Jo's junkyard prowled forward to sit against her left leg. Bobcats and bees. Oh my.

Mavis hadn't woken her honeybees.

And I was glad.

Because along with the wise folk, ordinary townsfolk had come out into the night. Daphne arrived with a squat, muscular man who must be her husband, the football coach. *He held her hand and helped her over the unfamiliar terrain.* He was here to help. Not like the Sect men, after all. Their presence explained the football players. The beer brewer from the fair appeared. Less jolly and obviously sobered by the night's events. Dozens more fairgoers came with him. Some in their nightgowns and pajamas. A few with random creatures on their shoulders, at their feet or in their arms. Raccoon. Fox. Mouse. Hawk. Chickadee. Beaks. Fur. Claws and hoof. Jeremiah Warren came over the rise surrounded by several waitresses and the lone Morgan woman who had stayed in her booth that day at the diner. She held an iron skillet in her manicured hand as if she was the one who had roused the diner to action. Ordinary? Had they somehow been compelled by my spell? Or was anyone in the town of Morgan's Gap really completely untouched by wildwood magic?

It was time. My tingling had built to a vibrating hum within my blood impossible to contain.

"Let me go, Mack," I said. He complied. Something in my voice too powerful to deny.

I slowly walked to the First Tree, determined to brave Ezekiel's flames. I wouldn't let him burn me or Pearl or the orchard. I'd seen my daughter walking into the orchard, holding Helen by the hand. Blessed Helen. Mother. Friend. But it was my shining birthday girl who was leading the way.

The right side of the First Tree was free from fire, but the heat from the left side was scorching. I gasped against it and then held my breath to keep from taking in the glowing firefly embers that might burn my lungs. I had left the needle box in the cottage, but I didn't need it when I had the source of its special wood at my fingertips. I placed my sewing hands on the bark of the tree that had first called me to the orchard. My tingling fingers had always transferred energy to the needle and thread as I stitched. Now they transferred all the energy my embroidery had absorbed today, for months, for years into Eigríoch. And not only from the wildwood tapestry. From every piece I'd worked throughout the town—apples and serpents, jaunty weasels, protective honeybees, fragrant honeysuckle vines. My work had been worn and carried, admired and loved, all over the mountain. Thousands of fingers had traced across the wildwood flora and fauna I had re-created with needle and thread.

"What's she doing?" Sheriff Long asked. He stumbled back as if the lullaby I softly sang was more dangerous than the fire.

"She's doing what she was called to do," Granny Ross said. "She's mending. She's been bringing us all together for weeks. Stitch by stitch."

Mack joined my song. Every wisewoman present and most of the woodsmen and even some of the townsfolk who knew the song, though they didn't know how or why, murmured softly in a chorus that was accompanied by the rustling of leaves. No one could ever say which happened first—the rush of wind or the moisture in the air. I only knew what I felt beneath my sewing hands and that was the First Tree breathing in a great inhalation sourced from the energy I gifted and then exhaling like a living creature would.

But it wasn't only Eigríoch.

The mountain, held together by miles and miles of roots, moved beneath our feet. Had the mines caved in because the wildwood moved the mountain for Siobhán? I was awed, but not afraid, even as the moss rose and fell beneath my feet.

The whole orchard breathed in and out.

The entire wildwood swayed and sighed.

And a misty, forest-fueled cloud formed above us all as if the forest had released a pent-up breath it had been holding all summer.

Silvery rain droplets like the ones I had sewn only hours before began to fall.

The flames sputtered, doused by a fine but dense fall of moisture from low hanging clouds the forest had generated from our combined energy. As Granny was stronger with her trio, all the wise folk were stronger when they were bound together—by the wildwood's roots and the wildwood-made creatures, by the sturdy birch hoop and my stitchery.

By the county fair.

Unlike the revival, the fair had included everyone, even when some folks had opposed that. By the end of the day, the entire town had come together under the stars to listen to Mrs. Rey play.

The lullaby had risen up and past my lips without any conscious decision. Eigríoch had needed to hear it. We all had needed to soothe ourselves and the orchard and the greater wildwood. Worship? Absolutely. If the orchard was the heart of the wildwood, it was a sacred one. Prepared and planted and prayed over for a century.

The wildwood abides, to be tapped into by different traditions in different ways. Some folks find God in the trees. Some folks find themselves. And some find each other and a connection to the universe that's larger than any one creed's definition of faith.

I had found myself and friends.

And I'd given Pearl a true home.

Ezekiel whimpered, perhaps from the sting of his burns or perhaps because of the pitiful sizzle as his beloved flames died out in the rain.

"The crone!" one of the football boys shouted, pointing toward the edge of the woods.

We all turned to see what had frightened him, but one of the other boys gave us the answer before we ascertained for ourselves.

"That's old Mary May, you chicken," the red-haired boy said with a punch to his sheepish friend's arm.

It was Mary May with leaves like a crown in her long silver hair and moss stains on her bare feet. As she came closer, I could see her smiling face, for all the world looking younger and smoother than it had before. Gone were the deep crags in her cheeks and the shadowed bags under her eyes. She moved lightly too, under the shadows of the apple trees, looking as spritely as a much younger fairy princess I knew.

"Witch!" Ezekiel screamed, but Cass was already pushing him back toward Honeywick. No one present cared to hear what he had to say anymore. Not even Sheriff Long, who followed his deputy with slumped shoulders and his hands in his pockets. He would lose the next election. He'd already lost Carol. She was a Ross and a Ross woman couldn't be kept. Not by force. I knew it as well as Mavis knew the secrets whispered by her bees. She'd given him a chance. More than he deserved. He was no woodsman. And never would be. In spite of his resistant charge, Cass kept looking at Carol. Now, him? There was hope for him. And I didn't blame him for being smitten by the librarian. All the Polaroids on the bulletin board at the library had shown the real Carol Ross all along.

"We tried to put the fire out," the frightened boy said. No longer scared, but certainly nervous.

"Thank you," Mary said solemnly, but there was a twinkle in her eyes. Unlike Granny, she wasn't put off by their fear. She accepted it as her due while gentling it away with her calm. A sudden bleat made us all look toward the rise and I wasn't surprised to see Billy running toward Mary, his horn as crooked as ever. He'd had a rest too, as a clay figure on the dresser in her turret room.

"I dreamed of Honeywick. Of Siobhán and Harry," I said quietly. She had come to stand near me. Everyone was distracted by the rain. Dancing. Rejoicing. Lifting their faces up to the sky to taste the drops on their lips. Worship, indeed.

"I always do. It's good to remember. To learn. Then move on," Mary said. "Some folks get stuck. Some in the good. Some in the bad. Right, Granny?"

The trio came toward us. They had been walking in a circle mumbling words I couldn't make out. They still held each other's hands, their connection unbroken.

"It was supposed to be Mavis, but Granny was put off by her bees," Jo confessed. The rain had only made her hair wilder and her movie-star face was dewy in the darkness lit only by football players' flashlights.

"It worked out. We do fine with Jo. Maybe not as powerful a trio as we would have been with Mavis, but needs must," said Truvy with an eloquent shrug.

Mavis sat cross-legged some distance away on the wet moss. Her eyes were closed and she swayed, enjoying the rain and no doubt listening to the hum of her distant honeybees. The Halls must have consumed so much wild honey. Its magic had been passed down through the generations. Mavis was as sweet and wild. No wonder Jo loved her. And I wondered how much of Mavis was a part of the trio through Jo's love in spite of Granny's trepidations.

Connections. As tangled as the wildwood's roots. Beautiful. Chaotic. And worth nurturing. Day by day. Month by month. Year by year. Community was worth the effort.

"Granny doesn't listen to the wildwood. She tries to tell it what to do. Restless woman. Never satisfied. Always afraid," Mary corrected. "It's good to have a plan, but…"

Granny could be ornery and mysterious. She could be cagey and disquieting. But Mary was right. Granny was driven by fear.

"She got stuck in that moment when Harry sacrificed all his bees. The horror. The danger. The dying. She could never get over it. Just like you got stuck in your fear of Ezekiel. For a long time. But you're not stuck anymore," Mary said. "It's time to move on. It's time for our daughters to know the truth."

Deborah had joined us. Her hair was stuck in damp dark curls all around her face. Pearl's hair was the same, but she was dancing and laughing in the rain. Fairy princess. Fae. Witch. I reached up to feel my own wet curls all around my face.

"Those damn bees. Haven't had a peaceful night's sleep in eighty years. I wanted to protect my girls. Anna almost died when she was little. Wasn't afraid. Not a bit afraid. Even after. They didn't even swarm her. One sting was all it took. If Grandma Hall hadn't been close by…she always could take the sting out…Anna would have suffocated. Eyes swollen shut. Throat closed up. After that…well, even wisewomen do unwise things, and no one can stir up trouble more than a Ross. I was hard on the girls. Difficult to live with. Kept 'em close. Any way I could. Always a pot of binding bubbling on the stove. As soon as they were old enough to undo the spells I'd woven, Anna and Deborah ran away," Granny Ross said. "Deborah came back pregnant," Granny continued. "She went off on her own and that was that."

"I thought Anna would follow me home," Deborah said. "She never did."

Anna. The Sect sisters had told me my mother's name was Anna. She had come to the Home for Wayward Girls for help. She hadn't known she would die giving birth and that the "home" would hurt me.

"Ross blood is stubborn," Granny said. "I was so worried about the bees. I failed to see the real danger until it was too late. I did everything in my power…"

"And plenty that wasn't in your power," Deborah said. "You've skirted the edges of things you shouldn't for years."

"You know as well as I do that wild magic is beautiful and dangerous. Better to teach them how to maintain the delicate balance of dark to light," Mary May said to Granny. "If you get lost in the darkness, how can you find your way or help them to find theirs?"

"Hippy," Granny replied. But her usual caustic tone was softened. Her cheeks were damp. She *had* helped me. Almost in spite of herself. Granny had told me to learn from all the wisewomen. She'd told me to take my hoop to the fair.

Knitting was her natural gift. As stitching was mine. I thought of Deborah's neglected weaving. The loom gathering dust in the corner of her trailer. How all the glass the crow brought her was the same colors. Like the Reys' music, our family had a way the wildwood spoke to us and through us. Threads. Twisting, twining, making something new. Mending. Warming. Bringing together.

Maybe we could also stir or brew, ward and bind, but our stitchery would always be true.

Deborah had come up to me and we had settled easily into our first hug as if our connection had never been tampered with. My aunt. Somehow I wasn't surprised. They had all begun to feel like family to me. Family I had found when I'd decided to run away.

*Away is a place.*

"Of course you came back. A Ross belongs in the wildwood. There's no stopping that," Granny Ross said. "Anna would have returned too. If she could have. I knew when I'd lost her for good. Felt the loss. Grief rustling in the leaves and chilling my bones forever after. Knew from the start there was something about you. A Ross knows a Ross."

"She has a birthmark on her shoulder. Just like Anna's," Mary May said.

"It's a strawberry," I said, trying to take it all in. The sisters had told me my mother, Anna, was a fallen women who had the mark of the devil and she'd passed it on to me. That's why they had always chosen that spot for the switch.

"Not a strawberry, Rachel. An apple," Mary May corrected.

I didn't have to reexamine my birthmark to know she was right. Even the Sect sisters hadn't been able to disfigure the small red oval.

"Anna craved Mary's apples. She used to sneak into the orchard in spite of the honeybees. She always said the apples were a gift," Deborah said.

"From Eigríoch. Not from me," Mary said, and smiled one of her Mona Lisa smiles.

Before I was even born I had been nourished by the First Tree. My mother had passed her special relationship with the orchard to me. The birthmark wasn't a mark of the devil. It was a promise from Eigríoch through her to me.

"And what will you do about Pearl?" Deborah asked.

"Helen is also her mother. We'll take it from there. Pearl's wiser than all of us put together and I'm pretty sure she already knows," I replied.

As if she'd heard me, Pearl grabbed Helen's hand and dragged her over to us. Mack reached down and lifted her up onto his shoulders.

"Good tastes like rain, mossy and sweet," Pearl declared. Even in this light, I could see starshine in her eyes.

The smoke had been damped down by the rain. I looked over to the rise.

The First Tree would live. Like Honeywick, it might be blackened, but it would continue on.

"The scratched hearthstone...what did it say?" I asked Mary.

"It said Mary May. Harry—my father—carved my name in the hearth. Siobhán—my mother—always said he'd heard it from his bees. She scratched it out ages ago along with the date of my birth. After many long sleeps. To try to protect me from a town that might remember to fear," Mary said. "He built Honeywick for me. The bees told him I was coming before he even met my mother."

Only then did I notice the flash of aged copper gone to burnished brown on Mary's middle finger. The hammered indentions of its crafting had softened and smoothed. The tree's branches and roots weren't as recognizable anymore. She'd always worn the ring, but in my dreams it had been shiny and new. Granny Ross coughed. She edged away from Mary. Jo and Truvy followed, letting her go where she would. Maybe Granny Ross would overcome her fear one day. She still had time. Maybe lots of it if she would let the wildwood have its way.

I'd seen Mary sleeping a deep, rejuvenating sleep cradled in the boughs of the wildwood. She had gone to rest right when I needed to rise. I no longer felt used up and tired. I was young with plenty of life left to live.

Crone was a goal. Granny was a title to aspire to.

"We should probably go home and get out of the rain," Helen said. Ever practical. Ever nurturing.

I hugged her and she hugged me back, her limitless supply of care expanding to take me in.

"What does the fairy queen say?" Mack asked jokingly up to Pearl. We all headed back to Honeywick. Only I sent one last lingering look at the First Tree to confirm that the tree was safe and sound and sleeping in the rain.

"I am the fairy *princess*," Pearl corrected.

And for some reason every person present turned to look at me the same way I'd looked back at the First Tree.

Morgan's Gap might be touched by the fae, but we'd made our community more solid tonight. I could almost feel roots expanding deeper and tighter into the mountain beneath us as the rain continued to fall. Pearl wiggled off Mack's shoulders and he helped her down so that she could run ahead of us. I didn't worry. I knew she could easily see her way in the dark because she was at home anywhere on the mountain.

*Happy birthday, Pearl.*

Mack reached for my hand and our fingers threaded naturally together.

The Home for Wayward Girls was long ago and far away.

And the roots I felt growing into the mountain were mine.

# Acknowledgments

I lost my mother in between the publication of *Wildwood Whispers* and writing *Wildwood Magic*. I'm thankful for all the friends, family, readers and colleagues who supported me with patience and understanding as I figured out how to live in a world without her. My husband, Todd, was ever constant. My children, reminders to keep moving forward. My agent, Lucienne Diver, and my editor, Nivia Evans, and her assistant editor, Angelica Chong, were invaluable.

But what better time to write a book about the importance of community and the magic of connection?

Every email. Every phone call. Every card. Every visit. Every charitable donation in my mother's name—every kindness—became seeds for the growth Morgan's Gap needed in their stand against divisiveness.

My mother was part of the Silent Generation. Born and raised in a time when girls were to be seen and not heard. She fought that notion her whole life while remaining beholden to it till the day she died. So *Wildwood Magic* also became about finding your voice and embracing your right to shine.

## ACKNOWLEDGMENTS

'd like to especially thank the teachers, professors, librarians and
tists who helped me find and embrace mine.

Like Rachel and Pearl, we must all shine on, come what may.

Never dimmed.

Never hushed.

# Meet the Author

Norris Hancock

WILLA REECE is a pseudonym for Barbara J. Hancock. She lives in the foothills of the Blue Ridge Mountains in Virginia, where stories are often told on a dark side porch in the flicker of firefly light.